I0642721

Fools' Apocalypse Part 1
BEYOND SYMBIOSIS

Written and illustrated by
Anderson Atlas

Published by:

Synesthesiabooks.com
br.peterson@gmail.com

Fools' Apocalypse, Beyond Symbiosis / Anderson Atlas
Summary: A virus destroys humanity and creates undead enemies. 6 main characters fight and escape a crumbling city and head down to Cuba, an island with the last remaining 'Safe' city on Earth.
1. Apocalypse- Fiction. 2. Zombie Horror-Fiction. 3. Political Thriller-Fiction.

ISBN-13: 978-1-949897-16-6
LCCN: 2016915333

Design and Illustrations by Anderson Atlas

Raves for

Fools' Apocalypse
Beyond Symbiosis
Previously Published as 6th Horseman

Thank you to all that supported me through this novel including my family for putting up with my writing and drawing zeal. Thank you to my critique group members: Pam, Elaine, Kate, Marilyn, Elise and to Karl, my first beta reader.

FOOLS' APOCALYPSE PART 1

BEYOND

SYMBOIOSIS

In the archives of history
One thing is clear,
Know your enemy
Without prejudice or fear.
For there is one thing we all must remember,
We are always at war
And death always near.

The Examiner Blogger

And the Wind Will Carry Us Away

This is my last blog. I've brought you breaking news and government scandals for years, so you know I speak the truth.

The world as we know it will be gone in a matter of days. Last night, June 15, 2019, at 8:00 PM EDST, the president, members of his cabinet, the Joint Chiefs of Staff, leaders of both houses of Congress, the governor of New York, the mayor of New York City, along with federal and state law enforcement, issued a joint National Terrorism Advisory System (NATS) Alert of Imminent Threat. This alert is a genuine, Red-Label Level-5–the highest there is for public issue–and nobody is saying when or if it will end.

The reason for this NATS alert is a viral outbreak on the island of Manhattan.

The Department of Homeland Security Containment Plan was immediately set in motion for Manhattan, giving local authorities no time to advise citizens of the specific dangers and how individuals should protect their families and themselves.

Minutes after the alert was issued, elements of the military and homeland security acted to forcibly quarantine over 10 million people, bombing bridges, flooding subways, sinking private yachts, and filling the Hudson River with destroyers and heavily armed Coast Guard patrol boats. Rumors of martial law being declared are rampant. No declaration from the president or Congress has been made as of this writing.

Now, news rags are reporting that the CDC issued a bulletin advising citizens to remain calm because the virus is non-lethal.

Other sources say the Containment Plan, unofficially known as "Operation Forty Days," stopped a deadly virus from escaping the island. They tacitly blame the CDC for "underestimating the virulence" of the disease for not allowing anyone, including medical and rescue personnel, into Manhattan.

Yes, once again, the "mainstream" news rags, parroting the official Homeland Security line, are reporting the containment has worked, the situation on Manhattan Island is "fully under control."

They spew lies.

This morning, I left my Long Beach home to get close to the containment line and was shocked to see both the Hudson River and the Lower Bay vacant of Navy and Coast Guard vessels. No New York National Guard personnel, active duty Army, Navy, Marines, or Coast Guard are manning any sort of containment line. They've cleared out completely.

And now I am sick with the virus. It's in every nerve, and my body is breaking down into a sickening mush. This contagion is lethal; the mechanisms it uses to spread and reproduce are unknown. No information regarding efforts to stop the spread, create a vaccine or medical strategies for treating the sick has been issued to the citizens of Manhattan.

I fear for the future of humanity and for myself. Darkness lingers in the corners of my vision. I am without hope.

Ian Gladstone

Height: 5'11"
Weight: 197 lbs
Race: Caucasian
Hair Color: Black
Occupation: Unemployed activist. Organized March on Washington 2016, wrote award winning papers and has socialist political tendencies.
Family: Lost Mother in 2015, estranged from father

Ian Gladstone

Chapter 1

Ian Gladstone
Soldier in the Making

The world is forever changing, that's what it's good at, so be a part of that change. That is the takeaway from the graduation speech. Ian Gladstone is in the front row, in cap and gown, trying to think past cheeky colloquialisms and motivational dribble to see if the speech applies to him. Post eye roll, Ian's eyes land on a shadowy figure hiding in an exit nook, just out of the warm yellow light from the stage. Normally, this wouldn't stop Ian's rather rapid thought process, but he'd seen this silhouette before: black trench coat, a cliché fedora, and black gloves. Some creep wanna-be from a bad nineteen-twenty's movie is following me.

The speech ends, and the parade of graduates begins. But as the minutes pass, Ian's uneasiness grows. *Who is this bastard? What the hell does he want with me?* However meaningful the ceremony is meant to be, Ian misses it, and when his name is called, he misses that, too.

A classmate nudges Ian, knocking a carefully placed curl of jet-black, neatly trimmed hair from his cap. He tucks the hair away and speeds up the steps to accept his master's degree. He glances at the exit nook, but the figure is gone.

Ian rushes off stage and grabs his briefcase. He doesn't notice the three-hundred-dollar flower arrangements, the gold trim on his professor's gown, or the bright-eyed alums in the crowd. The image of the man in the nook is burned in his mind's eye.

He must be singling me out because of Mother. She's the public figure, after all. However, she isn't around and can't be bothered to show up for the ceremony. No, that shady jerk was watching me. I'm gonna kick his ass the next time I see him. I swear to god.

Today is a big day, and time is tight, thanks to dragged-out stupid ceremonies. Ian can't worry too much about a creepy fanboy. He shakes off his paranoia and pulls out his phone. He texts his mother as he waves down a cab. He fires off a text to the Senate staff assistant and the event coordinator, his revised time frame, all in the few seconds between standing, sitting, and door closing. He was good at his job.

"Webster Hall," Ian says to the driver.

"Webster Hall, here we comin'," the driver responds. "That be the famous Queen Anne-style theater that gave birth to labor union rallies, weddings, dances, and lectures. Hell of a landmark. What happenin' there tonight?"

"My mother is Senator Gladstone. Going to win re-election tonight. I'm sure you heard of her."

"Hell yeah. How's it being the son of the most powerful woman in the legislature?"

"Fine. Listen, I'm my mother's campaign coordinator and speechwriter, and I'm the reason she's won election after election since I was fifteen. You heard that right. I told her her rallies were boring, and she listened. Now, I need to make her speech tonight not suck, so if you don't mind."

"Sorry ta bother ya. I could tell you're important. I know the drill."

The cab slowly pushes through heavy traffic, allowing Ian to tighten up his mother's acceptance speech. He's a good writer, knows the right words to say, and can bring about shouting as easily as tears. The trick is to know how to blend lies with the truth in order to paint the most powerful story into people's minds—just remember to be fact-check proof, too.

Ian pays the driver, tips heavily as always, and then gets out of the cab. He pauses, waiting for traffic to clear before heading across the street to Webster Hall.

Thunder rolls overhead.

Webster Hall has a redbrick façade and its weather-stained marquee is as old as the city itself, but that's the charm. You can miss it, if not paying attention. Quite a symbolic place for an acceptance speech, paying homage to the working class and immigrants in the Lower East Side neighborhood. Now it's a bumping nightclub and concert hall but still fills with blue collars most nights.

A man in a dark suit steps in front of Ian.

"Excuse me," Ian says, trying to swerve around the man. He stops short. Is this the creep?

The stranger's skin is deep tan, their glasses

mirrored, and their hair is cut short. Not the dark figure that had been tailing him. "Walk with me a moment, Ian Gladstone." The man turns Ian's shoulder forcefully, and the two head away from the theater.

"You been following me?"

"Following? That's a bit egocentric, don't you think? I don't care about you or your silly speeches. I want your mother. You could have a bright future ahead if you cut that anchor." He didn't waste time. "Your mother got the virus, son."

"What the hell are you talking about?" Ian flushes with irritation, smoldering into anger. "I've got shit to do, man."

"Not a real virus. A mind virus. She's clinging to a romanticized idea that authoritarian power can solve everyone's problems. And because of your mother's wandering eye and greedy hands, she's getting into trouble. Her playing with the wrong people will set her up to spend twenty years in federal prison. Did she ever talk about someone named Zilla?"

Ian stops dead in his tracks.

The man continues to walk but turns. "Don't be a fool, Ian. Get your mother to turn herself in, and we'll go easy on her. Otherwise, she'll go down as a traitor, as will this Zilla person. They're messing with fire, Ian. Don't you get burned. I'll be in touch." He turns and walks off.

The anger in Ian's chest vanishes, replaced by stabbing fear in his stomach. Who is Zilla?

Ian finishes editing his mother's acceptance speech, albeit distracted and confused. He helps coordinate the team setting up the decorations in Webster Hall, verifies street closure and press pool area, and makes sure the food and wine are being handled. He checks the polls, but they're handsomely in his mother's favor. There's no worry there, so he goes home to wait until evening.

Time falls off the clock like tumbling bricks, but eventually, the polls close, his mother's success is announced. Ian feels no relief. His mind searches, thinks, uncovering suppressed memories, ignored emotions. The human brain loves patterns. It also notices breaks in those patterns. Is she really in trouble? Or was that guy trying to scare me?

Ian's mother, not shy about talking on the phone around anyone, had begun to shush her conversations when Ian entered the room. She went places at night, alone, and had been increasingly stressed this election—though it was a landslide.

Circumstantial. Ian shuts the worry off like a leaky hose bib, dresses in his most expensive tux, and rushes off to celebrate his mother's success.

The limo drops Ian off at Webster Hall amid a hundred reporters and fans. There will be some pop stars in attendance tonight, and some deep pockets.

The music thumps the walls, the wine and liquor flow, and the balloons eventually drop. Flower bouquets crowd the stage, and the backdrop is a huge American Flag. It reminds Ian of his graduation ceremony, one he barely had the time to enjoy, let alone share with his mother. He's here for her, but not the other way around. Ian is more bothered by that fact than he initially thought. Is she that selfish? Could she be breaking election rules to get ahead? Mingling with someone named Zilla? Sounds like Godzilla. Obviously, some fool with an ego the size of the Asian continent. If she's in deep, it won't be just her career that ends. It will be mine.

Minutes before midnight Ian leaves the celebration with his mother. She's drunk, her eyes red, her sway pronounced.

Ian didn't have a drop. He shifts nervously, never having confronted his mother before, but finally spits out, "I was approached by some guy that looked like a Fed."

His mother sits up. Her blue satin dress shifted; the carnation pinned to her dress fell to the dirty limo floor. "Intimidation. Those filthy Republicans."

"Are you in trouble? You have to tell me."

"Pffff," she says. "You know how the shitheads play. It's all fucking lies. Don't worry about a thing."

Ian helps his mother to her room and lays her on the bed, stripping her shoes off and tucking her feet under the sheets. "Goodnight, Mother." He leaves a glass of water next to four ibuprofen on the nightstand and heads to the balcony to smoke. Something doesn't feel right. She's not acting like herself. First off, she doesn't cuss, and secondly, she had popped some pills earlier that Ian had never seen her take before.

The night glows with streetlights and backlit windows. Cars zip by, zipping through shallow puddles noisily unfazed by the late hour.

Halfway through the cigarette, the fed steps from a black SUV parked across the street. He stands in the middle of the road and looks up, puffing on his own cigarette.

Ian heads downstairs, out the front door, and to the sidewalk.

"Who are you? What agency are you with?"

"FBI." The man pulls out a badge and holds it up, but it's too dark to see. "Are you going to help your mother?"

"By turning her in? Are you fucking serious?" Ian shakes. He's afraid but trapped.

"Make a deal with us. Tell us everything you know, and she'll get a slap on the hand, and your career will not get hit. Win-win."

"Nothing's win-win."

"What do you know about the Stone of Allah?

"What?" Ian spat. Getting more irritated by the second. "What stone? Nothing. Never heard of it. Why?"

"Good." The fed hands Ian his card then tosses his smoke onto the road and smashes it. His foot twists and twists until the butt is nothing but filament.

"What does a Stone of Allah have to do with my mother?"

"Not sure yet." He leaves.

Ian paces on the sidewalk. The more he thinks about it, the more he knows his mother is doing something illegal. She's tied into something, justifying what she's doing, and a heartbeat from getting caught. I can try to dig it out of her. No. She'd never give in to my pestering. She's too stubborn.

Ian can't sleep. He smokes, tries to watch TV, tries to exercise, but it's all too much. Every minute that passes feels like an eternity, and every breath inflates his resolve to confront her about what she's into.

At four in the morning, Ian hears the back door slide open. His mother, still in her blue cocktail dress and no shoes, slips outside with a large black briefcase and a shovel. She digs a hole under the rose bushes, quickly, and buries the case. She tries to fix the grass so it looks untouched. She fails.

She returns to the house and takes a shower.

Ian slips out of the shadows he'd hid in, digs the case up, and opens it with a screwdriver, revealing stacks of documents and a dozen USB drives. "Of fucking course. What the hell else would be in here?" He mumbles, reflecting on the fact that his parents were filthy rich and didn't need any money, let alone an amount that could fill a small briefcase. He flipped through the documents. Missile designs. "Jesus. Selling defense secrets? Why? It's not like we need the cash, Mom," he mumbles, sweat trickling down his forehead. Ian stands and turns just as his mother steps outside. Her hair is wrapped in a purple towel, another one around her body.

She doesn't say a word.

Ian tips up the briefcase and dumps out the papers and memory chips. The prints flutter to the damp grass. "Who's Zilla? And what the hell are you doing for him?"

She stiffens like a statue, her eyes dark in her pill-drunk state. "You can't tell anyone about this or about Zilla. I'm sorry you heard his name," she says, stifling tears. "I tried to keep my conversations out of earshot."

She doesn't know the Feds are talking to me. "What did you do?" Ian yells. "Are you taking me down, too? Your own son?"

She shakes her head because she's at the top of the steps, and she looks down on Ian. "The less you know, the better. So stop snooping." She whips around, heading inside, but pauses. "Pick all of that up and rebury it. Do it quickly." She stomps upstairs without another glance back.

Ian doesn't bury the case. He sets it on the breakfast table, shedding dirt on the table mats. I can't go to jail. She won't take me down with her, will she? He makes a cappuccino and, while steaming the milk, slips his hand in the pocket of his slacks, thumbing the Fed's business card. All Ian can do is sit at the breakfast table and think.

He has seen some unusual activity. Strange meetings, large bills. Last year, Lester Comings of the New York Post was found shot in the back near Central Park the very day he dared to ask questions beyond what Senator Gladstone agreed to answer. Could my mother Have had something to do with his death? It was never Ian's place to ask about inconsistencies or discrete meetings, so he never did. But as his mind unwraps suppressed memories, he realizes how many secrets his mother is keeping and there are many.

As six rolls around, the doorbell rings. Ian pulls his exhausted body off the chair and slogs to the front door. He's so tired but vibrating with an alien weight hanging on his shoulders. He swings the massive, red, oak door open, letting a massage therapist inside—the therapist knows where to go, lugging his table and bag to the stairs.

"You're here early," Ian snaps.

"So are you."

Ian would normally retort with an equally vitriolic statement, but he's too tired.

His mother startled him, standing at the top of the stairs. "You're done. I'll be replacing you as of today." She spun on her heels after the massage therapist lumbered past her, following him into her bedroom.

Ian swelled with anger. "She's fucking up my career too. God damn her."

The world is a strange place. People are strange, but like animals, self-preservation is the number one rule. Ian dials the FBI and steps onto the porch. "I'll tell you everything I know."

A dozen agents arrive in minutes. They interrupt the massage, take the documents and USB drives, and haul the newly reelected senator out the front door. She's not mad. Sadness fills her eyes and streams down her cheeks, but her jaw is locked tight.

\#

She's indicted on half a dozen charges, including racketeering, perjury, conspiracy to sell Department of Defense trade secrets, and others.

Ian moves out of his home, an order from his enraged father, though regret fills his heart, growing over the ventricle like a killer octopus.

Mrs. Gladstone pays the million-dollar bail and returns home to await trial.

Ian can't stay away. He has to see her, to apologize and admit his act of preservation was the most selfish thing he's ever done.

"Mom!" Ian calls out as he pushes inside the mansion.

"In bed," she responds.

She stands in her bedroom doorway, wearing red silk pajamas. Ian notices how thin she looks, how her top sits on her bony shoulders like she'd forgotten to take out the hanger.

"I'm sorry," Ian mumbles. "For turning you in. You fired me. I was oissed that you were betraying us, this city… this country. I-I couldn't flush my life down the shitter."

She motions him through the door and closes it. "I understand. I brought you up to follow the law. Drink this." She hands him a scotch on the rocks.

Ian downs the drink in one gulp. "I feel like shit."

She sits on the bed. "You should." She breathes deep. "There's one thing you don't understand. The rules are bent out of shape. They're like an airline wreck, just a mess. I broke them to gain the power to fix them. But I see my folly. Humanity is a caterpillar begging to cocoon and hatch into a butterfly. The whole system must be destroyed in order for a new one to emerge. Fighting from the inside of the system is futile."

Ian listens. Shocked at the revelations. He never heard the skeletons in her closet rattle, but someone heard their seductive whispers.

"You are going to hear things about me tomorrow or the next day. The news will break that I transferred classified satellite defense documents to the Chinese government."

Ian knows that part is true, but the question of why still confuses him. "Who is Zilla?"

"The truth is vastly more complicated." She shifts

her eyes away, looking out the window.

"What's really going on then?"

She refills his tumbler and her own. They drink. Her eyes flutter. She's pale, skin and bones. "I will lose this fight because the right-wing military industrialists' powers are too strong. I must pass the torch to you now."

"Wait a second." Ian sets the glass on the nightstand among dozens of photos of him with her, from his newborn pictures to now.

She turns Ian's face so he can look into her eyes. "Take the torch and run with it. We're close to changing the system, so close. Don't distract yourself with anything. Not girls, drugs, or greed. The system has cracks, so use them to smash the walls to bits." Her eyes roll, and she sways. "The powerful need to be checked. They are the future thieves, your future. Someone must stop them."

"You're stinking drunk." The booze was certainly going straight to his head. "I guess I can't blame you."

She collapses, folding into the down comforter like a stone.

"Jesus, what's wrong?" Ian touches her arm, then her forehead. Clammy.

"I love you. I'll be watching. Go make me proud, and don't feel sorry for me. This is okay. I will never go to jail. Not ever. Zilla will contact you. Trust him."

"What's going on? I'm calling the ambulance. You look terrible."

Her grip tightens on his arm. His heart pounds and swells. Dizziness rolls through his brain as his veins flood with molten lava. The room darkens like shadows closing in. She pulls him down and hugs him hard. Ian pulls away, crying. "I need to get help," he slurs.

"I remember you as a baby and a boy. I remember your first bike, your broken arm when you were at my swearing-in ceremony. . . I'm sorry I missed your graduation ceremony. Master's is a huge step up."

Ian climbs off her bed, feeling as if someone had strapped bricks to his chest. "Phone, Mother! Fuck!" He pulls his phone from his pocket, swipes the screen open, and tries to focus on the icons. They're blurry and swimming over the screen. Ian moves toward the door but can't pick his foot up off the carpet.

Her voice softens to a whisper.

Ian falls to his knees and struggles toward the door. "Mother! What ju-do to me?" he says, slurring.

"I love you, and I forgive you. Take my torch," she says over and over. "Trust Zilla."

Ian turns back to her, then loses all sensations before crumpling to the plush carpet.

She dies in her bed, sixty years escaping in one last breath.

#

Initially, the press had thrown Senator Gladstone under the bus. Shockingly, the reports took on a gentler voice after her suicide. She left a twenty-page document expounding her innocence, and her loyal community believed every word.

Ian knew she was into something with this Zilla guy but tried to remain open-minded until finding out exactly what Zilla was about. He knew his mother. She wasn't evil in any way, mixed up maybe, but not evil.

The more he played back the events in his head, the more he realized he should not have turned her in. She had only fired him to keep his ass clean. He should have trusted her, listened to her, and insisted she tell him the truth.

Zilla contacted Ian six months later through email. The note was simple: a generic greeting, a dozen dates and locations. I never said Zilla, but Ian knew it was him.

The list was a sort of itinerary. Ian couldn't resist and followed it to the letter.

He found himself tumbling through chaotic, backroom political rallies, self-avowed communist organizations, and unsavory, less-than-legitimate activist groups.

He let his hair grow long and forgot about suits and campaigns. Growing in his darkening heart was the desire to come at society from behind.

#

One year to the date, Ian gets an email from Zilla.

I can see you want to be a part of the change, Ian. Real change. Like your mother wanted. The email reads. I have a tough job only you can accomplish. Are you willing to get your hands dirty?

Ian smiles. "Hell yeah."

Chapter 1.1

Ian Gladstone
As the Clock Stops

Ian stares at his phone, his eyes a little blurry and tired from working all day crawling through, cleaning duct after duct, and planting Zilla's surveillance gear. He had taken so many risks to get the job done. Now it is. Eight months of effort are coming to an end. Untraceable bugs have been set up in offices across New York. *What now? What do I do?*

Maybe Ian can breathe deeply again. No one will know his name, but he will see the part he's played. When Zilla and his lawyers gather enough solid evidence to prosecute the corrupt bastards in the city and state government, Ian will revel in being the shadow warrior, the virus in the machine, and the window washer. He is the spy in the dark who will never get credit for good deeds. Then, with Zilla's help, Ian can find a way to infiltrate the Feds. Spying is in his blood now, a fuel he didn't think he could do without.

Ian doesn't even think about the fact that he's never met Zilla, never looked into his eyes, never heard his real voice. *Whoever Zilla is, how can I be sure he's one of the good guys?* Ian shakes off the doubt. *The country will know Zilla soon enough.*

Ian orders a latte. A dude with dark circles under his eyes and pasty skin cranks out cup after cup of steaming espresso and milk and flips coins at people. The guy *seems fine working ten-hour days* and *making less than a livable wage, but he shouldn't be.*

Finding a seat on a knee-high wall bordering a grassy patch and a tall metal sculpture that needs to be recycled in a bad way, Ian watches people pass. A woman pushes through the crowd, running down the street like a lunatic, but she's not the only one acting weird. Ian senses energy in the crowd but can't quite name their mood. Everyone has their phones to their ears—entirely normal—but their faces are tight and contorted. It's like the crowd is collectively cramping with gas in their guts.

A guy in a tacky plaid shirt and a flat cap yells into his cell phone, "Yeah, right! The military satellites are down. Trust me. I've got a source at the *Times*. The government is peeing in their pants." Ian stands and follows him, eavesdropping. "Yeah, well, if the government satellites are that vulnerable, then this virus will start crawling across the Internet. . . Yeah, I'd unplug it and sell off your SEC antivirus stock."

Ian turns around and heads home. Everyone he passes looks worried and agitated.

"Mornin', Mr. Gladstone." The doorman opens the door and tips his hat.

"It's Ian. Mr. Gladstone is my father." Ian tries to return a smile, though he can't stand having doors opened for him. He's a man of the people, not some rich guy.

The flat-screen TV in the lobby is on, and the volume is high. Ian stops to listen to a blonde woman spouting off: "We are getting reports that an attack targeting the satellite infrastructure of the United States is underway." Ian holds his breath. *She's not talking about my little spy game, is she? I didn't infect anything with a virus. Just planted bugs that intercepted communications.*

"The computer virus is labeled Salt and Pepper. Aptly named because it is corrupting servers with error codes at an astonishing rate while leaving nude photos of pop stars on the controller's desktops." The reporter said.

The satellites are failing, and my last job for Zilla was in a DOD satellite control facility. Is there a connection? There can't be. Why would Zilla bother bugging offices if he was just going to send out a computer virus?

The elevator doors open, and G. Mason, a slick businessman addicted to the call-girl type, stands against the back elevator wall. He shakes his cell phone at Ian. "I was about to make ten thou on the UK stock exchange," he complains. "But the satellite dropped my call. Smart-ass hacker needs to get a job."

Ian nods because his throat is too dry to speak. Every time he hears this guy talk about losing money, Ian feels triumphant. They switch places as Ian gets in the elevator.

"I better check my accounts," Ian croaks sheepishly. That came out wrong. *Why do I feel so nervous? Oh, right. I always feel this way after committing a federal crime.*

"Hacker's probably some punk living in his mama's basement, eating animal cookies for lunch. I hope they throw him in jail for the rest of his life." The man hurries away, smacking his gum like a hyperactive cow.

The doors close, the elevator rises, and Ian murmurs, "*You* are one of the reasons this world is so screwed. I hope you lose your entire fortune with this computer virus." *Maybe I'll piss on his door.* Ian shakes his head, regretting that thought. *Time to check out; I'm frazzled.*

The elevator door opens, and a man pushes past Ian. Ian steps off the elevator and freezes. He spins around. The man is wearing a pitch-black trench coat, a fedora, and black gloves. *That's the creep* who *had been following me the year before.* Ian thought it was the Feds but never got confirmation.

"Hey!" Ian yelps. He dashes to stop the elevator doors, but they close. Ian slaps the call button, but the elevator is on its way down. Ian looks to the other elevator doors but knows there's no way to beat the creep to the first floor. *Who the hell is that guy? Why is he following me?* Ian walks to his door, wrapped in confusion.

A red package and a bottle of Blue Label Johnny Walker scotch lay at the foot of his door. The scotch has a nice black bow tied around it. Ian scoops up the package and the bottle and slips inside his condo. He then relocks the lock and turns his security bar until it clicks. He sets the red box and the scotch on the coffee table and stares at them. *It's gotta be a gift from Zilla. Who else? Today was my last install. Ha! The man in the fedora. He's Zilla.*

Ian opens the red box and finds a red-tinted syringe. Ian's brain can't process what he's seeing, so he opens the scotch and takes a long swig. Creepy to give someone a shot. It could be Zilla's idea of a joke. Ian pushes the box aside and flips on the TV.

Two-hundred-dollars-a-bottle whiskey begins working its magic. The burn in his throat sends icy shivers along his nerves, the rest of his body anticipates the whiskey glow. Ian immediately takes another drink, savoring the heat. He feels the stress flake off his consciousness like weathered paint peeling in the sunlight.

The news about the computer virus rages nonstop until two in the morning when the TV fuzzes out. Ian laughs when the cable news channel finally gets the bug. Blondes in suits should have expected the virus to attack their computer systems. He takes two sleeping pills and passes out.

The next day, Ian wakes up with a bad hangover around eleven, which is too early to get up. He tries to turn on the lights, but they don't work. He lumbers to the bathroom, but the lights don't flick on either. Ian pisses, flushes, but the water doesn't refill. Something is wrong in the building. The sink faucet is dry, too. *Damn, what I really need is a hot shower.* He picks up the TV remote and tries to turn it on. *No electricity, dummy.*

Ian's watch is dead. Confusion sets in as he slips into panic mode. He leaps to the nearest window, throws the curtains open, and peers down. A five-car pileup clogs the street in front of the building. The traffic lights are out, and crowds gather in the middle of the street as if in an anxiety parade.

Adrenaline kicks in; Ian runs to the closet and riffles through boxes until he finds his binoculars, a sixteenth birthday gift from Dad. The binoculars are six-hundred-dollar peeps, still unused. He rips open the box and runs back to the window. The street is a mess. People are yelling at each other, hovering around the car crash when another car bangs over the curb and sidewalk, smashing head-on into the building across the street. At the same time, two guys throw punches at one another in front of the barbershop. No one tries to stop them.

Ian runs to the lobby, taking the stairs two at a time. It's empty. No bellhop. No annoying rich neighbors. The street is a different story. Thousands are running, walking, or stumbling up the street like rats fleeing a sinking ship. Cars are jam-packed, and some people are scrambling over the tops. A motorcycle weaves in and out, pushing pedestrians out of the way without a word or gesture, while sirens and horns and screams drown out the voices pleading for help. Ian paces in the lobby for a minute, then goes outside. *Someone has to be able to give me some news.*

Ian is immediately attacked by a very sick man.

Nope, not gonna stay out here. Ian ducks back inside, fearing the intensity of the crowd. He can't hear anything over the thumping in his ears. His stomach tightens as he flies up the stairwell and ducks into his condo.

The house is so quiet without the TV. Ian tries his battery-operated MP3 player, but it doesn't work either. *What the hell?* Anxiety builds. He pours a drink of scotch and watches the world from the window. The crowd in the street continues flowing like a river. The street has bloomed with fear, and the mass migration is never-ending except for the bodies left behind. People fight, push past each other, and trample the slow and the weak. Total chaos has erupted, and no one is in control. This is the end reel; the credits will run soon enough.

Gunshots echo through the noise. Machine guns. A Humvee tears down the street, rams a car wreck, slows, trying to push past it, and people swarm it. Ian can't look away.

A boom shakes the building. Shock keeps Ian anchored to the floor.

A body—a woman—falls from above, straight past his window. His heart stops, and he drops his drink.

A jumper? Or was she pushed off her balcony? Ian finds her with the binoculars splattered on the sidewalk like a stomped orange. His circulation feels thick like mud, and his thoughts are dull. The sound is muffled as if he's anchored to the bottom of a great and heavy sea. He wants to shut down, hit his power button, and blink out of existence. Did he have something to do with what's going on outside? *Is this Zilla's next phase? Has Zilla gone too far? Have I?*

Storm clouds part, and a jet plunges toward the ground, smoke pouring from the engines trailing behind like a tether to hell. It crashes a few blocks away, behind some apartments. A moment later, the window rattles. A plume of black smoke grows like an expanding balloon, rising to greet the other smoke and ash coalescing along the skyline. At this rate, there won't be a skyline. It will crumble to rubble and dust after the fires have their way. Ian gulps more scotch. *What will I do if my building catches fire? I won't have anywhere to run.* His father lives upstate and hasn't spoken with him for years. The only contact with him comes in the form of checks that pay for the condo. *Is my father worrying about me?*

Ian is alone now, so he has time to think about himself. He sits, but his insides spin like a neutron star. If he could get just a little sleep, a few hours, he could think better. The scotch won't knock him out. The medicine cabinet has the answer. He takes two sleeping pills and leans over the sink in case he throws them up.

The pills hit like a kick in the head. Time becomes meaningless. He forgets about the world and has no more inclination to leave the condo. He dances, makes jokes, and goes utterly mad for four or five hours. Ian ends up face-to-face with one of his writing awards clinging to the wall

in a two-hundred-dollar frame his father insisted upon. It reads: *High Literary Achievement Award from Columbia University. Awarded to Ian Gladstone.* The type is printed with shiny metallic ink and has an official-looking gold insignia and fancy borders. Ian rips it off the wall and stomps on it.

He tries to sit on his sofa, misses the cushion completely, and lands on his ass. The room spins, and he laughs so hard his head tightens like it's in a vise. His eyes tear. The world is so funny. It played a joke on him, and he just got the punch line. It's been too long since Ian laughed like that—he's taken everything so seriously for years, acting as if he were the only one who could fix this broken culture. His part is genuinely infinitesimal.

The door bursts inward, and five men hustle into the living room, two carrying a police battering ram, all of them wearing bulletproof vests, pistols, and batons in their belts, but they aren't officers. They're thieves.

Ian gapes, frozen as a bronze statue.

The guy with the wife-beater shirt under his vest and intricate tribal tattoos covering his body comes at Ian.

Ian knows he should be able to raise his hands to defend himself or his home, but he's too fucked up.

Tattoo-man's baton clocks Ian across the head, and he twists and sinks into an abyss of dark swirling pain.

One guy says, "No food."

Another snap, "We're not here for munchies, fool!"

The closet door bangs open, and Ian's desk drawer is flung into the wall.

The pounding in Ian's head increases; warm blood drips down his forehead. *Shit.* The spinning doesn't stop. He wants to pull out his phone, call the cops, an ambulance. *Ha!* He's railed against the police state in blogs and articles for years, never thinking he'd need them. Now, here he is, wishing they would or could save his life.

Ian cracks his eyes open and watches the guys move to the door. They've got armfuls of his expensive clothes, suits, computer, backup hard drive, guitar, and a box of jewelry his mother left him—everything of monetary value Ian has in the world. He should tell them the computer stuff is as valuable as a burnt toast. Well, it doesn't take a genius to be an asshole.

The tattooed man returns to Ian, slips off his Rolex watch, and brings the baton down on his head again.

\#

Ian's eyes open slowly. Light infiltrates his bruised brain as the early morning sun squeezes through the gaps in the blinds, barely pushing back the dark. His once-tidy apartment is completely trashed, and everything of value is gone. Ian is naked now; he has nothing left in this world. He used to rail against consumerism, but now he wants all his stuff back.

Getting up, Ian goes to the mirror to examine his wounds. His blurry reflection is thin, covered in blood, and shaking. Ian uses water from a bottle to clean off the blood and then takes a handful of ibuprofen.

Not a sound enters his ears—no cars, no screaming or crying, no computer fan or air-conditioning unit—nothing.

His head spins, and he sits awkwardly on the floor, putting his head between his knees. When the spinning stops, he moves to the window and whips open the blinds so that light penetrates every nook and cranny of the condo because he doesn't want to be in darkness anymore.

The New York skyline is still, cold, and silent, like the model on his dad's development table. The beginning of the new day, the dark new day, is here. The sky is a swarm of blackened clouds, and the buildings look dingy and old without lights. The stillness is far from tranquil. Sadness hovers in the air, tears fly on the wind, and silent screams stick in the throats of millions. No birds fly, no cars honk, and no dogs bark.

Ian doesn't know how everything went wrong, but he instinctively knows that things are worse than he ever thought possible.

Ian forces himself to go downstairs, taking the steps slowly, and emerges on the street like Rip Van Winkle.

Car crashes still clog the street, and the Humvee's windows are shattered. Soldiers' bodies are splayed on the pavement, beaten and trampled. Ian walks to the corner of Ninety-Sixth Avenue, where a broken water main floods the street.

A nearby door bursts open. A red-haired woman wearing a pink robe runs toward him, choking so hard she can't speak. She collides with Ian, her eyes bloodshot and her skin pale blue. She grabs his arms, her grip tightening.

"Hey, hey, I...uh," Ian croaks.

She slumps to the sidewalk, trying to pull Ian down with her. Bubbles form on her lips as she tries to speak, but her eyes cloud over, and she dies in his arms. She was waiting for someone, anyone, to hold on to so she wouldn't die alone.

Ian is dizzy. At first, he thinks seeing her die is making him ill, until he coughs, splattering blood into his palm. He's sick! Ian remembers the red syringe Zilla sent him, switches into full flight mode, runs to his building, up all twelve flights, adrenalin smashing through his nervous system. Ian whips the door open. The red box is not on the coffee table.

The men. Did they grab it? Ian scrambles around like a drug addict, searching for a fix. The box is by the wall, kicked there and ignored. Ian opens the box, hands shaking, and removes the syringe. He unfolds the paper under it. It depicts an arm with an arrow pointing to the shoulder, along with the following text:

> Just so you know your actual contribution, all those cameras, listening, and data collection devices you set up in the police stations, the National Guard, the defense contractors, and the satellite control facility were filled with a deadly virus released in an aerosol micro-spray. The virus is unstoppable, and so is our progress. A cure is in the syringe. We believe in rewarding our soldiers. Thank you for your service.
> ~Zilla

Closing his eyes, afraid to wait one more moment, Ian plunges the needle into his shoulder.

A deep thud shakes the building. Ian looks out the window and sees a Bradley fighting vehicle roll over cars, smashing them into piles of junk. The tank hits the sidewalk, its tracks kicking up debris and smashing concrete curbs. Ian is surprised to see the vehicle alone, with no support troops anywhere. A man emerges from the hatch, his long hair lifting in the breeze, smoking a fat cigar.

Ian turns from the new city, the one now run by oppressive thugs and opportunists, those whose only ability is to take from the weak, and faces his empty condo. The walls seem to shrink and push in on him.

Ian's mind fills with the echo of Zilla spitting his conspiracy theories. His promises for a better future, a better humanity. But Zilla is the liar, the crook, the greatest of evils. He has staged the biggest terrorist attack in all of history.

Ian retches until nothing remains in his stomach.

Zilla is somewhere, relishing his madness, a red syringe at his feet. But Zilla *doesn't deserve the mercy. He deserves to die alone, infected with his own virus, not all the innocent lives just trying to get along in this crazy world. He'd hunt Zilla down.* But hunting him is a fool's errand. Zilla will go unpunished. Ian folds his arms tight across his chest. I never even saw his face.

I need to get out of the city and far, far away.

How did I get so manipulated?

After Ian's mother's death, he needed to rescue his mother's reputation. In his mind, he couldn't accept her folly. She had always been so bright. Her death affected him more than he thought. His world had shattered, but he thought he was uncovering the truth. How grief twisted his mind.

That's why Ian did what Zilla wanted. Ian couldn't see reason through all the lies fed to him by Zilla and other merchants of conspiracy. He wasn't even looking.

CHAPTER 1.2

IAN
THE PATRIOT FOOL

Ian wants Zilla dead, strung up, and bled to death. Whipped, tortured, and made to hurt for his actions. But who is the mass murderer? Ian had never seen him. *Fucker shouldn't get away with this. Who was Zilla? Were any clues left behind?* Ian revisits his only close encounter.

    #

Eight months before the viral outbreak, an email from Zilla set Ian's fate in motion. Zilla crystalized and funded the political rebellion Ian so desperately wanted. Zilla despised, as Ian did, capitalist tyranny and believed the filthy rich Wall Street moneymen corrupted the entire

US banking system, which led to currency manipulation, shadow courts, and wars for oil. Zilla wanted to see the power given back to the ninety-nine percent—the *forgotten man.*

Zilla articulated the problem of greed better than Ian did, which was rare. Sometimes, they'd chat online for hours at night, agreeing on every political issue.

After months of dialog, Zilla divulged his plan. Ian remembered Zilla's words perfectly: "Man's indifference and plunder of this Earth is over. American wealth held by the gluttonous, indolent capitalists suppresses global change. These wicked puppet masters are too powerful."

"Are you talking about the Bilderberg group? The G8? Illuminati? How do we even know which one controls our government?"

"We must know who the puppet masters are!" Zilla blurted. "We must find corruption wherever it hides. But we have to start small and think logically. Spy on the pawns, follow the money, find the knights and bishops, let them lead us to the kings and queens."

Zilla continued, "We must identify every single double-dealer feeding at the trough. This is where you come in. I have bugs in White House offices and bedrooms, the vice president's residence, West Wing offices, and all the offices in the Eisenhower building in Washington. However, the elite are careful to conduct their shady business in discreet restaurants and private clubs that are regularly swept for surveillance devices. But we have to find a way to get this information. We must know the orders the masters give to the police, the military generals, the national guard, and defense contractors."

His request hit Ian like a sledgehammer to the groin. "You want me to bug the cops and the military?" Ian had asked.

"Yes. With undetectable cameras and wi-fi data interceptors, we can tie down the conspirators, who they employ, and how they communicate. The corrupt are in control. Identifying the crooked leaders and their followers is essential to our plans to destroy capitalism."

Ian loved the idea of a "gotcha" move that wouldn't hurt anyone but reveal the hidden power hierarchies, so he signed up.

Ian was stoked, on fire, expectant to change the world. He followed his mother's lead but believed he'd effect more change than she had in her twelve years in the US Senate and two in the House. And he would not get caught.

Ian ducked into the fancy bathroom at Aldea in the Flatiron Building, wondering if his faded jeans and secondhand button-up shirt turned any heads. The bathroom was bathed in gold light. The three stalls and two urinals were enshrined in marble, with no attendant. Ian's shoes squeaked as he rushed into a stall and closed the door. The toilet, though clean, looked like every other toilet. *People piss and shit the same*; no *bloated bank account or trust fund will ever change that. The rich and the poor were separated only by corruption, bad ideas, and stupidity.* He sits.

He was anxious as he waited, letting his mind flitter about. He smelled some kind of fragrance. *Hmm. Woodsy musk mixed with a sharp Irish Spring kickback.* His nose wrinkled.

The bathroom door opened. A man entered the next stall. Ian peeked at the shoes: rich brown, dark stitches, and glossy as a mirror, probably made of lambskin or some other miserable animal's hide.

"Ian Gladstone?" A computer-altered voice came from the speaker on a cell phone.

Ian cleared his throat. "Yeah, that's me."

The man sat an overstuffed, black duffle bag on the marble floor. Gloved hands slid it over.

Ian dug through the contents, feeling like a drug dealer inspecting stacks of bills. "Zilla?"

"Pardon my paranoia, but you can't know who I really am. I must maintain my position of power to affect change."

"I get it." Coveralls, a tool belt, a clipboard, and a square toolbox were in the duffle. "Everything we talked about is in here? ID, too?"

"You're all set." Zilla's voice sounded like Darth Vader speaking through a tin can. "Did I ever tell you how much I respected your mother?"

"No. We usually keep to politics. Though she did tell me to trust you." Ian wanted to see Zilla's face, see the man behind the curtain, and know how much power Zilla really had and how famous or infamous he was. It's like seeing cake through the glass without money to buy it. No. It's worse. It's smelling the cake only.

Ian had told himself it was okay not to know who Zilla was. What mattered was what Zilla said and did. *Actions define men, not flesh and bone.*

"She was smart—a good leader. You have done well following her lead," Zilla commented.

"Let's get this done before someone comes in. I'm ready."

"The consequences will be yours if you fail. Wait five minutes before you leave." With those final words, the man stood, opened the stall, and walked out of the bathroom.

Ian slipped into the navy coveralls. They fought back because he refused to remove his shoes, and the uniform was one size too small. After wriggling around, the uniform seemed to fit.

As Ian left the stall, he stopped at the mirror. His

nerves were strung tightly, sending a humming sound throughout his body. It was a good hum, like the resonant decay at the end of a good song. A stitched logo embellished the left chest, and a clipped-on ID badge declared his name: Alex, Air Conditioning Specialists of New York.

Ian wet his hands and ran water through his jet-black hair. He was a soldier now, powerful and untouchable. Rebelliousness always felt good.

He tossed his T-shirt and jeans into the garbage and left the bathroom. His vision was acute, and his heart pounded rhythmically as adrenaline snaked through his body at record speed.

The pretentious lobby bar was packed, even though it was early afternoon. The suits and preps surrounding the overstuffed leather chairs probably didn't have jobs anyway.

#

Ian chokes on the memory. *Pretentious preps. I'm such an* asshole. He wants to run to all the people he thought poorly about and take them into his arms. Even dealing with assholes is better than everyone around him dead or dying. *Regrets. Yeah, they're mounting.*

#

The preps were watching a game on an eighty-inch TV that commands the crowd's attention. Ian's watch said he had some time; the phone in his breast pocket would buzz when he was clear. He took a seat at the bar.

The cute bartender nodded at him. Her bright red hair was braided and held together by a metal clip with sharp talon-like protrusions. Her eyeliner was thick, and her lipstick dark red. Ian couldn't stop looking at her, imagining her becoming a bonfire on a beach at night, with flames so bright they transformed the surrounding crowd into meaningless shadows.

"Need something, or are you still on the clock?" Her

45

voice was forceful but oddly soothing.

"IPA, thanks. Anything local."

She drew a pint from the tap and set it on an embossed napkin. "This is my favorite brew, Boulevard IPA. Let me know if you like it."

Ian gulped without tasting and smiled at her. "It's good."

Someone scored, and the crowd burst into cheers.

She leaned in and said, "It's got orange, grapefruit, and a hint of lime."

Ian adjusted his coveralls again, then looked at his watch.

"Little nervous? Are you starting a new job, Alex? Need to take the edge off?" She winked.

Looking uncomfortable was a bad move. Ian forced a chuckle and touched his ID badge. "Ah, no. I'm off the clock." His brain raced as he tried to find a reason for his apparent jitters and sweaty forehead. "I've got money on the game." That should work. "I need to change. This uniform doesn't quite fit. Temp job. My day job is event organizer for Red Stars." Ian snapped his mouth shut and looked away. *Damn it, I'm Alex, not Ian, the political activist. Instead of being in spy mode, I'm blabbing to some girl at a bar! Maybe I should walk away and go home.*

"Oh, my god! I subscribe to them. Read their RSS every day." Her eyes widen, big and bright, and her cheeks flush.

His mother's familiar words sounded in his mind. "Girls and family are distractions. You're a political architect. Your noble action is selflessness, and your sacrifice will be remembered throughout history."

For noble reasons, Ian's mother neglected his father, her sister, and the Gladstone extended family. Ian wished she could watch him change the world for the better.

46

The girl at the bar chatted away, but Ian wasn't paying attention. He nodded and smiled enough to keep her going while she served beers and made drinks for impatient patrons. His phone buzzed, startling him. "I'm sorry," Ian said, cutting her off. "I'd love to continue our chat, but I've got to go."

Unfazed, she put down a fresh napkin and wrote her name and number. "Call me?"

Ian smiled and touched her finger as she handed him the number. "Yeah." He hefted the duffle bag over his shoulder and left the bar, pausing in the Flatiron Building's shadow.

Ian looked at her number and sighed. She was so cute. Sighing again, he wadded it up and tossed it in the garbage. Time to make history now. No distractions. His real work was just beginning.

Ian walked to the subway and boarded a train to the Brooklyn Bridge, dodging the tourist crowd. He walked briskly up Pearl Street, passing the slower people and the weekend photographers. His first job was at One Police Plaza and the police commissioner's office.

Ian passed a van parked in a unique permit space at the curb, the logo identical to the one he wore on his chest.

A woman wearing a tight, dark blue skirt and a white-collared top walked toward him. Her green eyes targeted and held him. Ian noticed a scar on her cheek that extended to her jaw. The moment they passed, she stumbled and grabbed his arm, sliding a set of keys into his hand along with a folded paper. "Excuse me," she blurted as she regained her footing and walked away.

Ian pocketed the keys and read the paper. It was a work order.

The craziest thing Ian's ever done was going according to Zilla's plan. If caught, Ian would go to jail.

Using the key to unlock the van's passenger door, Ian set the duffle on the seat. Hands shaking, he unzipped the bag and took out the tools.

Ian crossed the expansive brick courtyard to One Police Plaza, a simple modern design, probably built to appear as solid as a bunker. Ian's father, the great architect, would hate it. On the other hand, it mocked ostentatious décor with its modesty and looked as blue-collar as possible. The building was thirteen stories tall with small square windows surrounded by red bricks, perhaps the most secure building in all of New York.

Ian passed metal barricades intended to funnel people directly toward the entrance. A hundred uniformed cops passed, going in and out, plus a hundred people in plain clothes and suits. No one even looked at Ian. He was trying to look as confident as he can. *Keep your head up and back straight, but be casual. You're just another guy doing his job.*

Near the entrance were a dozen cops with machine guns slung from their shoulders, muzzles down, chatting and gossiping about the game or some other bit of drama.

Ian handed the work order to a uniformed man at the exterior entrance, who read over the document and returned it, pointing to the front door. Ian passed through the gold-framed revolving door and entered the front lobby. Giant vertical banners towered high over his head. One said "HEROES," and another displayed a representation of an NYPD badge. Ian crossed to a side door near the elevators, swiped the card Zilla gave him through the electronic card reader next to the handle and waited. The card reader's light turned green, and he entered the small, windowless room. There are no chairs or adornments, just a door and a guard in a white shirt wearing a bulletproof vest and carrying an M-16.

"You're not Redmond. Where's your ID? Put your tools down and get your hands up."

Ian's throat filled with his stomach, but he did what he was told. The back door, plain white with more security locks, flew open, and another cop marched in. He was overweight and red-faced, so red he looked like his skin was about to burst into flames. He approached Ian, snatched the ID card, and studied it. After a moment, he looked up. "I'm sorry about the inconvenience, Mr. Hadley. We had a bomb threat in the building this morning and are running hot around here." He moved to the back door quickly. "Stay put. We need to run additional security checks. It's protocol, that's all." The two guards left him alone.

Oh shit, Ian thought. *I'm going to jail.*

Sweat poured from Ian like Niagara Falls. He couldn't shake the image of vomiting in the corner. *Why haven't the guards come back? Did Zilla screw up my ID? Why am I doing this? Risking so much?*

Staring at the camera mounted to the corner ceiling of the little room, Ian imagined spending the next ten to twenty years in prison. Planting surveillance cameras and microphones in One Police Plaza broke a dozen state and federal laws. Ian thought about turning, throwing open the door, and running far away. *Bad idea. I've already broken a half-dozen laws to get in this room. They'll plaster my face over the six o'clock news, and my life will be over. Just follow through. I'm not hurting anyone here. It's not like I have a bomb on me.*

The far door opened, and the same guard entered, strode to the corner, and morphed into a statue, deep-set eyes cold as ice. Ian's eyes watered. *Blink, Damn it!*

The portly man stepped inside, handing the ID back to Ian.

"New with the company?" His face was chubby and

wrinkled from decades of stress and too many tumblers of scotch.

"Yes, sir," Ian responded. "I've taken over Central."

He smiled, drawing his lips off his whitened teeth. "Good. Redmond was always late."

Ian wondered where Redmond was. *Is he on vacation? Was he fired? Or rotting at the bottom of the river? How did Zilla get me into this company anyway?*

The portly man waved to the guy in the corner, who took the toolbox.

Ian's heart thumped so loudly; the beat should be audible in the quiet room.

The cop rifled through the toolbox, set it aside, and patted Ian down.

The portly man handed Ian a paper. "Now then. You've got crybabies on two and six saying they don't have heat. So, get to it."

The man opened the door and led the way to the elevators.

Ian inspected vents in ten offices and planted five bugs just behind the grates.

Thankfully, no one was the wiser.

The heat kicked on two hours later, and people thanked Ian as he exited the building.

Most of these people were good, hardworking city employees. Ian was only interested in the crooked one percent.

#

Eight months since he bugged thirty-five offices. Well, not bugged at all. According to the note with the syringe, he had set up devices that spit out a deadly virus into the AC ductwork. Ian had been proud of not leaving a trace. Zilla didn't leave any clues behind either.

Ian looks over his trashed condo, listens to yelling

and gunfire on the streets of New York, and smells the acrid stench of smoke seeping into his once-safe place.

The note Zilla wrote lies along the sliding glass door to the balcony. Tears come to Ian's eyes. All he wanted was to spy on the leaders and uproot their corruption. Instead, she helped to take them off the board altogether. He tears the note into the smallest pieces he can manage and slides down to the cold tile.

Dried blood on his forehead was now cracking and stiff, and the pounding in his skull was like a taiko drummer up close. *I've got to get out of this city before I'm caught up in the storm of panic.*

Josh Connor

Height: 6'
Weight: 185 lbs
Race: Caucasian
Hair Color: Dark Brown
Occupation: Journalist
Mother: Lives with
Josh
Political affiliation:
Libertarian.
On Watch List

CHAPTER 1.3

JOSH CONNER
BREAD CRUMBS

Finding humor, disgusting things, and pointless drivel on the Internet is easy. Uncovering actual conspiracy, however, requires either strict tenacity or dumb luck. For Josh, finding accurate information is the latter.

\#

It all started eight months ago when Josh was browsing a germaphobe site. He, being a germaphobe himself, visited this site often, especially after the last pandemic.

Buried among a dozen Q&A feeds were some insane comments by a supposed Columbia University professor.

WashTwice34

I will never again walk down a crowded mall or airport. People are constantly coughing. Viruses fill the air! The thought makes my skin crawl. We need to educate people about the actual dangers of viruses. They kill and cause cancer and death!

Nancy89NY

Maybe u shouldn't even open your window or leave ur house for that matter.

WashTwice34
What are u even doing on this thread? This is for people who know the truth and want to do something about it.

Nancy89NY
I am a window shopper, I guess. U are truly insane. It just sucks how extreme fear-mongers like u want to scare everyone into hidey-holes. U make me sick. Ur just weak.

ProfessorTooGood01
WashTwice34 has good reason to be afraid. Last year, I worked on a project adding a specific protein to the cellular wall of a mild influenza viral strain. It's called gain-of-function. Though the US government won't fund it because the public has lost confidence in the ability to be safe with their newly created viruses, we were funded by the Gilden Group. Our new virus lived five days longer, flew farther in the air, and resisted known antiviral therapies. We believed making the virus more communicable to humans will help us learn thereby helping us fight the next deadly viral outbreak.

WashTwice34
Why on God's green planet would you make something more deadly? Do u know how many lab mistakes happen every day? Given a long enough timeline, the likelihood of escape is 100%.

ProfessorTooGood01
I used to believe that learning how things work is

the purpose of science. We do not fully understand how viruses mutate, but we know viruses change their surface proteins. Knowing how a specific protein changes a virus isn't possible until we make the new virus and study it. All was working so well. Until...

Josh couldn't resist commenting:
JoshP8484
How did you test the virus's ability to travel in the air? Did you spray it and track how far it flew?

ProfessorTooGood01
Yes. We developed a small aerosolizer that simulated a sneeze. High-speed camera footage was stunning and... scary.

JoshP8484
You don't believe in gain-of-function anymore?

ProfessorTooGood01
No. We have become far too good at it.

Josh decided to write an article about the professor, so they emailed back and forth. Josh thought the piece would be exciting until the professor divulged a secret that truly frightened Josh. The aerosolizer was stolen. Josh offered to report the theft and investigate further but received no more emails from ProfessorTooGood01. He vanished like a cat in the dark.

Josh researched aerosolizers, general to specific, but the theft trail went cold. He even tried to find the professor's real name and any data he could, but that failed, too. The cloak of anonymity is thick on the internet and near impossible to unveil someone's true identity—unless they're teenagers who post every single moment of their lives on threads and social media.

Josh became busier than ever, a senior writer at *Liberty Values*, a libertarian think tank full of back-alley philosophers and out-of-the-box thinkers. Josh's job was fighting the icebergs of socialism and ignorance on the web. He had moved on with his life, but the aersolizer theft stayed in the back of his mind like a tick feeding off his mental energy one tiny sip at a time.

\#

Josh types a response to someone inquiring about one of his articles.

People tell so many lies disguised as "commentary" or write articles written from the perspective of "concerned" citizens and "unbiased" journalists. Yet, many online personas hide under a mountain of Marxist philosophy and ignorance about history. I am trying to expose the frauds.

Whenever I find a piece about so-called socialist-democracy, I post links to my article, "Failed Socialist Countries," a list of fifty failed democratically elected socialist governments. The article contrasts countries that use free, or close to, free-market principles to guide production (zero failed) to socialist countries, (nearly eighty five percent failure rate). Capitalist countries decline when they adopt socialist policies, but do they teach that in school? Hell no. No one likes to be wrong, especially teachers.

I'll share with you another resource detailing the progress and success of capitalism often ignored. Socialists insist on parading sob stories about the people left behind as capitalist economies thunder ahead. But numbers don't lie like people do. People left without jobs or health insurance or buried alive by abject poverty are a far lower percentage than the grinding poverty socialist states create. Pseudo-socialist states like France, theoretically combining the best of capitalism and socialism, don't eradicate poverty. Their ghettos, *banlieues*, once promoted as worker utopias, are slums dominated by colossal concrete housing projects concentrating the residents in poverty and social isolation. Stick around. I'll blow your mind with some of the articles. I've got coming out this next year. Let's keep fighting for libertarian ideals.

Josh sends the email and proceeds to read his other messages. They're hate mail—he's used to getting some pretty vile messages, so he simply trashes them without a second thought.

Josh shuffles to the kitchen, lifts his stained mug out of the dishwasher, and pours a cup of coffee.

"Don't drink it all! Make a new pot when you do," his mother calls from her room, using her shrill, I-know-you're-an-inconsiderate-son voice. She moved in with him when her rent-controlled apartment was infested with bedbugs last year and never returned to her home.

Josh shrugs and empties the coffee pot. It's too early for a night bug like him, but he has a deadline today.

The shades are still drawn, a steady stream of dust parading through the light shining through the slats. His computer beeps, signaling a new email–a spike of dopamine orders his feet to rush him to his room.

The email is a chat request from a hacker friend.

GigglyPuss666
Hey, man, I found your viral aerosolizer.

Josh's coffee cup almost fell out of his hand.

GigglyPuss666

A manufacturer in Taiwan is selling the specs for a new, improved, more miniaturized design on the Dark Web.

Josh stares at the text on his screen, paranoid thoughts filling his mind. A dirty sensation crawls over his sweaty hands. An insane scientist could culture a virus, pack it in the device, and spray it anywhere. Everyone, not just germaphobes like Josh, should be frightened to learn about a gadget like that.

JoshP8484

Oh my God. We have to tell someone. Maybe they can download the design from the Internet. Can you find out if someone bought this thing?

GigglyPuss666

No. But this is Hansel and Gretel-ville. Breadcrumbs are everywhere if you know what to look for. I ran a search on a hundred chat servers looking for anyone talking about the device or spreading a virus into crowds and found some fucked-up shit.

JoshP8484

Isn't the Dark Web already full of fucked-up shit?

GigglyPuss666

Not like what I found. Or didn't find. Eight, nine months ago, people were talking about the device stolen from Columbia U, and some were saying spooky shit about using it. After every post by this guy, Zilla, the thread vanishes. Threads like these don't just stop. See, the Dark Web is full of shit-breathers. Boards like these fill up for pages. Not when Zilla comes around. He cuts the boards down like a samurai hacking off heads. It's weird, like his posts have some kind of corruption capability attached to them. Kinda looks like he doesn't want people to talk about it."

JoshP8484
You look into this Zilla guy?

GigglyPuss666
Come on, who do you think I am? Zilla is everywhere. He's supporting socialist ideologies over here and anarchist movements over there. He's a democrat and republican, Dahmer, and McVeigh all in the same breath. Big tatas, little tatas, the guy can't be pinned down.

JoshP8484
What is his game? Speculate. I know you have it in you.

GigglyPuss666
From what I can tell, he's trying to make friends. He's like a political call girl, dressing up in whatever ideology you like, then taking their chats offline. See, some people think he's just some crazy dude talking out of his ass. But I think there's something else going on. I've been reading his posts all morning and it seems to me he's trying to kill the threads that are talking about spreading a virus around. When he kills the thread, it weakens search results. If no one is refreshing content boards about virus pandemics or this aerosolizer thing, the subject isn't listed high enough on search to gain any attention. Unless you're looking for it

and have hours to dig, like yours truly.

I found a few threads that had left over links to proxy server addresses that no longer exist. Then, I found one that was live. A year ago, he was using a server in South Africa almost exclusively. Fucker was chatting in Chinese, Italian, Russian. Something in his Russian post that got me freaked.

JoshP8484
You speak Russian?

GigglyPuss666
I was born in Ukraine, brotha, before coming to the states. Pay attention. He transferred over two million bitcoin to a transpacific freight company. A week later, the boat left a Chinese port filled with microprocessors bound for San Francisco. Not too weird, except I found out the boat had one very cold, very secret package on board.

JoshP8484
How do you know it was secret?

GigglyPuss666
It wasn't on the manifest, but some clown in the crew snapped a pic of it and tweeted it.

JoshP8484
What was so special about the package?

GigglyPuss666
Oh, biohazard symbols, coolant lines, locked up behind some fancy door, no one's supposed to talk about it. That kind of thing.

JoshP8484

But he's talking about it.

GigglyPuss666
Not really. Facial recognition software picked up the biohazard image in the background.

JoshP8484
So, if you found the image, NSA knows about it for sure.

GigglyPuss666
Yeah, probably. Still kinda spooky. Some guy shipped a virus to the states the same time some thingy that sneezes it into the air gets stolen. I'd keep outta Times Square for a while. Hey, gotta go. I'm sending you some of the threads I've read. See for yourself.

Josh reads for hours. His mind races as the importance of this story clarifies. *People need to know about this, and now.*

Suddenly, Josh's computer flicks off, snapping his nerves like wound-up rubber bands. The desk light is still on; his clock still blinks so the power didn't go out. Josh pushes back from the desk and stands. "Hmm. My power supply must have just died. It's practically brand new." His keyboard isn't lined up straight anymore, so he squares it with the monitor, adjusts the pens laid neatly next to the printer. "Guess I'm going to Circuit Mart."

His hands itch, so he cleans them in hand sanitizer. *GigglyPus knows, so the government knows. The NSA have rooms of computers scanning these docs and pics and analyzing them, right?*

The front door slams open, followed by his mother's scream. Josh, startled, rushes toward his bedroom door.

"Mom?"

In the living room stands a hulking man, wearing a black suit over a bulky armored vest, sweeping a gun around. The man points it at Josh, forcing him back. The hulking agent follows Josh as he backs into his bedroom.

Another man, no gun in his hands, enters, scans Josh's room with ice-blue eyes, says, "Sit, please." He flips a badge wallet at Josh, too fast to read. "I'm with the National Security Agency."

Josh croaks, "You're required to give your name. Show me the ID again, slowly." His mouth goes dry like he's been water-boarded with flour.

The man ignores the request. "We have evidence that you've been in contact with a known radical felon, screen name GigglyPuss666. We've learned interesting things from him, and we know he's told you interesting things." The agent folds his arms across his chest. "We need to know what you've been told. Truth carries favor. I'm sure you don't need to be told that."

"First, what did you do to my mother?" Josh croaks, glancing at the door.

"She's fine, don't worry about her–right now." Ice-blue eyes agent answers his cell. "Understood." He hangs up. "Small change in plan."

Three more men in dark suits, white shirts, and skinny ties barge in, dismantle Josh's computer, haul it and all the peripherals away. One of them takes out a hand-held device, waves it over the drawers until it beeps and then pulls out thumb drives and backup hard drives. They scan the entire room. "We're going to need your passwords."

Josh tries to stand, but the agent with the gun forces him down. "You have no right to take my property—"

Agent blue eyes replies, "Your little career is over. No more articles about liberty or freedom or your precious

Jefferson. No more rebellious comments, no more hacker friends, and in return, you won't go to jail, your mother won't go to jail, and maybe your sister in Ohio won't go to jail, either. If you publish anything or go to the media, your family will be ruined."

"You can't do that."

"The Patriot Act gives me more authority than even you know. You might even try to use a weapon on me, forcing me to put you down like a dog." The agent moves his jacket aside, exposing cuffs tucked into a leather belt pouch. "I might just take your mother with me. Or I could visit your sister…no? Then we have an agreement?"

Josh can't do, or say, much with the gun pointed at him. He's never felt so furious, but so helpless at the same time. He nods, swallowing his resentment and bitterness and fear.

"Now, go get yourself a nice easy job and move on with your life." The agent with the ice-blue eyes follows his men out of the home.

Josh runs to his mom. She's on her bed, crying, her face smashed into her pillow.

"Are you okay?" he asks.

She looks up, her eyes puffy and red. "What have you done?"

Josh turns and kicks the wall, smashing a hole in the drywall. His jaw is painfully locked in anger. "I dissented, that's all." He chucks. "I guess that's everything."

    #

Josh goes out of his mind within a week. He uses a landline to check his messages. Every call is from his friends complaining about missing emails and texts. His boss fires him, reluctantly, because Josh insists he can't write anything political anymore. He is miserable, his tongue effectively cut out, but his mother and sister weren't hauled off to some secret prison, or worse.

The clock becomes Josh's enemy when he has nothing to do. Every tick is like a nail being driven into his hand, sending his brain into dark places, exacerbating his phobias and paranoia. Twice, he sees the classic black car parked outside his building, and his landline clicks suspiciously.

Everything around Josh gets dirtier, in spite of him washing constantly and sanitizing surfaces daily. He can't make himself leave the house for bottled water or anything else, even though the tap water looks like it's crawling with bacteria.

His mother finally notices his odd behavior, tries to dig out his problems, but Josh can't tell her anything because he loves her. Her life is on the line. Yeah, she's annoying at times, but he can't let anything happen to her, even if he's relegated to shining shoes for a living.

Two weeks after the NSA visit, Josh wakes at two in the morning. He dreamt about Zilla again. *Does he know the NSA hobbled my life?* Did Zilla send men to Josh's apartment, pretending to be NSA? Haunted by these questions, Josh can't survive without some answers. *Maybe I can investigate, as long as I'm sneaky about it, very sneaky.*

Dawn arrives, finally. Josh throws on a long sleeve shirt, long pants, a surgical face mask and heads out into the summer heat. The New York hustle and bustle seems particularly frantic, but he's a poor judge of normal. Ducking in and out of alleys, looping back twice and making sure no one follows him, Josh finds the local library.

The reading rooms are packed with unshaved, unwashed, unbrushed types. Germs fill the air like confetti, but his face mask is the kind that inactivates viruses, and he has hand sanitizer in both his shirt and pants pockets.

Josh sits at the only available computer and roots around in message boards. GigglyPuss666's posts are a week old and useless. Did the NSA or Zilla get to him? Somebody else Josh hasn't thought of?

Someone coughs nearby. Josh wants to flee, forces himself to stay. *Zilla, where are you?* He visits some popular chat sites and some boards that GigglyPuss frequents. Nothing.

The keys stare at him, their worn-off letters crying out to be used for good. Josh, shaking and overheated, considers his next move. If he tells anyone about the NSA taking his computer and threatening him, his family is at risk. But if he says nothing they win, right?

Josh looks around; no one is paying any attention to him. Good. He creates a free email account and types a message to his boss and best friend. He pauses the mouse at the "Send" button, sweat rolling down his cheek. He's got some savings, his mom does too. If he sends this email, detailing the NSA threats, prefaced with strict instructions to let him get out of town before investigating Zilla and GigglyPus's disappearances, he'll have time to escape, right?

Josh hits "Send."

The clock in his head strikes midnight. Josh's witching hour is now though it is only six in the morning; making his great escape from New York is unavoidable.

He steps away from the public computer, dumps a handful of cool, fragrant sanitizer into his palm, massages it over his hands and wrists, unbuttons his sleeves and does his arms.

Some toothless guy taps his shoulder. "You done, man?" His breath is as foul as a sewer pipe.

Josh recoils and heads for the door. Outside isn't much comfort. His paranoia has increased exponentially, but he didn't realize how much until he's out in public. The sidewalk is too crowded; everyone with their steaming, bacteria laden breath, huffing, and puffing as they sped, walking to and fro. *My apartment is a block away, only a block.*

People he passes, every one of them, look agitated. Sirens wail in the distance in unusual urgency. The streets are gridlocked. He jogs to his building and ducks inside.

Thirty-five stairs up and a stubborn lock later, he's inside his bedroom, trying to catch his breath. He flips on the TV and starts season four of the *X-Files,* cranks the volume so he can't hear the weird chaos outside and the bugs in the apartment can't pick up his packing. He knows there are bugs.

Time to get Mom. She's not on the couch, nor in the kitchen. He walks to her bedroom, finds a note taped to the door:

Couldn't keep it zipped, could you? We warned you.   ~Zilla

Josh nudges the door open, finds his mother on her bed, glossed-over eyes staring, overflowing with thick yellow mucus. Bloody snot bubbles from her nose and mouth. The skin on her arms and legs is dotted with red welts. "Mom? Mom!" No response. He watches for any breathing movement. None. Her chest rise or fall, doesn't even twitch. She's dead. "Oh mom. I'm sorry I couldn't keep you safe. This is all my fault."

The front doorbell rings, over and over.

"My husband! He's sick. He needs a doctor, but I can't get through. I need your phone, Josh! Please! Maybe you can get through." His too-friendly neighbor, Mrs. Beckle, won't give up.

"No. I'm sorry. I don't want to get sick, too." Josh screams through his facemask, through the door.

His suitcase stares at him from the bedroom. *Damn it.* Tears stream down his face.

He hears Mrs. Beckle fighting another neighbor, Mr. Hobbs, in the hallway. He's coughing, trying to get in his apartment. Mrs. Beckle won't let him pass. She's crying for help, screaming for someone to help her husband.

Josh runs to his utility closet, tossing stuff around until he finds a fat roll of duct tape. The buildings power goes off.

Trying not to panic, Josh tapes grocery bags over the cracks around the front door and his mother's door. He grabs food and water from the kitchen, runs to his bedroom, tapes that door shut. More chaos and screaming come from the street three stories below. Instead of peeking, he pops a valium, chugs some water, and collapses into the corner.

"This will be over soon. This will be over soon," Josh mumbles over and over.

Ben Leman

Height: 6' 0"
Weight: 285 lbs
Race: Caucasian
Hair Color: dark brown
Occupation: New York water treatment employee
Family: Father: Building Engineer, Mother: Laboratory Scientist,
Political affiliation: None, manic and deep anger issues

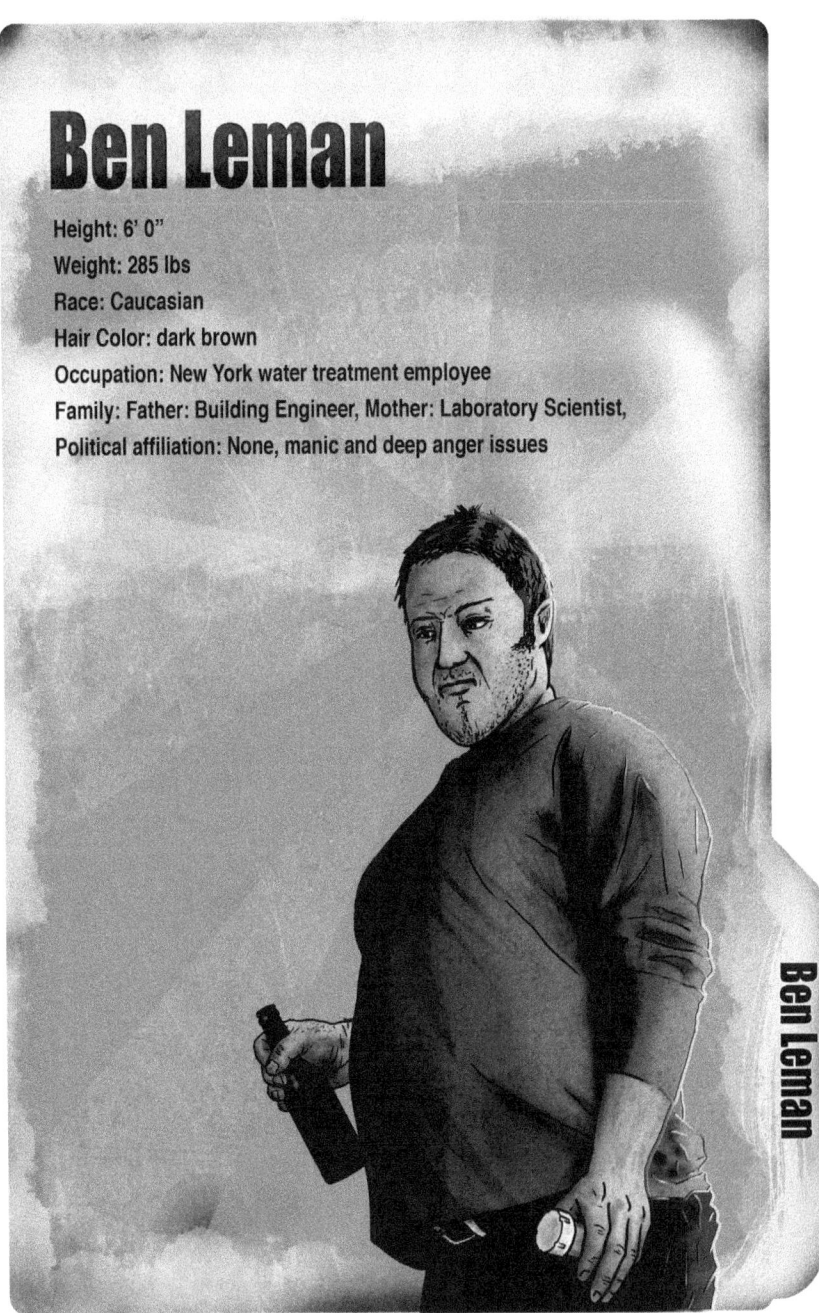

Ben Leman

Chapter 1.4

Ben Leman
Two Days Before the Extinction Event

Ben doesn't like it when people look at him too long. He turns away, peeks, and they're still staring. They're jackasses, or they just don't have a fucking clue where their pupils have decided to rest. Either way, it's their fault, and he wants to slap the shit out of them and throw them off the Brooklyn Bridge.

Today, the bank is full of shit-eaters. Half of 'em already stared at him too long. He'd say somethin', but he doesn't wanna get thrown out. He looks at his feet to cool his nerves, thinkin' maybe somebody noticed the stain on his shirt kinda looks like Jesus.

Finally, the teller calls him to the window. "How can I help you today?"

"My freakin' card doesn't work at the ATM," Ben says loudly because there are three inches of bulletproof polycarbonate plastic between him and this broad with a 1960s hairspray hairdo.

"To withdraw money, you have to slide your card," she says, pointing down to a card reader next to the tray at the bottom of the plastic window.

70

She didn't hear a fucking word I just said. "Card no workie." Ben slips the card into the metal tray under the bulletproof glass.

She looks at him weirdly.

"Come on! I don't have all day," yells some construction worker from the line.

Ben turns, his eyes bulging. "I'm fucking trying. This babe can't hear me through the sludge cloggin' her ears." He turns back and gets the look that says, 'I've decided you're an asshole, so I'm going to sit here and pretend to type out shit just so I can waste your time.'

So, he waits.

"I'm sorry. Your card doesn't work."

Ben's head is ready to pop. "Dammit, bitch. I–" He shouldn't have said that.

The security guard rushes over. "Sir, you have to leave." The guard puts his hands on his hips like he's Captain America.

"I'm not leaving until I get my fuckin' money." Ben really needs the cash, and his fuse is burnt to nothing. Two other guards grab Ben from either side, drag him to the door, and shove him so hard he falls to his hands and knees, off-center, so he rolls on his shoulder and lands on his back.

It's raining. He looks up and sees brick buildings towering overhead and gray, pregnant clouds. The rain is rancid and bitter, not fresh. He rolls back to his hands and knees, stands, and damn near trips on his busted flip-flop. He kicks, and the thin rubber sole goes flying, slapping the bank's glass door.

Ben searches his pockets and finds cigarettes.

A gangster walks up, pantyhose on his head, his fucking pants hanging so far below his ass they were hanging off his knees.

Ben isn't some conservative fuddy-duddy, but some

people just look like, well, dumb fucks.

"Hey, bro. Got a smoke for an old friend?"

Old friend? In some neighborhoods, having cigs turns you into a lighthouse that beckons broke assholes to your shores. Ben hands the cigarette over to the total stranger.

"Thanks, bro." He backs up. "I was gonna ask you if you had some change, but you ain't even got shoes." His eyes shimmer with humor. "Gotta light, at least?" He never takes his eyes off Ben.

The gangster freaks Ben out. *This asshole'll be first off the Brooklyn Bridge.*

"Yeah. Let's get out of the rain, shall we, bro?" Ben guides the "bro" down a narrow alleyway, turns, socks him in the gut, and knocks him on his ass into a puddle. Ben kicks him in the ribs and snatches back the cigarette.

Gangsters don't intimidate Ben. No one does. Ever since he was in school, he was king of the playground. Not much of a king now, but whatever. The attitude stuck. He rips the dude's shoes off. "Fucking Adidas Micropacers. Who'd you steal these from, eh? Well, now they're mine." Ben marvels at how well the fancy shoes fit his fat feet. He turns to leave, but four more gangbangers block his exit. *Shit.* "I knew you thugs were nearby planning to take me down. I can smell your stink. Like a skunk. Can't help but spray after every step."

They come at him, and the fight is on. Ben lands a few punches, but not enough. He's laid out with a head butt, lands on his back, the wind knocked out of him. One of the homies, or whatever they call themselves, rips off the shoes; another reaches into Ben's pocket, pulls out his wallet, digs through his cards and photos, tosses the empty leather at his face, and runs off.

When the world stops pulsating, Ben sits up, tasting

blood in his mouth, seeing the new stains on his shirt have messed up the one that kinda looks like Jesus. *I almost had those gangbangers. Next time, for sure.*

"Are you okay?" Ben couldn't quite register the stranger's voice over the ringing in his ears and the traffic noise. This is, after all, New York. "Hey, do you need me to call an ambulance?"

The voice is sweet. Its owner is slender, wearing a red dress covering her prominent curves, and has bright matching lipstick. Her hair is pretty and brown. Oh, and a curious scar runs from her cheekbone to her jaw, a gnarly one at that. An umbrella keeps off the drizzling rain.

"No–Shit. I mean, no thanks."

"Did you just get mugged?" She kneels right next to him and holds out a golden lighter.

The cigarette still in his fingers is half-broken and wet, but what the hell. He rips off the filter, puts the other half up to his lips, and she lights it. After a deep drag, he chuckles. "Some fuckin' day." Ben tries to haul himself to his feet, needing help because he weighs over two-eighty. The lady pulls him up; her strength is surprising for such a delicate-looking female.

"Do you want me to call the cops?"

Ben shakes his head. "Right, that would be another nail in my coffin."

She shrugs. "You wouldn't get your shoes back anyway, I suppose."

Ben wiggles his toes. *Ha, if you only knew.* "I just want those gangbangers to die a horrible death. You know? Where's a piano when you need one?"

She laughs. "What would you do with a piano?"

"I'd drop it on their fuckin' heads, that's what."

The lady hands Ben her card. A phone number printed in foil is under an hourglass icon, with all the sand on the bottom. "Call me. I have a piano you might be interested in."

"Figuratively speakin'?"

Her smile flattens like a heart dying. "No. Not figuratively speaking." Walking away, her ass swings back and forth like the pendulum of a grandfather clock.

That night at the bar, Ben can't think about anything but the lady in red. Absent-minded, he stares at her card, rattling the rocks left over from his whiskey sour.

"You want another one?" Shane asks. Ben's favorite bartender is thin as a stick-bug and just as ugly, but he's funny.

"I told you, I don't got any more money."

"You're in here almost every night. I know you're good for it," Shane replies. He pours a new drink.

After two more, Ben needs a woman like a bee needs a flower. He looks around the busy but not crowded bar. A large chick with blonde hair and lovely jewelry is at a table with one of her friends. Ben catches her looking at him. Sweat beads on his forehead like he's birthing sand crabs from his pores. He stands and wobbles toward the blond, cramming the lady-in-red's card in his pocket. The blonde meets him halfway.

"Hey, babe," Ben says to the woman, then finds the nearest seat. He'll look less like a douchebag if he's sitting versus swaying. "I was wondering if you'd take a drink and drink it with me."

"Sure, darlin'," the overweight blonde says, her Southern accent soft, drawn out.

Ben laughs. "I can do a Southern chick!" he says a little too loudly. Her expression tells him he just stuck his foot deep in his mouth with less skill than a sixth street hooker. She douses him with her drink and stomps back to her table.

Ben's feet take him home, one stumble at a time. Halfway, a car horn startles him, crossing the street. "Fuck off, asshole! I'll kill you. Kill you like the motherfuckers you are!" he yells and stumbles. The wind picks up and cools his wet shirt and sweaty skin. *I need to chill. Gotta get home. My bong is waiting for me. Oh, but where is that lady in red?* "Lady in red?" He sings loudly. He fumbles in his pocket, finds her card, and stares at the number. Finding his phone takes less than ten seconds but seems like forever. Finally, it's ringing.

"Hello, Ben." Her voice soothes his nerves. "I want you to talk to my friend, the owner of the piano." The phone clicks.

"Wait, wait. What's your name?" Ben yelps. He is profoundly disappointed when a man's deep voice comes on. "Hello, Ben. My name is Zilla."

"Um, I'd rather talk to the lady."

"I know. But talk to me for just a moment because I know how alienated you are."

"I don't really wanna talk about my feelings, dude."

"That's okay. But, you're gonna wanna hear what I have to say. Trust me. Sometimes, in life, we get an opportunity like no other. A ray of light is shining on you today. You're like me, a cog in the machine just turning and clicking. You're as overlooked as a gray sedan in a sea of exuberant sports cars. But I've stopped at your door, and I'm in that shiny red Ferrari, Ben. Here are the keys. So, the question is, do you want to take it for a ride?"

"If you were really tossing me the keys, I'd burn some fucking rubber, dude." Ben isn't quite sure what Zilla's talking about.

"Good. Just because I own a Ferrari doesn't mean I don't know how your side feels. I want the world to feel the pain we've felt."

"Feel? You talkin' about. . . shooting people?"

"No. Nothing like that." Zilla's voice is soothing but threatening at the same time. "I want to play a fun little prank, make everyone in the city throw up, and I need your help to play it. We'll make history in a very clever way. Neat little bacteria will grow in people's water heaters, so when they do dishes or take a shower, the bug will make them sick. A city-wide barf-fest! It'll be fantastic, make the national news! Maybe the BBC! Will you help me? Will you help us?"

"I ain't going to jail."

"No, you won't. When you're done, we'll erase any camera footage and smudge the entrance logs. We're good at that. We need you on the inside. Simple, effective. Afterward, we'll fly you to Florida to stay on my yacht. You in?"

"Hell, yes," Ben says without a millisecond's hesitation. The phone goes dead.

He holds his cell phone at arm's length and squints at it, still drunk. Revenge sounds good, but he's still confused about how. "How" doesn't matter. People pass him quickly, looking at him funny. "Wha' 're you looking at?" he barks at a man in a business suit. Ben doesn't get respect unless he busts faces. Women don't like him, nothing good happens to him, and everybody else seems to have a golden ticket but him.

Stumbling around the corner of his apartment building, he sees a streetlight illuminating a shiny, cherry-red Ferrari.

Ben walks closer to the Ferrari and looks it over, wondering how long it's been there. Not long in his neighborhood, for sure. The passenger door opens, and the

lady in red steps out. He squares his shoulders, trying to look manly and tough, swaggering up to her.

She doesn't say a word; she holds the keys in one hand and something in the other.

Ben takes the keys and lets her push a medicine bottle into his palm.

She steps close and whispers into his ear. "Take a drive, Ben, to *work*. Take out the guard in a friendly way; you're not a murderer. Then, pour what's in that bottle into the circulation tank and come home. Take the long way home if you want. You've got two hours."

Her perfume wafts into his brain and sends heat through his body. The jingle of her earrings is light, delicate, and sexy. He grabs her waist and pulls her close until her breasts press against his chest. "Okay," Ben whispers, weak in the knees. "You know where I work?"

She kisses him on the lips, then pushes him away gently, her graceful hand on his chest. "The clock is ticking, tiger. We'll talk when you are successful."

"You're gonna scrub the cameras, right? They're all over the place, like Russian spies."

"We'll take care of them. And the log, too. Team effort. Can you do this, Ben?" Her smile fades, and her gorgeous eyes bore into him.

"I got this." Ben adjusts himself, whips open the Ferrari door and then falls into the seat. The rich smell is almost as good as her perfume, almost.

The woman walks off, her heels clicking on the concrete.

A bottle of vodka lays in the passenger seat, along with a white bottle labeled "Chloroform." He guesses chloroform is the "friendly way to take out the guard." Good thing the night guard is one of his buddies. He'll forgive and forget and might even enjoy a nap on the job.

Ben starts the engine. The radio clicks on and pumps Crusaders out of the speakers. *My favorite band. How does Zilla know that?* Ben's blood morphs into rocket fuel. He revs the engine, grabs the vodka, and swigs. "Let's do this fuckin' deed!" Ben squeals the tires and fishtails into the middle lane. Buildings blow by like he's in a fighter jet, passing the snails on the road. Speed is the fuel of dreams. Ben laughs, living the fantasy.

Ben stops at a red light, still packed with cars at butt-o'clock at night. He waits, thumping the steering wheel to the music. A cop drives by, checking everyone out.

"Get lost, copper," Ben says. "No one wants you here."

The song ends, and the engine purrs. He feeds the beast under the hood with the gas pedal. The light turns green, so he releases the clutch and slams the gas, spinning the tires until the tread catches the pavement. He simply flies, swerves around fools, and catches a few middle fingers in the rearview. The car spins around corners like it's on a track.

Ben chugs the vodka, gunning the gas all the way to work.

He parks the Ferrari a block from the New York City North River Water Treatment Plant. Typically, he's cleaning ducts and replacing old water lines and filters for a living. Fantastic career: great union, benefits, hours. Unfortunately, it doesn't impress the ladies.

Ben hits the buzzer on the treatment plant front door and watches a digital panel light up until Stanford—no relation to the rich bastards or the university stiffs—answers. "Hey, Ben. What's up?" Stanford's watching from the closed-circuit camera under the awning.

"Gotta get some shit from my locker. I'll only be five minutes."

"What shit? You look blitzed."

"Extra set of house keys. Gotta get home and hit the sheets, you know."

He buzzes Ben in and meets him at the front entrance. Stanford's built like a freight train and, like Ben, has eaten his share of doughnuts. Ben reaches out and rests his hand on Stanford's shoulder.

"Phew, you're not driving, are you?" Stanford asks.

Ben flips the soaked rag from his pocket like a switchblade and slaps it over Sanford's mouth. Ben's arm wraps around the guard's neck, putting him in a chokehold faster than he can fart. Stanford struggles for a moment before collapsing.

"Sorry, Stan." Ben drags Stan to a side room and locks him inside. Ben's blood is hotter than it's ever been. *Fuckin' fun!*

Ben slides his ID card through the electronic lock at the main floor entrance and waits for the green light. The door lock clicks and the green light blinks. It's quiet and dark, but Ben knows his way around. Red lights shine from the ceiling like glowing bat-eyes. His stomach clenches. *They better follow through on their end and clear the tape. If they don't, I'm goin' on the run. Probably have to move to Canada or some shit.* He stumbles down the metal staircase into a forest of tanks, pipes, gauges, and warning signs. He knows one more guard is walking around, so he has to be quick.

Ben grabs a hammer drill from the maintenance storage, fixes the appropriate bit, and runs toward the huge tanks on the ground floor. He shuts down the additive tank that mixes the chlorine, fluoride, and food-grade phosphoric acid into the tap water. The tank blades slow and stop, setting off an alarm. He takes the drill, pushes the bit into the top of the tank, and drills a hole. He carefully pours the pill bottle's contents into the giant water tank, not spilling any, and starts the circulation blades again, spreading the liquid into all the clean water that feeds millions of homes.

Zilla said the liquid is a bacteria that'll make millions of people barf their guts out.

Ben pauses momentarily, guilt pricking him, as if someone is sitting on his shoulder, wagging their finger. *Tsk, tsk tsk.* Ben shakes his head and flips off the imaginary angel, scattering visions and thoughts like shaking a snow globe. *They're just gonna get sick, is all...just a big, fat prank, nothing to feel too guilty about, right?* Ben punches the side of the tank to erase his mind, like wiping a blackboard with a wet rag. *Oh shit! That hurt.* Cradling his knuckles, he runs out of the maze.

This'll be a hell of an entertaining night, flipping through the cable news channels and *watching the joke get everybody. Like that fat bitch at the bar.* Ben runs back to the Ferrari, hoping to get some miles between him and the chaos about to hit, but the fuckin' car is gone.

"Shit, guess my two hours of fun are up."

Hana Scottfeild

Height: 5' 8"
Weight: 135 lbs
Race: Caucasian
Hair Color: dark blonde
Occupation: New York Officer
Family: Adopted at age 10. Father: retired New York Police, Mother: retired school teacher, Political affiliation: Democrat

Hana Scottfeild

CHAPTER 1.5

HANA SCOTTFIELD
PULLING THE PLUG

At three o'clock in the morning, Hana's phone rings. She groans, having just got off a sixty-hour week. She'd been looking forward to a couple of days off. Tonight, she dealt with a highly intoxicated man trying to chase down his ex-girlfriend. He cut his leg intentionally and flicked blood on Hana as she moved in for the arrest. "I got AIDS!" yelled the drunk. Sobering up a little in the back seat of the cruiser, he admitted he didn't have AIDS, but it scared her half to death. After taking AIDS-man in, Hana responded to a bomb threat at Mt. Sinai Hospital, an attempted suicide at an apartment on 121st Street, and a large-scale protest in Central Park that got ugly. Her good work earned her a pile of paperwork too tall to see over. The shittiest shift she had ever worked. Something foul in the air. *Is the moon full or something?*

Still lying in bed, she looked at the phone. Her ringtone used to make her smile, and now, she wants to throw it through the window. She instantly thinks of three possible crimes she'd be committing: littering, pedestrian endangerment, and destruction of private property.

Damn this Zilla. Hana is expecting his call.

Zilla contacted her for the first time last night, claiming he's a whistle-blower embedded in the CIA, desperate to prevent the CIA, feds, and Homeland Security from killing a lot of people in "the ultimate war game, unlike any the government has played before."

Hana couldn't help but be curious, knowing she had a friend in HS that could confirm or deny the allegations.

Zilla had said. "Homeland Security is trying to justify an attack on the newly discovered oil reserves in the mountains of Sudan. We can't let the manipulation happen again." After a much deeper explanation, he added, "I've confided in you because of your pivotal role in the Richardson case last year. I'm impressed with your honesty and courage to do the right thing."

Richardson was the NYPD deputy chief and was as dirty as cops get. He and six subordinates, including two lieutenants and one detective, took bribes from Russian gangsters distributing illegal drugs all over New York. Hana responded to a deal gone bloody, but one dealer spilled the set-up to her before he took his dying breath. She and her trusted team set up a sting and took all the crooked cops to jail. She could have taken the money. There was certainly plenty to go around.

Last night, a package was left at Hana's front door. Inside is a stack of documents labeled "classified" and a bunch of CDs. She scanned the official-looking documents—a collage of famous names, black ink marks, and other classified filing stuff. Hana inserted one of the disks into her laptop and dug through file after file of surveillance videos.

She played through dozens, stopping when she recognized the Secretary of Defense talking with the

President in an office that was certainly not the Oval Office. There were no windows, no paintings, just walls of books. The surveillance film was grainy, and the camera angle was down from a high point, but she saw and heard the two men discussing an attack on Manhattan that would happen in the next few days.

The Secretary wanted to sell the attack to the public as a Sudanese terrorist plot, justifying the US government's plans to invade Sudan, just like Afghanistan. The truth was the perpetrators would be a homegrown activist group tied to a Green Peace.

Hana huffed, awash with skepticism. But her attention had been poked, more like stabbed, with a hot poker. She continued watching.

The terrorist attack will be a non-lethal bacteria released into the water supply. It will scare people, make them sick, and prove some point about overpopulation. The government will exacerbate the situation, quarantine all of Manhattan, and justify a new war.

The plot is a conspiracy so deep that it rivals the Mariana Trench.

Who is Zilla, and can his information be legitimate? *How can I really know?*

Hana had called her friend in the CIA, but her phone had been disconnected. That coincidence did not sit well with Hana.

Consequently, she doesn't sleep well; her neck is tense, and she must have been clenching her teeth for hours because her jaw feels like someone used it as a punching bag.

Hana is so confused that she shuts down. She can't tell what's right or wrong. *Would the President lie to everyone to start a war?*

What do you do when you can't do anything, when

you are hopeless, lost, and on the verge of tears? You don't answer your phone when you know the caller will say something you don't want to hear.

Hana lets the call go to voice mail. Zilla will have to find someone else to help him. She stands and walks to the window. The night sounds are more aggravated than usual—traffic is heavier, and meandering night owls and drunks are louder and more aggressive. She parted the curtains and saw the city, an orderly universe of blocks, lighted as usual. The streetlamp below her window illuminates a couple arguing, and she feels jealous of the petty, narrow problems.

Hana sees dust on the windowsill, snatches a rag from her linen closet, and wipes it clean, wishing she could easily wipe away her thoughts of treason, betrayal, and war crimes. The phone rings again; dispatch.

"Scottfield here." She tries to be professional but sounds like a twelve-year-old.

"Get to the station. Five guys already called in sick. Dispatch and nine-one-one are flooded with calls," the dispatcher says.

Hana moves reluctantly to the bathroom. Zilla said this would happen.

Hana stares at the tap, biting her lip.

She flips on the light and gasps. *I look like shit.* Age seems to have shriveled her skin overnight. *When did these wrinkles get so deep?* Hana grabs the bottle of water left by the sink, washes her face, slips out of her nightshirt into a sports bra and comfortable panties, and pulls an undershirt over her head. Her armored vest goes on next; it's too tight, and then she dons her police uniform. Her fingers automatically unlock the safe and lift her weapon out. She checks the safety and magazine before sliding it into her holster. She takes a moment to disguise the bags under her eyes with powder, adds mascara, and wraps her hair into a bun, cinched tight until it pulls on her scalp and won't interfere with her peaked uniform cap. Ten minutes total, she's out the door.

Hana slams her front door as hard as she can. *Shit, I should have answered the phone. Could I have done something to stop this?*

People run down on the sidewalks in the street. Panicked. She jumps in her cruiser, turning the key. The engine roars, and the radio bursts to life. She races out of the parking spot and onto the crowded street. Move people! She beeps the siren as she pushes through the crowd. The cruiser's bright headlights and spinning red-and-blue lights illuminate the panicked and twisted crowd like a demented disco.

Someone or something slams into the cruiser, and screams come from behind her, but Hana does not respond because she has orders to disregard everything. "Two-eight-M-niner, respond to 59th Street slash Queensboro Bridge entrance. Complete quarantine is in effect. No one, repeat no one, is allowed to leave the Island."

The radio signal explodes into a grating fuzz. *Are cell* towers *out?* Hana can't respond to the order.

Hana yanks open the center console and retrieves a ham radio issued by Homeland Security that is set to the Emergency Broadcast Channel. A looped recording plays over and over. Hana turns up the radio, hoping to catch some details before she gets to the bridge. The gist she catches is confusing: Civilians with flu-like symptoms are flooding already overwhelmed hospitals. A computer virus corrupted several military satellites and cell networks, disrupting military and civilian communications. Even wi-fi connections were disrupted. NYPD computers are down.

So, is an actual *virus going around along with a computer virus? Shit. Two fronted attack. This is big.*

"All able-bodied police personnel and civilian employees are ordered to report to work."

Hana wonders how many other officers are sick and how many will decide to stay home with their families. Hana's tired, not ill; even if she were, she'd go in. Her duty, above all else, is to help save lives.

A car careens off the street, jumps the curb, and smashes through the glass doors into a high-rise lobby. A woman stumbles from the dust cloud, only to be overcome by the fireball erupting from the car. The explosion tosses her into the street, her lengthy hair and skirts aflame. Hana swerves around the victim, using every ounce of self-control not to stop and help. *I have orders. Don't look back. That woman is probably dead.*

A skinny guy in a suit jumps in front of her cruiser. Hana slams on the brakes, and angry people mob her vehicle, banging on the windows, shouting, and attempting to climb onto the trunk and hood. Hana hits the gas and then the brake, rocking the big car. She blips the siren in two-second intervals. People stop pounding to cover their ears. Switching on her public address speakers, Hana says: "Go home! Shelter in place. A quarantine for the Island is in effect until further notice. You all will be safer at home." Her voice, projected by speakers under the hood, reaches for blocks. Some people scatter. Most don't care or distrust her authority.

Hana resumes driving. She might be sent home, too. If martial law kicks in, the cops go home, and the military takes over everything. "Speaking of," Hana mumbles as a convoy of five Humvees and two Bradley fighting vehicles force her off the street and pass, ramming cars and anything else that doesn't move out of their way.

Hana wishes this were a dream but knows it isn't.

She thinks about her family, glad they live far from

the city. But there's Mira, her perfect friend. Hana thinks of calling her, but the cell towers are down.

The yellow streetlamps illuminate the heads and shoulders of the people in front of the crowd, and a thin layer of smoke hovers over the rest like fog.

Blaring her horn and blipping her siren, Hana drives up the shoulder of the on-ramp of the Queensboro Bridge, pushing her cruiser past cars and a flood of pedestrians. She arrives at the barricade and pulls in tight against the two other patrol vehicles, leaving her lights flashing. She shrugs out of the car and sees the crowd eyeing her with fear and suspicion. She takes a few moments, breathing deeply, to fully regain her composure. An older man bumps into her. "What's going on?"

"I suggest you find your home, sir. And fast."

The man looks at her, his wrinkles deep, dark circles under his eyes looking like football eye paint. He backs away as she walks around to the trunk. Ten people stop and gather around, firing question after question, shouting over one another, stumbling on their words, drowning Hana's responses. They quiet down after she pops her trunk and lifts out an M-4.

Hana glances over the bridge's edge while taking the short walk to the barricades. A mass of cars cluster at the lower entrance. Dozens, maybe hundreds, of people are out of their vehicles, milling around after trying to cross the bridge on foot, being turned back at the barricades by officers. She continues to the upper road, pushing past a dozen people. Officer Denton, a bald man wearing a surgical face mask, opens the barricade and lets her through.

Two other officers arrive on foot. "Can't get our cruisers through the traffic jam."

A man with a shaved head, wearing a black jumper, approaches. "What the hell is going on?" he yells. More

people join him. "You gotsta get out of my way, Po Po!"

"Go home!" Hana replies.

"I gotta get to my baby! She's just over there in Woodside! You can't keep us here, yo!"

"Yeah!" echoes another man in the crowd.

"If I were you, I'd be at home, hovering over the TV, watching the Emergency Broadcast System!" Denton yells and coughs.

"I live in Brooklyn, foo! You won' let me go home!" the man in the do-rag yells. A mean-looking woman spits at

Hana. She dodges the gift and slips on her face mask.

She looks at Denton, flushed and sweating heavily, coughing hard.

"You okay?" Hana yells.

Denton is as tough as they come, but he looks like hell. "I'm fine. Get your head in the game."

The man in the do-rag continues yelling, but Hana tunes him out. As more people gather, more cops are needed on the bridge, or the police will be overrun. The two forces are like tectonic plates pushing against each other. When the pressure releases, it will be the cops who fall.

Hana listens to the chatter in her earpiece linked to the ham radio. Crowds continue to grow, fires burn, car accidents go unchecked, and lethal force is permitted to stop unruly citizens. Mobs attack the marinas and overload the boats, hoping to escape to New Jersey via the Hudson River. One yacht doesn't turn back when ordered and is sunk by an Apache helicopter.

"Martial Law?" Hana yells over the loud crowd.

"We'll know soon enough."

Five o'clock comes fast. More and more people pack the Queensboro Bridge on-ramp, mad as hell, coalescing, getting pushier. The leading edge of the mob is inches from the razor-sharp barbed wire on the barriers, but the crowd facing Hana surges forward anyway. People scream and cry out for help as they're shoved into the wire and cut. Spilled blood enrages the mob, and they keep pushing.

Hana flips the safety off her M-4.

So far, everything has happened exactly as Zilla predicted. Emergency channel reports even say the attackers may be Sudanese terrorists.

Hana glances at Officer Getty. He looks sicker than before. All the police officers are getting sick except Hana.

Zilla told her not to shower, use hot water, or drink anything unless it was bottled. He spared her.

Finally, the emergency bulletin announces the CDC says the bacteria in the water will make people ill, but it is non-lethal. That is the information Hana's been waiting for.

Officer Denton shrugs and yells. "What the hell are we doing if the thing isn't deadly? Why aren't they lifting the quarantine?"

A woman screams as she's trampled. Hana shoots into the air, but the stampeding mob doesn't slow. A man falls against the razor-barbed wire, his flesh sliced open like butter. He can't get loose. People push from behind, using him to protect themselves.

"I can't wait for central. Pull the plug!" Hana yells. No one hears over the roar of the mob's noise. She repeats herself loud enough to squelch her tears. She shoots another burst into the air. "Open the bridge!"

"What?" Denton shrieks. "We're ordered to keep this locked up."

"I'll take full responsibility!" she yells, knowing it's what Zilla wants her to do, but also her best judgment as a cop, too. "The quarantine is *creating* the panic. The tension will be relieved if people can get out, saving lives. Open the bridge! Let everyone go."

She lowers her weapon. The other officers follow her lead. She's their senior and has never led them astray. Denton pulls the barbed wire away, and the crowd spills past like a river after a heavy rain. Hana is pushed against the huge meal girder. The crowd continues flooding across the bridge, thousands of terrified people. None of them know the bug is harmless.

Hana pushes her way back to her cruiser through the thinning crowd to see if she can get it out of the way. Once inside, she fires up the engine and pulls off the road to let traffic through. People drive across the bridge recklessly. After a few hectic minutes, the crowd finally becomes manageable. Hana relaxes until she sees an alarming sight.

Thick, white smoke arcs into the sky. It must have been a rocket fired from a rooftop nearby. The rocket burns deeper and deeper into the atmosphere and disappears. A cold sensation infects Hana's spine. Everything is about to get worse.

Hana's cruiser dies. She tries the ignition, but nothing. The cars around her stop, and the traffic lights blink out. The emergency channel stops mid-loop. Hana pulls out her cell phone, dead. The rocket must have been an electromagnetic pulse. *Shit. Zilla never said anything* about *an EMP! Every electronic chip for god knows how many miles around will be fried. Is this just another thing to blame on the Sudanese? Bullshit!*

Movement to her right catches her attention. A Chevy truck, so old it has no electronics and was unaffected by the EMP, is heading right for her! It hits the on-ramp going forty miles an hour, aiming for the gap between her cruiser and a red Honda. Hana grabs her seat belt and clips it as the truck slams into the passenger side. The force knocks the cruiser off the ramp and tips it over the rail, nose first. The impact crumples the front, the airbag fails to deploy, but the seat belt cinches tight. The car topples, smashing the roof. Hana covers her face as the windows shatter into small honeycomb patterns.

The cruiser finally settles to a complete stop. Hana assesses her body. *Not badly hurt.* She unclips her seat belt, falls onto the ceiling of the cruiser, and looks outside. Her cruiser rests atop two other vehicles. Both doors are smashed, so the door handles won't budge. She can't squeeze out the front windshield, and the steel cage prevents her from crawling out the back. Hana's anxiety surges, and she screams. The exertion makes her dizzy, so dizzy she gasps for breath. *I'm gonna die. I'm gonna die just like my mother.* Hana rips off her uniform shirt and vest so she can breathe.

When Hana was young, her mother drove herself off a bridge into the river. After her body was recovered, tests showed her blood alcohol level above three percent. Even if she'd survived the crash, she would have continued

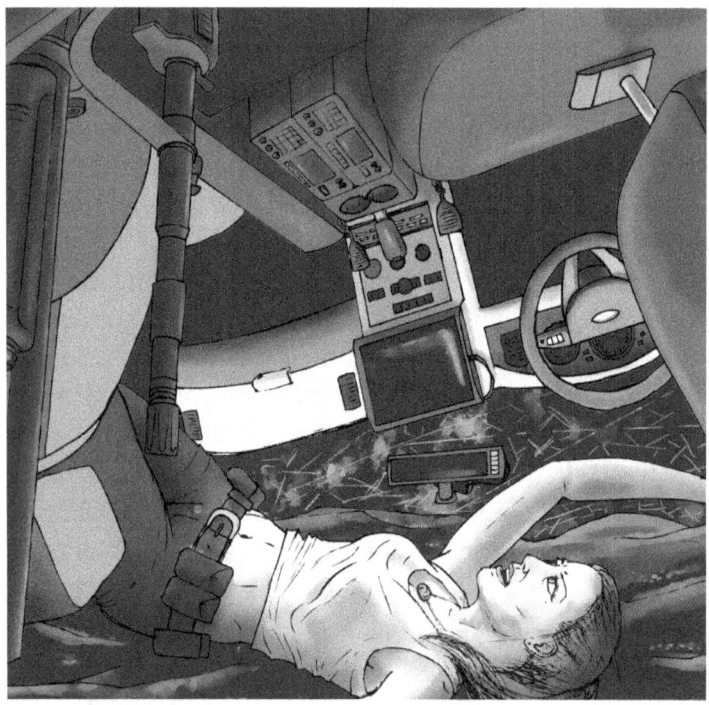

going downhill mentally. She was a slow-motion wreck.

Hana was first taken to a group home and spent the next year bouncing from foster home to foster home. Most of her foster parents saw her as a paycheck, and she occasionally had to be fed.

Beth, her mom's cousin, and Ricky, a cop, adopted Hana and quickly became the best Mom and Dad in the universe. She was definitely one of the lucky foster kids: She got out of the system and never had to go back.

Hana failed her freshman year in high school but went back, graduated with honors, and, with Rick's help, became one of the best cops in New York.

Ten years on the force prepared Hana for all kinds of situations, but tight spaces still unnerve her. She extracts her necklace, which Ricky and Beth gave her for graduation from the academy, from under her t-shirt. The engraving in Japanese kanji means *Peace and Love through Truth and Strength.* Rubbing the silky wood between her fingers and thumb, feeding off its calming effect, she considers her predicament. *How do I escape?*

First, she kicks the door with controlled leg thrusts, but it's crumpled and inoperable. Next, she tries getting to the back seat, but the metal access door between the headrests doesn't budge. She can't squeeze through any opening or force any of the metal. *Gonna take the Jaws of Life to get me out of here.*

Hana hears a moan. Someone is in the car below. "Hello! I'm here!" Hana yells.

"I– I'm hurt," sobs a woman, her voice weak and wavering.

"You're gonna be okay. Stay awake. Keep talking. What's your name?"

"Jan–ice," the woman cries, then screams, "I'm bleeding! Oh God, what is happening to me?"

"Stay with me, Janice! Help is on the way," Hana lies. No reply. "Janice!" Hana drums her heels on the cruiser ceiling, tears flooding her eyes. Janice doesn't answer.

Hana tries not to think about how long it will take

for help to show up. She might be locked in a prison of smashed, useless cars for days. People are yelling and screaming, but no one checks on the overturned police car on the Queensboro Bridge ramp.

Hours go by. No one comes. *Why?* Nothing makes sense. Hana likes to think she's as tough as they come, but she's not. Sitting with her eyes closed, trying to think of other things isn't working; relaxing isn't possible. Worse, her blood sugar crashing makes her shake. She squirms around and pops open the glove compartment, hoping her granola fix will tumble out. Instead, a red box she's never seen before falls out. She opens it to find a red syringe and a note:

Use or die. The New World thanks you. Your service was indispensable.

~Zilla.

Markus Coburn

Height: 6' 1"
Weight: 220 lbs
Hair Color: gray
Race: African American
Occupation: Preacher
Family: Wife, no children.

Markus Coburn

Chapter 1.6

Markus Coburn
Seven Years Before the Extinction Event

Markus Coburn locks the door to his church and staggers down the steps to the sidewalk, squinting in the bright sun. Jordan stares at him, her judgmental eyes digging under his skin.

She cares, maybe too much. "It's fine, J," Markus tells his secretary.

"No, it's not fine. We don't have to cancel Wednesday's service yet. You're being lazy. All we have to do is double our efforts. We could go door to door again," she offers, trying to act cheery.

"I can't pay you. We have no volunteers, and Regional has cut our stipend again." Markus follows the sidewalk to the street, stops, and turns. "I don't like preaching to empty pews." He shrugs. "It's over."

"Mrs. Clare is there. And old man Donald." Jordan is a young, proud black woman who always wears fashionable pantsuits to church like an uptown lawyer. Her enthusiasm masks her naivety, but that's youth in a nutshell.

Markus chuckles softly and shakes his head. "I guess we'll talk about it later. See you Sunday."

He detours on his way home, hoping to get a muffin

and a cup of coffee at the café, so deep in thought he crosses the street without looking. A car screeches to a halt and nearly crashes a parked car. The angry driver blares the horn and gives Markus the finger, but it doesn't faze him. His church sits empty, thugs run the neighborhood, and Markus doesn't feel God in his life anymore. *Does He even exist, or am I just a stupid old man?*

Markus sees misery everywhere he looks. The people in his pews seem forever sad because Jesus hasn't helped them. Markus has lost—lost the *souls*—of one hundred and four parishioners God entrusted to him. The downward attendance freefall tells Markus he's failing, comforting no one, bringing no one to Christ.

Markus heads for the café, looking forward to drinking coffee with his friend Ramid, one of the few things he still looks forward to.

Markus met Ramid a year ago, sitting at a table alone, drinking coffee and reading. He was a portly man wearing a full-length white kurta, a flat white skull cap, and a long traditional beard. Markus simply approached Ramid.

Ramid could have been obstinate, rude, or ignored Markus, but his smile was welcoming. He motioned for Markus to sit as if reading the preacher's mind. "I know the look. I've been there myself." He sipped his coffee confidently. "You are living with the suffering of hundreds upon your shoulders. It is common for men like us."

"I feel–" Markus looked at the passing cars, searching for the right words. "God has abandoned me, maybe this town."

"Coffee?" Ramid asked, waving to the waiter. "I am Ramid Aheed Mohammed, and you are?"

Their first conversation was a complete pleasure, cementing a lasting friendship. A whole year passed like wind before the storm. They settled into a routine of having coffee twice a month. Ramid, the senior Imam of the Islamic Center of New York, is a proud Muslim, retaining his dignity even in New York City, where he usually gets less than positive attention. Ramid, even more than Markus's wife, understands the pain of running a congregation. It seemed they were cut from the same cloth. The man has helped Markus through dark times, though he still has not found peace.

Markus finds a two-top table on the patio and waits for Ramid, who arrives on time, as usual. "Hello, Ramid. How are you?"

"I am very fine today. The summer weather suits me here." He ordered an espresso. How is Jordan? Is she still trying to fix everything? She does not know why the people stay away. She will."

Markus nodded. "She's so very young. Reminds me of me."

"Ah, being young is never so sweet as when we are old enough to taste it."

Markus chuckles. He sighs and chooses his words carefully. "I've decided to leave New York."

Ramid frowns. "Let us discuss the meaning of this." The waiter delivers the espresso. Ramid takes a bag of sugar cubes from his pocket, places one on his tongue, and sips his espresso.

"I haven't told my wife yet. When I look out at the streets of New York, I see only a blur of meaningless activity. Tired, empty shells instead of people. They meander and seem hollow and Godless, weak, like foil figurines. I admit I may be projecting, peering into a reflection of my soul, since I haven't spoken to God in quite some time."

"I cannot say that I did not see this coming." Ramid's dark eyes are kind, but today, they are red in the corners. He has his own stress.

Markus immediately feels guilty for dragging his problems out so early in the conversation.

Ramid's phone rings. He stares at the number for a moment and stands. "I will return." The cleric steps away to answer. The wind whips open his notebook, blowing loose papers off the table.

Markus collects them quickly and puts them back in the book. He notices a fax labeled "URGENT." It's hard to ignore such a compelling title: *Three stories re: Stone of Allah in European press past year unacceptable. Previously unknown records at the Vatican. Make them go away. Budget increased tenfold. Pick me up on the 10th,* 2:00 PM, *flight 2564 LaGuardia. ~Alban Aarif*

The Imam returns to the table, more somber than before, his face grim.

Markus explains: "Your papers blew off the table. I collected them for you. I think I got them all." He wasn't going to say anything about the message but blurted, "What is the Stone of Allah?"

Ramid looks down, his face veiled by shadow. He doesn't sit; he scratches his beard and peers down the street as if he were waiting for the bus. "You were not supposed to see that, my friend."

"Care to satisfy my curiosity? It will be between us and God," Markus says, counting on their friendship to smooth over the moment.

"This is a personal matter. I'm sorry, but I cannot discuss it." He excuses himself and makes a call.

When he returns to the table, his demeanor has changed again. "Markus, will you come to my car? I was rude and will tell you something about the stone."

"Certainly." Markus pays the bill and follows Ramid to the alley, stopping beside a black sedan. "Quite a risk parking here. The ticket is hefty," Markus says, looking around.

Two olive-skinned, bearded men dressed in tasteful black suits step out of the sedan. One wears a gold necklace, the other a thick diamond bracelet, and a massive gold ring. They approach.

Ramid turns his back and walks to the other side of the car.

The men move fast, grabbing Markus's arms. Their grips hurt, but their dead-eyed stares frighten Markus to his soul.

"What are you doing? Owe! You're hurting me."
Markus is forced into the back seat of the sedan.

Ramid gets into the passenger side, ignoring Markus entirely. The driver drives to a nearby parking structure. Markus pleads for an explanation but receives no response.

Ramid parks the sedan on the top level of a parking structure. His two helpers pull Markus from the vehicle, drag him to the edge of the building, and force him to look over the edge to the asphalt below.

Markus fumes with outrage. "What do you people think I've done? Why Ramid—I thought you are my friend." Markus struggles to free himself and manages to turn his head to look at Ramid.

Ramid stands there, watching, a weak smile on his face. "You should not have seen that," he whispers, lowers his head, and looks away. "This is partly my fault. I've become too open with you."

"What are you talking about? This is insane."

The stranger on Markus's right presses a pistol barrel hard against his temple. Traffic is flowing; people are going about their day.

God, please let someone see me.

"I am sorry, friend. My carelessness costs me the life of my friend. We are fighting a war, and I am loyal to Allah. I will mourn your death."

"No!" Markus pleads. "I don't understand a thing! Please, I have a family. I have a church. I can forget what I saw."

After a moment, Markus is pulled away from the edge. The man on his right hammers Markus's back hard, nailing his kidney. Pain erupts inside him, and he drops to the grimy rooftop.

Ramid waves the man away and crouches down to pat Markus on the back. He sighs and waits for Markus to catch his breath. "You are my friend. I will honor that one time. But you must leave town. This is no longer your home. You would do this anyway, so this is no great hardship."

"I promise." Markus cringes in pain. "I'll leave."

"Keep your word, and you will live. Stay here, or seek to understand the words you saw on that fax, and you will lose everything. Go to the police, and we will find you and exact revenge. If we cannot find you, your wife's life is forfeit. I give you this one chance because we are friends. We will be watching you. The war has found your shores, my friend. We'll be watching." The Imam and his thugs drive away.

Markus, clutching his side, waits for the pain to subside. When he's breathing more easily, rage fills his soul. He's dealt with thugs before, neighborhood dealers, and thieves. This is different. *A man of God! Threatening Marian! I've never felt so violated and insulted in my life. I pray that the anger that wells up in my soul will not swallow me whole.*

Markus's cell screen is smashed, but the phone still works, so he calls a cab. Minutes later, a yellow taxi pulls up. Markus practically throws his old bones into the back seat.

Crowds block the intersection near his church, but the cab pushes through. Towers of flames crawl up the steeple; black smoke pours from broken windows. A fire truck roars past, lights flashing, sirens blaring.

"Can't go farther, sir," the cabbie says. "Sir?"

Markus can't move, can't look away.

"Twelve-fifty, sir," the cabbie says impatiently. Eventually, he speaks again, "The meter is still runnin'."

Markus makes no movement or sound.

"Sir?"

"Please take me home," he mutters, giving the driver the address.

"Ah, finally, he speaks."

###

Midnight comes, and Markus is still at his home office desk. Strangely, he isn't sad. Rage courses through him. He puts the nearly empty fifth of vodka hidden in the desk drawer up to his lips and takes a swig. "Benjamin Franklin said beer is proof God loves us and wants us to be happy. He should have included vodka," Markus says aloud, taking another swig. "God lets evil exist because He wants us to choose, to earn our place in Heaven. What does he want me to choose? Lord, why are you so silent around me now?" Markus wonders if there might be another way to earn his stripes. He'd build a pyramid or a city of gold for the Lord. If only he'd deliver him from pain and sadness. He knows his thoughts are desperate but can't help thinking about them.

The next day, Markus and Marian seek refuge with an uncle in Birmingham, Alabama. He chooses not to tell anyone about Ramid or his threat, but Markus thinks of little else. Weeks go by. Marian eases his anger with her touch and kindness and her excellent cooking. His old parishioners do a fine job, cheering him up with handfuls of letters. The insurance agrees to pay to rebuild the church.

One thing continues to trouble Markus. He has not confided his crisis of faith in Marian. She does not know her husband's doubts about whether he can be a preacher anymore, and he no longer talks to God. Though Marian is miserable in Alabama, returning to New York puts both their lives at risk, a fact he cannot articulate.

Markus's hatred for Ramid smolders like coal fire, robbing him of sleep at night and peace of mind. The devil is at the doorstep, waiting for Markus to succumb to his whispers.

Markus tries to ignore the fax about the Stone of Allah and forgets Ramid's words. But if there's a war and he has to choose sides, his former friend is the enemy.

Ramid is a wise *man who should know secrets beget curiosity. What's so different about this Stone of Allah? If it is of God, why does an imam join a campaign to erase the existence of a holy relic? Who told Ramid to threaten my life and my family and burn my church? There must be a reason, but is it religious? How can knowing the name of a relic make me a threat?*

###

Unanswered questions run around Markus's brain like caged gerbils. One morning, staring at burnt toast on his plate, he realizes he has to know what the Stone of Allah is, or he'll never be a whole man again. He takes a cab to the far side of Birmingham to a cyber café, careful to drive the cabbie in circles. Markus uses a gift card to pay for the Internet connection because he is certain Ramid and his thugs have people watching him and his family all the time.

His first order of business is information. An online search for the Stone of Allah yields nothing, but his lack of online experience can't hold him back. He needs a library. A big, old library.

Markus is out of bed when the sun rises the next day, determination filling every cell. Marian silently watches him pack a bag, hurt and confusion marring her beautiful face.

"I need some answers, Marian. You know me." Markus tucks pressed white shirts into a suitcase and throws some ties on top.

Her expression speaks for her.

"We will discuss everything when I return, I promise. Why we left New York, the fire, this pilgrimage I'm making, our plans for the future."

Marian smiles, hugs her husband, and kisses him gently. "All right, Markus. I'll wait, but you be prepared to talk the second you step off that airplane."

###

The fax Markus saw said the Vatican has records of the Stone of Allah. *If Ramid and his cronies weren't able to destroy the records, I could dig them up. I can't believe how much time I've wasted hiding in this house. If the Lord has any grace, he will forgive me for giving whoever Ramid's bosses are time to ferret out the records and destroy them. I will find every scrap of scripture, legend, and fairy tale* that *still* exists *about that stone. I will know why it has the power to turn a friend into a foe.*

Markus arrives at the airport an hour later, pays cash for a ticket to Rome, and boards a plane to Italy. Settled in his seat, he opens a book about Islam, hoping a better understanding of its beliefs and history will help him identify and understand the war Ramid says he's fighting.

Isabella Torrioni

Height: 6'2"

Weight: 155 lbs

Race: caucasian, Italian descent

Hair Color: Dark Brown

Occupation: Security, Columbia University, SPEC

Personal security for Professor Cott.

Family: Estranged from father and mother.

Dishonorably discharged from the Army in 2003

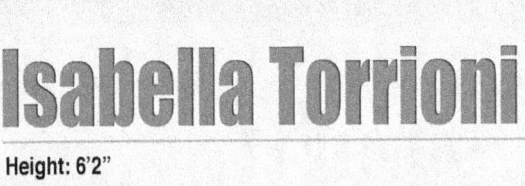

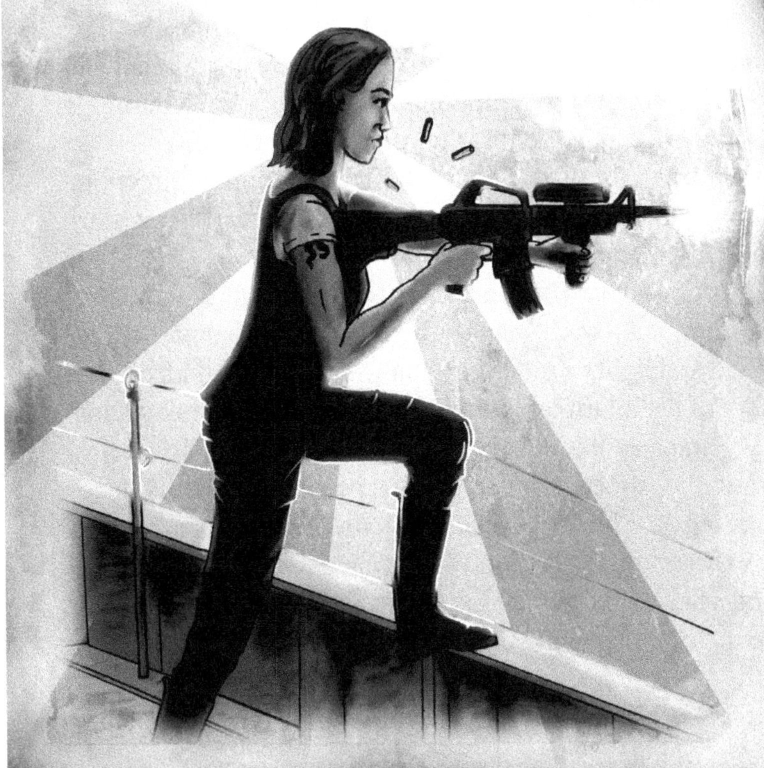

Isabella Torrioni

Chapter 1.7

Isabella Torrioni
One Million for One Job

A crowd as big as New Year's Eve at Times Square floods the street, sweeping over the intersections and sidewalks like a fucking tsunami of destruction, burning, trashing, fighting, yelling, crying. Panic is expressed in visible patterns, like flocks of birds changing direction. Enough to make one swallow their tongue if they start heading your way.

Unless you are Isabella Torrioni. She isn't scared of a fight, but a mob? That's different. No one smart hangs around and fights a mob. Isabella watches the mob from the safety of her apartment window as if Macy's Thanksgiving Day Parade is passing. Some dude stands at his window across the street, watching the chaos, fear in his face. Glancing up, he locks eyes with Isabella for a moment, his expression pleading, *"What's happening down there?"* Thousands of people run the street, all in the same direction, like the running of the bulls. Only, where were the bulls?

Part of this is my fault; here *I am, as unprepared as those poor bastards. No food, no water, no plan to get outta Dodge. Stupid.*

No better time than now to make a plan. I need supplies. I need them before they're all pilfered.

Isabella runs down the empty stairwell into the madness on the street. The corner market entrance is clogged with other people looking for food and water. She socks a guy in the gut and forces her way through the mob into the already-trashed store. Food and soda cans roll around; smashed juice and milk cartons, shattered glass jars, and bottles add their sharp edges to the slippery mess on the floor. Smokes, booze, wine, and beer are gone. Isabella grabs bread, peanut butter, and some pads and makes her way to the medical aisle at the back of the store.

Some shithead was there stuffing his pack, clearing the whole shelf. He stops to rub his bloodshot eyes and wipes snot dripping into his goatee onto his sleeve. Isabella grabs him and slams him against the cooler door. He coughs up goop and burbles something incoherent. She reaches into his bag. He struggles, so he gets her elbow in the nose. That stops him. She lets go. He falls to his knees, cussing, blubbering threats he can't deliver.

Isabella turns, grabs acetaminophen and aspirin from the bag, and pockets them.

An old man cries out. He's sheltering his wife from two thugs with pistols and just took a thump to the head. The man hands over all his shit. Isabella rushes behind the thugs and escapes the store. She wonders for a moment if she should've helped the man and his wife. Shakes her head. *Two strangers aren't worth me getting shot in the face.*

Mobs still flood the street, flowing around and over abandoned vehicles, trampling the dead bodies that spot the pavement like sprinkles before the rain.

Watching from her window hours later, Isabella sees sprinkles turn to showers as people drop dead, fall from buildings, roll down steps, or simply cough until all the breath leaves their lungs.

And the shitty thing is, she's just earned a million dollars. *If I'm not able to collect, someone's face is gonna get bashed in just to make me feel better.* Not very ladylike, but Isabella hates ladylike.

When night falls, banging and screams, gunshots, and explosions fill the air, a dark and twisted version of the Fourth of July celebrations. Thugs too cowardly to be seen in daylight are on the loose. Isabella is too smart to hide behind her flimsy apartment door. Sneaking onto the roof, she finds a large woman, a few teenagers, and an older man huddling against the parapets.

Isabella counts three fire escapes she can reach easily and makes a mental note of how she can get to the rooftop next door. She can escape. Now all she's gotta do is wait for the right time.

A dozen others come up top, frightened, complaining that thugs forced them out of their homes. "We've lost everything," a woman moans.

Isabella doesn't say a word.

Jet fighters roar overhead, firing rockets from their bellies, destroying the bridges. It's only been a day since the EMP, but a day is all it takes for a scared government to rationalize dropping bombs. Explosions shake the very bones of the building. Columns of red fire rise into the sky, surrounding the rooftop in blooms of hellfire.

Isabella grits her teeth, closes her eyes, and waits. Tonight is not the first time she's waited out a barrage of bombs.

Later, she eats a slice of bread with peanut butter and drinks some water, making sure no one sees so they don't ask for any, and so she won't have to fight to keep it.

The wind carries chaos and the sounds of distant cries. Power is out all over, but fires keep the skyline alive at midnight.

The street below is packed with dead people and dead cars. Most everyone still alive has cleared out. A single person bolts from a building, leaps on top of a car, and heads into the darkness, a predator hunting for weaker, more vulnerable victims.

Half the group on the roof is coughing up shit, and some dude, a self-appointed leader, tells them they have to leave. The sick ones leave, their heads down, shoulders hunched. The large woman lumbers up to Isabella. "Do you have any painkillers?" she asks.

Isabella shakes her head, and the woman shuffles to someone else. People move away, and the leader shows her the door.

I gotta get outta here, even if it kills me.

\#

Morning arrives, and the quiet is more unnerving than the chaos. Isabella stayed awake all night listening to the cries of people around her fall silent, like dogs in crates succumbing to confinement.

The city still burns; buildings funnel black clouds into the sky like massive chimneys.

Time to go. She heads down the dark, musty stairwell, stopping at her apartment to grab a broom. She unscrews the brush and tosses it aside. The stick is a simple weapon and effective.

The soft morning light can only lift the veil of darkness a little, the dark smoke preventing the full onslaught of sunlight from reaching the ground. Isabella's the only person alive on the street, the only one for miles, it seems. Many dead bodies lie on the road, under eaves, and hang out of cars. She wants to run as fast as she can but doesn't. *Keep a cool head, go easy, go carefully.*

A block away, a National Guard bivouac is surrounded by sandbags. Five dead guys wearing camouflage hazmat suits, their face plates splattered from the inside, almost obscuring their twisted expressions, lay silent. They must have suited up too late.

Isabella drags a shotgun from underneath the big guy and collects two nine-millimeter pistols and some ammo. Now she's set. *Somebody better fuck with me. Please, I need a distraction.*

There are survivors, but few. Most of them cower in their apartments, their eyes staring out, waiting, fearing.

A guy bursts out of a department store with a handful of stuff. He looks at her for a moment too long, probably sizing her up. Isabella gives him her coldest stare and opens her arms.

"C'mon, asshole!" she yells and shakes her broomstick at him. He runs. "Get outta here." She decides to call this stick her Beater.

Someone orders Isabella to put up her hands. She does so, turning slowly. Two men in t-shirts and shorts, both carrying M-16s, stand a dozen feet away. Isa has to comply because the looter distracted her. *That won't fuckin' happen again.* A Bradley fighting vehicle pulls out of the side street and stops behind them, its massive tank tracks cracking the pavement and curbs as it inches forward. One guy grabs her bag and rips it open.

He's bald and buff. "I got your shit." he looks her up and down. "You are a bitch, aren't ya?" He laughs. "She's got guns and food!" he says, inspecting the contents.

Isabella grinds her teeth, waiting for an opportunity to get at this guy's throat.

The other snarls, "Hurry the fuck up! We don't have time for you to dip your dick!"

"She'd rip it off for sure." He swings at her, but she

steps aside and grabs his wrist, twisting it until it cracks. He screams just as someone knocks her head from behind.

She wakes some time later, pissed as hell, with a dried trail of blood running down her neck and onto her shirt. She stands and waits for the spins to ease. "Fuck. I lost everything. Damn it to hell." She begins the long hike north, which is the fastest and easiest way off Manhattan Island.

Smoke clouds hover like watchful phantoms. Visibility is less than fifty feet, and the smells burn her nose. Inside a nearby burning building is a furnace. The once-precious paperwork has curled up and dissolved into ash. No doubt computers have melted into blobs, cubicles full of memories all gone. Fire doesn't care. It just feeds and grows.

Farther from her apartment, it is more of the same, except no more spies watching from windows, no more looters. Everyone else is dead. The bodies are almost stacked on top of each other.

Had it comin'. People suck. Most of my family sucks, guys are assholes, chicks bitch too much, and weren't we killin' the planet by overpopulating it with assholes? The sun is still gonna come up and go down, with or without them.

Her thoughts are random, zigzagging from extreme sadness to aggression to paranoia, and back again. It's more tiring than walking all day.

Maneuvering through the maze of smashed cars, trash, and dead bodies is harder and slower because Isabella stops frequently and checks her six. No one is gonna get the drop on her again. Her ears tune in and focus. They hear creaking and a crash that she feels in the concrete under her feet. These buildings are coming down. *Conspiracy theorists don't think fire can melt steel and drop the Trade*

Towers. Ha. Fire is the ultimate destroyer of worlds.

Isabella picks an M-242 shell casing up off the street. The M-252 machine gun crowns the rotating turrets of Bradley fighting vehicles. Finding the shell makes her feel better. *I'm gonna run into those fuckers that stole my shit, and I'm not even trying.* Isabella smiles. *I'm gonna kill 'em. They are going to pay for taking everything: my shotgun, pistols, and food. They even took my damn pads and aspirin. What the fuck are they gonna do with pads?* It was a slap across her face.

A Bradley fighting vehicle has a pretty big footprint, so tracking it is easy, and she's getting close, too. *No guns, just my Beater. I gotta come up with a plan that involves more than just smashing their heads in. I gotta get the jump on them this time. I guess if they take me down with that M-242, then so be it. Just throw me in the gutter with all the other dopes.*

Isabella sneaks past an overturned, burned-out yellow cab and spots the Bradley smashed through the front of a drugstore. The men inside are stealing everything they can. She runs, half bent over with the Beater in both hands. There is no movement in the APC; the men are all inside the store. The back is locked, so they aren't all that dumb. She braces her foot on the tank tread, grabs a small handle above the back hatch, and climbs to the top. The overhead hatch flips open, and a mole head pops out. *Eh, so there's someone left behind after all.* Isabella spins the Beater and brings it down on the fool's head. The vibration she feels in her fingers, as the wood cracks bone, stings. The man falls. She sets the Beater down and slips easily into the Bradley. The man groans as her foot lands on his head, so she gives him one more knock. Now he's out.

The back of the Bradley is filled with sodas, beer, pills, and piles of canned food. Isabella's backpack sits on

top. She yanks it off their stash and checks to see if her pads and aspirin are still inside. They are, so she adds a few cans of soup and beans and slips her backpack onto her shoulders. Man-sweat hits her nose, and she gags, needing fresh air immediately.

She wasn't always so uptight. Ever since she got cornered by a dickhead outside a bar, she reacts this way. Fucker caught and pinned her behind a dumpster, a big hairy guy, that same musky smell all over him. She would have been raped if she hadn't head-butted him. *I hope he's lying in a ditch now.* Isabella shakes off the memory, burying it.

Two pistols and the shotgun hang on the wall of the crew compartment next to an assault rifle, so she takes them all.

As she climbs out the top hatch, she sees the jerk who yanked off her backpack and laughed. This guy should have died with all the others. He's scum, guilty as charged, so he gets the death sentence. Isabella flips the cover off the M-242 trigger, pulls it gently, and delights in the *Crack, crack, crack, crack!* Shaking the whole vehicle.

She rotates the turret and unleashes more hell, massive bullets shredding everything in the store—shelves, toys, candy bars, and all the other crap they sell explode in a million pieces. Life as confetti. She pumps a few more rounds into the man who stole her stuff, splattering his guts.

She knows how to drive the vehicle and considers taking it, too. *No, I know better. The Bradley takes three to operate efficiently and a support squad of six. One person can't keep the roaches from swarming it and taking me out.*

The other guys start to return fire just as Isabella ducks down the hatch. She dumps an ammo box onto the floor, grabs a belt of three grenades, pulls the pins, and exits through the back hatch.

With her pack, an assault rifle, and a shotgun slung over her shoulder, two pistols in her belt, and her Beater in hand, Isabella runs down Lexington Avenue. The explosion in the Bradley sets off two more, flat-lining the APC for good.

She wants to get to Central Park before noon, an hour or so away and set up some kind of camp for the night. Squatting in a building only to have it burn down or trap her like a rat in a maze isn't an option. The park sounds safest, has fresh air blowing around, and has enough open space to see any fire coming. She thinks about heading north but decides against it. One, thousands of New Yorkers headed that way, trying to escape the city. A ton of dead and rotting bodies will be up there. Two, she doesn't swim very well, so she's not gonna be able to cross the river. And three, when the military rolls on through, she wants to see them comin' so she doesn't get shot.

Central Park looks empty, but recon always comes first. She crouches among the trees, surveying the open areas until she's certain no one else has claimed the space. She sets up camp in the middle of a baseball field with a one-hundred-foot perimeter of noisy booby traps: soda cans, plastic bags, and egg cartons. Feeling secure, she lets her mind wander. *Has my family survived? I don't even know* most of them. *It's not like we all hang out at reunions or anything.* She tries not to think of her father but can't help it.

He was a strict Catholic, the head of an import syndicate connected to cartels south of the U.S. border. God must have looked the other way when her father's clients laundered money, hid cocaine in legit import deals, and sold illegal guns to thugs. Hypocrite. He was worse than just a hypocrite; he was a beater who'd "whoop" her and her mom. She remembers the day he learned she'd failed her algebra class at her swanky private school. He beat her so badly that he had to lock her away in his cabin on Lake Rockland until the bruises healed. "This is for your own good. You'll be a better person when you learn to behave," he'd said. "You either make the rules in life, or you follow them." He didn't think she'd be making any rules, hence the need to learn to follow them. *Bastard.*

Wanting—needing—to smash somethin', she turns to the trunk of a tree and punches it hard. Her skin splits, but she punches it again. "If you're alive, Papa, I'll show you some new rules. *My* rules." *Shit. Time to get some* shut-eye*, not get all warped.*

###

Isabella was tough, but for some reason, memories could get under her skin and fester. They had gotten worse after getting kicked out of the army. Sure, she could drink away dark thoughts, but eventually, she'd run out of money and have to get a job. She always ended up hating the bosses and was eventually fired by men with big egos like her father—the ones who wanted to pull on her puppet strings, but she wasn't no puppet, especially for hypocrites who always broke their own rules.

One evening, after punching this bitch out at Eve's, her favorite bar—she started it—a pasty, white dude with a bright white beard, bald head, and thick glasses calling himself Professor Cott approached Isabella. "You've got a good right hook,' he said, handing her a beer.

" I know. Got me through basic training, Iraq, this hell hole. People don't expect it because of how I look. I get a jump on 'em every time." Isabella was a little drunk.

"I need someone who has some guts to work for me. Are you looking for work?"

It took a moment for Isabella to respond. "What kind of work? I won't run drugs. Nothin' to do with exploiting hookers or beating up kids. No matter how bratty. And I ain't gonna sell myself like that, either."

"Nothing bad," Cott said. "A physics lab at Columbia University. We've had break-ins and threats on our department. Hippies don't like us playing with quantum stuff." Cott rolled his eyes. "Kids can be quite ignorant these days."

Isabella accepted the job as the security guard for his physics lab on Columbia University's campus. He and his grad students did top-secret stuff, even had the military stop by a few times to gawk at some trash-can-sized piece of tech with wires and dials and pipes. The job was good, allowed her enough solitary time in her shift to spike her coffee with a little Irish cream and not have to deal with anyone other than one other security officer.

She didn't see Cott for a while. Until one evening, there he was, standing in her doorway, looking dopey but smart, holding two coffees.

"You're doing good here. On-time, accurate notes, not a single snafu." Cott handed her one of the coffees. "But I remember you saying you were good at busting heads. But no one would see you coming."

"Yeah, I remember. I was the one that said it." Isabella took a coffee and took a sip. It was good, even though it didn't have any alcohol in it. "Why do I get the feeling you're workin' up to askin' me somethin' that may or may not be breakin' some of my rules?"

Cott chuckled his nervous laugh. "No, no. What I need is a personal bodyguard. I need someone that can get in the door, that doesn't look like a thug, but can hold her own if need be."

"No drugs? No sex stuff?"

Cott shook his head. "I won't break any rules. Trust me."

Turned out he was a man of his word. He turned out to be a political activist. The professor had more of a nightlife than most college students, going to bars and clubs, sometimes shit-hole warehouses in Jersey, or he'd end up in back rooms with shady-lookin' people. He called Isabella if he was afraid or if someone was causing trouble. Most of the time, she had nothing to do except be alert and ready, but hey, that's the security business for ya. The year went by, and life was good. She got in three, no, four fights for this guy, always after some late-night meeting he attended. The side work earned her fifty grand a year. Couldn't beat that. Over the year, she earned Cott's trust and vice versa.

However, someone did ask her to break one of her rules. Offered to pay her one million dollars. She only said yes because it was a very small rule. Not one of the big ones.

Two weeks before everyone started dying, Cott met with an activist group called People for Stable Fairness, a bunch of weirdos who dressed in all black like dead poets or something. He disappeared into a Jersey warehouse with the head honchos and told Isabella to stay in the alley.

An hour passed, and Isabella paced, bored out of her mind. A limousine was parked at the end of the alley, blocking her car. If Cott needed a quick escape, she'd have nowhere to go. "Oh, this asshole is gonna have to find a new spot," she mumbled, stomping toward the limo.

The driver-side window rolled down, exposing a woman with red hair and large, dark sunglasses. "Hello. You're Professor Cott's guard?" she asked.

"What's it to you?" Isabella asked, resting her hand on the pistol grip in a shoulder harness under her jacket.

"How would you like to make a million dollars on a one-time job?" she asked.

"Fuck you," Isabella snapped. "Now, I'm gonna have to insist you find a new parking spot."

The woman stepped out of the vehicle, dressed in full camo gear, not some slick cocktail dress. "This is not some sicko offer." She smiled and took off her glasses. Isabella saw a fighter's eyes, a long scar on the woman's right cheek ending at her jaw, that gave Isabella goose bumps. No, the woman was not some bimbo.

"Come, sit for five minutes. My boss would like to explain his proposal. The easiest and most money you'll ever make." She motioned to the backseat of the car.

"Fine, one minute. But I ain't getting in the car. Roll that window down and speak up. I have a little tinnitus from being fuckin' bombed over and over."

The window rolled down. In the back was a shadowy figure. No lights to illuminate his face, dark suit, gloves. "You understand that a well-funded power base runs our country. We don't elect them, and we don't cut their checks. They run the country without consequence or conscience."

"The deep state. Yeah, Cott blabs about them all the time. Seems like you and him should have a cuddle."

"What I need from you, only you can do. It has to do with destroying something the military-industrial complex is researching and funding. Destroying this device will save lots of lives. It's being developed in the physics lab where you work. Now, do I have your attention?"

"You're gonna pay me one million bucks to trash some weapon researchers are slapping together? Where the fuck do I sign up?"

"This job has a very specific due date. It must be destroyed by midday on the 15th. No later than noon."

"Who the fuck are you?"

The woman in a lipstick red dress handed Isabella a fat envelope.

125

The shadowy man chucked. "I am like you; I was used and discarded after Operation Freedom in Iraq. The Deep State proved they do not do the will of the American people or the soldiers. They use us. They used you and spit you out. I want to stop them from doing any more damage. You may call me Zilla."

Isabella stared at the fat envelope. Snatched it, flipped through five bundles of one-hundred-dollar bills, a healthy advance. "I ain't going to prison for nobody, not Cott or you, Mr. Fuckin' Zilla-man."

"There will be no prison. You already have the access to the physics lab, you know how to get around the security because you know where the access points are, the servers that store the video feed, the schedule of the other guards. If you don't do this job, the Deep State will have one hell of a powerful weapon that they can turn on anyone even US citizens because no one even knows it exists. No one else will know about your part but you. Follow the instructions in the envelope and see how perfect my plan is," Zilla said.

The woman handed over a metal square the size of a brick. "Wave this over the hard drives that store the camera feed, and all the data will be wiped clean."

The window to the limo rolled up. Zilla was done talking.

"The only way to cure cancer is to cut it out. Wouldn't you agree?" The woman said.

Isabella did. She had that same thought many times. "You will help us destroy this weapon?"

With trepidation and distrust, she accepted the job, sliding the fat envelope into her pocket. The metal brick was heavy and solid, with not a single wire showing, but it fit into her other jacket pocket.

"I know you respect free thinkers. Time to prove

you are one of them," the woman said, returned to her seat in the limo, and backed out of the alley.

Cott came out of his meeting, and Isabella drove him home. He was in a weird mood, didn't talk as much as he usually did, and trudged inside his house without saying goodnight.

Isabella sat in the car in his carport, wondering about Cott's behavior and Zilla's promise of one million dollars for a single job. Eventually, she opened the envelope and flipped out the note from Zilla telling Isabella how to destroy the weapon the brainiacs in the physics department at Columbia built. The deed had to be done in two weeks, exactly. She read the detailed instructions twice: the trash-can thing was a low atmospheric rocket that could deploy a sonic weapon that could cripple the people of an entire city. Zilla wanted to destroy any advanced weaponry that could be turned on the American people without their knowledge. The note said this device was only one of a dozen projects he will target in the coming decade.

Isabella did not want to care about Zilla's end game. But she did. The military made her into a weapon, and the one time she went off the rails, they threw her away like a piece of trash. The brass was always looking for new weapons, and they sure didn't care about the people who got in the way. *Fuck them.*

But she could go to jail. She valued her freedom too much. *Who are those bastards? Are they trying to entrap me?* The feds weren't supposed to do that, but she had heard them break that rule dozens of times, and not all conspiracy theories. Many of the Fed's dirty deeds were on record. What stops the US military or the CIA from doing the same?

Isabella lit a cigarette with her U.S. Army-engraved Zippo lighter, touched the glowing embers to the paper, letting the flames lick her fingertips before tossing it out the window. *No, thanks. But hey, you just try and get a refund for your deposit, Zilla.* The brick the woman said would clean the hard drives remained in the back seat.

Two weeks went by quickly. Isabella got an eviction notice from her landlord and a letter from a law firm informing her that she was being sued by the family of an Iraqi man she'd beaten while on duty in Iraq. The family was holding a grudge even though they were now living the good life in Wisconsin, and their boy didn't have a scar to boast about. She might have to pay out thousands of dollars in restitution. That fifty grand she got from the chic with the scar would vanish like a dandelion in the wind. That million dollars suddenly looked pretty good.

The morning the bacteria in the water supply made everyone sick, Isabella went to work as usual, leaving her apartment at five in the morning. She had no idea what was happening, but something was different that day. The street was jammed with cars, and people were rushing somewhere. She avoided everyone, as usual, and cranked the volume up on her earbuds, jogging down the stairs all the way to the subway stop. No one was down there. *This place is a ghost town. Weird. Hell,* it's *better this way. I'll take it.* She turned down the music as she got on the sparsely populated train that was usually packed. Some lady hopped on at the last second. She wore a face mask and moved as far away from everyone as possible.

Shockingly, the trains were on time and got her to work by five-thirty. Even at this early hour, the campus usually had kids and workers millin' around, but not today. Isabella strolled up to the plain white building, wondering where everyone was. *Those brainiacs like to start early. Is Guillermo not guarding the door? He's usually on time.* She used her key to enter the building and shut off the alarm. *No front desk guard either? Okay then.* Someone is guarding *this place* twenty-four-seven. She stashed her lunch in the refrigerator and went to the front desk. At least one guard had shown up. His shit was all over the place: a book, a crossword puzzle, an ice-cold cup of coffee.

Isabella was stationed at the front desk until after seven. Usually, there were all kinds of people in the facility, but today, no one was showin' up. *What a perfect time to… to…blow up a baby rocket and earn a million bucks.*

She visualized the million dollars in her bank account. *So many zeros.* Excited at the prospect of so much money all at once, she took off toward the physics lab, adrenaline rushing. *If I do this deed, it'll have to be quick.*

Isabella unlocked the door to the lab and shut off the alarm. The rocket was at the far end of the room, locked behind four-inch-thick Plexiglas. The thing was much longer than she remembered; an extra piece had been added. She drew her sidearm, aimed at the Plexiglas, and stopped. It's probably *bulletproof, and my gun's registered and identifiable.* Searching the lab, she found a metal bar in the supply closet and chipped at the lock. Finally, the stainless-steel clasp broke. She ripped the small latch off and flipped open the four corner clips. The entire side cover fell open and noisily slapped the tile. Isabella tried to roll the entire plexiglass crate, but it was too heavy. She retrieved a dolly from the closet next door, tipped the rocket on its end, and walked it onto the dolly. She simply rolled the thing to the elevator. This thing wasn't something NASA geeks would cream over; it was more like a hobbyist toy, but it was sophisticated enough. *Could this really shoot out shock waves and make* everyone *in a dozen miles get sick or die?*

She wondered why she had to take it to the roof

to destroy it, but the note in her instructions was explicit. *Probably not trying to burn the whole building down.*

Isabella rolled the rocket out of the elevator toward the roof access door.

A note stuck to the door read:

You have exactly fifteen minutes to destroy this weapon. If you beat the clock, you will be able to get away. Good luck, soldier.
~Zilla

Isabella's heart jumped, and her pulse quickened. She rolled the rocket to the middle of the roof and carefully walked it off the dolly, knowing it was full of rocket fuel. *Why fifteen minutes?* She wondered. What did Zilla know that he didn't share? Isabella was flushed with suspicion. This is way too easy. She no longer liked this game but wasn't the type to walk away from a job. The self-destruct button was on the side. All she had to do was press it and hold it until it started flashing. It would supposedly burst into flames and melt the components into unrecognizable goo. *Easy.* She pushed the red button at the bottom of the cylinder and held it until it flashed. She backed off and watched three legs fold out of the base.

A police helicopter approached, flying in her general direction. Were they coming for her? She looked at her watch. *Eight minutes.* The rocket stabilized automatically, adjusting its legs.

"You don't look like you're getting ready to self-destruct."

Sirens wailed in the distance. Lots of sirens.

Five minutes.

Isabella watched the fuel ignite, thrusting a column of fire under it as it shot into the sky as smoothly as unsheathing a sword.

Isabella blocked out the sun with one hand and watched the rocket rise, climbing and climbing and climbing, until the bottom half dropped off and a second-stage engine ignited. The rocket disappeared: no explosion flash, sound, or falling debris. Well, those fools said it had unconventional tricks. *Should I assume the rocket is gonna self-destruct in the clouds so it won't hurt anyone? Right?* She should be right, but she didn't feel that way in her guts. She felt like she did something bad. Something stupid.

Think about it later. First, get to the control room and erase the camera footage.

The nearby police helicopter's rotor stopped turning, causing it to coast over the stadium and explode. Isabella's jaw fell open. Sirens went silent like God flipped

a switch. Truck and car noises ceased; faint screams and yelling floated on the quiet breeze.

I still need to delete the surveillance records. She reminded herself and ran to the door. A red box hung from the doorknob of the roof door, "Urgent" printed on its side. A red syringe and a note were inside:

Use or die. The New World thanks you. I knew you'd come through. Your service was indispensable. ~Zilla.

Isabella was about to toss the syringe over the edge of the roof, but a little voice in her head spoke up. A thousand heartbeats passed, an eternity of reflection. The mysterious morning started to click into focus. *Shit is going down. Bigger than some mysterious sonic weapon. Fuck, there is no god-damn money, is there?* She stuck herself with the needle and compressed the plunger, believing she didn't have a choice.

Flinging the roof access door open, she jogged down the dark stairwell, trusting herself not to fall.

There is no *way the building's out of power*; the *lab building's backup generators should already be running. That rocket that launched did this. Happened at the same time. Mother fuck. I did this.* Panic sent her jumping down four, five steps at a time, smashing her shoulder into the far wall but not stopping. *Destroy the records*; gotta *hurry.* Bursting through the B-1 door, she found the data room and caught her breath. Computer stacks lined the wall, silent like stone towers. She had no idea which one to disable. *I'm so fucked. They probably back up the servers* off-site. *I'm such an idiot.*

She left, knowing her only chance to avoid prison was to go on the run. When she got outside, she froze. Cars choked the street; traffic lights were dark, and people were standing around yelling at each other, waving their cell phones in the air. A loud engine whined to her left, and Isabella turned just in time to jump out of the way of an old Chevy truck swerving all over the sidewalk, people running to get out of its way until it disappeared around the corner.

Isabella ran in the opposite direction. *Time to go bug out.*

###

Isabella's part in the extinction event is clear. Now, holding her knees, sitting in the middle of Central Park, well-armed, surrounded by cans and trash, she cries. The biggest mistake of her life was trusting Zilla and that bitch with the scar. *That rocket was an advanced EMP. I wouldn't have launched it if I'd known the truth. No one deserves this… shit.* Isabella tries to put the consequences of her stupidity into words but cannot. Her chest tightens as a wave of sadness fills her heart.

The grey skies darken as night comes. She shakes it off, mostly. *They're dead. I'm not.* She just needs to forget about her little rocket incident and focus on surviving. *I'm not sick, and I'll probably stay that way… if that syringe was filled with an actual vaccine.*

The breeze smells rotten, burnt.

So, this Zilla guy declared war on New York, huh? I guess that makes me his soldier. You'd think he'd want me to die like the rest of New York so I can't tell anyone what I did for him. Unless…he has something else for me to do.

CHAPTER 1.8

TANIS HEART
THE DAY THE SATELLITES DIE

Tanis Heart heads up the steps at the Fifty-Ninth and Lexington subway exit, the mid-day sun beating down. The city is bustling with people, all doing their thing, going here and there. Tanis loves this city, a metal forest filled with giants. Only, he lives in Forest Hills and doesn't get into the city much. When he does, it's bliss. He's only fifteen, but when he walks around New York, he feels free and in charge of himself like adults must feel.

His cell rings. "Hello, Ma. . . yeah, I'm gonna surprise Dad at his office. Eh, I just took the subway into town. I've done it by myself loads of times. You're freaking out. Come on, Ma, I'm not a baby anymore."

He finally gets Ma off the phone. She worries too much. New York City is as safe as any suburb, maybe safer. He crosses the street shoulder to shoulder with a bunch of other people. He unwraps a lollipop as he walks and pops it in his mouth. Today is a typical New York summer day, semi-cloudy, not too hot, people doing what they always do: eat at cafés, take their lunch breaks, hop in and out of cabs, and whatever else adults do.

Tanis's father is a colonel in the Air Force and the smartest man alive. He is military through and through but doesn't wear his uniform anymore because he works at a secret Department of Defense building in the city. He mostly manages the staff and the liaisons between the facility and the USAF but does other stuff he can't talk about. Dad is on the job more than he's at home, but that doesn't bother Tanis. The whole country exists because of the strong military.

"The problem"—he's told Tanis a thousand times— "is the military doesn't have enough power. Civilians run the military. Civilians elected by cash donations from the biggest corporations on the block." Tanis agrees, would go a step further. The whole voting thing is so lame. People should be told what to do because they're too stupid to think for themselves. Most kids are as dumb as rocks, and they'll be the ones voting in a few years.

Tanis's school holds an election for student council president and other leadership positions every year. "Leaders." *Ha!* Truth? They're just the nerds who run the bake sales and organize school rallies and stuff. Anyway, voting for the most popular person to run meaningless school functions is lame. Just give someone the presidency and let them and their squad run things and leave the rest of the students alone.

Tanis believes the United States is run the same way. The president is elected by popularity, not by what he's done, can do, or how smart he is. Tanis even buys into the rumors that the electoral college is nothing but a secret group of rich guys who decide the winner, so they have a puppet on strings to do as they say.

Jimbo, Tanis's best friend, didn't believe elections were rigged. So Tanis, who considered himself a pretty good computer hacker, programmed a simple code into the main computer so that no matter who won the majority vote, Alexia would win. Alexia, the nerdiest and least-known candidate, won student council president by a landslide. It was too easy, but that move made Jimbo a believer. Tanis believes elections in the real world are rigged, too.

It's all so stupid. The government lies to everyone, his teachers lie, his friends lie, and so on. Lies, lies, and more lies. The only people he trusts are his dad and mom.

Tanis runs to the front door of the DOD building, a tall, slate-gray skyscraper with a million shiny windows. The guard at the metal detector greets him with a high five like he's three years old. *Dork.*

Tanis sets his backpack on the conveyor belt and steps through the detector, knowing it won't beep at him— it never does because he knows what not to carry in his pockets.

The guards behind the lobby counter playfully salute Tanis, letting him head for the elevators. A man with long, black hair emerges from a room carrying a tool bag. His shirt says he's an air-conditioning guy. Behind him, an armed guard packs a full-auto M-4 snub-nose rifle. *Nice.* Though it's kind of a red flag. Anyone who knows anything knows civilians aren't allowed to possess full-auto rifles. It's totally obvious this is a military installation disguised as a civilian.

The elevator bell dings, and the doors slide open. Tanis steps in, followed by the other two. The AC guy with the black hair smiles and nods.

Idiot, Tanis thinks. *You're basically a plumber for cold and hot air. Shave that beard, cut your hair, and get a life, Alex.* The A/C guy gets off on ten, but Tanis heads to the top floor offices, just below the penthouse.

He knows everyone in the office, so it isn't weird to make his way past the cubicles, glass-partitioned offices, and all the friendly people to his father's office door. Tanis bursts in, grinning, pleased at shocking the hell outta Pops.

Mr. Heart is sitting at his desk, looking surprised, but he doesn't move. Tanis raises his hands to illustrate the surprise, but Mr. Heart just looks scared or something.

"Come on! I got you," Tanis said, approaching the desk, enjoying the surprise.

Mr. Heart sits up straighter in his chair, still looking like Tanis flipped the old man the bird or slapped him or something.

Something thumps under the desk. Someone squeals.

Mr. Heart rolls his chair back violently. A woman stands up, wiping the corners of her mouth.

Tanis stares at the huge boob hanging out of her shirt, nipple and all.

Mr. Heart, as quickly as he can, pulls up his pants and zips his fly.

"I thought you locked the door," the woman hisses. She tucks her boob into her bra and buttons up. She's buff-lookin' and has a nice scar on the right side of her face running to her jaw. She fluffs her hair, stomps out of the room, and glances at Tanis with a crooked smile like she isn't mad at all.

Mr. Heart gets up and grabs Tanis's arm, digging in his fingers. "You just screwed our whole family!" he snaps. He pushes Tanis roughly into the chair in front of the desk. "Stay here. I'll be back." He chases after the broad with the big tits.

Tanis had stifled the shock and pain when his dad manhandled him, now, he cries. *Dad's a liar, too. How could he do this to Ma? They're like soul mates, happy, always on each other like they've been in love forever.*

Knowing his father has betrayed Tanis and his mother fills the boy's heart with aching poison. Tanis stands and paces, drying his tears on his sleeve. So now his parents will get divorced, and he'll have to go back and forth between them like a yoyo. He kicks the desk, hard. *Like hell I'll go stay with him. Not a chance now.*

The boob broad bursts into the room, beelines to the desk, picks up a thin leather satchel from the edge, and turns, says, "Your father's a great man."

"Get outta here." Tanis looks away but glimpses the logo imprinted on her satchel. He recognizes the simplified graphic logo with INA Global printed under it.

Someone starts beating a bass drum; oh, that's his heart.

She's still staring and smiling but covers the logo by holding the satchel against her skirt. "Your dad made a mistake. It won't happen again. Don't tear your family apart because of one mistake." She turns and walks out of the room, swinging her ass like a pendulum.

Bitch! Not because she was sucking off his dad, but because INA Global rumors have been all over the chat rooms lately. A company that doesn't exist officially but builds satellite weapon systems. This chick is a corporate spy. She's got to be using his dad to get information. *How could my dad be so stupid?*

What's her game? Tanis pulls out his tablet, clicks on the external keyboard, and logs onto Blacknet, a hacker site on the Deep Web. It's not a place for the weak-minded, but he goes there to learn and chat with other hackers, not to browse porn, gamble, or hire a hitman. That shit is for losers.

His contact list is flush with people available to talk, but he's looking for Zilla.

Two months ago, on a chat with a few guys from Anonymous, discussing the hacker war between the U.S. and China, people said the DOD was hiring anyone with half a brain and paying good money to combat the daily security breaches Chinese hackers were making. Then this Zilla guy popped up on the board. He didn't just have two cents to contribute; he uploaded documents! It was risky, but Zilla didn't seem to care. He was smart enough not to lead the NSA to his door.

Tanis had never seen classified stuff before, and it blew his mind. He was especially interested in this company called INA Global. They built a kinetic bombardment system capable of launching projectiles from a satellite, hitting any target on Earth. The speed the shells would gain traveling from space to the ground gave them so much force that they would rival the biggest bombs on the shelf.

Space-based weapons are totally against international law. Plus, Tanis's father doesn't approve of them. They're too easy to use as a weapon of mass destruction.

Zilla's documents prove INA Global is looking for a buyer, accepting bids from China, Venezuela, and Russia while lobbying senators and congressmen. Zilla insists corporate spies are working in the State Department and the DOD.

And Tanis just found one.

TN*8 (Tanis's handle):
Zilla, I've got news.

Zilla responds instantly:
All eyes, bro.

TN*8:
I saw this woman try to conceal an INA Global logo. She was acting weird. She's in my dad's pants, and I think she's using him.

Zilla:
Your dad is her mark. This is what we've been talking about. INA can't sell its system to the US, so it's

140

gone to Russia or China and probably installed it in the next-gen satellites. INA wants total power in the thermosphere. Once it knows where the US satellites are, it'll sell that information for a premium. This can potentially pull the US's pants down.

TN*8:
I guarantee my dad isn't in on this. She's distracting him, using him to gain access.
I don't know, man. This is big, too big.

Zilla:
Too big for you. But not for me. Give me access to your dad's computer, and I'll find out what she's been doing. She's probably hacked his network and relaying data off site. I can track where those bits go. I may even be able to get enough docs to prove that INA exists in the first place. That'll get the Fed's heads rolling for sure. You gotta get me in his box.

TN*8:
I could get in trouble. I should just tell my dad and let him handle it.

Zilla:
Dude, he's not gonna believe you. INA doesn't exist, remember? He probably thinks his network is hack-proof. You gotta remember, if INA has a spy in the office already, your dad and his staff are being manipulated. This is an outside job.

Tanis trusts Zilla. He's got Einstein's brains. Dad's computer stares at him, still logged on. He's maybe got thirty seconds before it logs off and goes to sleep.

Zilla:

Hurry, before your dad comes back. We only have one chance to hack this system, to follow the breadcrumbs.

Tanis plugs a specialty USB cord into his tablet, pauses, plugs the connector into his dad's computer. *Will I go to jail? Is this right? Will my dad get in trouble?*

Zilla:

Do it now. Be a hero. This is a once-in-a-lifetime opportunity!

Tanis slams the USB home. Both computers blink out. He wiggles the connection, but it's in. "What the—?" he whispers, startled.

Dad's monitor comes back online, displaying a text box.

Nice work little dude. Pack up and get out of New York. I'll find and reward you. ~Zilla.

"What? That was fast." *Something's not right.* Tanis pulls the USB cord from the computer, yanks the keyboard off his tablet, crams them into his backpack, sits back in the chair, and waits. The office quiet makes him uneasy and anxious, so he stands and paces to calm himself. *Zilla said, "Little dude." How does he know I'm short? He said, "get out of New York." I told him my dad works in an office in Washington, DC.*

Tanis glances at the camera on top of the monitor, covered with a square piece of plastic. *Zilla can't see me now, but obviously, he knows who I really am, who my dad really is, and where I am right now. No, no, no.* Tanis's heart sank. *I gave him access to Dad's computer. All I did was save Zilla the trouble of hacking into it.* The trust he placed in Zilla evaporates in a single breath.

Trying to distract himself from his own stupidity, Tanis paces, listens to the door. People are yelling. But he can't leave. He has to ride this out. Eventually, he retrieves his tablet, turns on a game. He plays for a half hour, but his character dies constantly. Sweat makes his hands slippery, and his attention to the game wanders when he remembers his dad's face. He wonders what his expression will look like when he realizes that his own son has betrayed him and ruined their family. The *click* of the office door lock startles Tanis, and he jerks upright.

Dad hurries into his office, not smiling, and drops a meatball sandwich from Pizzano's in Tanis's lap. The heat of the marinara burns through the fabric of his pants.

"Eat. I've got to handle a small crisis, but I'll be right back. We need to discuss this little incident." He leaves, slamming the door.

Tanis tries to eat, but the sandwich is dry in his mouth. More time passes, and he's ready to bolt when an alarm goes off and someone yells. He stands from his dad's chair, backs away from the desk, pressing his back against the window. His heart jumps around in his rib cage like a monkey on speed. *Crap, I'm goin' to jail.*

Dad throws open the door. His face is as intense as Tanis has ever seen it. "Big trouble. Do not leave!" he orders, slamming the door again. The lock tumblers *click* again, like a jail door clanking.

Tanis looks out the window, down to the street, fifty

stories below. "Please, God. I don't want to go to jail," he whimpers.

The lights blink off, darkening the room except for the daylight. Emergency lights come on in thirty seconds, flinging red over everything.

I need to get out of here. I'd rather go on the run than to jail. Maybe Zilla can give me a place to stay until whatever this thing is blows over. Shit. Should've thought this through before listening to Zilla. Tanis runs to the door, can't unlock it, puts his ear to the thick slab of wood, and listens to some guy yelling at the top of his lungs.

The words are muffled, but Tanis hears, "The Constellation is down, sir. Every satellite! The North American workgroup. The European one, too. A computer virus took over the bios, wiped out our onboard memory, erased our protocols. No communication at all. Internet servers are down all over. We're sitting ducks."

Someone else yells, "Level ten has shut down the building, sir. Our contamination alarms have gone off. There's a virus in the building."

"What are you talking about?" yells some other dude. "A computer virus or a biological one?"

"Biological, sir. An unknown substance is setting off alarms on level ten. APS ventilation system has taken over and is initiating anti-contamination protocols."

"What substance?"

"Not sure, but the system didn't like something in our ducts!"

Tanis is a caged rat. *Is this my fault? I'm fifteen. Can they try me as an adult? Hell yeah, they can. I'm a sitting duck, too.* He Looks around for a place to hide. His tablet dings. Tanis flips open the screen.

Zilla:

Big trouble comin'. There's retaliation. Safer for you to get out.

TN*8:
Can't, doors locked.

Zilla:
Use the vents. Hide. I'll send help, but you gotta get gone. And now.

The vent is above the desk. It's big enough to crawl into. Tanis grabs his backpack, pulls out his Swiss Army knife, jumps on top of the desk, kicking off the potted plant and the framed photo of him and Ma. He unscrews the cover and pulls himself up and inside. *Hide? No way. I'm outta here.* The next office over shouldn't be locked. If he can crawl a few feet to the next vent, he can climb down and make a break for the stairwell.

Tanis squirms along the duct, getting close to the next office. He gets to the office vent and looks through the slats. No one is in there. Tanis, sneezes on the dust, his chest tightens. He crams his knife into the edge of the vent cover and tries to wrench it open. It doesn't budge. He pushes on it with his shoulder but can't force it open.

A fan he can't see, but hears, fires up and wind rushes around him. It's sucking, not blowing. A roll-down shutter turns on and closes over the vent. They're locking down the ventilation system. *Shit!* Tanis screams in his head, his heart pounding, fear filling his chest so fast his asthma kicks in full-force. He crawls backward towards his dad's office, but that way is closed off, too.

Tanis can't breathe! He reaches behind him, pulls his inhaler from the backpack, sucks on it twice, three times, but the albuterol doesn't help. *I need out!* Tanis stops thinking like someone pulled his power cord.

CHAPTER 1.9

BEN
ADJUSTING TO THE DARKNESS

Ben doesn't have a Ferrari to drive anymore. He thinks about walking home but changes his mind when, in a moment of clarity, he realizes Stanford can identify him. *No doubt I'll be popped for this ssstunt. Maybe the judge'll be lenient and only give me two lifetimesss for poisoning millions of people.*

Ben sits at an empty bus stop, considers his choices, and decides to turn himself in instead of running. *I's need t' get thisss over with. Three sssquares a day doesn't sssound too bad, eh? Maybe I plead insanity. Feelsss kinda true right now.*

Ben stumbles back to the offices again and runs his badge to gain access to the mixing room. The alarms still blare, but he doesn't mind. Descending the metal stairs, he sings at the top of his lungs to drown out the racket. Two steps down, he slips and falls to the bottom, nailing his head on the concrete floor.

###

Waking up, lying in complete darkness, Ben touches his head, feels a dry crust he thinks must be blood in his hair, and winces when he tries to look at his watch. A headache the size of the Chrysler Building makes him dizzy, so he stays where he is for a few seconds. *What the fuck time is it?* He can't see his watch face, so he presses the light button. Nothing.

Confused and disoriented in the dark, Ben wonders why the alarms were off. *Must have been screeching for hours. Unless somebody turned them off. Where are the workers? Why haven't the cops found me yet?*

Ben crawls, fumbling back to the stairs, and climbs them slowly. He has to stop to rest. "Fuckin' booze. I hate this part." He sits on a stair tread and puts his head between his knees to keep dizziness from making him fall again. The stairs guide him out of the tank farm, up to the offices, then the street level. *Guess I'll go home. The cops can pick me up there whenever the hell they get around to it.* The office door stands wide open; no lights are on there, either. The entire building is dark. *Why didn't the generator come on?* He gropes with his arms in front of him until he finds a wall and stumbles along, hoping it's the right wall to take him to the closet he stuffed Stanford in.

Ben moves slowly, still disoriented, wishing he knew exactly where the hell he is in the building. He finds a door, gropes for the knob, and opens it. It's so dark he has to kneel and run his hands on the floor. He feels a face and a person. "Don't hate me, dude!" Ben yells. "I'm so fuckin' sorry I knocked you out. I'm goin' to the cops, I swear. I don't know why I did it. I'm an asshole."

Confessing out loud relieves Ben's guilt for a minute. *Huh, I don't feel good, ever. Why did sayin' what I did out loud make me feel better?* "I'm a drunk and a loser. But I'm turning myself in. I totally swear."

Stanford was still crammed on the floor of the closet. "Wake up, dude. And whatever you do, don't turn on your tap for a few weeks."

Stanford isn't moving. Ben leans closer and shakes his friend's shoulder. "Get up. Go home. You're lucky I knocked you out. I did you a favor 'cause you won't get sick now. I'll explain when the cops get here."

Stanford doesn't respond. Ben slaps the guard's face gently, like people in the movies, but gets no response. Stanford's skin feels too cold. Leaning closer, Ben doesn't hear the guard breathing. "Stanford... buddy?"

"Hey, what the fuck, dude?" Ben slaps him across the face. No reaction. He hits harder, then leans close.

Stanford is dead.

Ben reaches for the doorknob and pulls himself slowly to his feet. He closes the door gently, turns, and stares into the dark hallway. A lump fills his throat like he'd swallowed a snake.

Now I've done it. I'm a fucking dumb ass son of a bitch.

Ben leans over and throws up bile, along with everything he's eaten, for what seems like a week's worth of fast food and microwave dinners. His body convulses, so he opens the closet and crams his big body next to Stanford, wanting to be dead, too. The pain, fear, and sadness wrack his brain, and darkness becomes a kaleidoscope of color.

This isn't a game or some prank. Stanford had kids. The guy was funny and carefree–most of the time.

After who-knows-how-long, Ben stands and leaves the closet. He heads outside in a deep state of shock. Every step feels heavy, like bricks are strapped to his feet.

Not a single light shows in the city; the streets are as dark and silent as the fucking back side of the moon. The tall shadows don't look like buildings but like walls of towering cliffs. Oh, but the stars are out, lots of stars.

Ben walks to Broadway and turns south, sweat bursting from his pores, drenching his skin. *Why is the air so fucking hot? Jesus, I must have descended into hell.*

The night-dark city looks like hell in the bright, full moonlight. Car wrecks hunch all over the place; dead people cluster in the shadows like scattered dolls.

Ben lives on the edge of East Harlem, seven blocks away. He jogs one block before he's out of breath. He leans against a building, gasping. "Fuck. I used to be able to run for days. When did I turn into such a bat slob?"

A fire rages in the upper floors of an apartment building. People are up there, shadows against the brightness of the flames. He wonders for a moment whether they need help but decides against investigating. *They're probably fucked. I ain't gonna kill myself helping strangers.*

Farther down 126th Street, panic overwhelms Ben when he wonders, "Are all these dead people, wrecks, bullshit everywhere my fault?" He shut his mouth, afraid to speak out loud the words he was thinking. *Did the bacteria Zilla gave me kill everybody? Is that even possible? People were supposed to get sick. Nobody's supposed to die.*

Ben races the rest of the way home. "A bunch of hits from my bong and shots of tequila will make me so numb I want even fucking care."

The front door of his building is propped open; a scrawny dude is sprawled on the threshold. Ben steps over the motionless body into the shadowy entrance lobby. The dark is like a solid thing. Somebody upstairs screams.

Ben wants to get to his apartment, crawl into bed, and wake up from this horror. It seems like a dream, a bad dream, a nightmare from which even pain cannot even wake him. Stumbling to the stairway, Ben climbs, keeping one hand on the rail, one ready to defend himself. A few floors up, he feels like one of the Ghostbusters climbing to the top of Central Park West. Three more flights up, he has to step over another body.

Ben pulls his shirt collar over his nose, trying to resist the rank smell that fills the stairwell. That fails because all he smells is piss. *God damn it. I must have pissed myself.* Ben finds his apartment and locks himself inside. His vices call to him like a siren. He submits.

###

Morning finally comes. Ben leaves his apartment because he's eaten everything in the house, smoked all his weed, and is going stir-crazy because there's no Streamflix or TV, or for that matter, running water or lights. One flask of whiskey left is just not enough to get him through the day.

Ben dresses, puts on his only pair of boots, and opens his apartment door. A package he didn't notice the night before was sitting on the floor, a bright red label on the front and the word *"URGENT"* stamped all over the box. Ben rips the tape off and opens it, finds a red syringe suspended in a plastic package, hi-tech looking, straight from the corporate machine. He picks up the note tucked beside the syringe:

Thank you for helping me take down the wicked city. Now, as your reward, inject the shot into your arm. Or maybe you'd rather die with the rest of them. ~Zilla.

Ben plunges the syringe into his arm. *Helped take down the city? Zilla lied to me. Fuck. I dropped the ultimate bomb on millions of people!* I didn't *just make 'em sick*; I *murdered them!*

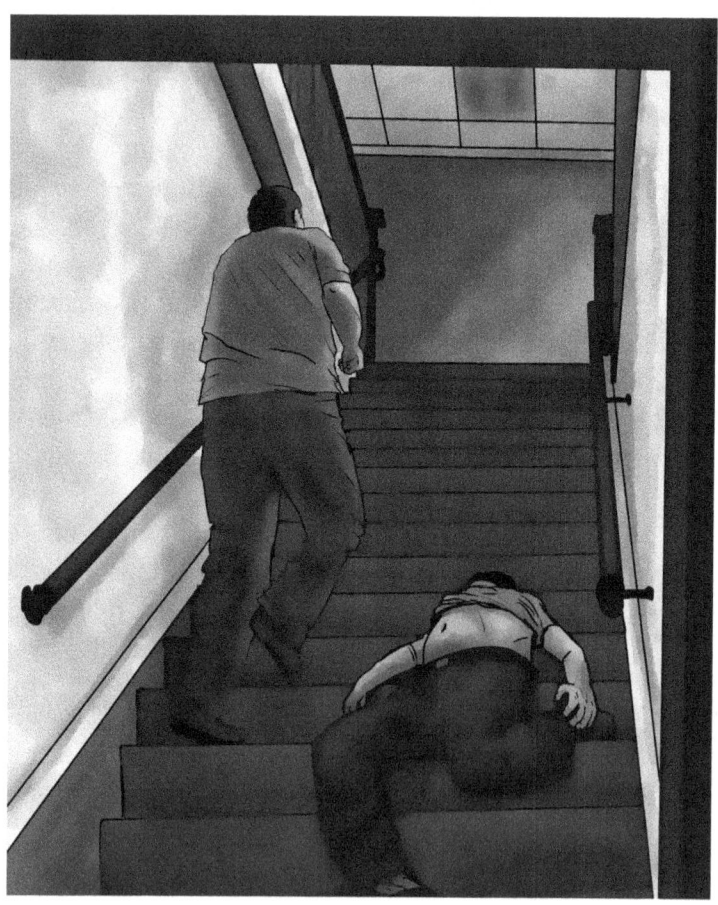

No, man. Ben freezes for a minute, then chucks the empty syringe, watches it fly down the hall, career off a door, and shatter on the opposite wall. The sound is oddly beautiful. It holds him in its echo for a moment. "I'm safe from dying, right? That was my get-out-of-death-free card, right?"

Ben descends the stairs, lighter on his feet, successfully checking his emotions into a lockbox labeled, "Do not open."

Outside, the air is sweltering. *Frickin' Hades out here.* Rain clouds swarm overhead, and smoke adds to the gloom, staining the sky and making it putrid yellow. Cars and bodies litter the streets and sidewalks. Trash and debris are everywhere, like the aftermath of a big outdoor concert—except everyone sleeping it off is doing it for good.

After looking around, Ben decides to walk uptown a handful of blocks to Francisco's Big Bellies, his favorite breakfast burrito place, hoping to find some leftovers. He rounds the corner and sees Francisco's front windows. Big, brightly painted letters advertise the Big Red Chick Pig Burro. He likes that one; he can't say its name after a bong hit or two, but it's made of eggs, a red sauce that makes his nipples hard, and chunks of sausage. The front door opens easily, chiming the bell. Rick ain't here, neither is cute Juanita. Maybe she survived. *She shoulda been my girl.*

Ben feels detached, disoriented, and so fuzzy in the head he can't think straight. But that's been his mode since high school. His old man told Ben, over and over, that he'd never amount to anything and probably couldn't get a job shoveling ditches. Ben would often think of his old man when he was drunk and starting to sober up. *Fuck you, Dad.*

You were wrong. I had a job. Leave me alone.

Francisco's chairs are knocked over, but plates of half-eaten burritos and empanadas still sit on the tables, covered in flies like party plates for the damned. Some have half-filled cups of coffee. Ben pictures Juanita sauntering out of the kitchen with a full coffee carafe. He used to watch her. Used to wonder if she knew his name.

Ben moves to the counter. The muffins behind the glass still look tasty. He grabs one, crams it into his mouth, and sticks one in his pocket for later.

"You guys take an IOU?" Ben yells, his mouth full, chuckling. He searches the kitchen and finds a cooler in the back with precooked food still on the shelves. The power's been out for, what, two days max? No eggs, but he finds a tub of potatoes and a package of precooked bacon, spreads the red sauce over it all, and wraps the goods in one of Francisco's famous huge tortillas. Ben returns to his favorite seat at the far end of the messy counter.

Francisco always kept a clean place. Wrong to let it go to shit.

Ben clears the counter with a wide swipe of his arm. "There you go, buddy, the counter is clean. Wherever you ended up, I hope you still makin' this mean red sauce." He bites the burrito nearly in half.

The cold food is heavy, hard to swallow, fucks with his stomach. Ben sways for a minute, staring at the cappuccino machine. *This'll be the last time I eat here. Shit, that's depressing.*

When the dizziness passes, he holds the burrito into the air, shouts, "Jesus-H-Christ. Frankie should have gotten a red syringe!"

The breakfast sits oddly in his stomach like he tried to cram a square through a round hole. He gives up on eating, leaving the two objects in his throat. Ben chugs some warm horchata and feels slightly better. He looks around, oddly reverting to a state of mind that feels like a damn kid. He giggles again for no reason at all.

An old man, dead as road kill, is lying half on the sidewalk, half on the street at the corner of Morningside Avenue, gripping his cane like it was made of gold. Ben pulls the cane from the old man's hand and walks on, swinging it over his head and twirling it in his fingers. Impulsively, Ben runs up to a car and shatters the window, cracking the cane. Pain resonates through Ben's bones like a tuning fork. He throws the cane aside and turns toward Central Park. A growing cloud of smoke obscures his view, but he's been all over this city and can navigate it with his eyes closed.

Ben walks along, feeling vulnerable. *Shit, I wish I had a gun. A real, big fuckin' gun. Someone's gonna pop out, and I gotta be ready to smack that bitch up.*" Turning the corner, his hope soars—a sandbag wall shelters a camouflage-painted New York National Guard Humvee.

Naturally, the Humvee doesn't start, so Ben checks the dead soldiers for weapons. They're stripped already, but he doesn't give up. These guys always have backups. He finds a small revolver in a dead soldier's boot, loaded, but Ben can't find any extra ammunition. *Well, I got six shots. It'll have to do. Better than the lint in my pocket.*

Ben walks a little faster toward the park, unnerved by the eerie silence, wanting badly to shoot something, but decides to wait until he gets to the grass. Maybe he'll try shooting a duck or something. Blowing something apart will make him feel better, if for only a moment. He's desperate to find a way to alleviate the feeling that squirms inside him, like tentacled things coiling his nerve endings, strangling his stomach.

Closer to Central Park, the corpse piles seem to multiply. People must have hung onto each other during their last moments. Some are heaped as if they all fell together in the same places. Others merely hold hands, like brothers in death.

The bodies tighten his chest, so he looks away toward the lake, searching for a duck. No ducks or any other kind of bird are moving around.

He arrives at the lake. *There are the fucking birds.* Two dead ducks, a sparrow, and a Canadian Goose lay along the lake shore, feathers muddied, bodies twisted.

This place is so creep. No people dead or alive. I hella appreciate that. But...but it's fuckin' still and empty, the way it is in the eye of a hurricane. Dark clouds thicken, turn, gather. The sky is almost black now; the sun can only spear through to the ground in random places.

Disappointed that there are no live targets to hunt, Ben walks back to the street and takes aim at a traffic light. Steadying himself, he aims the gun and slowly squeezes off a round.

Boom!

The traffic light burst into shards. It's satisfying but doesn't get rid of the dark feeling growing inside him. The feeling is kinda like when he takes too big a hit off his bong and can't breathe.

Just gotta ignore it. But the black guilt is in his veins, thumping and swimming through his body like death trying to crash the party. He takes a swig of whisky.

"Hey!" Some guy yells from across the street and hurries toward Ben, jet-black curly hair flying. The guy's got a black beard, too, and, as he gets closer, jet-blue eyes. Damn prepared, toting a huge hiking backpack with water bottles clipped to the shoulder straps and a pistol in one hand.

"Have you seen the military?" he asks. "Cops? Firefighters? Anyone?"

The guy looks like a regular enough dude Ben could take in a fight if he had to. "Nah. Nobody but dead stiffs." Hearing himself say the words, remembering Stanford, Ben wants to barf. He breathes deeply until the urge passes. "Where you headed? Looks like you're gonna hike a mountain." Ben tries to sound as pleasant as he can.

He doesn't want anyone to know he's the killer of all these dead people, the mass murderer, the blade of the sickle.

"I'm getting out of the city. Everyone's dead. The fires are getting worse, and I think I heard a building collapse." The guy looks Ben up and down as if trying to decide if he's real. "The smells are awful and getting thicker."

"Yeah, no shit," Ben says, looking around. "Guess I'm gonna do the same." Ben is surprised he actually feels better now that he's not alone.

"My name's Ian."

"What's up? I'm Ben."

CHAPTER 1.10

TANIS
ESCAPE INTO HELL

Tanis wakes, drenched in sweat, still locked in a pitch-black vent. The darkness is so complete he isn't sure his eyes are open. He's been out for a long time, drooling on the dusty metal. Not a sound can be heard. *Damn the Man. I wasn't dreaming, was I? I really fucked myself.* Memories of the awful things that happened in his dad's office rush back, filling his brain. Tanis yells for his dad and screams for Ma, cusses every word he's not allowed to say, and kicks and screams some more.

"Dad. Ma," Tanis whimpers. Breathing is hard.

"Where are you, Dad?"

No one comes to his aid.

Tanis thinks about other places he had considered worse. Until now. Now, his worst memories pale in comparison to being trapped in this duct. Like when he was forced to go to the opera with his class and his mother tagged along—or bullied into riding a stinky horse. Or his mother making him put on a tie and go to church. None of them seem terrible at all anymore. *Hell, I'd rather be in jail or at church. Or freakin' school. Or on a golf course during a thunderstorm! Anywhere but here!* Tanis felt as though he was pinned underneath a Sumo wrestler. *I'd rather be on the sinking Titanic!*

The walls swell tighter around him. *I gotta get outta here! Now!* He gasps, overtaken by panic, and passes out.

Tanis wakes, having no idea how long he's been unconscious. Weak, he checks his cell phone; there is no signal. The bright light hurts his eyes but is somewhat comforting. He finishes his water, and luckily, there's a candy bar in the front pouch. It's smashed but good.

Time seems frozen. Tanis has no idea what to do next.

He hears a noise and shouts, "Heeeeelp meeeee!"

Someone's enters the office below.

"Help me outta here!" Tanis yells, smacking and kicking the metal.

An axe blade punctures the vent cover. The hole worked open.

"Oh, god, thank you. I thought I was gonna die in here."

The person widens the split. It's weird that he isn't saying anything. He twists and twists until the roll-up door breaks off the track. Tanis inches up and looks through the gap. The person wears a black hoodie. He snaps his head toward the door. A noise from deeper in the building must have startled him. Instead of finishing ripping off the vent, the person puts the axe down and sprints out of the office.

"Hey! Where you going?" Tanis yells.

The man is gone.

Tanis pounds on the vent some more. This time, he's able to knock out the cover. He squeezes through and falls, knocking his knee on a chair and sending it across the office.

He wants to hug whoever cracked that vent open, but they're gone. *Who were they? Why run? You saved my ass only to ditch me.* The axe leans against the wall next to a box with a red label. The label reads:

To the brave soldier who stood on the front line. Stab this into your arm. Otherwise, you die. ~ Zilla

A red syringe lays inside the box. Tanis hates shots almost as much as cramped vents. He looks at the vent. *Nah, I hate that vent more than anything—including shots, clowns, or that bimbo jockin' my dad.* But I ain't stupid. He pockets the needle.

The entire floor is quiet; no hum of computer fans, no chit-chat, no yelling. He runs to his dad's office; the door is still locked. "Dad?!" No answer. Tanis checks the cubicles, but no one is around. He tries the conference room. That door is locked as well. But the frosted glass window by the door shows the room occupied. A hand is pressed against a glass. "Hey! Hold on. I'll help you." Tanis runs back and gets the axe.

The hand twitches.

"Get back!" Tanis hacks at the doorknob with the axe until it flies off. He shoulder-rams the door with all his strength, but the opening doesn't get very wide. A dead, bloated woman blocks it. He covers his nose and mouth with his shirt, trying to block out the putrid smell, but can't. It's too strong.

Every person inside looks dead. His dad is lying on a woman at the far end of the pile. The dead people's eyes and noses are crusted by thick, dark-brown, gooey stuff, their mouths wide open.

Tanis steps back, tremors rolling inside him. *No, Dad.* Tanis turns and bolts as fast as he can, clutching the axe to his chest. He's down the stairs as fast as a spooked rabbit, leaping two steps at a time until he gets to the lobby. The big glass doors are locked, so he swings the axe, battering the glass. The axe buries into the spiderweb cracks, but the glass doesn't shatter. It hangs on the doorframe held together by security film. Tanis hacks and hacks until his arms ache and there's a wide enough gap to push through.

He carefully squeezes through the hole in the glass and steps outside, stumbling to the sidewalk, weak and tired.

Cars pack the street, but the drivers have ditched them or are dead at the wheel. Bodies are everywhere. *Everyone is fucking dead!*

The shot! He pulls out the red syringe and, without hesitation, jams the needle into his arm. He clenches at the sharp pain and shoves the plunger down. Heat travels through his shoulder and into his neck. He sits on the concrete, puts his head between his knees, and fights waves of the pukes until they go away.

A horse bolts from a narrow alley. Tanis leaps out of the way, but it follows him. It's a cop horse, badge on the saddle and all, and it's sick. One eye is filled with so much pus it looks like a baseball has landed in its skull. Tanis manages to jump away just as the animal rams the building. The horse falls to its front knees, making seriously strange sounds.

Tanis runs hard, tears streaming behind him. Some guy on the sidewalk chokes on phlegm. "I can't help you, dude. I don't know what to do. I can't fucking help anyone." He needs Ma. She always knows what to do.

The smells of smoke, burned plastic and wood, sour garbage, and ashes choke the street. Tanis pulls out his cell. *God damn it!* Still no signal. He looks around. No street lights or working vehicles. He dashes to a pay phone, but it doesn't work. He spins around and around, searching, seeing unfamiliarity though he knows the city well. *Home. Which way is home?*

He starts jogging north. He checks his cell phone again and again, but there is still no signal. He even holds it high, but nothing changes. Someone's Blackberry is sitting two feet from their dead hand. Tanis checks it, but it doesn't even turn on. He looks around again, his brain putting the pieces together. *Someone set off an EMP. The only reason my cell works is because I was stuck in the vent. The surrounding metal acted like shielding, a* Faraday *cage.*

Tanis's guts hurt, like knives chopping them into sushi. Bile bubbles up in the back of his throat. He's starving but can't imagine eating around so many people stuck in frozen torment. The last thing he thinks he'd be looking for is a cheeseburger, but he can't help it.

First, find something to eat, then bounce on home. He passes a digital camera store, then a hotel. Finally, he sees a small market and peeks through the security shutters. Food. A man is lying in the middle of an aisle, not moving, sprawled in a waft of lingering smoke. Tanis uses his Swiss Army knife to try to pick the lock with the blade, but it doesn't work. He needs something thin. He mumbles a saying his father was fond of. "Look for it. Find it." A woman is lying half on the curb, face first into the pavement, hair in a bun. Tanis sprints to her and kneels at her head. He can see a bobby pin. *Right there. Just grab it.* He swallows a throat full of bile, shuts his eyes and… fingers shaking…pulls out a pin.

Almost an hour later, the lock turns. Tanis is mildly pleased. A few years ago, Dad gave him a set of lock picks for Christmas and taught him how to use them. Learning the skills took patience but was fun. He never thought he'd actually *need* to pick a lock.

Inside, the shelves are loaded with soups, beans, chocolates, gum, and sweets. He takes as much of his favorites as he can fit in his backpack and fills his mouth full of little powdered donuts. "Sorry, but a kid's gotta eat, even as the world burns. Bitch to God about it," he said to no one in particular.

The man in the aisle is an old guy lying in a puddle of barf. *Akkk.* Tanis's stomach turns. The man is holding a photo of a young girl at a barbecue, cheering hotdogs with him.

The man's ear twitches.

"Dude, you alive?" Tanis's mouth is still full, and he can't seem to swallow.

Carefully, Tanis nudges the man. "Hey, can you hear me?"

Movement down his jaw line.

Tanis lifts the shoulder.

The man's head pulls off the floor, mouth open. Something in his mouth bulges. Something white, covered in blood.

Tanis jumps back and chokes on the doughnut,

spitting and spitting. He bolts out of the store as fast as he can, wanting to scream some more, to hit something. The sugar sticks in his throat.

Tanis stands in the middle of the cluster-fucked street and cries like a baby. He sobs hard, so hard it hurts his entire body. He has to *get home.* Everything he knows is there: safety, familiarity, Ma. He walks, trying to get his bearings, but he usually passes these streets in the subway. Six blocks later, he sees the first of many signs for the Queensboro Bridge.

The closer the bridge gets, the worse his body feels; pain twists his guts, his head thumps, and he's wheezing. He jumps a low iron fence surrounding a restaurant patio and sits at a table. The black metal chairs and matching tables are covered in ashes and dust, looking hundreds of years old. He chugs some water.

The wind picks up, brushing away the sweltering heat, but the gross odor in the wind worsens. He's ready to see another person alive, ready to be home, ready to wake up, ready to be slapped across the face.

A deep explosion goes off somewhere toward Central Park, followed by a bunch of pops. *Someone's alive over there.* He'd look for them, except he doesn't want to mess with anyone packing a machine gun. Tanis decides to leave the patio. Call it instinct, but he moves faster and closer to the buildings, trying to stay out of sight as best he can.

"Anarchy is a game only thugs win," another of his father's fun sayings.

Tanis wishes he had his twenty-two caliber hunting rifle. It has a sweet scope and an insulated barrel for quiet recoil. He's a good shot, too, because his cheating old man took him to the gun range a lot.

At the corner of 2nd Street, a massive buildup of

cars clutters the on-ramp. *Navigating this mess* would *be impossible unless I had a monster truck.*

Tanis jumps on a red Jeep and skips onto the hood of some old, crappy car, hop-scotching to the straightaway. Most cars are deserted, but a few still have people buckled inside. They're all stiff like crash-test dummies, looking like they're sleeping. He hops on a beat-up yellow cab, then into the bed of a blue truck.

A smashed, overturned cop car lays upside down on top of other vehicles, looking like it probably tumbled from the upper ramp. *Maybe there's a weapon inside, at least a nightstick.* Tanis works around the pile of cars, looking for a way inside the cop car.

The cruiser's doors are crumpled inward, and the bent-up hood of the Lincoln below prevents the cop car's passenger side from opening. Tanis wrestles the metal hood, careful not to slice open his hands. Doesn't budge.

"Hey, you! Help me!"

Tanis ducks like an idiot. *What the hell am I doing? I'm not the trapped one.* He stands and looks into the cruiser. *A cop! The cop's still in there, alive.*

He runs to the front of the Lincoln, braces his foot against the side, above the wheel, and pulls as hard as he can on the hood. Sweat pops out on his face and his whole body strains.

"Don't leave. Keep trying."

"Yeah, okay. Hold on." *Gotta get her out.* His dread of being trapped inside the metal duct coffin returns, and he feels the adrenalin rush of strength in his arms. The hood budges, but barely and not enough.

A sign pole is lying in the middle of the ramp, broken at the base. Tanis grabs it, slams it into the gap, and uses the leverage to wrench the hood off the door. One last push, one more heave against the groaning metal … "I got you!"

Finally, the hood bends back enough to unblock the cop car door. Tanis climbs closer, grabs the handle, and tries to wrench the door open. It's jammed.

"Oh my god," a lady cop yells. "You've got this. You're doing good." She kicks the door like a rabid dog who'd have chewed its own arm off to free itself.

"Can you, like, kick at the same time as I pull?" Tanis asks.

"Grab the handle," she says. "I'll count to three."

They simultaneously kick and pull. The door creaks loudly and finally opens a third of the way. The cop wriggles into the tight gap, gasps when a jagged piece of metal rips her shirt and cuts into her side. She takes it like a champ. She's a cop, after all.

She jumps down to the ground and then hugs Tanis fiercely. "Thank you, thank you so much. I didn't think anyone would come around. I thought I was going to starve to death in my own damn cruiser."

Tanis offers her a bottle of water. "No prob. I'm Tanis."

"I'm Officer. . . scratch that, just call me Hana." She's in bad shape and looks like he feels. She's pretty for a cop. Dirty blonde hair, nice lips, green eyes, and thin, wearing a white tank top and dark blue slacks.

"You been in there for a while?"

Hana nods, reaches back into the car, and grabs her blue uniform shirt. She balls it up and presses it against her wound. "I'm not sure how much time has passed, but it's been over twenty-four hours." She takes a drink of water, closes her eyes, and looks like she might faint, but she drinks some more water.

Tanis holds out a stick of beef jerky. "Somethin' to munch?"

"Thank you." She devours the salty meat and drinks

more water.

"I got trapped, too, in a building. I have no idea how long I was in there. I don't even know what happened," he says, pulling out his cell phone. "Towers and sats are down, so my clock isn't updating." Tanis intentionally leaves out how he helped Zilla bring down the satellites. He never even questioned Zilla's intentions; he opened his father's computer like a gullible, obedient little geek. *Stupid! I helped that monster upload a computer virus that wrecked the satellites and left the military blind. Yeah.*

Blinded the only people who could've protected us. Now, the city is wiped out, and everyone is *murdered. I'm the biggest moron in the whole freaking world.*

"Your phone's working? Everything in my car is dead." Hana takes his phone and holds it up–an ingrained reaction.

Shame and remorse overwhelm Tanis. *I could confess to this cop, and she could arrest me. Someone will figure it out and then hunt me down—the FBI, the CIA ...* his heartbeat thumped hard and he felt sick. *The DOD, for sure, because they've probably already figured out that Dad's computer was used to upload the virus that crashed the satellites. They'll say letting Zilla into Dad's computer is a terrorist act. Maybe it is. But I didn't fucking know that's what I was doing!* Tanis vows never to talk about Zilla, or the computer virus, or the vaccine, or *anything* about this horrible day, ever again. *This secret will die with me.*

The lady cop hands the phone back.

Is she looking at me funny? Do I look guilty? Tanis clears his throat. "I, uh, was locked in my dad's office building ... I had to bust out... " Tanis hangs his head and feels the blush creeping up his neck and face.

Hana tries to smile. "We're lucky." She takes another drink and looks around. "No one could hear me yelling, or they just ignored me. I heard huge explosions, close enough to rock my cruiser." Her face flushes white as the blood drains from her cheeks. "When the explosions stopped, everything went quiet."

Tanis tries not to watch her adjust her sports bra and reaffix her thick, black belt to her waist. *She's nice lookin', that's for sure. Gotta be half Ma's age.* Hana checks her pistol and sits it back in her holster.

A woman lying between the cars twitches. "Hey," Hana says, rushing to the woman.

Tanis follows. The woman's hospital mask is dangling by one ear. Her eyes are bloodshot, and her chin is covered in mucus. Her skin looks white and leathery, and the blood vessels are dark and swollen. *The woman is very, very dead. Why the hell did she twitch?*

"What happened?" Hana asks. "It wasn't supposed to be like this."

"I don't know. But the whole city is burnt toast." Tanis looks away, choking down his guilty knowledge. "I walked through a million bodies."

"Whatever made people sick ended up killing them. But the CDC said the bacteria was non-lethal." Hana mumbles to herself, looking into the smoky sky. "All this death…it was much more than a bacteria in the water. I saw a rocket launch. I think it was an EMP attack that killed all the cars and the electronics. This was a well-planned, well-funded act of war, maybe genocide."

"Yeah, totally fucked everyone. TKO," Tanis mumbles, feeling shame in every nerve and twist in his guts. *If I had not believed Zilla, nobody would be dead. Zilla would have failed. The military would have hunted that fool down like a dog and thrown him in Gitmo. Zilla is the* actual *terrorist.*

Hana's head sags. It looks like she's crying. She pulls a handkerchief from her back pocket, blows snot, and dries her eyes. "Where were you going?" she asks.

Tanis pretends not to notice the quiver in Hana's voice and nods toward the Queensboro Bridge. "I live across the river in Forest Hills. I'm going to find my ma."

"I live in the city. Something tells me I'll never go home again. My folks live in Long Beach. I can go with you until you get home. Then I'll split up and find my folks."

"Cool."

Tanis and Hana climb to the bridge deck, weaving

around the cars. The old bridge is epic. Massive steel beams crisscross overhead, held in place by steel rivets with heads the size of golf balls; the whole structure is laid across solid brick towers. Tanis loved this bridge, but now the metal is warped from fires, leaving sooty black wounds on the tan girders.

When the cars are too tangled to navigate, he jumps on the hood of a Mercedes Benz, intending to hopscotch again, but stops short. Hana jumps onto the hood, grabs Tanis's arm, and steadies herself.

The section of the bridge crossing Roosevelt Island has collapsed. What's left is mangled, bent down toward the river, girders twisted like spiral noodles. Across the river, the rest of the Queensboro Bridge is nothing but broken concrete and rusty rebar, tangled and useless.

Hana hops off the Benz. "I was afraid of this. There's no way across."

The current far below carries debris and bodies in the muddy water. Tree branches and trash, a couple of small boats, and a child's stroller are snagged in the rubble left when the Roosevelt Island towers were obliterated.

Tanis has never imagined a sight so scary, so wrong. The bridge is a ruined heap. Smoke and dust swirl in the air, rip at his throat when he breathes. A faint shudder rumbles through the wrecked structure like anxiety coursing through nerves. Queensboro Bridge is a corpse.

"How we gonna cross the river?" he asks. "Use the subway?"

She scans the sky, the bridge behind them, and the water below. "No. The bridge was destroyed to stop people from leaving. This kind of thing has to be approved by the highest authority. It would be a last-ditch effort. The only reason to do this is if all exit points were hit simultaneously. Bunker busters on the subway tunnels, included." She looked worried. "The quarantine of the island might have been ineffective. I don't see anyone across the river." Her hand on Tanis's arm shook slightly. "Still, we're gonna have to swim it to get you home."

"I'm not a good swimmer. I'm a nerd. I do my thing on computers." Tanis watches the dirty water. "Probably cold and polluted and full of huge, mutated catfish and river sharks. Besides, the current looks freaky strong here, we could get carried out to the ocean."

She nods. "Well, if you aren't a good swimmer, the river might be a death trap. We can try going north where the river is narrower. I can help you cross it. Maybe we'll find a fishing boat up there."

"That sounds cool. Don't think we have a choice, huh?"

"I don't think so."

Traveling companions by tacit agreement, Hana leads Tanis north in the heat and the stink, both wanting to go home to ball games, crap on the TV, and good dinners.

Chapter 1.11

Isabella
Cheers from Iraq

Fat raindrops land on Isabella, jolting her awake. She's tucked tightly in a sleeping bag in the middle of a field in Central Park. It's been two days after the attack on New York. She doesn't get up but opens her mouth and lets the rain splash on her tongue.

Raindrops should taste sweet, but these are rancid, like the butt of an old cigarette. When she gets to her feet, pain spikes in her lower back. She ignores it, grabs her bag, and digs out a bagel. Dry, cold, and stale, it's still delicious.

Dark clouds churn above, heavy with moisture. The drizzle will soon turn to rain; maybe the city will be saved if enough rain falls and puts out the fires. She stretches. *I think I need to find the quarantine line today. All this silence is starting to get to me.*

She loads up. *Let's go North. The jets and the explosions were the bridges being destroyed, no doubt the subway, too. So going north, crossing the river at its narrowest point, is my best option. I'll probably have to fuckin' swim, but what choice do I got?*

Jogging through the park, the only sound she hears is the damp grass and mud squishing under her feet until a massive explosion erupts somewhere around Fredrick's Circle. The muffled *whump* shakes the ground, rattles the trees, cracks the pavement, and sends clouds of debris into the sky. A roaring ball of fire rolls up over the dense tree canopy between the tall buildings. Fresh black smoke fills the sky.

Woah! What the *hell was that? Metal hawk dropping munitions again?* She couldn't see or hear any jets. *Na. The flyboys have left this place to rot. There's a gas station up there ...maybe the underground tanks blew?*

Isabella raises the barrel of the assault rifle she nabbed from those fools in the Bradley and checks the breech; it's loaded, and the clip is full. She verifies that the weapon is set on semi-automatic, looks down the sight, and sets off. Checking her gun is a reflex, a good habit, just like when she was in Iraq.

She avoids the burning gas station and jogs toward 7th Avenue northbound instead. Seventh feels like a good choice because the median with trees gives her a wider playing field and some cover. She doesn't worry too much about an attack from above. Looters aren't usually hiding out in apartments with sniper rifles. This is not an insurgency. But habits are hard to break.

###

Isabella did well in Iraq, at first. She was infantry, one of the few women on the team. She loved being a soldier, kept her wits about her, learned fast, honed her sixth sense. Her job was supplying the front lines with ammo, food, water, replacement radios, and medical supplies, but they engaged the enemy just as much as anyone, especially in Fallujah.

One night, the enemy circled the front line and awakened her team at dawn with sniper and AK-47 fire. She snapped into focus, a veteran fighter after surviving weeks on duty. Infected cuts covered her hands, her eyes were dry and irritated, and she smelled of black powder and gun oil and cramped from a bad period, but she shut off the pain like a light switch. She could still hear, see, and fire straight. When she signed up, an army recruiter asked her if she had something to prove. Hell yeah, she did.

The sun had not yet fully risen, so she flipped her night-vision goggles down and followed her company to the south courtyard, keeping in the deeper darkness next to

the walls, to secure that area for a supply delivery.

Everything was quiet until one crazy towel-head ran out of the alley she'd just exited. They must have been hiding in a hole. A dozen rounds should have plunged into her back, but he was a lousy shot. Isabella spun and hit the trigger, nailing twenty rounds into his chest and spraying the wall with blood.

J.C. walked up to him and shot a 9mm round into his dead eyes just to make sure. That was one of ten, maybe fifteen, Haji suicide fighters who came out to play. Her team secured the supply line, driving it through bone and blood.

The sun was hot by 9:00 a.m. When the fighting wound down and the dust settled, her company fell back to base for downtime.

Active duty is lonely for most soldiers, hot battles interspersed with waiting. Time to think about what they'd left behind: Ma, Pa, brother, sister, lover. Downtime wasn't lonely for Isabella. The quiet was as sweet as that first shot of whiskey. She felt her heart beat like a robot. Her vest flattened her chest and hid her body. Here, with her hair pulled up under her baseball cap or hidden by her helmet, she was just another soldier, not male, not female. Her gear was heavy, but now, propped up on a brick wall full of bullet divots, she didn't feel hot or achy, just relaxed. She slept soundly and deeply as if she'd died.

Three hours went by like a heartbeat. Rodriguez shook her awake. She crammed food down her dry, swollen throat before the team patrolled the neighborhood and set up a forward base in a luxurious mansion built like a fortress. Stocked with battle-rattle, MREs, smokes, and medical supplies, their new base camp served soldiers as a relatively safe place to patch their wounds, reload, eat, and rest before heading back out.

Skirmishes rocked the night; explosions surrounded them, some a block away, some a mile away. The wind smelled like blood and burned rubber. Wounded were carried in, some without arms or legs, some with just holes, all covered in blood, leaving crimson trails as they arrived and were carried away. Guarding medics and exfiltration was more than dangerous; it was messy and fuckin' loud with screams and barking orders…the occasional cry.

A week later, Isabella and her team were redeployed to the Green Zone in Bagdad, where she guarded a checkpoint eight hours a day. Fallujah was bad, but she got to run around at night, clear houses, and protect convoys on the move when the sun wasn't so evil.

Green Zone Grunt work was daytime work. Shit, hot work. Plus, every driver and passenger who passed her vehicle checkpoint were potentially militants prepped to blow off her face. Many of the towel-heads that passed had bloodlust pooling in their eyes. They hated her, not because she was American, but because she was a woman who carried a gun and barked orders they had to obey or risk being shot.

Day after day of that bullshit, she finally snapped. A man wearing a dirty thobe and sandals walked toward her checkpoint. He looked like every other Iraqi, except he hid his hands. Isabella yelled, "*Raweenee edeek!*" "Show me your hands!"

He either didn't listen or didn't care. He kept his hands hidden.

"*Ogaf bmkanek la tetharek!*" "Stop where you are!"

He didn't stop. When she raised her rifle to blow off his fucking head, he stopped and held up his hands. She made him pull up his robe and spin around. No bomb, no weapon, so she waved him on.

But at the moment he passed, he shot her a look that might as well have been a punch to her face.

She bashed his head in with the butt of her rifle,

leaped on him, and didn't stop hitting him until her buddies intervened. That dirty Iraqi looked inside out when she was done with him.

She raged inside, like the sun, eager to release her pent-up resentment and hatred of these men who treated women like brainless property. The ali babas around her stared, but less hatefully than before. They were afraid of her, finally.

She was transferred to unit HQ, where she was tried and formally kicked out of the army. *Whatever. Fuck 'em. I don't regret a damn thing.*

###

Isabella exits Central Park and steps over the knee-high brick wall surrounding the grounds. She moves cautiously across the road, looking to the left. A cloud of smoke still rises from the gas station and the circle. She sees no other movement and continues up 7th with her assault rifle at the ready.

Chapter 1.12

Markus
When in Rome

Markus thinks he might never recover from the long flight to Rome. He retrieves his baggage and heads to the street, sore but glad to be on his feet.

Cabs lined the pullout. He doesn't have to choose one; the driver seeks him out and drags him to the nearest cab. The small car's trunk is too small for his luggage, so the driver clips it onto the roof rack and drives Markus to Vatican City.

The first thing he notices in Vatican City is that it's

as bustling as New York but venerable. The people go about their business serenely, without the hunted, withdrawn look of so many New Yorkers. Markus immediately falls in love with the city, wishing he'd brought Marian. She would appreciate his sense that ghosts of a thousand centuries still wander the streets, treading where once cobblestones paved the ground.

The taxi follows streets winding around blocks of old brick apartments and office buildings, cluttering the city like a packed bookshelf–the city's beauty only broken by occasional graffiti. The streets and sidewalks are filled with Italians zipping up and down the narrow streets in their little cars. People love using their horns. Everyone honks at each other. He laughs. His mother, God rest her soul, would have loved the homemade feel of this country.

The driver speeds faster and takes corners more recklessly the farther he gets from the airport, turning Markus's stomach. "We're not at a carnival, son. I didn't pay for a roller-coaster ride." The driver nods politely but doesn't understand. Markus doesn't speak Italian and is too nauseated to read his phrase book. "It's fine. Just, Lord, get me to the library alive."

The Vatican gates look like a medieval portal, leading travelers into history's bosom. Its three-story-tall brick archway is topped with grand sculptures of Roman figures and ornate shapes. Such history. It's such a grand old city. So grand, Markus feels young and small among the monumental structures. The Sistine Chapel is more impressive, as are all the classical buildings Markus read about on the plane. *Feeling small and inconsequential is deeply rooted in Catholicism. Catholicism will always foment false idols with its gold-trimmed cathedrals, praying to statutes of saints and confessing to priests garbed in robes as ostentatious as their ceremonies. However, I will keep my criticisms to myself while I am in their house.*

Markus's map leads him directly to the Gallery Library. He walks inside and pauses, struck by the quiet: the soft tap of his feet on the solid marble floors, the occasional echo of a whisper, and papers being shuffled. The library is bright, lit from all angles by strategically placed windows nearly two stories tall. Its high-arching gold ceilings made Markus gasp, as did nearly all of the Renaissance paintings that adorn every available space. The library is stunning. Such treasures don't belong hidden away in the city of grandeur…but that's an argument for the ages.

Walls and walls of ancient and contemporary books beckon to him. The Internet has nothing to compare to an actual paper-and-ink library. Markus walks past the index section to a service librarian's desk. "Hello, my name is Markus Coburn. I've an appointment at two with an archive *seigneur*."

"*Buono cera, Signore Coburn*. We are expecting you."

He quickly learns the works he came to see are kept in the basement. The researcher assigned to help him hands Markus white, lint-free cotton gloves and a map of the archives. The researcher then helps him choose twenty books to start and replaces them six hours later with ten more. Time slips through his fingers like sand on the beach. Markus suppresses his hunger by focusing and pushing through information as easily as a drill seeds wheat.

He opens the next book and skims the pages. Halfway through, he discovers a transcript from the Eighth Crusade detailing how the port city of Caesarea in northern Israel was conquered. It was written by a scribe from France's King Louis IX's Army of God.

The first attack on Caesarea was an abject failure, but the second army succeeded quickly. *Why? What made the second invasion so successful?* Markus turned the page. The answer surprised him. Because no one resisted the attack. The strange account describes the second French army entering the city, finding only dead people and dead animals, no gold, no treasure, so survivors. Caesarea was a wealthy port city named after Herod the Great for his mentor, Caesar Augustus.

Markus turns back a page to find out why the first attack failed, but there are no details, only the statement that the first army was led by a great leader, John the Mighty. *If he was so great, why did he lose? Come on. There's got to be more than this.* Markus rubs his tired eyes and then continues reading.

Louis IX's second army piled the Caesarean bodies high and burned the dead because they were afraid of a curse. The army burned everything in the city before moving north to capture Acre.

Markus was bothered by the lack of information regarding the first attack, not to mention that he'd not found one reference to the Stone of Allah.

He turns the page and scans the end of the account. King Louis IX, angry after losing his first army to an inferior band of godless soldiers, thanked God for victory in the presence of his retinue and privately questioned the loss of his best soldier, John the Mighty. *Who is this John the Mighty?*

Markus looks through a different book for references to the first Army of God during the 8th crusade that attacked Caesarea. He finds none and wonders how many other volumes he'll have to scan. He chuckles to himself. "I really have gone off track. I'm here to find the Stone of Allah. I can't get sidetracked whenever I find a little mystery in these history books. Otherwise, I'll be here for years."

As closing time nears, the lights dim at the far end

of the library. More lights go out. Only the walkway to the exit and the one above still glow. A priest emerges from the dark and approaches Markus.

"I guess I got to go?" Markus replies, dissatisfied. "I'll be finished in a moment."

The priest wears a black robe with the typical backward collar. Deep wrinkles and a scrunched nose hold up his thin gold-rimmed glasses. Speaking English with a thick accent, he says, "I see you are interested in the Eighth Crusade."

"Yes, well, I think I'm sidetracked. I'm sure you hear this all the time."

"It is true that a passion such as history must be allowed to wander many paths to find truth. I was told you are looking for an artifact called the Stone of Allah."

Markus nods. "Yes. I was given a stack of books archiving mid-eastern artifact lineages. But I'm afraid I don't find any references. Every story seems to have dotted I's and crossed T's. I'll except for this story of Louis the IX's first attack on Caesarea."

"So you find this path. And something in your heart tells you to wander it?"

"A path is meant to be taken," Markus says, smiling. "Though I'm unsure if it is my heart speaking or just blind curiosity."

"I do not believe in such things."

Markus thinks a moment about the priest's statement. "All right. I guess I don't believe in blind curiosity, either. The Lord knows me better than that." Markus opens the last book he read, flipping to the paragraph that seemed to be missing information. "King Louis the IX was left in an awkward situation because he borrowed a fortune, plus an army of troops from the Knights of the Cross, to conquer Caesarea, only to find everyone dead and no treasure to repay the Templar. How did the Caesareans defeat his first army, and why aren't there any accounts here about what happened to the victorious Caesareans? How was it that King Louis the Fourth's second army walked through the gates of Caesarea?" Markus places his palm on his notes. "Something is missing."

The priest slips a worn, thin book from his cassock pocket, sits across the table from Markus, and slides the book to him. "There is only one copy of this text. The original has been lost."

Markus looks, then slides it back. "Is there a transcript? I don't read Latin."

The priest smiles. "Picture this. You are John the Mighty, a loyal and fierce warrior in the court of King Louis the IX. You ride up to the great stone walls of Caesarea on your massive stallion with an army of ten thousand men behind you, flying the French colors, secure in your unshakeable faith that God is on your side. Your body is covered in steel armor, as is your horse. Your army has counterweight trebuchets, steel weapons, thick armor, and is better-trained and more experienced than any other."

Markus nods, the image vivid in his mind.

"You see, the Crusades were retaliation against the Moors, attempts to take back the parts of the Mediterranean they conquered in the Middle Ages. Just because the Muslims and their forbears had the land for over a thousand years does not mean it was theirs in the first place. They were the first to soak the land in blood. Retaliation is the truth that John the Mighty fought for, as did most of the Crusaders.

"The first order of business in any siege is to surround the city gates, then launch attacks by arrow and trebuchet. After a few weeks, the Caesareans should have been hungry, weak, and easy to conquer. Everything was going according to Louis the IX's plan. John and his soldiers were so confident they played games and ate and drank during the evening hours. The translation says, 'the heavens shined on their efforts a quarter moon after the siege began, with a great light show in the early morning.'"

The priest leans closer and continues, keeping his voice hushed. "The light show was a meteor shower. Thousands of burning, falling stars fell in two days. John rejoiced, believing it was a sign. The morning of the third day, before the sun rose, John gathered a group of his best warriors and approached the main gates. He was almost at the siege line—"

Markus interrupts, "What is the siege line?"

"The Caesarean archers didn't have much range. Their maximum distance was marked on the ground and called the siege line. If you crossed the line, their arrows could hit you. Stay behind the line? You are out of harm's way."

Markus nods. "Please go on."

The priest smiles and continues. "John did *not* cross the line. He was too smart to deliberately put himself in danger. He stood well behind the line and called for surrender. John the Mighty waited for an answer. It is said that he grew impatient when no one acknowledged his presence or answered his demand for surrender." The priest paused and took a breath. "Then the most amazing thing happened. He was struck in the chest, killed instantly."

"An arrow struck him?"

The priest held the thin volume in his hand. "No. This document says a meteor struck him. The official account says arrow, but it was a stone from the sky. The chest plate was penetrated as if it were made of paper."

"Why do you believe it was a meteor?" Markus asks. "That would be a huge coincidence. Is there any evidence?"

"This is the oldest account we have. It is much older than Albert of Aix-la-Chapelle's account. He wrote his in the eleventh century." The priest flipped to a page and pointed. "It says here that the French army found the meteor under John's dead body. It was reported to be a clear stone shaped like two arrows joined at the haft, with a rusty cloud in the heart of the stone that glimmered, even in the night, as if it had a power unto itself." The priest tucked the book back into his cassock. "The French were confused, disheartened, stunned. There was no retreat strategy because, in their arrogance, none was prepared, and the Caesareans promptly slaughtered most of the French in a bloody assault, took the meteorite, and hailed it as the Stone of God."

"Then why did King Louis the IX find the city dead after he came back with his second army?"

The priest shrugs. "No one knows. The city's inhabitants probably died from some disease. Maybe their food and water supply were contaminated during the first siege. Probably dysentery. 'Twas common back then to die of such things." The priest nods, "Fascinating isn't it? Striking an individual man with a meteor would most surely be the will of God. Hence, God's Stone."

"The Stone of Allah. You were right. This path was set for me." Markus says.

"As are they all. Unfortunately, I cannot let you take this book. It is the last of its age, and it is far too precious. Other texts have gone missing, and this one will not find the same fate. I hope you find the answers you're looking for. For now, I must bid you good night.'

Markus thanks him for his time and finds his way out of Vatican City to his hotel. His room overlooks the River Tiber, running through Rome.

Markus spends a week in Rome, searching the archives every day from the time the library opens until it closes, without finding the answers he sought. Obsessed with why and how the Caesareans died, he studies other siege conquests and speaks with the priest four more times. No other reference to The Stone of Allah, or where it ended up if it really was a meteor.

One night, watching the city lights from the balcony, thinking about his conversations with the priest, Markus considers how Caesarea was saved from the first Christian attack by the Stone of Allah. *No wonder the stone became a precious icon to* Islamic *people. Did other meteorites showering the city kill the people? Did the Stone of Allah's fame bring thieves to the city? Maybe a civil war? So many unanswered questions. I would not survive being a historian.*

I am not entirely comfortable with so many unanswered questions. Markus looks into the sky. *Don't suppose you'd help me with this one?*

Markus returns to the internet, reading up on the fabled King. It would seem, years later, King Louis the IX claimed his brother pushed him to go to Tunisia for one last victory over Muslim occupiers. But Louis died in the tiny Mediterranean country, perhaps from dysentery. *Another dysentery reference.* Markus circled the word in his notebook over and over.

Loud popping and lights bursting in the night almost stop his heart. Another noisy pop—fireworks declaring a celebration. Markus watches the show and wonders why he is so obsessed with this mystery. *What is God trying to tell me? I need not ask questions to which the answers, I know, will present themselves.*

He turns to his laptop and moves the mouse. He accidentally clicks on a picture of an ornate crown called The Holy Crown of Jesus Christ in the margins of a Wiki article. *Catholics and their gaudy symbols and vestments. It's the main dividing line between Protestants.* He looks closer to the image. *Bowing down to idols for centuries. Hmmm. This crown looks too large and heavy to be worn.* Reading the caption and the date, he mumbles, "The Holy Crown of Jesus Christ was commissioned after the Caesarea attack and bought by King Louis the IX. The crown is on display at Notre Dame in Paris." Markus finishes the last of his drink. "Looks like I'm going to Paris. I must follow every lead, and this is a lead."

He rides the Eurostar train to Milan early the following day, staring out the window like a kid who'd never seen vineyards or fields of grazing sheep. Awe washes over him as he spies a hilltop castle surrounded by centuries-old buildings that appear to function as they did hundreds of years ago. The train flies by a shepherd in dirty clothing, beard to his chest, speaking on a cell phone, and a wealthy man in a limited-edition BMW at a crossing, tapping his fingers impatiently on the steering wheel.

In Milan, Markus transfers to a train to Paris, dines on fresh bread, Fourme d'Ambert cheese flavored with mixed nuts, and a glass of Pinot Grigio in the lovely dining car, and takes a nap. He arrives shortly after eleven at night, full and alive, his adventure filling holes in his soul he never thought were there. His small, quaint room at a five-hundred-year-old hotel was soul-warming.

After the warm sunrise, Markus takes a taxi to Notre Dame de Paris after eating fruit and pastry for breakfast. Notre Dame de Paris defines Gothic architecture; the church's shadow looms over him as he steps out of the taxi. Two square towers adorned with arched windows stand as the front entrance to the church. The Grand Gallery, centered between the towers, has a pointed roof with a circular stained-glass window at the apex. Girders extend from the roof, continue over the sidewalls, finally arching to the gardens as "flying buttresses," he reads. They look like the ribs of some enormous creature. The bell tower, adorned with pointed archways and steeples, is beautiful. Markus marvels at the grotesque gargoyles and studies their fantastic creature faces carved on the downspouts.

Markus enters the massive front doors behind a group of tourists. Craning his neck to see the vaulted ceiling and elaborate stonework makes him dizzy. Walking down the side aisle between richly stained wooden pews and lines of strange faces, he finds the crown easily. It has an elaborately formed open circlet of pierced gold, sitting on a round challis shape, resting on a gold pedestal circled by carved figures on thrones. Jesus Christ is depicted in the center, the Virgin Mary on the left, and some other figure

Markus doesn't recognize on the right. Perhaps it represents the Holy Spirit in human form or John the Baptist. It's about a foot and a half tall and as detailed as anything Markus has ever seen.

A young woman stops next to Markus and stares at the same crown. Her darker skin, straightened black hair, thick glasses, and bookish looks put him at ease. "Beautiful, isn't it?" she says, her accent from New England, maybe.

Markus nods, but only slightly. He dislikes these pieces paid for with money the church stole from the people. *God would not appreciate the corruption in the Catholic hierarchy that paid for these commissions with the sweat and blood of the populace.* Markus mumbles so she can't quite hear, "You shall not make for yourself an idol in the form of anything in heaven above or on the earth beneath or in the waters below. Exodus 20:4."

"Louis the IX bought the piece from Baldwin II, who ruled Constantinople at that time. It's incomplete. If you can believe that," she says. Obviously happy to speak with another American.

"Is that right?" Markus replies. "What more could they do? This is already filled with too much detail. I think it would make my mother faint; God rest her soul."

"It's a decorative status piece the king would have carried with him on occasion. This crown was said to contain the power of God." The woman stands on her toes and points through the gaps in the goblet-looking part. "There are four clasps inside this top part that are bent inward, around a gold cup."

Markus follows the angle of her finger and peers closely at the clasps. "I see. Big. Looks like it could hold one of those small foam footballs."

She nods. "Clasps like those usually hold a precious stone." Her eyes widen. "Must have been made for a large stone."

Markus studies the clasps. *Did Baldwin II recover the meteor in Caesarea, commission this crown to hold the stone,* and *then sell it to Louis the IX? The transcript said no jewels or* treasures *were left in the city. Could that single meteorite have been kept secret because it* embarrassed *King Louis IX and his holy army, a stone he would not part with? Maybe he kept it because it humbled him. The man was canonized as a saint, after all.*

Markus pictures the king carrying the absurdly large crown.

The woman's eyes are bright and eager, and her mind is full of information she is primed to share. "I read

that after this crown was completed, it went missing. Stolen, I believe, kept inside a church in Reims until the entire congregation mysteriously died. That brought the gold crown and its large stone back into the hands of the King."

Goose flesh flowed over Markus's skin. "Don't tell me. They thought the congregation was killed by dysentery."

The woman nods. "Fascinating. Isn't it? The crown followed King Louis the Ninth around until his death in Tunisia."

Markus doesn't respond. He's not able to. The woman smiles and moves on to the next exhibit.

Markus finds a seat on a wooden bench. Light filtering through a window hits him in the face. The light warms him. *Dysentery, huh? Tunisia.*

Night arrives, and Markus has no appetite. He calls Marian early, eager to hear her voice.

She sounds concerned. "You're telling me you're going to stay in Italy for another week?" she exclaims. "I'm worried about you, Markus."

"I've got to see this through, Marian. I have a purpose now," Markus emphasizes, feeling more alive than he has in years. "When I return, you will understand. Please trust me." He ends the call.

Speaking to himself aloud, he says, "I'm going to find out what this Stone of Allah is and why men will kill to keep it a secret. I will bring this story out of the shadows and into the light, and maybe Ramid's War will end, and I can go home."

He doesn't lie to Marian often, and this was a big lie. He consoles himself and promises to make it up to her and God when he returns, then dials the airline and books a flight to Tunisia.

Chapter 1.13

Ian

Emerge, the Parasitic Tentacles

Ian walks to Central Park, a couple blocks east of his condo, planning how he will get out of the city. His pack, loaded with hiking gear and as much water as he can carry, weighs about sixty pounds. It's quiet—too quiet.

A few years ago, he spent two weeks deep in the Chimborazo Mountains in Ecuador on an Earth Expedition with the Sierra Club and fell in love with hiking. Getting out of the city and into nature is his religion. He yearns to get away from crowds and traffic and eight-dollar lattes. What he's experiencing now is not anything like "getting away." Nature's silence is rich, real beauty filled with subtle sounds. This dead city is more than quiet. It's ominous, deeply absent of life—no cars, horns, bikers, no alarms or sirens, no birds, rats, crickets, no church bells, no music, laughter, or children playing, not even anyone shouting or arguing. This silence is sickening.

Ian rounds the corner of 100th Street, hears a shot, and ducks instinctively. He creeps toward the noise, staying low, and finds a thirty-something, overweight guy looking pale and sweaty, holding a six-shot revolver. Ian wonders if the man is sick until he swigs from a flask. He isn't sick, just drunk.

Ian considers heading in the opposite way, but he'd like some company. He approaches. "My name's Ian."

The man turns, startled. After a moment of silence, he says. "Hey, I'm Ben."

He crams the gun under his belt, which Ian is glad to see. Ben seems to be rather normal for the time being, though he looks uncomfortable in his own fried-bacon-toned skin.

"Are you sick?" Ian asks hesitantly. He doesn't quite know what else to say but is tired of the dialogue in his head being his only companion.

Ben shakes his head. "Na. Just buzzed."

"You made any plans?"

"What do you mean?" He puts his hand on his forehead. "Sorry, I'm slow. Rough couple days." A moment passes. "Plans to get the fuck out of dodge? I guess I gotta get off this island before it starts to reek all to hell."

"I was thinking the same," Ian replies. The two fall into step, walking north. "I need to find food first. Maybe pick up other survivors on our way out."

Ben avoids a dead guy lying in the street. "Yeah, let's find living people. Real people, alive, would be a fuckin' good start."

"Getting out might be a challenge. I heard the jets and the explosions. I think they took out the bridges," Ian says.

"Government's gotta have a quarantine line set up," Ben slurs and drinks more from his flask.

"Hopefully." Ian grabs his stomach, trying to be subtle about it. "Seen any markets not cleared out?"

"I made myself a bacon and potato burrito a while ago."

"Precooked?"

"Yeah."

"Was there more?"

Ben nods.

"Take me there," Ian said.

"I think there's enough for a few more burritos."

"Good." Ian isn't sure how to phrase the question in his mind. Finally, he simply asks, "Do you know why you're not sick?"

Ben's face reddens to a deeper shade as he looks away. "I must be immune or something."

"Yeah. Me, too."

They follow the street surrounding Central Park, stopping at Fredrick's Circle roundabout on the northwest corner. Ian's stomach pinches from hunger. "I'm starved. I don't think I can wait until we get to your burrito place. I'm stopping at the gas station."

"Yeah. Cool, man. I'll grab some shit to go. I never thought I'd need a go-bag, so I ain't prepared like you. I don't even have a backpack."

"I was caught flat-footed, too. This pack was completely empty. Even my fridge was bare. Hell, all I had was some spicy mustard packets."

"Yum. I'd eat that shit without anything else. Just

squish it in my mouth."

Ian hurries off the roundabout toward a BP gas station. Cars crowd under the canopy, silent, like sculptures of cars. People had been lining up to fill their tanks to get out of town when the sickness swept through the population. A blue Volkswagen is on the raised island, wedged between two pumps, crowding a truck and a motorcycle. The motorcycle driver lies next to his bike, wearing a brown leather jacket and jeans, the gas nozzle still in his hands. A grey-haired woman is slumped in the front seat of the VW, the bodies of a girl around eight holding a younger boy in her arms in the back seat. They're so still.

Ian chokes on his own bile. He's never seen such a young dead body. Such sadness. Innocence robbed. He feels slightly better when he looks away.

"You see the back seat?" Ben asks.

Ian nods and continues to the store.

"Fuckin' unbelievable. This shit hit fast, man. Get sick, then, like, twenty hours later, you're coughin' up and choking…then…dead. I can't believe it," Ben says, shaking his head.

Ian runs to the convenience store, anxiety filling him. He flings open the door, rattling the bell hanging from the handle. The sound is so loud it seems to rip into Ian's brain. He stops the bell with his hand. He squeezes his eyes shut, trying to burn away the image of the two dead kids, but it will stay with him until his own clock runs down.

Darkness swirls around him, penetrating his skin, spreading all the way to his toes, absorbing his whole body in pure sadness and shame so painful he wants to die. *What did I do?* Ian cries like he's never cried before, sob after sob erupting from him as he slides to the floor, covering his face and hands. Ashamed to be breathing, alive, walking around when those two kids are dead. No one else except him and Zilla will know who unleashed the airborne virus, committing mass murder. *Is that fuck, Zilla, walking around laughing* at *his evil deed? I wish I could find him. Make him pay. But he's probably long gone.* Ian argues with himself. *He's not gone. He's around. Probably soaking up his handiwork. I should try and find his ass. Then turn him in. Turn him in `to whom? First, find civilization. Then*, get to the hunt.

Ian breathes deeply and opens his eyes.

Ben is at the other end of the store, grabbing beer and chips. "Sorry, dude. This shit is sad. It's fucked up. Don't sweat trippin' out."

W*hy is he immune? What's so special about him? Some drunk is spared, but not those kids? It's not fair.*

Ian's desire to kill Zilla burns in his belly. Any doubts Ian might have about the man's motives flitters away. Ian wants to rip the monster's throat out and watch his light fade to nothing.

Zilla didn't tell Ian the "surveillance" devices really delivered the virus into the air people were breathing, but Ian can't lay all the blame on Zilla. First, Ian was gullible enough to lie, sneak into offices, play spy, and release the virus into the world without vetting the faceless stranger whose orders he obeyed. Ian's choice to follow blindly and the consequences—unintended mass murder—are his responsibility. He stands, but the swimming feeling in his gut hasn't quite passed, so he presses his back against the glass door.

Ben walks up to Ian with this kid-in-a-candy-store look on his face, arms overflowing with booze and junk food, chewing a mouthful of something. He stops walking; his eyes widen until the whites surround his irises. His face turns grey, then stark white.

Ian is confused by Ben's reaction. *Never seen a person cry? Doesn't he feel the sadness everywhere, covering everything like rust?*

Ben drops the bottles and packages. The glass crashes and breaks, throwing beer across the floor. Keeping his eyes on Ian, Ben claws the revolver out of his belt. He raises it slowly, pointing it at Ian. Despite using both hands to hold it, the gun shakes wildly.

Shocked, Ian raises his hands. "Woah! What're you doing, man?"

Ben doesn't answer or move.

Ian ducks aside, hands covering his face. "The fuck's wrong with you?" The gun doesn't follow Ian but stays aimed where it is, at the front door.

Someone's on the other side of the glass. It's the motorcycle guy. The dead motorcycle guy.

"Didn't we…see…that guy at the pumps?" Ben whispers, hands white-knuckling the pistol grip.

"Uh. Yeah. He was one hundred percent dead."

"What is that then? You see him, right?"

The motorcycle guy stands on the other side of the glass door, blood and snot-covered leather jacket and worn jeans, his face pale with sunken cheeks and eye sockets. His eyes are gone but not voids. Behind his eyelids, something moves. The man pushes his body awkwardly into the glass. His left lower lid tears, and out pops a thin white tentacle, protruding like an albino baby octopus, which has burrowed into his eye like a hermit crab. Black liquid leaks from the man's torn eyelid. Also, from his ears.

If it wasn't completely clear that he was dead before, the fist-sized chunk of his hair and scalp that's missing, leaving part of his skull exposed, seems to clarify.

But he's not dead. He pushes at the door with his clumsy arms.

Ben can't speak as the door shakes, ringing the small bell over and over. The motorcycle guy gets his foot wedged into the door gap, keeping it open. He's able to flop his arm inside the store.

"Dude, he's looking right at me," Ben shrieks.

"How? He has no eyes," Ian answers.

The man pushes inside and clumsily takes a step toward Ben. Ben is transfixed, and so is Ian.

The motorcycle guy slides up to Ben and lunges, grabbing him. "Hey! Fuck! Stop. What the hell?"

Ben shrieks, pulling away.

Ian grabs the motorcycle guy's shoulder and spins him away, sending him stumbling until he falls on his knees.

"Are you okay, Ben?" Ian asks.

"This is really happening? I'm not trippin', am I? What the fuck is wrong with him, Ian?" Ben yells. "No, really?"

Ian steps toward the man and hands out. "Hey. Mr. Relax. We can help you. What happened to you? To your eyes?"

The motorcycle guy pulls himself upright, slow and clumsy, using the counter edge; he sways for a moment, his head moving side-to-side as if he still has eyes. He lifts his arm, reaches out, and gurgles a sound like death trapped in his throat.

"Come on, Mr. Let's sit down. I'll call the ambulance…or I can try." Ian steps back, the horrible thing happening in front of him worse than anything he's ever imagined.

"This shit really happenin'?" Ben repeats.

"Yes."

Ben lifts the gun and fires. *Boom!* Half of the

motorcycle guy's skull explodes from the .38 caliber round. A thick root-like thing, bright white and almost glowing under the contrasting black blood, flops out of his skull and hangs on his cheek. His body continues to move toward Ben, white tendril twitching, shrinking back into the motorcycle guy's skull, pushing out a glob of brain matter that splatters on the floor.

Ben fires again and hits the man's chest. Dark liquid pours out the hole, but the body lumbers, one relentless step at a time, at Ben.

Ian backs into a rack of chewing gum and knocks it over. The clatter startles him.

"I shot you, dude!" Ben yells, firing into the walking corpse again. "But you're already dead! Aren't you?" *Boom!* "Why the fuck is he still comin' at me?"

Adrenalin floods Ian's body. He turns, grabs the nearest wire potato chip stand, raises it over his head, and brings it down on top of the motorcycle guy. Dead hands reach for Ian, graceless but strong.

"Over here, dude!" Ben holds the door to the cooler open.

Ian turns and shoves the dead guy into the cooler as Ben slams the door shut.

Though muffled, the cooler is echoing with crashing cans and shattering bottles.

Ian sits down to catch his breath, his heartbeat stuttering so painfully that he thinks it might stop.

Ben shuffles to the front door and looks outside. "It feels like we're in some game show, dude. But with fuckin' primo special effects. Shit, can they make it this real? I blew his fucking head off! Can that be faked? Am I hooked up to a machine or something? Maybe this is virtual reality." Ben drones on and on.

"It's impossible to reanimate dead tissue." Ian inspects the cooler door handle, making sure it won't open from the inside. The dead *thing* bangs around, knocking over bottles and boxes of food, still making pitiful noises.

"Pffff. Impossible, huh? Just look outside."

Ian runs to the door. The grey-haired woman has climbed out the broken window in her VW; the kids are stirring in the back seat like they're waking from a nap.

"God damn it," he mumbles.

Lightning whips around the dark clouds, and thunder follows. Rain chases away accumulated smoke, revealing more of the nightmare scene.

Ian senses, more than clearly sees, movement behind a wrecked truck on the roundabout, next to the park's brick wall, and beside the gas station garage. He blinks, trying to clear his brain fog. *Shit.*

"I don't feel so good, dude," Ben mumbles. He turns and throws up on the magazine rack by the door, heaving and gagging, tears and snot running down his face.

Sympathetic nausea overcomes Ian, and he joins Ben's unwilling purge.

Ian watches those dead kids trying to get out of their car. Watching their reanimated agony brings tears to his eyes. "Fuck this," he snaps, pulls his huge pack on, flings the door open, and runs, clumsy with the weight. Passing a body slowly, trying to get to its feet, he shouts, "Stay dead!"

Ben follows Ian silently.

Slogging through the rain, they get wet, but don't care. The clouds are as dark as oil, foretelling the storm worsening. Ian rounds the corner of a redbrick building and slides his pack off, fumbles for the lighter in the middle pocket. "Stay right here!" Ian orders Ben and runs back to the gas pumps.

The grey-haired woman limps toward Ian, her clothes shredded from her unrefined motor skills. Under the cloth, tears were bloody scrapes, some very deep, her blood also black. Her head swivels slowly from side to side, like a dog listening to the wind, and stops moving when her root-filled eye sockets point right at Ian.

I have misused "abomination" when writing about conservative nut-jobs. This is an abomination. An alien, malignant parasitic life-form taking dead people for its

204

host, animating the bodies. But why? What does this ...
parasite want?

The grey-haired woman is stiff and clumsy, slow
enough for Ian to run around her to the gas pump. He
kneels, his hands shaking, flicks the lighter's flame into the
gasoline pooled under the motorcycle, and hurries back to
Ben, screaming, "RUN!"

Ian swoops his hand through his backpack strap, hefts it onto his shoulder and follows Ben down 110th Street, bordering Central Park.

Seconds later, the gas station's holding tank explodes, the blast deafening. Ian slows, looks over his shoulder, and watches the roaring fireball billow and roll above the red brick building blocking their view of the gas station.

Wiping rain from his eyes, Ian still senses movement behind windows and doors. He can't see other dead people moving in their homes and in the businesses, but knows they are there, stumbling around, awakening.

"What the hell are you stopping for?" Ben yells, looking over his shoulder.

"I have to see what happened." Ian runs back toward the fire, stopping at the red brick building's corner, kneels, and peers along the wall, heart thumping.

Ben huffs to a stop and falls to his knees. He leans over and squints toward the fire. "Good call. I wanna see how their faces melted off in that fireball."

"So you're, like, a sicko?" Ian asks only half seriously.

"I guess so."

The explosion had tossed the woman half a block. Her clothes were on fire, but she wasn't thrashing. She crawled through in the middle of the roundabout as though her melting skin meant nothing. The blue VW had been hurled into the middle of the street, roof pancaked, glass shattered. A small arm hung out of the back window, black as tar, twitching.

The rain damps the fire, but the flames still flickering in the rubble might burn for days. The gasoline vapors and chemical stench irritate Ian's eyes and lungs. He covers his mouth and nose with his shirt collar. The lines of abandoned vehicles burn, empty of movement, life, and hope. "Looks like fire works better than bullets," he says to Ben.

Ben leers. "Nice work, Commando."

"Don't celebrate just yet. If everybody turns out like these people, ten million zombies are gonna wake up soon."

Ben looks around. "Fine, I won't smack your ass just yet. But don't call 'em zombies, 'cause that's too damn weird. Nope, something else's goin' on. I still think we're being punked or drugged or somethin'."

Ian recognizes the hint of terror in Ben's voice. "Something more is going on. The roots inside their eyes. Maybe they're puppets of them. Let's get outta here."

Another explosion rocks the ground. Ian runs harder, feeling lucky he isn't blown to pieces. Turning on 7th Avenue, he slows. The sixty pounds bouncing on his back is weighing him down. Half a block later, he gasps for air, cursing himself for not being in better shape.

Ben can barely run at all. What he is doing is lumbering along, choking for breath. He nears Ian. "Good god. I'm glad you're walking now. I'm a fat bastard, you know."

An older-looking, bald black man in a dark-gray suit stands alone in the middle of the intersection at 7th Street and 111th, a baseball bat leaned against his leg, gazing into the sky, his arms outstretched, hands open, as if he's beseeching God to sweep him up and take him to heaven.

Ten, no, eleven Puppets stalk the black man.

"Hey," Ian says to Ben. "That's Markus Coburn. My father's company rebuilt his church after it burned to the ground. The new church is the largest one built in New York in fifty years. Pretty cool building, too. Spared no expense. My father said that he was supported by a global corporation out of South Africa called Cantel Corp. Or something like that." Ian watches a moment. "He's gonna try and fight the

Puppets off with a bat. What is he crazy?"

"He certainly is nuts. I've seen the church. Damn huge."

Markus picks up his bat, and his prayer is apparently finished.

Ben yells to Markus, "What are you doing, dude? There's, like, a bunch of dead fuckers comin' at you! They're gonna try and eat your brains or claw you to death. Your bat ain't gonna do shit!"

Markus kicks a Puppet away, swinging his black-goop-crusted bat into the skull of another.

Ian runs to Markus. "Come on. Our only choice is to burn them or run, and you don't have fire." He pulls on Markus's arm.

Ben is close by. Puppets surround the three, forcing them closer together. The dead reach, grab, blindly try to rip them apart. The Puppet's dead hands are strong. The three fight frantically, desperate to get away.

A young man Puppet, long braids falling from a do-rag, grabs Ian's collar, pulling him close, screaming shrilly. White roots stretch from his eye sockets, undulating like anemone tentacles in a tidal pool. Markus grabs a handful of braids, jerks the Puppet off Ian, and hammers the creature's head until the skull implodes.

Ben shoves another Puppet to the asphalt, punches his chest, stomps, breaking ribs. The Puppet doesn't respond to pain at all.

Puppets stumble away, colliding, tumbling into heaps, locked together by their flailing limbs.

Ian, Ben, and Markus run, searching for a way north through ever-increasing crowds.

Everywhere Ian looks, he sees more dead people clamber to their feet.

Markus puffs, "Thank you, young man. The demons

surrounded me faster than I thought possible. I'm Markus. Who are you?"

Ian glances at Markus and sees no fear or confusion in his eyes. The preacher is a rock.

He believes God has his back. "Ian," he gasps between breaths.

"You look familiar—ah, your father! Photos of you on his desk. Did great work on my church."

"Had," Ian whispered.

Markus doesn't answer.

Ben, so out of breath he's incomprehensible , croaks, "Got a…extra baseball …bat? Or… flame thrower? Church…apocalypse proof?"

"Sorry, son."

The three jog in the center of the street, rain-soaked, sweeping their eyes right and left, wary of all movement.

Ian, glad for the cooling shower, jogs, pacing himself, the heavy pack digging at his shoulders.

Ben's gasping is louder, hoarse, and he's slowing.

Markus shows no signs of fatigue or strain.

Gunshots, rapid-fire bursts, ping, and rattle behind them. Ian hopes the Marines or the army or someone is coming to help. He's wrong again.

Chapter 1.14

Josh
Venturing Out

Josh has been huddling in his apartment for days, hungry, sad, and stir-crazy as a beetle tied to a string. He measures the long hours in heartbeats. Sleeping is oblivion, but it is only possible for a few hours at a time. Every time, he awakens to the same lonely four walls.

It would be better if he could go to sleep and never wake up again. He considers taking his own life but decides that would be stupid. He prides himself on his intelligence.

Amassing the courage to peek out the window takes an entire day.

Finally, he pushes back the bright yellow curtains his mother insisted on. The sun hurts his eyes, but they adjust. "Holy shit." He regrets his decision to look because what he sees is death and destruction.

Bodies, wrecked cars, and broken buildings. Smoke and trash.

He mourns the dead strangers. Every one of them. He'd cried for his losses for over a day, but now he feels the sadness of them all: for the dead pedestrians scattered in the streets, dead drivers trapped in their coffin-like cars, and the dead he cannot see in the buildings.

The skies are black from dozens of fires in the city; smells of wet ashes, rotting garbage, and death penetrate the seals around the window. He tries not to think about how the seal he'd managed the day of the outbreak wouldn't last. In fact, it was probably leaking already.

Pacing. Always pacing. Checking seals. More pacing.

"If only I had my computer...hell, any working electronic device would make me feel better." He assumes an EMP destroyed everything with a circuit because none of his stuff functions. Not his watch, his tablet, or his smartphone.

His stomach rumbles loudly. Sleeping keeps his hunger at bay, but his body is already absorbing itself. His concave belly and ribs with no flesh feel like a skeleton, and he can count the knobs of his vertebrae down his back. Hunger is as much his enemy now as the disaster outside his apartment. He frees the plastic liner from the cheese cracker box, licks the salty crumbs, and gives the mini-donut bag the same treatment. He's glad for the sugar, but the chocolate smears barely taste like anything.

"I must leave the safe zone. Somewhere, the destruction ends, and normal life continues. The truth must be rooted out and shared, and I must be the one to tell it all. How Zilla spread the virus. Killed my mother to shut me up. The whole world needs to go on a manhunt for him. Bring him to justice." He stands, looks around his gloomy cave, forcing himself to think clearly. "Now, if I'm going outside, I need a plan."

Ideas don't come easy. Hours later, he realizes he's stalling.

"I'm not going to shrivel up and die in this apartment, damn it," his booming voice is louder than he expected.

Sounds of movement inside his apartment startle him as if his ears, clogged with his self-imprisonment, pop open. The shuffling is human-caused.

Someone's ripping down his tape!

Josh turns, leaps over his bed, and hides on the other side, trembling. A door opens. It can't *be my front door. I have two locks and a security bar. I know I didn't leave it open.*

Josh finds a face mask saved from the pandemic lockdown in his desk drawer and slaps it over his nose and mouth, pinching the metal nose clamp tight.

More scraping sounds. His bedroom door isn't tapped up, and he has the entire apartment to roam, but he did wrap his mother's body and sealed off her entire room with tape. Taking a deep breath to get his nerves fired up, he edges toward the door and peaks out.

His mother is shuffling stuff around in the kitchen cupboards, her back turned, and she is probably looking for a snack.

"Mom?" Josh takes a few strides toward her.

She turns at the sound of his voice. Long white worms protrude from her eye sockets. Black streaks of blood leak from sores on her mouth and ears. She screams, long and shrill, and flops toward him; her gate is uncoordinated, her back hunched. She was broken but angry like a predator. Josh retreats to his room and slams the door, flicking the lock. *What the hell?!*

She claws at his door.

"Mom. What's going on?"

She streaks in response.

That's not my mother. Not anymore. The virus is mutating her DNA into...into what? A zombie. No two ways to put it.

"I need a weapon."

His closet full of crap is his best hope. Inside the first box are old photo albums, books, notes from college, and some science fair awards. Hefting the award like a club, he tosses it aside because the plastic figures are brittle and useless. He picks up a notebook and hacks the air with it. No good.

The box of camping gear is more promising. He drags the big grey plastic tote out rifles through it: four cans of sterno, a folding knife, a sleeping bag, a foil thermal blanket, a first-aid kit, an emergency water filter, and a small electric chainsaw, a gift from his sister. He pockets the knife and sets the chainsaw aside, thinking it wouldn't have survived the EMP. *Too bad. This chainsaw was a little beast.* He remembers sawing through a twelve-inch tree trunk in no time. He flicks the sharp, green-stained blades with his finger, admiring the compact little machine. He opens the battery cover and pulls the plastic tab he'd fixed covering the six "D" battery contacts–the proper way to store long-term electric devices. He presses the trigger. Nothing, of course.

His mother is still clawing at his door, but someone— or something—else screeches in his building. There are more walking dead. Probably a lot more.

Slashing the sharp chainsaw blade through the

air, Josh's fingers touch a small lever. Remembering the safety trigger, he pushes it down and pulls the trigger simultaneously. The chainsaw spins to life! *How the hell?* He looks at the camping great now strewn on the carpet. *The thermal blanket must have shielded the circuitry! I'm so lucky.*

I have to be smart about *how I use this thing. The "D" batteries won't last long.*

Josh flings open the door. Mom, or something that once resembled her, rushes at him, arms outstretched, black blood leaking from broken fingernails and scratch wounds on her arms.

Revving the chainsaw, horrified tears running down his face, Josh swipes the sharp blade across her grasping hands, ripping her fingers open in jagged cuts. She falls aside, arms and legs flailing. Josh's eyes close, but he forces himself to look, plunges the chainsaw into her head, pushes with all his strength, and drives the spinning blades into her surprisingly soft skull.

I'm sorry, so sorry. But you wouldn't want to live like this.

Chapter 1.15

Isabella
Tossing Brains

Isabella counts ten dead people on the ground, beaten and mangled but struggling to move like broken puppets with their strings cut. Something slithers and twists under their skin, raising creepy bulges in unnatural shapes.

A crazy-looking headless body covered with black shit shambles right up to her. She raises her assault rifle chest high and pumps a burst of three rounds into the thing. It doesn't go down.

This has gotta be a fuckin' joke. Maybe I'm drugged. Isabella flips the rifle to full-auto and pulls the trigger hard, unloading the entire clip into a group of creatures stumbling toward her. But they keep coming at her, streaming onto the street from alleys, buildings, and cars.

Isabella slings the rifle strap over her shoulder and grips her Beater with both hands. *Time to vent some aggression.* Running straight into the knot of Puppet-people swinging, she cracks some dopey-looking woman's head and jabs the next sucker in the throat, getting her Beater stuck in the soft tissue. Isabella jerks it free and spins, striking the headless fool across his knees and taking him down. It feels good: her muscles vibrate like perfectly tuned guitar strings. She turns again and punches the Puppet flesh with everything she's got.

The air fills with weird, wordless, wild screaming as she spins and fights. Black blood splashes everywhere. Her senses heighten as she stabs and bashes. Fire rages in her soul. Her muscles burn with strength, stronger than any man, stronger than these Puppets. Isabella dominates the fight.

The headless guy comes for more, and she gasses out. She needs to back away, breathe, and lower her heart rate.

Fuck. These bastards aren't staying down! One of the Puppets grabs Isabella's ankle and squeezes, breaking her skin. Isabella's Beater is ripped away, her right arm nearly torn off. Another hand grabs her leg, tearing her jeans. Powerful fingers tangle into her hair, tearing at her scalp. *Shit, shit, shit.* Fear is bitter in her mouth.

Isabella is immobilized. Time dilates and stretches as she watches a white worm-like creature as thick as her middle finger slink up her arm, leaving a tacky, slimy trail. She forces her eyes down, but sees another worm slither out of a nose, weave around in the air like a snake tasting the air for prey, leaps onto Isabella's shirt, wriggles toward her face.

Rain and that black shit, the things bleed nearly blind her; a hand squeezes her throat, shutting off her air. Struggling frantically to get free, she feels more worms fall on her, trying to get inside her, to push through her skin!

The light in her mind is fading when she hears her drill sergeant scream, "Limp, soldier. Go limp. Drag 'em down with your weight!"

She slumps. The hand stops choking her, and she collapses.

Far away, a motor revs and idles, revs again, like one of those little chainsaws she used to clear rubble.

Cold, sticky blood splashes all over her, and the hands let go. She shakes her head to clear it, groping for a rock or something to use as a weapon. The second wind fills her lungs, lighting up her entire body. Her hand falls on her Beater. Fury powers her jabs and swings from the ground; she tries to roll, rubbing her face against her shoulder to clear her eyes.

The chainsaw revs, freeing her leg. She rolls to her belly, crawling like she learned in boot camp, but in the obstacle course, there weren't body parts and dead things.

Isabella wipes her face on her sleeve until she can see. Worms are all over her! Trying to bore into her skin through any available opening. *No fuckin' way!*

She furiously slaps them away.

Satisfied she's worm-free, Isabella looks around and sees her rescuer. A thin guy, wearing a medical mask over his nose and mouth, wipes his face on his sleeve. His curly, dark brown hair is matted with sweat, and his thick glasses are splattered with black shit. He chops the last puppets and turns to Isabella, extending his hand.

Isabella grabs his hand and stands. She's still gasping for air.

The man is tall but scrawny and looks like the typical gamer dork who plays video games until sunrise. He sports a stupid *Ghostbusters* shirt and tight jeans. *Dork or no dork, he just saved my life.*

"We need to keep moving." He holds her hand as he takes off, helping her balance.

Pain tears through her ankle, arm, and ribs. More cuts and bruises complain. Those bastards almost tore her limb from limb. Stopping for breath, she leans over, hands on her knees. One last worm clings to her boot. Isabella slaps it off and stomps it into a tiny puddle of goo.

"See any more? The fuck if any of those things are gonna dig into my skin!"

The guy looks her over. "Don't see anymore."

Isabella doesn't scare easily, but these worms freak her out. "They seemed smart, like tapeworms with brains."

"Don't have eyes, either, but behave like they can see. Take over their host bodies completely," the guy says.

Isabella doesn't know what to say. She's having a hard time accepting the whole walking dead crap.

"Fucking things are parasites or something. Body snatchers."

"Jeez. You think? The worms in their eyes could be…controlling them?" Josh says. He sounds like he's gagging.

"Don't know. I do know they're not human anymore. That's pretty fucking clear."

"This is so impossible."

"Is possible. Is happening. Get your head in the game."

More Puppets emerge from the buildings, cars, and alleyways, moving slowly, which makes her feel better.

Isabella hobbles along, forcing her brain to ignore the injuries.

"You're welcome by the way. My name is Josh," he says quietly.

"I had it covered," Isabella snarls at the boy. He looks away.

"Where are you headed?" Josh asks.

"What's it to you?"

"I can help you get out of the city," he says. "We can help each other, I mean."

She looks at him hard. He obviously is looking for company. "I don't need help." Isabella's reluctant to let him tag along; she doesn't need some geek mooning around her. She looks herself over. She's covered with cuts and bruises, her arm and shoulder are almost useless, and skin is ripped off her ankle deeply enough to expose tendons and muscles. *Shit.* "Fine, you can shadow me, but I move fast."

Isabella drops onto the bottom step of an apartment building, tears a strip of cloth from her shirt, puts the cleanest part against the wound, wraps it around her ankle, and cinches it tight.

Josh nods, watching her face. "Even with only one good leg, huh?"

"Just watch me."

She scrambles to her feet, and they speed walk, not touching. Pain shoots up her leg with every step, but she's good at ignoring pain. It isn't too hard; you focus on something else, close off the pain, lock it up, and move on.

Puppets are still coming out of the buildings and alleys and cars, but their reaction time is as quick as a doped-up fentanyl junkie.

Isabella picks up speed. Josh stays close to her—the two rush past more and more Puppets. Isabella casually looks over her shoulder. "Come on," Isabella hisses. "We ain't movin' fast enough. They're all on our trail like bloodhounds."

Josh slows. Isabella can tell he's out of shape. He's also whiter than white. He either doesn't get outside much, or his pigment has high-tailed it out of his skin from fear. Both are likely.

After a few blocks, she has to slow down again. Hot pain clutches her calf muscle each time it flexes. Isabella reaches out and grabs Josh's shoulder for support.

He doesn't seem to mind. "So, you didn't get sick?" he asks her.

"Neither did you," she snaps back.

"I've got a condition…" He's still wearing his medical mask.

"You don't say."

"I'm afraid of germs, okay? When my mother died from some crazy infection, I sealed my apartment with tape and plastic. But she came back to life. I knew I couldn't stay locked inside anymore. Then I saw you needed help."

He's so proud of himself that it makes her ill. "Told you, I don't need help."

"Yeah, okay. I just wanted to talk. I haven't seen anyone in days. Well, besides some gangsters. I did see a tank come through with a handful of mean-looking guys."

"Yeah, I saw those fools, too." Josh reminds her of a guy she served with in Iraq. Her friend was smaller but had the same look on his face. Smart, but not too smart. Anyway, Josh isn't all macho or always staring at her tits, so she's okay with him.

They hustle down 7th Avenue like they're late for a court date. It's raining hard, but she likes the torrents washing the black shit off her skin and hair, even if the rain isn't clean.

They'll get to the river soon, but Isabella has no idea what to do after that.

CHAPTER 1.16

TANIS
NOWHERE IS SAFE

By the time Tanis and Hana reach North Harlem, he's tired of walking.

Hana's tired, too. They need shelter, so she runs around looking for a safe place. Most people locked their doors when the shit came down—shuddered windows, fixed security bars. Not a door could be opened. If either of them made a racket busting a door down, the dead would know where they were and pile up like a snowdrift of rotting flesh and worm thingies.

Hana finally returns and leads Tanis down a side street to a half-open roll-up door. They duck under the door, finding a metal workshop where gates, balcony railings, and security bars for windows are made. The building is quiet, and there are no dead bodies around. She tries to close the roll-up door, but it's jammed. "This is out of the way. So, I think we'll be safe here. At least for a bit…and if we stay quiet."

They pass a large, open floor space with worktables and racks of gates and metal bars. She goes to a door that leads to a lobby. "I need to make sure the front door is secure. Stay here, okay?"

"Yeah, sure, whatever." Tanis looks around. But then rushes after Hana. He's not interested in being alone at this moment.

Windows run the length of the shop's front wall, all covered with decorative security bars. So is the glass door. It looks pretty secure to Tanis. He stops next to a gumball machine and stares into the gloomy day. Normally, people would walk by, and he'd hear car horns, garbage trucks, or airplanes. Now there's Nothing. A dozen cars are parked on the street, as still as ruins, dead people inside their tombs on wheels. Bodies litter the sidewalk, as close to each other as stepping-stones.

"I miss the sound of cars," Tanis says. "The sound of a normal day."

Hana stands next to him. "I kind of like the quiet. Besides, the sounds that I like are long gone."

"What sounds?"

"Old trains, the hiss of steam engines, noisy cafés, or the clinks of china at a fancy meal where everyone is so engrossed in what they're eating they've forgotten how to speak. I haven't heard those sounds in a while."

"You're not eighty years old. Since when did you hear old trains?"

She breathes deeply and closes her eyes. Tanis can tell she's going far away, back into the memory parts of her brain.

"My adoptive parents used to take me on upstate train tours, pulled by classic steam engines, to Canada and back, through beautiful forests. I've never been so happy."

Tanis turns from the window, not wanting to see outside anymore. Continually seeing dead bodies keeps his chest tight and stomach sour.

The roll-up door they entered rattles loudly as someone enters their hideout.

Tanis drops quietly to his knees and crawls behind the front counter.

Hana pulls her gun and heads for the lobby door. Too late. The door crashes inward, and people funnel inside. Hana's caught in the open!

"Fuck, man. We gots us a little lady hidden in here!"

Tanis hopes the intruders can't see him. He's short, so he feels hidden. *Hana's a cop*, so *she'll know how to get us* out *of this.*

"Drop your weapons, guys. Tell me what you want. I don't have anything here, but what I found is yours. Let me show you where my stuff is." Hana tips up her gun's muzzle and opens her fingers. She moves toward the men, out of Tanis's field of view.

His chest tightens more every time he hears her take a step; every breath feels like he's sucking air through a straw.

Hana yelps. The lobby door slams shut.

Tanis listens, but their voices are muffled. There's no *way I'm standing around while they attack her! I gotta do something.* Staying crouched, he scuttles over to the metal factory door, stands, and risks peeking through the small window.

Three men stand in front of her, pointing National Guard–issued rifles, but these jerks aren't Guard. Hana is on her knees, her fingers laced behind her head. One guy dumps Tanis's backpack out on the floor and kicks the shit around.

"You said you got something for us."

"She's got somethin' for each of us, that's for sure." The guy touches his long goatee, like stroking a cat's tail.

"No way, man. Look at her pants, her belt, her shoes. She's a cop! We gotta get gone," the man with a baseball hat says.

The short one moves to the roll-up door. "Yeah, let's go."

"Look around! There ain't another cop for a hundred miles. There are no soldiers either. They blew the bridges and the subway tunnels. They left us here to die. They left her, too."

The dude with the baseball hat joins the short one at the exit. "This is fucked up. I ain't staying." The two duck out and are gone.

The remaining guy steps closer to Hana, his rifle trained on her. "So, you're the po-po? I guess this is my lucky day," he says, and his hand goes for his belt. "Get on your back."

Hana nods and slowly lies down, her hand up, palm open.

Shit. I gotta *do something, but what? What would Hana want me to do? Jump out, throw shit at him? I could crack him over the head with something. Bust his creep-skull open.* His asthma kicks in, choking him. *My inhaler is in my bag! Damn it. I need a fucking machine gun!* He drops to his hands and knees, his vision darkening at the edges. And in that small circle of light, a metal rod almost glows. Tanis grabs the heavy metal bar, returns to the glass door, opens it carefully, and slips into the lobby. His lungs are so tight he can't breathe very well, but enough air gets in to keep him from blacking out.

The guy straddles Hana, trying to get her pants undone with one hand, awkwardly cramming his gun into her cheek with the other. "I've got a bullet with your name on it, cop unless you stay nice and still."

Tanis runs at the guy and plunges the metal bar into the back of his head. "Ahhhh!" Pushing the weapon as hard as he can.

Hana bucks her hips, and her attacker topples over, his face making a wet sound on the concrete floor. She glances at him and makes sure he's down before she runs to Tanis.

Tanis slowly folds himself down to the floor and curls into a ball.

Hana rifles through his stuff and hands him his inhaler. He takes a few puffs and feels the air fill his lungs. She pulls his head onto her lap and hugs him hard. "It's okay. You did good. You did what you had to. You saved me twice. You can stop now, okay? Breathe. Nice. That's good. Keep doing that…How about I save you next time?"

Tanis chuckles, barely able to make a sound. "I couldn't let him hurt you."

"We're all predators; some of us are cannibals, too. Gotta watch out for the gobblers." She laughed. "Funny how I used to say that all the time, that we're all predators, but some humans are cannibals. It's not literal, you know."

Blushing, Tanis sits up. "Yeah, I know what a metaphor is."

"What's funny is that it's true now. With no law and order, evil people have the power. They have free reign over people like us. Smaller, younger women. The predators are coming to eat us."

Tanis shook his head. "Don't say that. I…*we* just need to get to the other side of the river. We'll sit in quarantine for a few days, and then they'll let us go find…

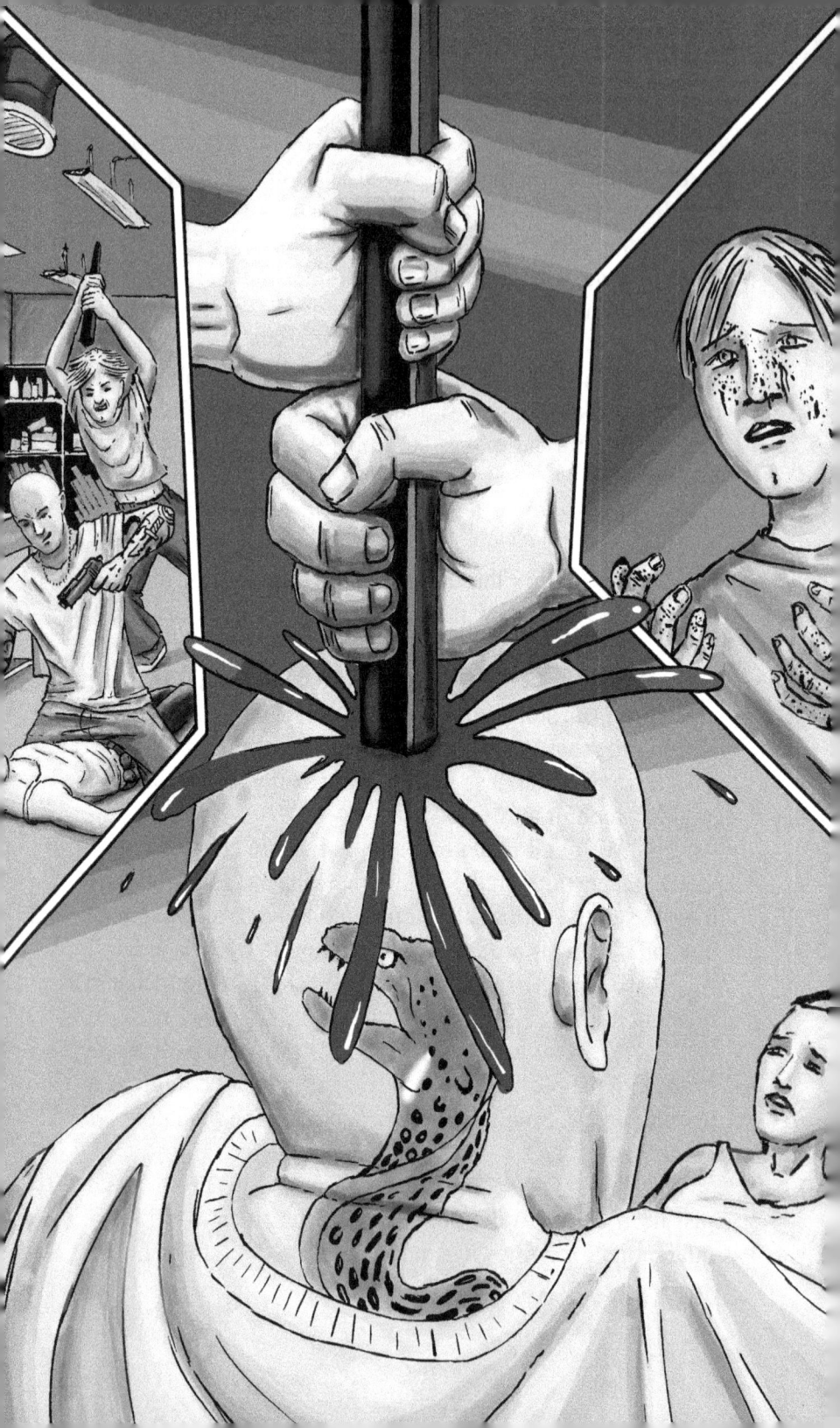

our families." He was about to burst into tears but held back.

Hana leans over and extracts a four-inch fixed blade, sharp on both sides, from her boot. "Don't think for a second I was going down without a fight. I was just waiting for my moment." She winks.

"I–never killed anyone before." Tanis wipes blood splatters from his face and steadies himself with his hands on the floor, waiting for the dizziness and nausea to pass.

"I'm glad. But don't worry; defending the innocent doesn't make you a monster. It only makes you stronger." She helps him clean his face and hands with water from his bag.

The two sit in silence for a while. Hana keeps looking toward the door. "We have to move. Those guys might come back looking for their friend."

Tanis nods in agreement.

"We need to get across the river," Hana says. "That means if we don't want to swim, we have to find a boat."

"Better find a boat, then," he says.

Hana nods. She snaps her fingers, looking excited. "I know where there's a boat."

"The Hudson River has docks," Tanis interrupts.

She shakes her head. "The boats docked there are too big and use electronics. Dead in the water. Plus, there was so much panic we'd probably have a hard time finding a boat left on this side of the Hudson. No, there's a nice boathouse north of here. Swindler's Cove's gotta have a rowboat."

"We're gonna have to row?"

"Either that or swim. The river's only four hundred feet or so wide there." She stands, shuffles to the small window, and looks out. "I think we can find a boat. I've seen Columbia University students rowing on the river hundreds of times, and they dock those boats at Swindler's

Cove. Worth a shot anyway."

The two head out, Tanis hoping the hike to the cove will take less than a few hours. The heat is terrible, like yesterday. The sun burns Tanis's face and neck and saps his strength. The bodies they pass swell with stink, and some look weird.

Tanis points to a white root. "Those things are covering the dead. What the hell are they?"

Hana shakes her head. "It's all so impossible. I don't understand any of it. So many dead." She's too emotional to say more.

"Oh god!" Tanis sprints away from a dead woman holding her dead dog.

"What?" Hana asks to follow. "Breathe deep."

Tanis shakes his head. "I saw a rat."

"Not unusual. They're almost official residents."

"It crawled out of that lady's neck." He gags.

The rats and worms aren't the only things feasting. The flies swarm the dead, not bothering to hide their gluttony. A few vultures have come down to eat, others remaining aloft on the updrafts of heat, maybe afraid to feast the flesh of the tainted dead.

Tanis stays wound tight, on the verge of freaking out the whole morning, hungry and sick to his stomach at the same time.

The highway is empty, except for a huge passenger plane, half-buried in the asphalt, one wing ripped off by concrete Jersey barriers. Eerie stillness surrounds the plane. The cop and the geek keep walking until they're close enough to get a good look.

Tanis expects to see emergency hatches open and slides inflated on either side, but there are no open doors. No slides. No one got out alive. "The EMP probably took them down. There is no warning, no way to survive. Bad way to go."

"The pilot did a good job landing on the freeway," Hana began. "…but not good enough.

Blood splatters the cabin windows. Tanis can't think about the fate of the plane's passengers anymore. He looks at his feet, silent, until Hana says, "Let's go."

"Yeah, alright."

The two cut across the highway, down a ramp, across a lot to an apartment complex, passing clusters of bodies like the terrible holocaust videos he was forced to watch in history class, blank grey dead faces with clouded eyes. Tanis wants to scream and run until he finds some dark, quiet place where he can climb into a CAT6 Ethernet cable and find the nearest server, cozy up to some funny YouTube vids.

His head droops, heavy, like he's firmly stuck in that Blue Screen of Death error mode where PCs go to die. He grabs Hana's hand and holds it tight, looking for a place to hide and rest.

But bodies are clustered in dog piles on the rooftops of the buildings or hanging out of windows, some not quite still. *Why pile up? What the fuck does that mean? Why go to the roof if you're sick? Or hang out your window? It doesn't make sense.* Tears roll down his cheeks. *This is a lot of dead people. Is Ma even alive? Pa isn't. His entire office is dead. Targeted? Someone knew they were military Space Force. It all started there*—an actual *virus along with the one I let Zilla spread. Wait a sec. Are people dying outside Manhattan Island, too?* He's glad sweat pours off his face so Hana can't see his tears.

He leans on her, trying to calm himself. He succeeds, barely.

They follow Harlem River Drive because it parallels the river. When they pass the Kennedy Bridge, they see it has been blown to pieces. Hana leads Tanis past the destruction, keeping between him and the site as though she were intentionally sparing him from seeing the depth of the truth, a very motherly action. Though she was a stranger, he felt more at ease with every step.

They keep walking. All the bridges are toast:

3rd, 138th, 145th, Alexander Hamilton, and the George Washington.

"We've walked over ten miles," Hana says.

"No kidding. I can't remember when I've walked this far, ever. My feet are messed up. Every very step is like piranhas biting a chunks off."

"Come on. One foot in front of the other. We'll make it. We have to."

The river narrows, and the city thins. Tanis shudders when he thinks about swimming across the brown, quickly moving water. He tries not to think of it, instead picturing himself safe and cozy in a boat of some kind.

Finally, the tree-lined road curved at a large hand-carved sign reading "Swindler's Cove." A few yards past the sign are a security gate and a shiny new aluminum footbridge that leads to a floating pier and a big boathouse two stories tall, freshly painted blue with yellow trim and bright red doors.

Hana pushes the security gate gently. Thankfully, it swings open.

"Help me find something to fasten this gate," Hana says, searching the ground.

Tanis finds a two-foot-long piece of rusty wire.

Hana closes the gate and wraps the latch shut with wire. "If there are looters, this might slow them down," she says.

The two continue along the aluminum walkway, their footsteps clanging, and move onto the dock.

"Awe, come on. The dock is empty. What happened to all the boats?" Tanis wonders, looking disappointed.

Hana points to the other side of the river. "Looks like people took them in the panic before everyone started dying."

"Just my luck." Tanis counts ten boats scattered

haphazardly on the opposite shore.

Hana hurries to the boathouse, breaks the window to the main office with her rifle butt, enters warily, weapon at the ready. The structure floats, moving gently in the quiet water. The bottom floor is a boat repair shop and storehouse, but only one wooden boat, resting upside down on construction A-frames, is left.

Hana eyes the boat for a while. "Yeah, this isn't going to work." She moves around the small wooden johnboat. "If we take this out now, it'll sink." She points at a hole the size of her fist in the flat bottom.

"Can we patch it?"

Hana looks around the storehouse and spots a workbench and metal cabinet marked "Flammable." Walking toward the tools, she says, "Epoxy should seal it. But we'll have to stay an extra day or so until the glue dries."

"Fine by me." Tanis searches a row of lockers, finds a towel, and dries the sweat off his face and neck. "I'm cool with hanging low. It's freakin' hot outside."

Hana moves through the boathouse, ensuring no creeps are hiding around the corner or upstairs. She returns, a smile on her face. "This place is ours. Come on, let's patch this boat," Hana says, breaking the metal cabinet open. Patching the hole with a wooden plug and stinky putty that smelled extremely flammable takes hours, after which they paint the repair with a blue epoxy sealant.

Hana finds a big bag of M&Ms in one of the lockers and snacks on them while she inspects their work. She laughs, making a smiley face with the candy in the thick sealant. She puts the last candy into the smile and says, "That should do it. Give us a little good luck."

Tanis laughs and adds crazy eyebrows to the smiley face. Hana elbows him, playing. *She's cool. Funny, too. Weird for a woman, weirder for a cop.*

They walk upstairs again, this time to search for supplies. The top floor has a lounge area, a meeting room, a small kitchen, and a bathroom. Down the hall are two other locked doors.

Now, looking at the doors, Tanis guesses they're storerooms or something. He still has that woman's hairpin in his pocket; he can pick the lock.

Hana busts the first door open with a swift front kick and peeks inside, finds a couch, TV, a radio set-up, and binoculars on the windowsill. The other room is locked with a deadbolt. She kicks, but the frame is too thick. "There's probably something of value here: life vests or keys or a motor or something. No big deal. We're gonna be out tomorrow anyway."

"I get the couch," Tanis declares, as though he's staking a room in a new house.

Hana gives him a crooked look. "You're gonna let the lady sleep on the floor? Some gentleman you are."

He chuckles, hot in his face. "Sorry, I guess you can have the couch."

She walks by and pushes him. "I'm kidding. You take the couch. You're a kid, and that beats the woman trump card." She looks Tanis up and down for a second. "What are you, like ten?" She laughs.

"I'm fifteen." His face burns. "I'm short, that's all. I haven't hit my growth spurt yet."

She laughs playfully, smiling at him.

"I'll forgive you for that one." He play-scowls.

The sun sets behind dark smoke clouds, and Tanis knows the sky will be really dark tonight. He's glad they're inside.

Hana snoops around while he sits on the couch. He pulls out his cell phone and plays one of the many game apps. The games aren't as distracting as he hoped. He still feels slow, sad, and dark inside.

Hana's cheering from the back room startles him. He jumps to his feet and rushes onto her. "What? You okay?" he asks.

She's head first in a crawl space in the back of the closet. "They got an old generator in here! If this thing is properly grounded it should have survived the EMP blast. It's a simple diesel engine." She retrieves a multi-tool from her belt, removes the front cover screws, and hands the panel to Tanis. "See these wires?"

He gets down on all fours and tucks himself as close to her as possible.

"They run down the inner walls to the first-floor framing."

"A ground wire?"

"Yes. Good," she says. "Plus, this cage has insulation that keeps the sound down. Perfect insulation from the EMP." She flicks the fuel-line switch, toggles the starter switch, and the motor fires up. She cheers again like a little girl.

"We have power! Whoop whoop!" Tanis yelps.

"I'm still paranoid about looters, so let's shut the blinds tight and no lights unless we have to."

"Sweet. We can also throw a towel over the lamp, right? Dim it?" Tanis asks.

"Great idea."

Hana and Tanis grow hungry despite feeling restless and on edge. Hana heads to the kitchen and tries the stove. It doesn't work. She lifts the lid. The stove regulates heat with a simple circuit on the control panel—a fried control panel.

Tanis shoves her playfully out of the way. "I got this. I built cool electronic kits when I was a kid. Anything with a chip became my friend." He frees the ends of wires from the circuit and touches them together lightly. Sparks fly, fed by the generator's power. Hana unplugs the stove and connects the wires directly to the burner.

"The electric stove uses the current and the coil to generate heat," he says, showing off. Hana plugs the stove back in. One burner turns bright red. They high-five.

Hana regulates the stove's temperature by plugging it in and out. She cooks little canned hotdogs and soup from the cabinet.

Tanis devours a pack of donuts and some more M&Ms for dessert. He feels less jittery and weird, and when his head hits the couch pillow, he passes out hard.

When he wakes, it's morning. He shuffles to the window and peeks out the blinds. Storm clouds have mixed with the smoke in the sky now stand still, as if waiting for permission to come crashing to land. Lightning strikes in the clouds, dozens of flashes at a time. A bad storm is coming.

Hana cooks hash browns she found in the freezer. They're not frozen anymore, but they're not rotten yet. She also finds a box of fake eggs in the cabinet. The breakfast is only missing orange juice and bacon.

"Can we stay here until a rescue team comes?" Tanis asks her. "It's such a nice hideout, and with the storm coming, I don't want to be anywhere else."

Hana drinks some tea and stares out the window. "Yeah, we can." She's deep in thought. "You know, I haven't seen anything in the air." She sips her tea. "That's kinda weird."

"What, like, you mean planes?"

"Yes. Helicopters too. If I were in charge, I'd have eyes in the sky. Even if people are scared of the virus, a sealed jet at twenty thousand feet couldn't catch the bug while taking surveillance and survey pics."

"Hell, military drones could be launched to take photos without anyone getting close to the virus. Don't they want to know what's happening on the ground?" Tanis adds thinking. The two sit in silence for a long time.

"I think we might have to stay here." She sips her tea. "Maybe for a while."

"What do you mean? You don't think they're sending

rescue teams?" What about getting to our families?" Tanis asks.

Hana shrugs. "I have a strong feeling the authorities have evacuated more than just Manhattan. Maybe for hundreds of miles beyond the river. They'd want a good cushion between the infected and the general populations. And what if they didn't stop the virus at all?"

"What do you mean *if* they didn't stop the virus?" Tanis asks, feeling a tingle flood up his spine. She doesn't answer him, and he doesn't repeat the question.

"Yeah, let's stay for a while." Hana decides. "It will be safer with this storm coming. Maybe we can find a radio that works."

Tanis smiles at her, snapping his fingers. "I made a radio with my dad for a merit badge. I don't know if there is everything here to make one like we did, but I think I can rig the one downstairs to work. We'll just have to rip out the fried circuit board."

"Boy Scout, huh?" Hana says. "You get to Eagle?"

Tanis shakes his head. "Not yet. I'm Life. But I still know things." He smiles and struts like a chicken.

"Let's do it. I would absolutely love a radio. Funny how the simple things become so important when…when there's an emergency." Hana barely finishes her sentence. She follows Tanis downstairs.

An old, beat-up, paint-splashed radio rests on the worktable downstairs. Tanis opens the plastic case, pulls the wires from the circuit board, and connects them directly to the diode and the power supply—which will work, thanks to the generator.

With Hana's help, he spends the next two hours remembering how the radio fit together. Finally, static flows through the speakers.

The celebration is snuffed like a candle flame in a

gust.

The gate at the end of the walkway rattles loudly. Somebody, or something, is making the metal clatter. Hana runs to the window, Tanis right behind her.

Five people are trying to get through the gate.

Hana draws her pistol and rests the barrel on the windowsill, watching. "Damn. I was afraid of this. Everything good is everything coveted." She slows her breathing, loosens her shoulders, straightens, and relaxes her back. "This might get ugly. Prepare yourself."

"Don't say that. Lie to me and tell me there are just schoolteachers, grocery store clerks, and crossing guards here to share a roof," Tanis says.

"I wish I could. Unfortunately, anarchy is wind under an asshole's wings."

CHAPTER 1.17

BEN
IN THE BATTER'S BOX

Ben runs longer than he thought possible for his fat ass. His cells burn at every level, and he can't hear anything but blood thumping in his ears. He stops and gasps for breath, hands on his knees, and throws up again. He's never thrown up as much as he has over the past three days. He thinks about how nice it would be to ditch Ian and Markus and go home, stock up on food and water, and find more weed in somebody's drawer. He imagines grabbing as much booze as he can find and fading out until the end of all things.

BEYOND SYMBIOSIS- FOOLS' APOCALYPSE PART 1

Markus and Ian return to Ben from their short lead. Ian reaches for Ben, but he waves Ian off. "I can't run anymore." Ben gasps. "Just can't…do it, dude."

Markus looks around, wheezing like a steam engine. "And on the seventh day, God rested."

They don't get to rest. Some bitch starts yelling from the roof of a six-story building, a kid hanging onto her leg. "Help!" she screams. "Hey, help us!"

Ben watches Ian and Markus run to the building. Ian flings the door open like an idiot. *Stupid do-gooders gonna get killed trying to rescue some dumbass chick and her snot-nosed kid.*

The building is an inferno, smoke pouring from the front door and windows. Ian isn't a fool. He runs back to the middle of the street and yells, "Use the fire escape!" She screams so loudly Ben expects the rest of the windows to shatter.

"I can't!" She screams.

Three dumbass Puppets inhabit the fourth-floor fire escape platform. Some look up at the woman, and some look down, even though they don't have eyes.

"Looks like they don't know how to climb ladders!" Markus calls out.

The Puppets pace back and forth like caged tigers.

"Well, fuck, if she can't fight off a few of those ugly things, she's gonna get everyone killed for sure. Leave them!" Ben yells. "They're goners!"

No one hears him. He watches Ian slip off his huge backpack and dash down the alley. Hero Ian pushes a dumpster under the fire escape and jumps on it like some kind of cat, pulls the ladder down, and climbs to the first platform; Markus is watching–probably praying for a miracle.

Maybe God could turn that Puppet into some weed

so Ben could smoke it. Now, that would be a miracle. Didn't he do that with wine at some point? Ben looks up at the dark clouds. "How 'bout it, God?"

No response.

The glass door across the street, opposite the stranded woman, falls from its hinges and smashes on the stairs. Puppets overflow the steps like a knot of writhing snakes pouring from their den.

Ben counts quickly. *Six Puppets, eight, no, ten.* He sprints to Markus's side. More Puppets appear out of the traffic jam, wobbling like baby birds hatching from the silent vehicles, pursuing him. "Hey, yo, borrow your bat? Hell, I'll even borrow your god for a bit."

Markus opens his eyes and sees the Puppets lumbering toward them, Ben's frightened face. "You need your own weapon, son." Markus points to the alley where the dumpster is. "I saw a two-by-four over there. Make expedient use of that."

Ben runs into the alley, finds and hefts the solid wood, and stands on the sidewalk swinging experimentally like he's in the batter's box.

More stupid Puppets lumber toward them, a crowd building up. "Come on, Ian!" Ben yells. "This shit is gonna go down any second!" Waiting at Markus's side, Ben counts twenty-one ugly bastards now. Two minutes more, they'll be surrounded. Thirty now. More stumble from buildings, alleys, and side streets. He fucking stops counting. "Dude, come on!!"

Ian yells from the fourth-floor fire escape platform. "Heads up!" He heaves a Puppet over the railing to the ground, and it explodes like a water balloon. Black shit goes everywhere.

Some of the crap gets in Ben's mouth! Ben cries, spitting and gagging. Markus is spared and conveniently sheltered by Ben. "You're welcome, dude. Bible seems to be workin' for you, at least."

The last two Puppets don't want to be tossed off the fire escape. Ian struggles and fights, kicks and punches. Finally, another one goes over the rail.

Markus shoves Ben out of the way, shouting, "Our escape route is closing, Ian!"

Ben and Markus back up into the alley

"Really fucking stupid, bro. There's no way out."

Another dumpster and a twenty-foot-tall fence box them in.

The last Puppet falls over the side and crashes to the asphalt, forcing Ben and Markus farther into the alley. The mob stumbling toward them closes off the entrance. "Shit, man. Where do we go?"

Markus and Ben climb onto the dumpster by the fence.

Ben looks up at Ian. Seeing their way out, the woman and the boy stumble down two flights of stairs. Fire erupts from the window facing the fifth-floor stairwell, so the woman and her boy can't climb down to Ian. The window behind them shatters, and black smoke engulfs the two.

"Hurry! Toss the boy to me!" Ian yells. They're only one platform up.

"No!" she screams, choking on the smoke.

"Do it or die!"

The woman dangles the boy over the railing by his hands and lowers him into Ian's arms, climbs over the railing herself, drops onto Ian, and lands on him hard, knocking the wind out of him and the boy both.

The Puppets crowd closer to Ben and Markus, but they hesitate for some reason. Maybe it's the fire inside the ground-floor windows. They don't like fire.

Ian, the boy, and the woman scamper down the fire escape to the bottom like Mario, Luigi, and Toad. Ian lands on the dumpster, takes the kid, and sets him on solid ground. A freakish noise fills the alleyway. Ian turns, looks up, and catches the plump woman when she jumps.

The Puppets must smell prey from such a short distance, close enough to lunge collectively.

Ian, the kid, and the woman evade the fumbling

undead, haul ass to Ben and Markus. "We go over the fence."

Ben figures as much, but there is no alternative.

Ian and Markus boost the kid and the woman over the fence. The kid makes it okay, but the woman bombs the pavement. She screams bloody fucking murder.

The Puppet horde rushes them. Ian grabs Ben's two-by-four and, Markus at his shoulder, bat heads like they're playing croquet or some shit. Ben leaps up the fence like a god-damned teenager running from the coppers and turns to go down the opposite side when he catches a glimpse of the alley. Hundreds of Puppets jam the space between the brick buildings. His heart stops ticking for a moment.

A tall, thin Puppet, moving faster than the others, has his radar —or whatever the hell it is they use instead of eyes—fixed on the survivors. Ben drops to the pavement. Ian and Markus jump down to the safer side of the fence and run to the main street. Ben waits, peering between slats in the fence for one last look down the alley. He expects to see the bastards leap-froggin' over the fence, but they don't know what to do with the dumpster. None of 'em climb on top of it, just pancake into it. *Dumb fucks.* Ben is about to turn and run when he sees that tall, thin one climb onto the dumpster.

The Puppet points his face through a gap in the fence like he's looking with his eyes. *Those fuckin' worms see me, I know it.* The Puppet shrieks and clambers awkwardly over the fence. The others follow: stupid monkey see, monkey do.

Ben runs and catches up to Ian and the others. Puppets pepper this street but haven't coalesced yet, so it's easy to weave around them.

A third-floor window in a building shatters, and a Puppet jumps, trying to land on the survivors. He gets close but misses, his body exploding on impact.

Ben gets soaked again, and Markus remains dry. "Kamikaze bastard!" Ben yells. Then another fucker falls, splashing his guts on the concrete.

Ben slips on blackened blood, rotten and full of mucus. His foot squishes on a string of intestines. He thinks he's going to barf again. *NO!* he orders his stomach. *Stop with this* throwing-up *shit!* More fuckers fall and splatter. One almost hits him, but he dodges it. "Why the fuck are they popping like water balloons? This shit is freaky weird," Ben asks rhetorically. The Puppets seem to have built up pressure inside their bodies.

"How should I know?" Ian snaps.

"They're bloated...but not. Their dead skin and muscles must be weakening with every minute they're dead," Markus says.

The five survivors sprint past an ever-growing crowd of the most fucked-up, sorry sacks of walking corpses anyone has ever seen. Two blocks away, the group slows to a fast walk with the corpses falling behind. Ben is hot and dizzy, and his low tolerance for pain slows him more.

Markus lets the woman hold on to his arm, and she's got the kid's hand. "Are you guys okay?" he asks. What are your names?"

She's plump but has a cute face and brown hair with dyed blonde streaks. Ben looks at her huge boobs and then at her designer nails. *I'd do her.* He stops himself from thinking about sex. Millions of people are dead and walking around with roots in their eye sockets, and he's thinking about banging this chick. He's not surprised at himself.

"My name is Rice," the woman says, out of breath. Everyone is out of breath. "This is Andy, my nephew."

"You guys don't feel sick?" Ian asks.

Rice shakes her head. The boy doesn't speak. His

brown hair is matted with crap, and he's got dark circles under his eyes. "When the news said something in the water was making people sick, I locked us inside my apartment. When they said it was harmless–I don't know–I didn't believe them. I didn't trust the radio reports."

"That was smart," Ian says. "They should have been able to quarantine the city. I've seen the government's contingency plans—the ones that direct the armed forces in case of a biological attack—on the Internet. The first order of business is to blow the bridges and tunnels to isolate the infected. If that fails, they firebomb the infected area. So far, there have been no firebombs, so they must have succeeded in closing a quarantine line. All we have to do is get there, spend some time in isolation, and move on with our lives."

The group continues walking. If Ian is right, Ben will be hitting the drive-thru somewhere soon and finding something to watch on HBO.

Markus nods. "They had plans, but it was for an identifiable viral attack on the city. What they found was some kind of bacteria in the water. Those tap water pipes fed other areas besides Manhattan Island. To control this outbreak, they'd have to seal off a five-hundred-mile area, including parts of Jersey and South Brooklyn."

"And it would have to be done in two days. That's millions of people behind the lines," Ian adds. "Tens of millions."

Markus points to a bunch of Puppets on an intercept course. "We have to run again."

"Shit," Ben says under his breath. Guilt courses through his veins. He remembers being very drunk when he was talking to the lady in red, getting into the Ferrari, and agreeing to put the poison in the tap water. But when he took out his friend Stanford, he was dancing toward sobriety, and nearly so when he poured Zilla's goop into the water tank. He hates thinking about that moment. He hates that he can't forget it all.

They jog at an easy pace, conserving their waning energy. The heat stifles Ben; sweat pours off him like he's taking a shower.

"If they blew all the bridges, we should find a boat," Ian suggests. "Getting off the island should be our top priority."

"Unless those ugly Puppets can swim," Ben mutters, panting.

"I know where we can find a boat," Markus says. "I do a youth retreat at Swindler's Cove every year."

CHAPTER 1.18

MARKUS
SUNNY DAY IN TUNISIA

The flight to Tunisia is short, and the landing is rough. Markus always breathes a sigh of relief when the wheels touch the runway, especially after flying over water. The stewardess hands out pamphlets warning travelers of a taxi scam and points out the toll-free help number. Markus is grateful to know he's not completely on his own.

The international airport is not a place he wants to get lost in; most of the signs are in Arabic and French, and he can't read them. His Tunisian travel book translates most of the signs, and he plans to hire an interpreter. He hears

French mostly, some English, as he bumbles his way out of the bustling airport.

"Oh lord, what am I doing here?" he asks rhetorically. "I'm following sickness. A trail of dysentery. From the dead city of Caesarea to a dead church congregation to the last known resting place of King Louis the Ninth. I'm making so many assumptions." He was making leaps of logic, but logic was not his forte. He was good at following the prompting of the Holy Ghost, who spoke loudly in his gut.

Markus assumed that since Tunisia is just north of the Sahara Desert on the map, it'd be hot and dry, but he feels a cool breeze, inhales ocean air, and beholds a bright blue sky. Seventy-eight degrees flash on a sign at the top of a big building. Lush palm trees, flowers, and rich vegetation are everywhere. He relaxes in the fresh air, eager to continue his grand adventure, grateful God is on his side.

Markus sees a somewhat familiar-looking sign, an arrow pointing to the taxi line. He approaches the nearest cab warily, thinking about the scam. The driver leaps out, runs up to Markus, takes control of his bags, bows elegantly, leads Markus to his old yellow taxi; a make and model Markus hasn't seen before. Rust creeps up the body from the bottom edge, and the tires are worn to the wire.

"Merci? Hello?"

"Hello, sir," Markus responds, taking the bait.

"Where are you going? I take you anywhere. You like ocean? Bar maybe? You play poker?"

Markus hands the driver a note listing the name and address of the hotel, written in French and Arabic.

The driver thumps the trunk lid on Markus's bags and settles into the driver's seat. "Yes, hotel first, okay, no problem."

"Thank you, Lord, for making this traveling abroad thing easy," Markus mumbles as he hops into the old taxi.

The interior smells of incense, and a lavish rug laid on the dash surprises Markus. There are pillows and heavily tinted windows. Comforting. Until the driver starts to drive.

Small cars and motorcycles zip everywhere. The traffic rules are suggestions ignored by most drivers, more than in Italy. Dusty, cracked buildings, tightly packed together, like the old, narrow, but maintained roads. Horns blare, others yell. The taxi driver responds in kind, then flings sharp French insults at others with ease. However, just like in Italy, the serene style, the cohesive architecture, and the flow of people and things impart a feeling of rightness and belonging that makes such bygone cities so beautiful.

Markus's hotel is five stories tall, looks brand new, and has fresh paint, and has lots of decorative lighting. Reflective glass panels arch over a warm lobby cluttered with plants, rainbow-colored lights, suited employees, and a comforting smell. Western popular music videos play on a flat-screen TV.

The bellhop leads Markus to his room and then sets his suitcase on the luggage stand. In poor English, the bellhop tries to explain how to operate the satellite TV, the refrigerator, and the small kitchen sink.

Markus waves him out the door. "This is perfect. Thank you, sir. I got it all. I'll manage with the grace of God."

Later, he heads down to the lobby, smells something so savory he literally follows his nose into the onsite restaurant where he feasts on curried lamb, a tasty yam and red bean stew and thought of nothing else. But it didn't last. As Markus finishes his tea he thinks of the Stone.

"What am I guessing I'll find here, anyhow? Surely, the Stone isn't in some dust mosque. No, what I need is another clue. But first, a drink."

Markus strolls into the bar for a drink when the

stage to the right lights up, and a beautiful olive-skinned woman saunters on stage. She lifts the microphone off the stand as the music begins. She sings in French, playing off the sparse crowd and her keyboardist and bass player. She's mesmerizing but not so much so that Markus is distracted for long.

He waves the barkeep over. "*Monsieur, Je voudrais vodka et tonique veuillez, merci beaucoup.*" His French is probably the worst ever spoken.

The barkeep slides over a wonderfully strong vodka tonic. Markus asks, "You speak English, young man?"

The barkeep nods.

"I would like to learn more about Islam and the history of this area. Where would you suggest I go?" Markus yells over the singing.

The barkeep cleans a glass while he answers in a thick accent, "I'm not Islamic. I'm Catholic."

Markus is taken aback by his answer. "I'm surprised to hear you say that."

"Not everyone here is Muslim. Protestants, Jews, and Catholics live here. We Tunisians are tolerant people, contrary to what the West says."

"I'm sorry for my assumption. I'm a preacher. I'd like to learn about how this area was affected by the Crusades. I'm on a learning expedition."

The barkeep gives Markus a phone number to the local parish. He finishes his drink and listens to a few more songs before deciding to retire for the night. He tips heavily, still feeling embarrassed by his ignorance. Markus prides himself on not being just another ignorant man from the West.

He calls Marian from his room. Immediately, she pleads, "You need to come home, Markus. I miss you. It's not the same. I…I want you with me in our bed."

"I know how you feel, my love. But this is important. I've never done…"

"Yes. You've told me a dozen times," Marian snaps. "You want me to trust you? Give me something. Anything. I need you or a reason to wait for you."

"Please. It's too complicated for a phone conversation. I promise to be in your arms soon."

Marian is trying to talk through tears. "I…I wasn't going to tell you this, but I must. The other night, someone broke into the house. They didn't steal anything, just rifled through our things. They left a card on your desk. It has flames on one side and your name on the other. What does it mean?"

"Oh, dear Lord." *They're harassing my wife. Ramid said her life could be forfeit.* Anger swells inside Markus, and he grinds his teeth. "I'm coming home. My flight is in three days. Until then, stay with your cousin. Don't tell anyone where you're going. Probably good to stay inside, out of sight. You'll be fine. God has a plan for me and for all of us."

"How do I fit into this plan?" Her quivering voice makes him more anxious. She's usually his rock, but she's cracking under the pressure he's created with his quest. He comforts her, saying, "Four days and I'll be home. It'll be okay. I love you."

Marian sniffles. "Okay. I'll go stay with Janet. Call me every day?"

"I will, honey. At our special time. I love you forever." Markus hangs up the phone. *She'll be safe at her cousin's house. Perfectly safe.*

The city lights dot the horizon. A cool breeze flows through open windows. Pacing, he admits that his wife needs him at home, but he also has to know why this God's Stone is worth murder to protect. "Three days is not a long time," Markus tells himself over and over. "Three days, and this ends."

Markus walks out of his hotel the next morning, pleasantly surprised to see the taxi driver from the airport waiting for him. The familiar driver and car are comforting. The driver winds through the old streets to a Catholic church on the outskirts of downtown Tunis, a small building with an ornate front entrance and a tall roof. Otherwise, the old church is unobtrusive and quaint.

Markus is met by the priest. "Hello, my name is Christian. It is nice to make your acquaintance." Christian, a tall, thin, blue-eyed young man. He's tidy, his dark blonde hair trimmed short, his clean, pressed cassock covering him chin to toes.

"Nice to meet you, Christian."

He shakes Markus's hand gently. "So, you here to learn about the Crusades?" His English is surprisingly good.

"I'm interested in the history of King Louis the Ninth." The two move to a desk inside the church office and sit. Papers overflow the desktop; books are stacked along walls bereft of proper shelves.

"Pardon my mess. Our library has a leak in the roof." He sits, the rusted old chair squeaking loudly under his insignificant weight. "I can show you our local records. However, you might have more luck in the Great Library at the Vatican."

Markus holds up his hands to stop him. "I've been there. What I need is local stories, legends, and maybe even rumors. I'd like to see the place King Louis died if that is possible."

Christian thinks for a moment. "His death place is, I'm afraid, lost to history. I do know Louis the Ninth brought his brother Charles of Anjou, King of Sicily, to Tunisia with ten thousand troops. They conquered the country, but King Louis died shortly afterward. The army made peace agreements with payment, left a garrison, and returned home with the king's body." After a short pause, Christian continues. "I have heard one odd story, though."

"Tell me."

"The king supposedly brought a plague with him. Historians believed it was dysentery, but I have been told the disease was new, so virulent the entire inner-city population died. Louis's remaining army declared the city cursed and burned every building to the ground. A mass grave was discovered on the Carthage side of town in 1920, the old villa. It contained as many as six hundred bodies— all burned."

Markus circles the word "burned" in his notebook. So far, two similar outbreaks occurred where the bodies were burned in an effort to control a plague. "Why do you think it wasn't dysentery?"

Christian shakes his head. "The symptoms, vomiting, internal hemorrhage, diarrhea, are similar, but who knows for sure? They had no tests back then. Dysentery takes weeks to move through a population, and many survive. This plague killed everyone in days."

"The deaths all happened in days?"

"Three, to be precise."

"The king had a particular crown," Markus changes the subject. "His brother, Charles of Anjou, took the crown back to his country after Louis's death, incomplete. A precious stone embedded in the crown was missing. This is rumor, of course," he says, trying to pass his suspicion off as confidence.

"I've not heard anything about a stone."

"Well, I believe a stone was blamed for the death of an entire city in northern Israel called Caesarea. The army feared the stone's power, its curse, and left it behind.

Curse notwithstanding, a precious stone large enough to fill the space in the crown on display at Notre Dame de Paris would most likely be stolen, not destroyed."

"I've not heard of this." Christian scribbles a name on a scrap of paper. "Call this Islamic scholar. He has researched the peace treaty signed with Louis the Ninth, his men, and this plague. He may have historical records regarding this cursed stone."

Markus leaves the Catholic Church and asks the driver about the man named Al-Ahem Mohammad Jahar.

The driver praises the scholar, talking eagerly as he drives Markus through the narrow streets to Al-Zaytuna Mosque, the largest one in Tunisia. "I wait for you," the driver says.

"That I can count on. Thank you," Markus says and steps out.

The mosque is beautiful. Dozens of columns line a bright, cobalt-blue, tile-covered prayer yard, overlooked by a tall, square tower decorated with ornate latticework. A single-story building surrounds the sacred space as well as a slightly taller entryway with an onion-top dome shining in the Tunisian sun.

An old man with deep wrinkles that line his sun-worn face meets Markus at the curb. He's wearing a colorful tunic and a long gown as blue as the summer sky.

The old man points out significant parts of the mosque, speaking English. "The columns, all one hundred and sixty, come from the ancient city, and date back to the time of Carthage." His guide's voice is hard, sharp, his words clipped.

"Beautiful," Markus says, growing uneasy. The wind picks up and spins dust in chaotic circles surrounding the two men. Markus's eyes burn. He quickly covers his nose and mouth with his handkerchief and sneezes.

"Al-Zaytuna is a famous university. Many scholars come here," the old man says as they walk past the Carthage columns toward the dome.

A younger man approaches and shakes Markus's hand, ignoring the old guide. "I heard you were on your way," he says, speaking easily. His white skull cap and sky blue-and-gold tunic look more natural on him. "Come this way, please."

The new guide leads Markus to an office and shows him how to wash his feet before he enters. "So, you're interested in the disease that killed King Louis the Ninth?"

"I'm studying the Ninth Crusade and am particularly interested in a crown missing an infamous stone."

The man's smile flatlines. He stares blankly for a moment before he excuses himself. Markus waits and waits. The office is mostly bare save for a single notepad and box on the desktop and a single small bookshelf holding five books. Markus leans in to read the spines. *The Quran* is obvious. Three other titles are written in Arabic on beautifully bound books. The last book looks worn out; the spine creased until the leather is nearly colorless. The faded title, written in French, is readable and says *Meteorology*.

Someone is very interested in rocks from the sky.

The young man returns but stops in the doorway. "I do not have any information about any crown. However, I have heard a story about survivors of the plague escaping to Gabes. That is all I've heard."

The old man bursts into the office, shutting the younger one up with a glance. The old man raises his hand toward the exit.

Markus understands he has clearly outstayed his welcome. He attempts to thank the younger man but is rushed out of the mosque as if he carries a plague.

Markus leaves the courtyard, confused. He squints

through the bright sunlight, looking for the yellow taxi. A dirty white van—the side Markus can see has no insignia, and the windows are covered with metal grating—screeches to a stop in front of him. A man wearing a dark blue uniform, with no patches or pins showing his agency or rank, steps out and walks toward Markus. He isn't alarmed until he sees the man's hard face, clenched fists, and determined body language. *I've not done anything wrong.*

"Excuse me!" the uniformed man says, "American preacher!"

Markus doesn't know whether to run or stand his ground. A woman ducks inside a small market across the suddenly empty street. Another uniformed man hurries forward, something dark in his hands.

The men grab Markus's arms, twist them roughly behind his back, throw a hood over his head, drag, and shove him into the back of the van.

Chapter 1.19

Hana
Holding Swindler's Cove

Hana's sidearm is at the ready, safety off.

Tanis hides behind the door, peering at her.

She peeks through the small glass window centered in the door. Heavy rain cascades down the window steadily, blurring the scene outside.

Five people are trying to kick down the gate she wired shut. Two armed men—one carries a baseball bat, the other a two-by-four—and a stocky woman, a kid, and a skinny guy make five.

"We have a good spot. We can't lose it," Tanis

whispers.

"I know, but we are just me. I can't hold this place against that many. We can share, but only with good people. Hana grips her weapon and thanks god she's armed. "Let's hope the intruders see the boats are gone and move on."

The gate opens. The man with the baseball bat, the other with the two-by-four, the woman, and the kid run down the walkway onto the pier. The skinny guy stays behind and closes the gate. Two-by-four rushes to the door. Hana ducks just as he looks through the window.

"There's a boat inside!" he yells.

This may get ugly. Hana's heart ramps up; she motions Tanis away from the door, mouthing, "Get upstairs!" Tanis disappears up the stairway.

Two sets of double doors open into the boat storehouse. She had already broken the window in the other door so they could get in easily. *Damn! Should've barricaded the doors. What if they're cannibals?* Surprise is her best option: hiding behind a tall storage cabinet, she waits.

The door opens, and the skinny guy tiptoes cautiously inside.

She lunges from her hiding spot and trains her pistol squarely at his chest. He raises his hands and yelps. Hana shushes him and directs him to the corner of the room with the barrel of her pistol. He goes to the corner quickly, his hands still in the air.

Two-by-four enters.

"Drop the wood!" she yells.

He drops the wood fast. "Ahh, I just pissed my pants a little!"

"It's okay!" the first intruder says, his hands still high over his head.

Hana puts her fingers up to her lips, ordering the

two men to be silent. She points her gun at two-by-four and nods toward his friend in the corner. She whispers harshly, "Keep your hands up. Make one sound, and I shoot you in

the leg. You can bleed out for all I care."

Baseball-bat comes through the door, his hands already up, his bat held loosely between his fingers. "I'm no trouble to you. Neither are my companions. We're here for a boat. My name is Markus, and that's Ben, and he's Ian. The woman is Rice, and the boy is Andy. We saved them from a burning building and two hundred or so zombies."

"Thanks, pops," Ben snips. "I also like long walks on the beach and the smell of rain in the summertime."

Hana lowers her gun at the sight of the preacher but doesn't bother pointing it at the woman or the kid. "Take the boat. I patched the hole in it yesterday."

Markus steps toward Hana. She brings her gun back up to his chest just in case he isn't so holy. He raises his hands back up and says calmly, "You're a police officer. I can tell. I'm a preacher. We're good guys, too. Please, lower the gun, and let's talk."

Hana lowers her gun. "Take the boat. There's nothing else for you here. All I ask is that you leave as soon as possible."

Ben drops his hands, "C'mon, lady. There's some crazy shit out there."

"You're not safe here. No one is," Ian says.

"He's right. Have you seen what's going on?" Markus asks.

"Obviously not!" Ben interjects. "She looks kinda messed up, but if she'd fought those Puppets, she'd be freaked like we are."

"Listen, the dead are getting up and attacking survivors." Ian takes off his pack and leans against the wall. "I don't know how it's happening or why, but it is. We fought hundreds of them. They don't die."

"What the hell are you talking about?" Hana snaps. "Who won't die? The dead?"

Ben steps toward her and stops as she tenses. "Listen, lady. Every dead body that dies gets up and walks around. Zombies!" He grabs his shirt front and holds it out toward her. "See this black crap? This ain't paint, lady. It's their blood."

"It looks like the virus took their bodies over. The victims of the virus now have black blood and white root-like things are growing in their bodies, replacing their eyes," Ian clarifies Ben's rant.

"It's all true," Rice adds, her voice shaky and weak. "They're everywhere."

Markus looks out the window. "They're followin'

us," Markus says, then adds, "Oh no. We have more company."

Hana returns to the door and peeks through the window. A woman with dark hair cut in a bob and two long guns draped over her shoulder is trying to break down the gate. Next to her, a thin white man wearing a medical mask, holding some kind of weapon, looks around nervously. The woman jerks the shotgun off her shoulder, bashes the latch off with the butt, and pushes the gate hard; it swings open wildly. "Do you know her?" Hana asks.

"No," replies Markus.

Hana moves away from the door. "Let her come in just like I let you. Everyone get in the corner."

Tanis runs down the stairs, panic all over his face. "There are two more coming down the gate. The girl's armed: shotgun, two pistols, and an M-16A4, standard issue army reserve assault rifle. The dude she's with has a chainsaw."

"Thanks, Tanis. I'd find that hiding spot again," Hana urges, looking out the window to confirm his report. "Take Andy with you."

Tanis leads Andy upstairs.

Hana studies the woman's movements. "She's not army reserve, though," he says over his shoulder.

"Kid knows his weapons," Ben comments.

"Yeah, he does." Hana answers.

Ian peeks out the window of the opposite door. "Definitely not reserve." The armed woman does exactly as Hana and Ian did—tries to lock the gate after forcing \it open. Now, the latch is broken, too, so she can only tie the gate shut with the wire.

"Let's avoid a gunfight. She looks okay to me," Ian says.

"Thinking like that can get us killed," Hana

mumbles.

The woman and man come toward the boathouse, wary, watching. The woman docks her weapon in her shoulder, stares down the sight.

She drops to one knee and scans the area slowly, her eyes hunting left to right. "Definitely military training, though," Hana adds.

The new woman looks across the river, maybe seeing the boats on the other side, stands and jogs toward the building. Veering away at the last moment, turning, hiding along the east boathouse wall.

Hana guesses the woman saw the broken window. The man stays right behind her, holding his chainsaw blade down by his leg, which is stupid. Plus, the thing is small and electric. He'll run out of juice soon.

Another double door is toward the back, presumably for launching and loading boats, but no one can get to it without going past the front doors.

Hana doesn't want a standoff and definitely doesn't want to shoot the woman. She's had to kill before, and it never leaves you. It changed her DNA somehow, altered her dreams, and aged her.

Ian yells as loud as he can, "Don't shoot!"

"Then start throwing weapons out that door!" the woman replies.

"We're wasting time. The Puppets are coming! We don't mean any harm," Markus yells. "I give you my word!"

"My name is Hana! What's yours?" Hana adds, thinking this is a better strategy than having a shoot-out.

"I just want a boat!" the woman yells back. "And I won't take no for an answer!" She fires a round into the air. "I've got sixty rounds here, and I know you don't have that much."

"This is so stupid," Ian hisses. "Can't we all use the boat together?"

"That would be wise!" Markus says. "Please, lower your weapon and come in. Plenty of room. It's a big boat, thank the Lord! Help us get the boat in the water!"

The gate rattles as people crowd it.

"They're here!" Ben yells. He runs to the boat.

"Come on! They're slow as shit but faster than you think."

"Ben is right." Markus joins him near the upside-down boat.

"Who's at the gate? You know them?" Hana asks.

"No time to explain now. We get in the boat, or we get swarmed, and we die," Ian yells.

Hana peeks through the broken window and sees the growing crowd. "Fine." Hana runs to the boat and helps flip it over, surprised at the weight. Had she and Tanis tried to lift it alone, it would have been very difficult. Hana counts the seats. It's big enough to hold everyone, barely. The boat slips into grooves on the floor. The grooves lead to the side door, which Ben opens.

"PUSH!" Markus yells.

Everyone slides the boat on its belly until it splashes into the water. Ian holds the line tied to the boat, preventing it from floating away. He steps out of the boathouse and into the line of fire.

The dark-haired woman runs up to him. When he doesn't move or raise his hands, she lowers her rifle. "Fine, we all use it. I'm Isabella, and this is Josh."

Tanis runs down the stairs, Andy following. Hana runs to the boys. "We have to go. It's not safe here."

Tanis points to the end of the walkway. "There are more people."

"Those aren't survivors," Ian says as he tosses his backpack into the boat. Isabella stows her weapons and her pack in the bow.

The gate rattles as more and more people arrive and shove on it.

"They can't get through," Ben says, watching carefully. "They're stupid as shit."

The gate is about fifteen feet tall, the bars made to look like boat oars, with solid metal arches on either side of the walkway. A long, heavy-looking sign hangs across the archway above the gate. The whole contraption looks impregnable.

"I had to bust the lock when we got here," Hana confesses.

"And I didn't have anything to reinforce it with, so it's weak. Put enough pressure on it, and it'll fly open," Isabella says.

The people surge against the gate until the wire tying it shut snaps. The gate swings open, and hundreds storm through.

Ben gets in the boat first and helps Markus onto a seat. Ian and Rice board next.

"I just want to stay here until we're rescued," Tanis complains.

"I know, but I don't think we can. We'll be sitting ducks. People who group up and form gangs can't be reasoned with. You know those guys we dealt with earlier?"

Tanis nods.

"That times hundreds. We can't win that fight. Trust me," Hana explains, holding Tanis by the shoulders. "We have to get across the river. There's probably a containment line—we get there, we're safe. Then we can find our families."

Eager, driven people push through the gate. Some drop off the walkway edge into the water, others more slowly but purposefully, like drunks trying not to stagger. More and more come until the entrance is packed, and the mob fills the parking lot and beyond.

"Hurry! In the boat, y'all, or lose your balls!" Ben cries.

Hana helps Josh, Tanis, and Andy aboard and hops in herself.

"Thank you," Josh says from behind his hospital mask. "For sharing your boat."

Hana nods and passes Ian and Isabella oars, keeping one for herself. Together they row the boat out of the dock area and into the river. The people mass on the dock and many, though struggling, find their way to the boathouse.

"Why are they like that?" Tanis asks. "What's going on?"

"They're zombies, dude," Ben says. "Better come to fuckin' terms with the fact that they seem to want to eat our brains."

Hana looks at Ben and frowns. "Let's not be too

dramatic and scare the boy. They're just a mob of vandals and drunks pillaging and stealing."

Ben tries to stand, rocks the boat, then sits. "Shit, lady. I'm not being dramatic. No reason to sugarcoat this crap. They're dead. All of them. Look at their fucking faces. We're all havin' nightmares tonight."

Hana looks away because Ben's glib, in-your-face remarks are making her mad. The only way he's coping is by being drunk. She can smell whiskey on his breath.

The attackers stop at the dock's edge.

"They aren't jumping into the water, which means they have *some* brains," Ian says.

"Maybe there's some human left in them," Markus wonders. "Maybe the people are trapped inside their own bodies, fighting the things taking over."

"You're all serious, aren't you?" Hana asks.

Ian turns to Hana, "It's true, they are walking dead people. But we call them Puppets. There are white roots crawling inside their bodies and heads, coming out of their eye sockets. The dead won't stop, and they don't have pain. Can't talk. It's…it's no good. We had to beat them into the pavement to get past them."

Isabella chimes in, "I've put rounds in their heads, and they keep comin'."

"You can expect me to believe that?" Hana can't understand anything she's hearing.

Isabella pulls up her rifle, flips off the safety, aims…

"You can't be serious!' Hana snaps. She draws her pistol, training it on Isabella. "Put the rifle down. I'm NYPD. You are going to listen to me. Those are people and–"

POW.

Isabella's one round hits the head of the closest person on the dock. Half of the head explodes, sending brain and blood into the face of someone else.

Hana gasps. She could've pulled the trigger on Isabella or, at the very least, ordered her to lower her weapon. But Hana says nothing. She looks past Isabella to the dock, shaking.

"Check it out, copper. You see that? You fucking see that shit?" Isabella says. "That look like a looter to you?"

The person is still standing, pacing the edge of the dock, a large white worm hanging out of the head wound like the brain had simply unraveled, which is impossible.

"I...uh." Hana gasps. "What is happening?"

Ian gently pushes Hana's gun down. "We're telling you the truth. All of us. They can't be killed. All that's left is for us to get out of here as fast as we can."

"Like we said,' Ben says. "The white things are their leaders now. Controlling the dead. That's why we call them Puppets. Got it?"

Hana nods and re-holsters her sidearm.

It starts raining harder, soaking everyone. Tanis's hair is plastered to his forehead, making him look about ten, and his eyes betray his fear. He's just a boy, someone's baby. Hana puts her arm around him. Hugs him. "Things just got a whole lot worse for us. I'm sorry."

"I...I want to go home," Tanis mumbles.

"I know. We'll try, okay? I'll do everything I can to get you there."

The boat nears the opposite shoreline when Rice screams, "There are more on this side!"

Heads pop up from behind the trees and bushes at the edge of Roberto Clemente State Park.

"Damn, damn, damn!" Ben yells as he rocks the boat heavily.

"Sit the fuck down!" Isabella snaps. "Back up! Row. Harder!"

"Christ be with us! There are too many to land here."

Markus presses his forehead to his Bible.

Ian pulls hard on the oars, so does Hana, Isabella, and Ben. The boat swiftly pulls back into the middle if the river.

"Let's find a different place to dock," Hana reasons. "There has to be a safe place."

The boat turns as they row. The progress is slow as they try to head into the current.

Ian is breathing hard. "We're fighting the water. We'll never get anywhere like this."

"The East River rises with the tides, but somehow the Harlem River—this river— mostly runs north to the Hudson," Josh says through his mask.

"I can swim faster than this," Ben whines.

"No, you can't," Isabella retorts. "Now, if you don't be quiet, you might get the chance to see how fast you swim."

Ben stands, red, flushing his cheeks. He looks like he might snap. Well, he looks like he's ready to snap at all times, but now he's closer.

Hana stops rowing. "Relax. Please," she pleads. "No one can swim in this current for very long. We don't have life vests."

Ben sits back down.

Infected people stumble down the rocks, oblivious to the branches and old fishing string and mud they're collecting as they wade into the water from both shores. These Puppets are more desperate than the ones at the boathouse, but none can swim. When the water is over their heads, they don't come back up.

"Dock over there," Markus announces, pointing to a rocky point on the shore where there are no Puppets in sight. Ian, Isabella, and Hana drive hard on the oars and angle the boat toward the open spot until a Puppet stumbles out from the bushes and throws itself at them. More gather and rush toward the water, an avalanche of gnashing teeth, worm-filled eye sockets, and desperately grasping hands.

"They're all blind? But they know where we are. How can they sense us?" Hana asks. She quickly counts twenty.

"Good question for which not one of us knows the answer," Ian says.

"God knows, but his plans are a mystery to me at the moment," Markus replies.

"Maybe we could fight off a dozen, but there are more creeping out of the bushes. My count jumps to fifty, at least. More are coming." Hana swallows hard. Her denial hovers at the edge of her thoughts but is quickly fading into sheer panic. *Keep your head,* she tells herself over and over.

"Back, back, back!" Ben yells. "Fuckin' back to the middle of the river!"

Their escape-across-the-river plan has failed, and they're floating slowly enough for the Puppets to keep up. Soon, thousands of them will be along the shores, trapping the band of survivors on the water in a rowboat without food or drinking water. Even after they row back to the center where the current is the strongest, they aren't going fast enough.

The boat is a tight fit, and Hana wants off. She's already on the edge of losing her composure when she hears Rice sobbing. They should've stayed at the boathouse, barricaded the doors and windows, and taken a stand. Now they're absolutely screwed unless the river takes them somewhere safe.

Hana looks at Ian. His face is tight, angry. She knows what he's thinking because she's thinking it, too. The virus is beyond Manhattan Island and is assaulting mainland United States.

CHAPTER 1.20

MARKUS
ESCAPE FROM HEATHENS

Markus awakes when someone rips the hood off his head. The room spins and swells as if time and space are expanding in front of his eyes. He can feel his brain trying to make sense of his situation, but his neurons are slow as molasses. When his vision clears, he sees he's in a shack—dirt floors, a curtain over the door, walls, and ceiling made of corrugated metal. Sunlight shines through cracks and imperfections in the panel arrangement, illuminating the dust hanging in the air.

His captors must've taken his jacket, pants, and shoes, but he's still wearing his t-shirt and shorts. His mouth is dry, and his head throbs like he's been drugged.

A man wearing a Tunis police uniform steps next to Markus and slaps him across the face. Stinging pain shoots throughout his skull, and the room starts spinning again. He's hit again from the other side. Nerves in his face start thumping and burning like his skin is on fire. He closes his eyes, bracing himself for the next blow. It doesn't come.

The man stands a few feet away, hand resting on the butt of his holstered pistol.

"You have been nosy in our country," the man says, his thick Middle Eastern accent harsh. He pushes the light so it swings like a pendulum. The shadow of the man moves with the light—back and forth, back and forth.

"I'm sorry," Markus says, the movement making

him ill. His voice sounds deep and hollow. This time, the blow is to his jaw. The sickening taste of salty blood coats his tongue and slides down his throat.

"Now, now, Mr. Markus Coburn."

"What do you want from me? I'm just a preacher. Born in Alabama. Son of a farmer who was the son of a slave. Been righteous in the eyes of God. I mean you no harm, brother."

The man lifts a hammer off a nearby table and places the end on Markus's knee. Another man behind him holds the chair. "You choose to answer my question with a lie, I shatter your knee. At your age, this will put you in walker for life."

Markus shakes violently. The room shrinks as pressure grows in his chest. He fears his heart will give out. "Whatever. . . whatever you want."

"Why you ask about Stone of Allah?"

"I...I'm studying the Crusades. The ninth one," Markus says, stammering. "I don't know anything about any Stone of Allah."

"The Catholic Church has all you need in their archives, but you come to Tunisia for research? Why you ask Christian about the sickness King Louis die from?"

"I...I wanted to know about the plague that hit Tunis and Caesarea," Markus says. "It seemed like a similar event. And I heard about a meteor that killed John the Mighty."

"Now we getting to truth," the man says. He walks to the man behind Markus, and they confer in Arabic. He comes back, striding casually, as though he is enjoying himself. "Tell me what you know about *Mehdi*."

"I don't know anything. I've never heard that word before."

WHAM!

Markus screams, thinking the hammer has been

brought down on his knee. The two men look to the door as an explosion goes off outside the shack. Gunfire follows. One entire wall rips outward, letting the bright sunlight in. Drawing their weapons, the two men run to the collapsed wall but too slowly. Shots ring out, and Markus's captors fall. Markus can barely see through the dust cloud, but a figure rushes in and frees his hands.

"Can you run?" a man asks in English.

"N– no," Markus answers, his throat dry and his voice barely audible. The man picks Markus up, drapes him over his shoulder, and hauls him away.

Gunfire goes off all around the fleeing men.

Markus is thrown into the back of a Jeep, hitting his head on the floor, then against the back as the Jeep takes off.

"Turn!" yells an American riding in the passenger seat.

Just as Markus manages to sit up, an explosion goes off in front of the vehicle. His vision goes white, and he feels the Jeep turn over on its roll cage. He tries to hold on, but he's tossed away.

Markus opens his eyes, sees a blue sky for an instant, lands hard in water, and swallows a mouthful as he descends into the brown stream. His panic eases when his feet touch the sandy bottom, and he pushes off. Thank God the river is shallow.

Markus climbs out of the water and glimpses three smoke stacks reaching high into the sky, spewing clouds of white smoke into the noonday sun. Someone he doesn't recognize is approaching, shouting, so Markus runs to a nearby building. The door is locked, too sturdy to break down barefoot. He looks around frantically and runs across a small parking lot into an ancient neighborhood of rows and rows of mud huts. Ancient, and a slum. A dog snarls, and a woman retreats into her home.

Markus can hardly run anymore. Pain spears his brain, emanating from his ears and eyes. He ducks into a hut and sees a back door opening onto a small courtyard. Markus runs through the courtyard, kicks over a bucket of water, snags clean laundry hung on a cord, and rips it down.

Another house opens on the back of the courtyard, and Markus runs into it. Still trying to untangle himself from the laundry, he wonders how close his pursuer is. The door closes behind him.

"Stop! We need to be quiet," the American hisses.

Markus stops and turns. The bearded, blue-eyed man bracing the door wears a white head wrap, ragged t-shirt, and jeans. His eyes are kind, and Markus feels at ease, the Holy Spirit telling him to trust his rescuer. The man looks out the crack between the mud hut and the wood door poorly hung on its frame.

"I don't think they saw where we went," he whispers. "We have a few minutes before we have to find somewhere safer."

"Who are you?" Markus asks, his chest heaving.

"Call me Mitchell. I'm with the CIA."

"What on God's green Earth led you to me?" Markus sits on the floor, the world spinning around and around.

"What matters is that you're safe. They were going to kill you, you know," Mitchell says softly. "They don't want anyone poking around, asking the questions you did."

"About the Stone of Allah?"

"Yeah. Whatever that stone is, it's being protected by Saudi Arabian money and some hard-core believers. They don't want any non-believers—meaning anybody but a very tight inner circle—to know it ever existed." Mitchell reaches behind his back, brings a pistol out, opens it by sliding the top back, and cleans the dust off the sides. "We've been trying to find out what's so special about that stone for years."

"It's a religious artifact. A treasure to them."

Mitchell rolls his eyes. "Right. But the part that confuses me is that the stone should be a bad omen. The entire population of an Arab-controlled city died after John the Mighty was struck, somehow ended up on an invader's crown, and another plague followed."

"Caesarea and Tunisia."

"You've been doing your research."

"I thought I was the only one."

"Good one. You're the only one smart enough to end up in Tunisia," Mitchell says sarcastically. He grabs Markus's arm and pulls him off the floor. "Time to go."

They run as fast as Markus's old bones can go down a narrow alley between mud huts bare inches taller than Markus. They pass a skinny, beaten-looking dog that doesn't even bark down another alley to the next cluster of homes in an abandoned-looking neighborhood, the glassless windows opening onto empty, dark spaces.

"Where is everyone?" Markus asks, panting for breath.

"Prayers. We need to find a hideout until nightfall."

They duck inside a small tin hut without a front door, clothing, cookware, or other personal items. The wall framing is rotten, eaten through by termites; the roof sags in the corner. The back door is weathered, with split wood hanging from rusted hinges.

Markus didn't notice at the time, but his CIA friend must have snatched some fabric from a hut they'd passed. "There," Mitchell says, fastening the drapery in the doorway, "That should hide us. If they find us, we go out the back door to somewhere else." He removes his white head wrap and uses his sleeve to mop the sweat off his head.

Markus is exhausted. "God, let us not be found." If they are, he will reassess the situation concerning God's master plan for him.

Voices, many voices, erase the silence. Markus sits in the corner and prays. No one comes. The residents seem to think everything is normal. Night arrives, and some of the heat drains out of the shack. Markus sleeps on the dirt floor, still sweating, while Mitchell keeps watch.

They should leave during the late hour, but it's

obvious they can't risk it. They sit in absolute darkness, unable to sleep, focusing on the small sounds of the night.

"Why can't the CIA get us out of here?" Markus asks, wiping sweat off his brow despite the cool night outside.

Mitchell sighs. "My resources are playing it safe, not wanting to alert the Tunisians of our presence." He shifts to lying on his back in the dirt. "I was ordered not to save you. My handler said you got yourself in this; you gotta get out. I don't know why, but I felt obligated to pull your ass out of the fire."

"Well, God bless your soul." Markus huffs. "I thought my government would spend a little more effort for a citizen in harm's way."

"Not these days. Tunisia is a tricky mistress. With so many Arab states on the edge of failure, and the political turmoil in the states, the CIA is keeping hands off. My partner and I were only reconnaissance."

"I'm sorry for your loss."

Mitchell doesn't respond. Finally, he says. "We're on our own. If we're caught, it's a firing squad for you and me, but only after they make us bleed from every conceivable pore. Do you understand the mess we're in?"

"I do."

Night after night passes. Markus never leaves. Mitchell steals food and clothing during prayers and snoops around at night. He leaves again at three o'clock in the morning and returns in good spirits hours later.

"Eight roads lead out of Tunis, guarded by about five hundred soldiers, a handful of A1-Abrams tanks, and a small helicopter field. It's busy out there. A temporary command unit patrols the roads, and there are lots of cameras."

That sounded bad to Markus. "How do they have American tanks?"

"The U.S. sold Saudi Arabia hundreds of tanks in an arms deal that kept the king on our side during the Middle East peace talks."

Markus huffs. "We prop up a country opposed to our Christian values and way of life. Seems kind of odd to me." He pauses, eyes thoughtful, troubled. "I guess it's true. The enemy of my enemy is my friend. Until they aren't."

"That's the way all governments work. The world is not black and white."

The next night, Mitchell goes out late again and returns at dawn with blood all over his arms and shirt. He doesn't say why, and Markus doesn't ask.

Markus is anxious, bored, and hates the sweltering heat inside the hut. He prays for patience but wants God to give it to him now. He recites his scriptures and thinks of Marian. His body lets him sleep—a lot—which he's glad for because when he's awake, he feels like he's going to crawl out of his head.

It's late; he's hot and sweaty and sour-smelling, and he hates waiting in the pitch-black night hours when he feels as if he's on death row, waiting for Satan to negotiate his fate. Markus paces, wondering if he's misunderstood what God wants him to do. Mitchell told him a dozen times to stay hydrated in the heat, so he drinks, eventually running out of water.

Later, he's tired and starts to wonder about the CIA man. Mitchell's comings and goings without explanations trouble Markus. The blood troubles Markus, too. *If he's CIA, why are we still hiding in this awful place?*

Markus lets his mind drift, not liking that his thoughts are taking him away from his trust in God. A crack in the far wall draws his attention. Markus crawls closer and studies how the crack in the mud brick wall separates into two long, thin lines barely wide enough to let in the nearby street light. The tiny lines spread around a rough oval before coming together again, the bright edges framing dark smudges. It looks like the face of Christ! Markus stares. *He's there! Smiling at me.* The more he looks, the more he sees the Savior's eyes, reassuring the preacher that he is still in God's favor. Markus rises to his knees and cries.

An hour later, Mitchell returns, impressing Markus again with his quiet entrance. "Hey," Mitchell whispers.

"Uh." Markus keeps the image of Christ to himself.

"Tomorrow night, we go."

"Now, why is that?" Markus sits on a blanket, rubbing his sore lower back. His fingers ball up bits of grime from his skin. He's never been so dirty.

Mitchell tosses a small loaf of olive oil bread in Markus's lap and slips into his makeshift bed of stolen blankets. Markus tears into the food. The bread here is the best he's ever had. Or maybe it's just that he's a starved old man.

Mitchell starts talking while Markus stuffs his face like a schoolboy after a fast. "I've been monitoring the troop movements. Tomorrow, a top scholar is giving an important speech at a big celebration at the outdoor stadium south of here. The troops will be re-stationed temporarily for the celebration, maybe six hours at the very longest. This leaves maybe five to eight troops covering the Ali Ben Abid Mosque and maybe a single unit covering the south road."

"Oh, Lord. Five to eight is no big deal. Just five to eight," Markus mumbles with his mouth full. He lies back down. Hunger satisfied, his body instantly relaxes. He's certain his fate is in God's hands.

"You know," Mitchell says, "I heard one of them talking about a big secret in the local mosque. The guy said he's normally stationed at the Ali Ben Abid Mosque protecting Allah's biggest secret, which I believe has something to do with the meteor that killed John the Mighty."

"I'm glad you can understand them," Markus says.

"You know we're in Medenine, right?"

"As you've told me."

"It's considered a holy city, has been for centuries. Its historic nature is the official reason there's so much Saudi money here. But there's also nearby oil wells, too. I'm one of the minority researchers who think the mosque is holding a dark secret, the Stone of Allah. After President Trump increased the CIA budget for Middle East affairs, I was given permission to try and get inside that mosque without causing an international incident. I've not found a way inside until now. I can't exactly say that the people interested in keeping the stone secret are a cult, but we do know that anyone who showed an interest in it has publicly disappeared. We have also linked murders to the group and old money. We can't investigate the deaths and disappearances officially, but as I said, you were in way over your head and in danger of being murdered or disappearing for good, too." Mitchell shrugs. "I guess I was impressed that a preacher got this far."

"I'm glad to see Big Brother is watching."

"Ha. If only you knew. I've studied Tunisia for the CIA for years. You found your way here pretty damn fast. You've got good instincts." Mitchell fluffs his stolen pillow and settles in. "A huge secret is kept here, and we want to find it."

"Your partner in the Jeep? I'm responsible for his death." Markus says solemnly, clasping his hands together and whispering a prayer.

"Yes." Mitchell pats Markus on the shoulder. "He was the fanatic. He knew we were finally getting close and was all in to save you. He wanted to know what you knew and was itching to go in blazing."

Markus's doubts return. Mitchell doesn't sound very upset at the loss of his partner.

"After all these years of looking, why do you see an opportunity now?"

"Something's changing. I've never heard anyone talking about the importance of the mosque until lately, saying it holds Allah's biggest secret. I think it's the reason for doubling the garrison. More and more people are being made privy to the secret, increasing the odds of it getting out."

"Naturally." Markus scratches his beard.

"I'm so close now. Closer than ever." Mitchell's brow tightens, but his eyes are radiant.

"This all sounds like a job you can return to after getting me home to my church and my foam mattress." Markus is tired of not being with Marian, sick of looking at the inside of this hot earthen box all the time, worrying when he hears voices or someone passes the front door.

"You lost your curiosity, huh?" Mitchell asks.

Markus has contemplated his quest for days and considers what to say to Mitchell. Markus's time in the hut has been a type of fast, fasting from modern comforts and food safety. But he's come closer to God here, seeing his Savior's face in the cracks and smudges on the wall. God brought him to Tunis, the fire of discovery smoldering in his belly. Markus had wavered, doubted, but knowing God had brought His preacher here to this place and put him with Mitchell, a CIA man with the same quest, stoked the smoldering coals to flame. Markus's desire to find the Stone of Allah and understand why a secret war is being fought over it is stronger than ever. He smiles at Mitchell. "Are you planning on stopping by this mosque before we leave town? Can we do it and not get killed?"

"Hell yeah! They don't even know we're here anymore. They think we left town." Mitchell has a smile on his face.

"Allah's biggest secret, and they keep it in a dusty mosque? Why not keep the thing in Mecca or Cairo or something? I don't quite understand."

"The mosque is heavily fortified. Plus, these people, whoever they are, don't keep Allah's biggest secret in a museum. They're hiding it for some reason."

"Then how do you plan on getting in there? Stroll on up and say, hi?" Markus feels like staying put until the job is done. He's pretty sure the Lord does not want him shot at anymore.

"I have intimate knowledge of the mosque," Mitchell answers.

"How did you come by this 'intimate knowledge' you speak of? Enlighten an old man, please?"

Mitchell clearly doesn't want to explain but does. "The French manufacturer of the vault at Ali Ben Abid Mosque sold the CIA all their product schematics, codes, and keys in order to survive the recession of 2009. Cost us half a billion dollars. I've studied satellite images of the area and know exactly how to get in, so this should be a breeze. Trust me. I'm the one who saved your butt—so you have to trust me."

"I don't feel saved yet!" Markus says, only half-kidding. He basks in the duality of the moment, angel on one shoulder, devil on the other. He's at the crossroads. *Will I die in a puddle of sweat and blood? Or will I find salvation? Even as blind as I can be, I march on down the foggy road. Is the future unwritten? Selfish? Or am I just the tool of the All-knowing Light that is God?*

CHAPTER 1.21

IAN

THE POLITICAL VOICE

Ian orders everyone to shuffle spots in the boat. "We've got to make room for rowing. I know it's tight. The faster we row, the better odds we get somewhere safe." The boat rocks as they play musical seats. He tries to relax when everyone is settled, and the packs and weapons are stored properly. The dark gray clouds turn black as the sun sets, and the darkness swarms around them.

Ian outlines their situation in his mind. Puppets taunt the refugees from both shores, the cliffs above the shoreline. Their yowls and screeches echo in the canyon, and their hollow, shrill voices bounce off the water and leap around the little boat. The unnerving sounds grate like microphone feedback.

Ian remembers a light in his pack that doubles as a lantern. He wraps the flashlight's strap on the end of Isabella's staff and tightens it with the clip.

When he turns on the flashlight, the darkness leaps away, and the bright beam makes everything else seem darker. None of the boat's occupants can see anything beyond the cone of light but can hear movement on the shores.

Ian rows because he needs something to do. The oar drags through the water, forcing his muscles to remain awake and help him relax. The oar becomes an extension of himself, one he won't part with for anything, no matter how tired he gets.

"Where's the containment line?" Rice asks, feebly.

"There ain't one," Isabella snaps.

"Now, we don't know that," Markus says. "It simply might be more inland."

"How are we gonna get off this river?" asks Tanis. "This shit sucks."

Ian glances at Hana and senses her hesitation. She doesn't know what to tell the boy, so he speaks for her. "We row until we find somewhere safe. Maybe the Jersey side. Maybe farther south." Ian issues orders naturally, as he did for years until Zilla started telling Ian what to do. He reflects on his life…

###

After Ian's mother died, he'd sought out some questionable like-minded activists. His mother tried to change the government from entering the front door; Ian was going to enter the back.

One night, his newfound buddy Reese and five other guys set out to do some "guerrilla protesting" to embarrass a law office that protected crooked CEOs.

Ian and his friends put on black suits and went to Club Tangle, next to the Law Offices of Sim and Mayers, who defended corporations, enabling them to oppress and betray workers.

Ian and his compatriots whispered to club guests that something big was going to happen next door at the law offices. People believed the rumor and followed the carrot into the street like sheep. Tweets and blogs passed around like a blazing joint, and the crowd doubled and then tripled, clogging traffic.

Ian sneaked away from the growing crowd, slipping on his black ski mask and leather gloves. He retrieved a backpack he had hidden behind a dumpster. He handed a rolled banner to each of his guys and led them down the alley into the underground parking lot. He pointed to the security cameras, and the group raised paintball guns, peppering the lenses with bright orange paint. One guy went into the front lobby to distract the guards.

Reese, jack-of-all-trades, picked the lock to the lower security elevator door using a cloned ID card. The group rode the elevator in silence, listening to the hum of the motors and pulleys.

The team planned to be in and out in ten minutes.

When the elevator stopped on the third floor, they ran to their assigned windows. Ian opened the one facing the street in the corner office, attached the top of the roll to the outer windowsill with duct tape, and kept the banner rolled tight with heavy clips. Making their statement was more complicated than simply showing people proof. The proof, in unmistakable form, had to be unveiled.

Ian tied the end of a two-hundred-foot spool of string through a grommet in the edge of his banner, secured it, hurried from window to window, connecting the string to each banner, and lowered the spool out the last window to the street. He was very careful not to let the string slip and unveil the banners too early.

Time was up. Ian could see police lights reflect and dance on the windows from the street below. The cops were early. Ian and the others hit the stairwell and ran down the steps to the street-level emergency exit. Ian bashed through the door like a sledgehammer. The alarm rang, but they'd done their jobs. The crowd successfully blocked the alley, and the activists simply separated and joined the mob.

Ian pushed his way to the front, where the police were holding the line. Somebody handed Ian a bullhorn. He pressed his back to the barricade and spoke clearly and forcefully. "Rooting out corrupt bastards means we have to follow the money!" His amplified voice, calm and authoritative, quieted the crowd.

"We see wrongs happening, and we see evil shit. Today we're highlighting the very law offices that keep corrupt men from going to jail!" Hands went up in the crowd, and glowing cell phone screens lit the night, cameras rolling. Ian and his friends ducked under the barricades, slipped past the cops, ran up the steps of the building and turned. Ian spoke into the bullhorn again: "Today, we show you what the media is too lazy or corrupt to tell you! We advocate for the Forgotten Man!" The crowd surged, forcing the cops to remain at the barricades.

Ian ignored the cops, who were yelling, "Get away from the building!" Police back-up would arrive in minutes.

Ian snatched the spool of string he'd lowered from the window and pulled. Banners unfurled from each window. They were images of everyday people. "FIRED" was written across photos of people with blacked-out eyes, and their "offenses" were listed: "Being gay," "Being a Democrat," "Being overweight," "Missing work caring for a sick child," "Being pregnant." Ian pointed to the posters, "Each of these people took their cases to court, and each case was thrown out by corrupt judges these guys paid off. The lawyers who work in this very building!" The crowd, angry and excited, booed.

Ian reveled in seeing their eyes reflecting their humanity, their desire to be right and feel a true sense of morality as strong as their beating hearts.

"But the government makes the laws!" yells a man in the crowd. "Isn't government responsible, too? How do you fix that by giving politicians more power?"

Ian didn't know how to answer the question. Even if the government was part of the problem, it had to be the solution, right? First, he was going to help tear down the system. Next, he was going to let others, those he trusted and respected, rebuild it.

Ian threw the remainder of the pamphlets into the air and ran. The propaganda confetti fluttered into the air, and the crowd exploded, dispersing from the cops like a flood, carrying Ian's message in their minds and hands.

Ian and his friends took those cops on a wild chase that night. He felt bulletproof, strong as titanium. He never forgot that night.

Eventually, he was arrested, along with fifty others.

Unfortunately, Ian's dad didn't let him spend the night in jail. Afraid of the negative publicity his company might reap in the press, he bailed Ian out and covered up his involvement. Ian hadn't spoken to him since, other than occasional texts and a brief visit at Thanksgiving.

Ian's organization grew after proving they could get shit done—The Red Stars, they called themselves. He attracted over fifty thousand people to march on Wall Street to protest banking corruption and the system itself. The core group camped out for days, and hundreds of supporters followed. One week turned into five, and fifty thousand turned into half a million across the U. S. Ian felt like a god, like he could do no wrong. The energy flowing through his thoughts kept him up at night, walking the streets, filling book after book with thoughts, opinions, and articles. Everyone knew Ian Gladstone's name, whether they hated him or loved him.

The night it all fell apart, Ian was halfway through a fifth of vodka, drinking and toasting their success, still faithfully camped on the National Mall.

The protest got a lot of attention at first, making people think critically and deeply before the media stepped in, distorting Ian's message, making the protestors look like crazy people.

True, some were probably crazy because the camp attracted homeless people, ex-cons, and predators who could take off work and sit around camping in a park for five weeks.

Protests in other cities—places with less focused leadership—failed more spectacularly. A guy in Orange County raped a woman. Cops tear-gassed parks, and robberies made everyone afraid at night. New York protestors jumped a couple of aggressive cops and bashed their heads in. Houston had a counter-protest next door, and eventually, people threw punches.

Every time media cameras flipped on there was a protestor who couldn't answer the reporter's question intelligently. With the lights illuminating dirty faces and microphones jabbing at hungry mouths full of peanut-butter-thoughts, the media latched on to the crazies. The YouTube whores took the incoherence viral.

The protest imploded, the media presenting the ineffectual protestors as leaders or true believers, ridiculing Ian's principles and political goals.

Zilla promised action, effectiveness, and money. Ian was more than tempted, he was sold. *Shit, I am a fool.*

###

Ian wants to scream and hit something until the bones in his fists break. The memory of who he was still haunts him. Ian used to write about the evil rich, their wealth gained at everyone else's expense. But Ian recognizes his error in judgment: he joined the very people he hated, and took everything away from everyone, including himself. Now he's surrounded by the shit storm he caused. Fucking poetic.

The rain eventually stops.

Rice whimpers, not even trying to keep herself quiet. Just after two in the morning, Josh falls asleep from exhaustion. Tanis sleeps, too. Ben passes out from drinking all day, little sips here and there. Ian's hoping he'll be more pleasant when he's sober. Isabella keeps her eyes wide open, chewing on a sucker Tanis gave her. Not surprisingly, the kid has a stockpile of candy in his pack. Markus doesn't sleep, either. He uses the light to read passages from his Bible. Ian and Hana keep the boat in the middle of the river by taking turns using the third oar as a rudder, rowing as little as they can, making the least noise and motion possible. Andy sleeps as well, but he's moaning like he's got a fever.

Ian can't tell how close they are to the shore, but every now and again, he sees eyeless faces moving along in the shadows, jackals working out how to attack them most efficiently, stalking them like wounded antelope.

"Shit!" Ian realizes the boat has drifted out of the center channel. "Center us. Back, back, back." Adrenaline floods his system. He turns the boat with one oar and rows with both until the shore fades from view. One of the Puppets leaps into the water, screeching until the twisted face fades to black.

Everyone is awake now.

"Can you not crash us into the shore?" Ben snips. "I'd rather not be Puppet food."

"I would steer better if I could see." But that was exactly what Ian didn't want. He needed a break from seeing the Puppets, their twisted faces, their snarls.

After reaching the Hudson, they float south toward the Atlantic Ocean. Ian doesn't want to get pushed out to sea in a rowboat, but the receding tide gives them little choice. He's worried but says nothing.

"Those Puppets must be able to hear us," Hana whispers. "They don't have eyes anymore, so I don't see any other way for them to track us."

Isabella speaks up, "Does it matter? They want us. We have to find a way to burn them all."

"Yes, it matters," Hana replies. "It matters to me."

"I think you're right," Ian cuts in. "They sense us differently now. They aren't human anymore. They must be hearing us. . . or seeing our heat. Maybe they have sonar, like a bat, or they can smell us and follow the scent, like search dogs. "

Markus chimes in, his calm voice reassuring. "Peter tells us about the apocalypse. 'The day of the Lord will come like a thief'—"

"Thanks for that," Isabella mumbles.

Markus continues, undeterred, "—the heavens will disappear with a roar; the elements will be destroyed by fire, and the Earth and everything in it will be laid bare.' In Thessalonians, the passage says, 'While people are saying, Peace and safety, destruction will come on them suddenly, as labor pains on a pregnant woman, and they will not escape.'"

"That doesn't make me feel any better, Markus," Hana mumbles.

"But we, all of us here, have passed through the fire. We are to become the righteous. We will rebuild the world."

"So you think there's no quarantine line?" Hana asks. "This virus is crawling across the entire Earth?"

"I don't know for sure. But these are the end times," Markus replies. "I know it in my heart. When there's no more room in Hell, the Lord will come, and the dead will walk the Earth."

Ian pulls his oar slowly through the water, steering them back to the middle of the Hudson. "I have to agree with Markus. This is the fucking end. If the army had stopped the spread of the virus, wouldn't we see planes in the sky? Wouldn't we see the full force of the U.S. military by now?"

"They should've firebombed the entire area," Isabella adds.

Rice sits up. Long lines of dark mascara streak down her cheeks. She looks like an 80s heavy metal rocker in the weak light of Ian's lantern. She asks Markus, "Why are we saved? I never spent one hour in church. My parents didn't believe in God. I never took communion or prayed!"

"God has a plan for all of us. It isn't quite clear to me yet, but I will see the plan. Stick with me. I'm in God's favor," Markus answers with a smile.

"Where do we go if the world has ended?" Rice asks. She wipes her nose on her shoulder and attempts to wipe her tears but only succeeds in smearing her mascara across her face.

Ian is an empathetic man, and looking at Rice makes his sadness resurface. It comes and goes, like the tides. He guesses it has to, or he wouldn't be able to fight, to survive. "Let's first find out if there's a quarantine line before we lose our minds. If we can find safety, we will," Ian reassures

Rice. She puts her hand on his knee and tries to smile. *Zilla would have survived. With fewer people in the world, I'll be able to track him down and stab him through the heart. I can't wait for that day.*

"Okay, how do we find out where safe is?" Rice sits up and composes herself.

Hana wakes up Tanis. "Hey, did you bring the radio you fixed?"

Tanis nods and hands his backpack to Hana. "Yeah, batteries still work, too." He lies back down on the floor of the boat.

Hana takes out the radio. "Tanis fixed this thing. It's not digital anymore, but he rigged this pin to scroll through the stations. If the world didn't end, we should be able to pick up a signal." She flicks the radio on and slowly scans for stations. Static erupts from the speakers. The noise is a shredded, irritating sound, but Ian listens, knowing there might be something faint in the static. Hana moves the makeshift dial slowly.

Ian had never really thought about how a radio works. Now, surrounded by burned-out electronics, silent silhouetted buildings, and darkened street lamps, it seems like magic. An ever-shrinking percentage of the population understands how a radio works, let alone how to build one. Ian marvels at the radio's guts and how Hana is moving the pin across a simple wire that catches the frequency.

The static breaks around 97.1, and the signal is weak but audible. "Need survives. Greed dies. There is an Eden," the somber, monotone voice says. "You have been chosen."

"What the hell?" Isabella's brow creases as she fixes her eyes on the radio.

"Let me recheck the rest of the dial," Hana says, but the rest of the dial is nothing but static. She tunes back to 97.1.

"Twenty-one degrees, forty-eight minutes, north. Eighty degrees, zero minutes, west," the voice on the radio says. Then it repeats the earlier message. "Need survives. Greed dies."

"It's an invitation. There are survivors gathering at those coordinates," Ian says, looking away from the radio. "That means the virus has circled the world." His voice cracks.

"How is that possible?" Rice asks.

"Everyone is sick now?" Andy mumbles. It's the first time Ian has heard him make a peep. His shock must be wearing off. His mouse voice is small and powerless. He must be eight or nine years old.

Ian's sadness peaks, a high tide this time. He squeezes his eyes shut and grips the oars.

"Shhh, Andy. Not everyone is sick. We'll find other survivors and your parents, I promise," Rice says.

"The virus works so unbelievably fast. Three days from death to reanimation. The same sickness has crossed oceans? Continents? Islands? How can it?" Ian says.

Josh adds, his voice rough from lack of sleep, "There are over eighteen million flights a year. That translates to roughly forty-nine thousand flights per day." He does more math in his head. "Average is two hundred passengers per flight,"

"That's over nine million passengers a day," Markus calculates.

"Doesn't take a genius to see how fast a virus could jump continents," Isabella says, "When it's carried at five hundred miles an hour cruising speed to all corners of the world."

"Especially for an airborne virus that has no symptoms in the first twenty-four hours of infection," Josh says.

"So, the world is dead," mutters Hana.

Ian pulls on his oar again, pointing the boat back to the middle of the Hudson.

Silence, other than the lapping of the waves on the hull, stretches as the survivors consider their position.

A scream spears the dark night. Then another, louder than ever before, more agitated. The darkness presses against Ian's back, the whole world threatening to destroy them.

"I suggest we get a bigger boat," Ian says, feeling like the water is the only real safe space.

"We must find Eden," Rice suggests, covering Andy's ears. "Anyone know how to read longitude and latitude?" She looks at Josh, who seems to have the biggest brain in the boat.

But Markus answers, "Those coordinates say that Eden is in Cuba."

Ian doesn't care how Markus knows the coordinates of Cuba without a map. "I guess we're going to Cuba."

Time passes as slowly as sap drips from a wounded tree, and like the sap healing the tree's wounds, Ian relaxes more, daring to hope the worst is behind them.

Hana touches his shoulder and points to the sky. "Manhattan hasn't seen such stars in over a century."

The clouds are moving away, exposing stars so numerous they're uncountable. *Are we special here? On Earth? Did I just fuck up the one grand thing in the entire universe?* Though Ian tries to hide it, he cries, letting his tears collect in his eyes and blur the starlight into obscurity.

Something bumps into the hull. Then, another bump. Ian sits up, grabs his flashlight, and holds it over the gunwale. He sweeps the surface, seeing a face in the dark water. Ian exhales like he's hit in the stomach with a tire iron. He's ready to scream when he notices there are no roots in the eyes.

"Ian," Isabella whispers. "Over here."

Ian stands and leans past Hana to look over the other side of the boat, tipping it a little under his weight. A mass of dead bodies is floating in the water, but none are moving, and none seem to be infected.

Josh speaks first. "The bodies are floating in a tight formation. A surface current must be pushing everyone together."

"They're all dead!" Andy yells, subsides into silence again.

Ian wants to cover Andy's eyes, but he needs to see it. He'll grow up in this dead world. *So look, kid. Really see*

this. It will help you survive.

Rice hugs Andy hard.

"It smells bad," Hana mumbles.

Isabella holds the light high to see as far as she can.

Josh says, "We're caught in the same current. We'll be floating with the corpses until we hit the lower bay and the current breaks up."

CHAPTER 1.22

HANA
BROKEN LIBERTY

The survivors float down the Hudson River, surrounded by dead, bloated bodies. The smell is sickening, thick, choking. Hana would throw up if she had anything in her stomach. Flies bombard her, swarming, biting.

Hana screams in her head, long and often. Squeezing her eyes shut helps drown out the world, but she can't keep them shut. Inevitably, they open. The lantern-lit bodies float in the same current, cradling the boat like they're ushering the survivors to the afterlife.

Ben stands. The boat rocks.

"What did I say about sitting down?" Isabella hisses.

"I have to piss. Geez, lady. Off my back."

"I'm gonna rip that thing off." Isabella looks ready to crawl over everyone and fulfill her threat.

"Fine, then get piss in your face. I'm going with or without a dick."

Ben unzips and pees.

Hana covers her ears, hating the sound of urine splashing on the body of some poor soul, defiling it further. *Maybe these people weren't poor. Maybe they had a more humane end than the Puppets. None of these bodies have roots growing out of their eyes. They must have died in the beginning before whatever reanimated the bodies spread. These people never chased, never tried to bite or tear, never had to starve to death like we might.*

The males take turns peeing over the gunwales.

Isabella somehow squats over the gunwale enough not to pee down her leg.

Hana holds it. The pressure in her bladder distracts her.

Rice leans her butt over the edge as Ian and Ben hold her arms.

Ian passes around his water bottle. Hana drinks because her throat is filled with razor blades. The liquid will stress her bladder further, but she's willing to endure the discomfort to keep from being dehydrated.

Isabella stayed at the bow all night, mostly silent.

Everyone else managed to get some sleep.

Hana did, too, for short intervals brought on by exhaustion. Ian let her have his shoulder for a time.

Eventually, the sky brightens as the sun rises. The same sun as always, the same ball of warm light, the same slow-motion revival.

Hana unfastens her ponytail, runs her fingers through her hair, and massages her scalp, enjoying the tingling until she realizes her hands are shaking. Cops see and experience scary things: perps with guns and no brains, AIDS patients cut and bleeding after downing a ton of pills, and, her favorite, stampedes in the subways from terrorist threats. Nothing compares to last night. Alien things have taken over the world, and they look too human to ignore.

The Hudson widens. Here, the current heads out to sea, which breaks up the flotilla of the dead, although a few bodies remain to remind them what will happen if they don't get out of this tiny boat.

The progress is still slow going. Hana has moved faster following parades. When the sun illuminates the landscape, she notices the Statue of Liberty on the horizon, the statute's arm and torch broken off, the wreckage of an Apache helicopter burned on the island's edge. She's broken, just like her country, just like humanity.

Tears fill Hana's eyes and spill down her face. She became a cop because Lady Liberty made her so proud. The statue's purpose inspired the world to go down the road of equal justice for all. Shes broken now. And there will be no justice for all the dead. Zilla won't see the inside of a jail cell. That thought makes Hana's blood pressure rise. She wishes she knew who he was so she could hunt him down. *Do I belong behind bars, too? I listened to him. What does that make me?*

She wipes her tears. The last thing this boat full of people needs is the resident cop sobbing with regret and fear.

The shore of Liberty Island is a couple hundred feet to the left. Puppets cover the small island and surround the downed chopper. They stop and stare with root-eyes, desiring the survivors with a simplistic frenzy.

Josh wakes as they near the statue. "We made good time," he says, yawning. "Must have been going just over two miles per hour on this thing."

Hana wonders if Josh's brain ever quits calculating. "We've been on this boat for thirteen hours," she says.

"Yup. And Swindler's Cove is about twenty-two miles. So that's about right. Two miles an hour," he confirms.

Ian wakes up, hearing their conversation. "Have you seen any boats we can use?"

"No. We passed a dock about an hour ago. From

what I could see, the handful of yachts were full of holes or half-sunk. A bunch of masts, too, stuck out of the water— probably sailboats."

"Government had to scuttle them so no one could escape," Josh said. "Obviously tactic of control, however naïve."

"While guarding the Queensboro Bridge, I heard the radio chatter about boats making a break for New Jersey. The National Guard fired on them, dozens of them, probably killing everyone on board. Image being that gunner and killing innocent people like that."

"We have no idea how much area the EMP affected, but I think it's safe to say there's probably a three to four-hundred-mile area burned out. We won't find any usable boats until we hit Atlantic City," Ian said. "We may find people rushed to get off-shore in the panic there, too. Finding a useable boat might be extremely difficult."

"I know where there's a useable boat," Josh says, his face bright, grinning like he's about to explode with excitement.

"Spit it out," Isabella snaps.

"Back toward the city, on the East River side of downtown, the New York Seaport Museum has old boats the EMP wouldn't affect—big sailboats, some seagoing ships."

"Don't you think someone would have taken those boats, or they would have been sunk?" Tanis asks, with worry in his eyes.

Josh shakes his head. "Those boats date back to the early nineteen hundreds and are difficult to maneuver in open water. Not great getaway vehicles."

"What are you, a fucking pirate?" Ben says.

"If they aren't great getaway vehicles, then how do you expect us to get away?" Markus asks.

Josh shrugs. "Different situation now. The main event is already behind us, and the Puppets are slow." Josh pushes up his dark-rimmed, thick glasses. "All we have to do is get off the dock."

"Worth a shot," Hana says and looks at Ian. He nods and cranks his oar through the water. The two turn the boat back to New York and pull hard through the current.

Rice starts crying. "I'm not going back there!" she exclaims. "Let me off this death trap first!" She stands, rocking the boat.

"Jesus! Can everyone just keep their ass on the seat?" Isabella orders. "Where the fuck are you gonna go?"

"I'm not going back there!" Rice cries and points toward downtown. "You can't make me! It's just death! Death!"

Isabella grabs Rice's wrist and twists it hard, forcing the hysterical woman to sit down.

"Yeah, hold your shit a sec." Ben stands up to protest. The boat rocks his way.

"If you don't sit down, chubby, you're gonna see my grumpy side real quick." Isabella's intent stare forces Ben to sit. He raises his hands in silent protest.

Isabella turns to Rice and releases her wrist. "I want off this boat and on a bigger boat. You're not gonna get in my way. You rock this boat again, I'll throw you over, no doubt."

Ian mediates. "Wait, hold on. Josh, is there another boat you know of that might be easier to get to? Maybe one that's not on Manhattan Island?"

"Yeah, but it's in Virginia Beach," Josh answers. "That's four, maybe five days south."

Hana shakes her head. "I cannot stay on this boat that long. We have no food, little water, we're shoulder to shoulder, and my muscles are already cramping."

Ian nods. "Sorry, Rice. We've got to get a bigger boat." Hana and Ian row harder. Rice closes her eyes and slumps down, whispering to Andy and running her fingers through his hair.

Half an hour passes. The boat hardly moves, but Josh assures everyone they're making good time despite rowing against the current. Isabella and Josh take the oars and row for a while. Hana leans back, resting finally. Her arms and shoulders ache fiercely, sending shooting pain into her neck.

The tall downtown buildings get closer, and with them a sense of foreboding. The anticipation of the horrors awaiting the group is torture. Ben and Markus take a turn, but it doesn't last long.

After too short a break, Ian and Hana take the oars again. Together, they churn through the peaceful waters of the bay.

As they near Battery Park, Hana can't see any Puppets. Trees fill the small park and block the view to the streets, which is the reason they were planted in the first place. Behind the arboretum are the huge, tall buildings of downtown, lifeless and silent, one on fire and near collapse.

The huge warehouse-like terminals for ferries crossing to Staten Island and Governors Island are quiet now, and none of the big boats are tied to the docks. The area is usually filled with tourists, workers, and school kids on field trips. They are the blood of the city; what's left is just skeletons.

Hana looks at the water for a while. The city's silence is so unnatural that waves of shivers come from somewhere deep in her soul. The water's shifting currents are soothing and orderly, so she spaces out on the ripples and reflections. She rows harder so she doesn't think about the strain on her muscles or the roar of her tainted blood.

As the rowboat moves around the end of Manhattan, Hana sees the heliport and the tall ship masts behind it. She'd seen these boats hundreds of times but forgot they were there because the heliport was so important. Presidents, heads of state, and celebrities landed there. She'd been assigned as guard many times when she was a rookie.

Puppets crowd the waterfront, many of them taking notice of the rowboat. Others gather on South Street. Hana wonders again how the sightless things sense the survivors.

No one in the boat speaks, but they're all wondering if there is any possible way to reach the tall ships safely. Hana sees Rice hiding her face behind her palms and shaking. The poor woman is unprepared for these horrors. Even Ben chews on his dry lips, trying to stay calm.

Isabella and Josh take over the oars, rowing against the current that is heading out to the open ocean. It's brutally slow, hard work.

More and more Puppets gather along the waterfront. They're hard to see, but they're obviously there, watching and waiting.

Hana unintentionally says, "Now, we're going to test our fate by trying to steal a wooden boat from a museum in daylight. I'm not so sure about this. Thousands of Puppets must be spreading the word of our little boat."

"We don't have a choice," Ian replies.

"The huge ship with the black hull. . . over there. . . is the *Peking*," Josh says proudly while rowing. "She's called a baroque, fast and stable. . . used to sail around Cape Horn, you know, the tip of South America." Out of breath, Josh hands the oar to Ian so he can talk and explain his plan to them.

314

"She's over three hundred and seventy feet, too big for us. And I'm not sure I've ever seen her on the bay anyway. I think she's permanently tied to the dock. *Wavertree* isn't an option, either. Non-operational. But right beyond both of them is the *Pioneer*."

The *Pioneer's* hull is black, and her deck is painted white. Her masts are black, but her bowsprit is white.

"Okay, Josh, she's a stunning vessel, but how are we going to sail the ship with ropes and lines everywhere, knowing that none of us have ever sailed a ship," Hana says.

"You wanna take that puny one?" says Ben.

"It's over one hundred feet long," Josh replies. "She just looks small because the *Peking* is so gargantuan. The *Pioneer* is a merchant vessel, a schooner-rigged with an eighty-foot mast."

"Keep it simple," Isabella says to Josh as she pulls the oar with every muscle. She and Ian work hard, though Ian stops and stares at the ship. "Pull your weight, Ian. The faster we get to the ship, the fewer Puppets we'll have to deal with."

"The *Pioneer* was like a freight truck on the sea because she delivered every sort of cargo, from sand to tea. She's strong, has an iron hull, is over twenty feet wide, and with her centerboard up, only four-and-a-half feet draft. She'll get us anywhere we want. . . and fast," Josh says.

"How do you know it'll still work?" Markus asks.

"Well, a diesel engine was added in the thirties and would have survived the EMP."

"Those dead people are following us again," Rice mutters. "They're going to be all over those boats soon."

"Let's hurry and sail away to some deserted island." Tanis's voice shakes, but he's brave when it counts, that's for sure. Hana puts her arm around him and hugs him from behind.

"This is all nice, but does anyone know how to drive that shit on the ocean?" Ben asks.

"I've sailed dinghies," Ian replies. "I was twelve, so I'm not a captain or anything. Plus, my father had a Sunray 501. He was overprotective and never let me take it out, but I've been on it with him a bunch of times."

"I've been on the *Pioneer*," Josh states, to no one's

surprise. "She's got lots of room. Plus, a couple of years ago, her rooms were totally decked out. You could even charter her with a five-star chef on board."

"The name is fitting," Markus comments. "*Pioneer.*"

Hana takes the oar from Isabella, buckles down, and rows fast and hard.

"Lots of Puppets on the dock," Isabella says, counting. "Nothing I can't handle."

The main dock is taller than the Pioneer's deck, but steps lead down to a lower wooden dock that is even with the *Pioneer's* deck.

The Puppets seem to eye the survivors thoughtfully, anticipating where the rowboat will dock. "Stop!" Hana calls out. "We can't pull up to the lower dock. The Puppets will overflow that area and could get on our boat."

"Pull up to the end of the taller main dock. There's a ladder there," Ian says. "It's far enough from the *Pioneer*, so we'll be drawing them away. We'll get their attention and push past them. Then we should have enough time to get to the *Pioneer* and cut the lines."

Markus pulls his bat off the bottom and hands it to Ben. "This is better than your two-by-four."

"Oh, I'm being volunteered?"

"Stay here if you want. I got it covered," Isabella says.

"What about your ankle?" Josh asks, but Isabella is already on the move.

Ian and Hana row to the end of the dock, knocking it into a wood pile.

Isabella slips on her backpack and two rifles grabs a ladder rung buried in the wooden pilings and climbs up onto the top deck.

"Hand me my Beater," she orders. Rice hands her the bloodied broomstick. "I'll clear the dock so you can run to the *Pioneer* as fast as you can. The Puppets are slow but strong. Don't let them touch you."

Hana likes the name "Puppets." They're empty vessels for those alien root things. *Do any of the Puppets* still *have thoughts or feelings? Do they still have souls? They move awkwardly, like baby fawns, scream like animals, and move like they're connected with invisible strings, so hopefully not.*

One Puppet reaches for Isabella before she gets off the ladder, but she grabs its sleeve and yanks it off the pier, sending it into the water next to the rowboat. Isabella leaps off the ladder, lands on her feet, spins, and cracks the Puppet, reaching for her across its skull, and thrusts upward. Her stick embeds itself inside the Puppet's jaw so deeply that the jaw, skin, and muscle rip off when she wrenches her stick upward. Black blood splatters her face, barely missing her mouth. She kicks the Puppet off the dock. Another Puppet reaches for her, and she pounds the side of its knee with her heel, snapping the femur, the jagged end ripping through the skin. Blood gushes out, splashing the dock like a ruptured water balloon. The thing still reaches from its crumpled, maimed body, screeching. Isabella steps aside, snatches the hand, twists it, and drops it to her knees, ripping off the forearm. Isabella tosses the arm over the side. It splashes into the water two feet from Hana.

Isabella pauses and looks down. "NOW!" She takes a few deep breaths and runs to the next Puppet, aims the shotgun at its knee, and blasts the leg apart. She runs to the next one and kicks it squarely in the chest so hard Hana hears its ribs crack. Another falls off the edge of the dock, creating a splash that rocks the rowboat. She squeezes off round after round, kicking, and pushing until the dock is clear.

Ian climbs up the piling, tying the rowboat's painter

to a rung so it wouldn't float away. Ben gets out first, without consideration for the women and boys, followed by Rice and Andy. The Puppet, whose kneecaps Isabella blew off, grabs Ben's ankle, and he cries out. Rice picks up Andy, settling him on her hip, and runs toward the *Pioneer*. Ben bashes the Puppet with the bat.

Tanis leaps onto the ladder, rocking the little boat,

scampers up as fast as he can, and runs past Ben.

Hana is behind him the entire time, her strong protective instinct filling her body.

Behind her, Josh slips on a pool of black blood, falls to his knees, and swears loudly. "Is this virus still airborne? Oh, god."

Hana turns back and helps him up.

Body parts are strewn everywhere, confetti of death, twitching, flopping, a macabre work of art painted in black, rotting blood. Hana jerks her pistol from her holster, knowing it won't do much good, but if one grabs her, she can buy some time.

Hana fires a shot into a Puppet with what looks like white sunblock smeared on its nose and a camera draped around its neck, a tourist come to see the Big Apple for all its worth. *Well, you got the rawest of deals, buddy. I'm sorry for you. For all of you.* The thing that was a tourist bleeds black, gasses off rancid smells that nauseate her. She keeps moving, aiming at broken, snarling faces as she hustles past. No matter how twisted, slashed, cut wide open the Puppets are, they're still reaching and grabbing, moaning, and screaming. *Why are they making so much noise? I can't stand this!*

Markus and Hana follow the others toward a metal staircase leading to the lower dock, which leads to the *Pioneer's* gangplank. Ian has already ripped down the small security gate keeping people off the stairs. Tanis, Rice, and Andy make it to the gangplank safely.

Hana stops and grabs Ian's arm, "What do I need to do?"

Ian looked confused for a moment. "Oh, on the ship. Just do what I say. We'll be fine." He flashes a quick smile. "We're going to move fast," he says.

"Good." She climbs down, crosses the lower dock, and pounds up the short inclined plank to the *Pioneer*. The ship hardly rocks under her weight, but she feels its motion on the water. The deck is huge.

Ian looks back at the rowboat tied to the dock. "We might need the rowboat if we have to abandon ship. I'll be right back." Without thinking, he runs to the rowboat, unties the painter, and sprints back to the *Pioneer*, guiding the rowboat along the dock. "God damn. Their screeching makes my teeth clench." Ian tosses the line onto the deck, looping it loosely over one of the safety ropes.

Isabella isn't surrounded anymore, but Puppets still approach from the main dock. She takes them down as they get close, tossing them off the opposite side of the dock, making it look easy.

Hana is grateful Isabella is with them because she's tougher than most men and does not hesitate to show it.

"Isabella!" Hana yells. "Time to go. You're done fighting for now. Get your ass over here."

The bloodied fighter turns and runs down the gangplank onto the *Pioneer*.

Ian is last aboard. When he's on the deck, he kicks the gangplank away from the ship.

They're all safe.

The sun beats on Hana's back, and she's sweating like a sponge being wrung out. She watches the Puppets massing together, some falling off the upper dock, some crossing the lower one, and is relieved. 'We made it. We're going to be safe." She inhales deeply. Standing on the *Pioneer's* wide, solid deck, she's glad of the large, spacious ship. Being in that little boat for so long robbed Hana of her sense of stability.

Screeching drags Hana's attention back to the horde. Dead people have overrun the dock completely. "Uh, Ian!

What do we need to do to get off the dock?"

"Hold on. I got this!" Ian runs to the front of the ship and unties a spring line. Isabella loads and pumps her shotgun and shoots a twisted face as the Puppet tears at one of the bumpers while others try to climb onto the ship.

Ben and Ian bat the dead off the deck. Isabella smacks them with the butt of her shotgun.

"There are two more lines tied to the dock, Ian!" Markus yells.

"Chop them!" Ian replies. "Chop them all!"

Isabella flips her gun around and shoots point-blank at a line. Hana runs to the last one and unties it. The *Pioneer* rocks away from the dock. "She's free!"

A handful of Puppets spill off the dock into the water.

Hana grabs the railing, her stable feeling vanishing again.

The *Pioneer* floats to the middle of the harbor lane, straight toward the huge ship, the *Peking*.

"Find the diesel engine and see if you can turn it on," Ian says. The ship is big and painted black. Its masts tower over the deck like colossal, tactical batons.

Sailing ships have always scared Hana. Ropes hang on hooks and in clusters by the masts and on the railings. Rope ladders lead up both sides of the masts to the top. Most of the deck is flat except for a companionway in front of the wheel and a waist-high sitting area mid-ship with another companionway. The long bowsprit—a large wood pole that juts out from the front of the ship—carries the forestays. All the sails are bundled in wads and stowed.

Ian shouts, "Hey! Somebody!" from the bow. He's using a long pole with a hook on the end, trying to snag the rowboat's painter.

Hana hurries to him.

"I gotta secure the rowboat. We may need it."

'I hope not," Hana mutters.

"Hold me. The line fell, and I can't reach it," Ian says.

Hana holds him by the waist, planting her foot against the railing, and Ian leans over the edge, snags the line with his pole, and pulls it in.

"Smart move, saving the rowboat," Hana says. "I would have let it sink to the depths."

"I figure, since none of us are too experienced, having a lifeboat would be a good idea. There's a small inflatable, but we all wouldn't fit in it comfortably." Hana follows him as he walks the painter to the back of the *Pioneer* and ties it to the rail.

"Like we fit into the rowboat comfortably," Hana replies.

"Yeah, well, the dinghy is worse."

"Cabin is locked," Markus says. "Can't get to the engine controls."

"Doors never stop me." Hana kicks the door open like she's raiding a drug house.

"Told you she was badass," Tanis says to Ben.

The doorway leads to a pilot house with a small table for charting courses, a panel of buttons and knobs, and a smaller wheel. Opposite the entry is a ladder leading to the engine. Hana doesn't go down yet. She returns to the panel of buttons. One is a radar, one is the radio, the largest is the engine control.

"No time to look for the keys, so let's find a way to make sparks." Hana removes her multi-tool from her police belt and pops off the control panel, revealing the electronic ignition.

"How do you know how to do this?" Ian asks.

Hana shrugs. "Wasn't always a cop. I was orphaned pretty young. Moved from house to house. I picked up some bad skills."

"Now a cop, eh?" Ben says, poking his head into the pilot house. "Kinda funny."

Hana shakes her head. "Finally got picked up by two good people. Showed me life is better when you follow the rules."

Ben laughs, and his face pulls away.

"No need for the electronic ignition anymore." She rips the ignition off and hot-wires the starter like at the boathouse in Swindler's Cove. The engine fires, sputters, slows. Hana pulls on the throttle, feeding it fuel carefully until it purrs solidly.

Josh works his way next to Ian and Markus. "I remembered it right. Dang, I'm good. It's a rebuilt Yanmar diesel upgraded at least once since the thirties," he said, reading a plaque near the companionway.

Hana looks at the wheel. It's not used any longer. There's no way to even look outside anymore. She goes back outside.

Ian's already at the wheel. He finds the transmission lever, bumps it into gear, catches the prop, and the boat moves forward

Hana falls on her butt before she can find her balance. Tanis runs to her and hugs her. She can feel his relief.

Ben yells, holding the bat over his head like a victorious warrior. Markus puts his Bible to his forehead and thanks God. Rice runs to Ian and jumps up and down, holding onto his shoulders. Josh swears at the Puppets receding into the background, and Isabella sits quietly and cleans her face and arms. Hana can tell Isabella is happy underneath that thick skin, radiating relief whether she wants to or not.

"You okay?" Hana asks Tanis.

"I'm okay."

"TO EDEN!" Ian yells as New York City slips away.

Chapter 1.23

Tanis
Going Home

Tanis had told Hana he was fine, but he's not. He feels better now that they're on this gigantic boat, but what he really wants is to see his ma. "Dad is probably one of those Puppets, but what about Ma?" Tanis said to himself. He doesn't have any brothers or sisters to worry about, but he has a dog named Kat and a fish named Birdy.

"What's so funny?" Hana asks.

Tanis tells her about his pet's names. "That's great. How did they get those names? Is there a story? Or is it just for kicks?" she asks with a big smile.

Tanis shrugs. "Just 'cause it makes me laugh." He moves to the ship's rail and watches the tall skyscrapers get smaller and smaller. Hana puts her arm around him. "I'm glad you got my back," he tells her and flips off the Puppets clustered on the dock, looking dumb as rocks.

Tanis sees Andy staring at him like a wounded puppy. "It's okay, buddy." He puts his hand gently on the boy's shoulder and guides him to the railing. "Go ahead and flip those bastards off. Put up your middle finger and hold

the others down."

Andy's eyes narrow. "I know how to flip the bird. I'm not a baby."

Tanis laughs. "Okay then."

The three of them flip off the Puppets and yell.

The three relax, standing quietly at the rail. Hana pushes Tanis gently. "What're you thinking?"

"I wanna go home." The engine's hum and the ship's speed are nicer than in the rowboat, but Tanis still feels like home is impossibly far away.

Hana takes a deep breath. "So do I."

"I'm going to find Rice." Andy walks away, his head low.

"How do I know Ma isn't locked up in our house waiting for me?" Tanis asks Hana.

"We don't."

"I wanna know. And Andy will probably want to know if his parents are out there."

Ian steers the ship through the Upper Bay. The small waves lap the hull.

Hana takes Tanis to Ian. "I need to know if it would be possible to make a pit stop," Hana asks.

Ian must be feeling jazzed and pumped after their successful battle for their new ship. "Full tank of gas. No way to get attacked by Puppets. Where are you thinking? Want to go to Greece?"

"How 'bout Forest Hills?" Hana asks. "Tanis wants to see if his mother survived."

"Whoa!" Ben says, butting in. "Let's stick with the plan. We go south until we find the containment line. If there isn't one, and this virus has crawled across the fuckin' continent, then we go to Cuba and find the nearest mai tai.

If civilization is Eden, then it's Eden or bust."

"You may not give a shit about your family, but I do," Tanis snaps. "What if Ma is waiting for me? She could be locked up in the house. You don't know."

"Sorry, Tanis," Ian answers. "I have to agree with Ben. This ship needs to get us to safety. Both sides of the river are infested with Puppets, and that means Forest Hills is a death trap. If we have to go thousands of miles south, we need to be smart about it. Any deviation may bring us too much trouble. We're in survival mode."

"Let's vote on it," Hana suggests. "It's only a short distance north and won't take us too far out of our way. You can stay on the ship."

"I can almost guarantee you, she ain't gonna be there, kid," Ben says.

Tanis wants to box Ben's ears. "You're here," Tanis says. He repeats Hana's idea, "Can't we vote?"

"This isn't a democracy. Not now. Once we get to safety, we can try to find a way to contact your folks." Ian folds his arms across his chest.

"What do you have against voting, Ian?" Markus approaches, his Bible clutched to his chest. "Maybe we should vote. It seems to have worked for our culture in the past."

Ian laughs. "Democracy rarely works! Voting lowered standards, increased bureaucracy, and rendered entire environmental efforts dead. Vote for a peaceful president; you still go to war. Vote for fair judges; they still get bought off. We vote, and we get shit. Politicians spend more time campaigning than actually trying to fix anything."

"You're freakin' right about voting," Tanis interrupts Ian. "It's too easy to cheat. So, let's not vote. Let me barter instead. Get me as close as you can to the shore. I'll be gone for five hours. Any longer, and you can leave without me."

"I'm confused. Where does bartering come in here?" Ben says in his ass-face tone.

"I'll bring us back at least twenty gallons of diesel fuel," Tanis says. "The barter, Ben, is fuel in exchange for time," Tanis says, sneering at Ben before he turns back to Ian. "I know where to get the gas. There are two marine depots on the way."

Markus pleads with Ian. "Let the boy try. He's a child in need of closure."

"I'm not a child, old man," Tanis snaps. "I know more than most adults. I can program a registry bug, squat on a multibillion-dollar corporation's website, rebuild any PC, operate it with style, and get a hacker into the mainframe control system of a secret Department of Defense's premier satellite management office." Tanis choked on his words. He gulped, hoping no one was really paying attention to what he'd just said. What the hell? I can't say shit like that out loud. Ever. "I mean, I could. If I wanted to." Sweat seemed to pour from his armpits as a pang of guilt about his last brag smacks him like some invisible hand reaching through his rib cage and squeezing his heart.

Ian nods, "Fine, little man. I get that you're smart. And it sounds like a good deal. I'll even help you."

"I will, too," Hana offers.

"Sorry, I ain't dyin' for your closure, kid," Isabella says as she crosses her arms. "But we do need the fuel. And some other shit."

Ben looks surprised and rolls his eyes. "Someone has to stay with the ship! It could get, like, fucking stolen, right?"

"Congrats. You get ship watch." Isabella snaps.

Ben nods. "Hell yeah. I'll keep her right where she is."

"We go to the house and bring back Tanis's mom, plus the fuel and any other supplies we can carry," Ian says, addressing everyone. He looks at Josh. "Up for a shopping spree with Isabella?"

"Um. Yeah, I guess," Josh answers.

"I'll help shop," Markus says. "Lord knows we need food and toiletries, and hopefully, there's medicine left on the shelves."

Rice looks at Ian. "I–I can't do it. I won't put Andy through that either."

Ian shushes her, "No worries, Rice. Stay with Ben. You three will be fine on the ship. Make sure it doesn't float away."

Ian points the *Pioneer* northeast, watching the compass turn in concert, slowly.

Tanis paces. *Shit in Shinola. I hope I'm not making a colossal mistake.*

Deep vibrations rumble through the air and ground, shaking the trees on shore. A building on the edge of downtown collapses, falling in on itself in slow motion, then faster and faster. Dust blooms from the feet of the skyscrapers, others look as if they're shedding skin, exposing steel bones to the yellow-stained sky.

The *Pioneer* is safe on the water; a few ripples fan out from the waterfront, but the survivors aren't threatened, just locked in sadness.

Ian sails—well, drives with the engine—down the Upper Bay and hugs the coast for twenty minutes.

Tanis can still smell the smoke, but for a moment, he forgets the undead and their root eyes until they near the Verrazano-Narrows Bridge. The suspension bridge used to be impressive, silver and baby blue, with tall towers that

looked like tuning forks jammed into the sea bed. Only the massive structures on either side of the sound remain; the middle is gone. Tanis tries to remember what it looked like, lit with vibrant blue lights at night or seeing fog and clouds hide the tall towers.

The houses along the rocky beach are hollow and dark, with no sign of comfort or happiness. The Coney

Island Lighthouse is surrounded by about a thousand Puppets stumbling around, looking for something to claw.

Ian steers the ship around the bend, toward Coney Island Beach and the boardwalk. Men, women, and children of every age stumble along the sandy shore, wearing shorts, t-shirts, and sundresses. A hotdog stand lies toppled on its side in the surf, beaten over and over by the waves where it will slowly disintegrate. A tall apartment complex behind the beachfront burns like the stub of a cigar; the neighboring building looks like tumbled blocks. The Colossus roller coaster, the rickety wooden one built in the early 1900s, still stands, and the aquarium is down the way, but the two are silent graveyards.

What about the dolphins? Tanis wonders. *Are they left in the pools? Are the hundreds of colorful fish in the tanks left there, too? Unfed, slowly dying one by one.* Tanis can't cry anymore because he's all out of tears, for now anyway. But in every heartbeat, he feels depression, begging his heart to stop.

The *Pioneer* passes under the Marine Parkway Bridge, or what's left of it. The span, blown to bits like the other bridges, is in pieces in the water, concrete pillars, metal girders, and long sections of roadway jut from the shallow waves.

Ian turns sharply to avoid hitting a twisted section jutting from the water, throwing everyone around, prompting a duet of complaints from Rice and Ben.

Tanis breathes a sigh of relief when the ship passes through the bridge veritable mine field safely.

Josh says, rubbing a bump on his head acquired from hitting the cabin after his spill, "Hey, the tide is high, so the small bushy islands in Jamaica Bay are at their smallest. Stay far away from all the land you see."

Ian navigates between the beach and islands like a

seasoned sailor.

"Ever swim out here?" Hana asks Tanis quietly.

Tanis shakes his head. "Hell no. Never went to the beaches out here. The water is freakin' way too cold. Plus, there are just a bunch of hippies always running around. At least, that's what Pa always said."

"Yeah. I never wanted to come out here either."

Ian slows the ship at the end of the bay, as close to the shore as he can, bitching about the EMP frying the radar and depth gauges.

Finally, they arrive at the end of Jamaican Bay.

A wooden dock juts from the beach, but it's too small for the one-hundred-foot *Pioneer* to tie up safely. "This is it," Ian says. "I'm nervous that we'll hit bottom." He idles the engine, runs to the bow, and releases the anchor. "I don't know much about anchors, so I hope this thing works."

"I'm sure it will. I have confidence in your abilities," Markus says.

One by one, Ian, Josh, Markus, Tanis, Hana, and Isabella climb down the stern ladder and transfer to the familiar wooden rowboat and row to the small wooden dock, probably used for fishing. Ian ties the painter to a cleat, and they disembark. Tanis follows Ian. Isabella and the other three are in a single file behind Tanis.

The shore is quiet, and the six survivors move warily down a sandy path that cuts through thick bushes, toward a line of trees concealing homes. Black smoke chokes the air. Tanis is jazzed, sure Ma and Kat are hiding in the house waiting for him. *I can't wait to tell them we have a huge boat we can escape on.*

Ian stops, shakes the sand from his shoes, saying, "Okay, Isabella, keep Josh from getting eaten and Markus no communion wafers. We need real food."

Markus shakes his head. "I'm not Catholic, young

man. I'm a preacher. Closer to a Protestant."

"I know. Giving you a hard time." Ian continued with his plan, taking a more serious tone. "Hana and I will go with Tanis to get his mom. We've got four hours. The tide will go out after that, and we don't need to get stuck in the bay."

Isabella hands Ian her shotgun.

"I thought you didn't lend out your guns," Ian says, smiling.

"I don't," she says, her expression flat.

Tanis wonders if Isabella ever smiles.

Tanis leads Ian and Hana up Cross Bay, passing businesses and houses, turns into Woodhaven Boulevard, the major throughway in his neighborhood. Tanis is surprised at the lack of cars on the street in front of the businesses or in the parking lots.

"Did the EMP hit out here? Ian, should we see if a car works?" Hana asks.

"Good idea. I would love to be driving." Ian runs to an old grey sedan, opens the door easily, slides into the driver's seat, and finds the keys still in the ignition. He tries the starter, but nothing. After a few more tries, he gives up. "Dead. They're all probably fried. We're not far enough away from the EMP hit zone."

Tanis leads them along the boulevard: houses to the right, more shops to the left. A cluster of cars jam the road near the park. Tanis, eager to get home, turns to Ian, saying, "Two more bl—"

A fat, white-haired woman wearing a yellow dress startles Tanis as he jogs by the front of a car. She grabs him! Tanis screams, trying to push her away, his hands sinking into her huge boobs, the rolls of fat closing over his hands to absorb him. He shoves as hard as he can; she stumbles back, and he slips away. She didn't feel real; it was more like pushing on a sack of water, not a person. She was bloated. Unnaturally so. Like a puffer fish riddled with the plague.

"Careful," Hana barks. "I'm not interested in seeing you bit open."

"Yeah. I'm fine. I'm not too worried about a few Puppets. They're slow as snails and easy to cruise around when there's only one."

"Where there's one, there's more," Ian says. He adds, thinking out loud. "Maybe the Puppets hear or

smell us, maybe both, but either way, they're aiming their carnivorous appetites in our direction." He points. "Yup! Like that guy. Watch it."

A guy in a baseball uniform, crouching between two cars, lunges at Tanis, but a smack across the face sends the Puppet reeling. "Hands off, fool!"

Ian runs around the guy, hot on Tanis's tail. Neither waste bullets. Avoiding Puppets is better and less attention-grabbing. Option two is to take down attackers by hammering their knees like Isabella did at the seaport.

Hana avoids them all, too, repeating her often touted saying, "save your fighting energy for the real battles."

More arrive every moment until dozens flank them, moving with intent but still fumbling over each other.

Forest Park is about four miles from the bay. Tanis slows at the edge of the park– thick woods and narrow walking trails could hide Puppets in a hundred places. Beyond a tree line are tennis courts and a golf course.

Tanis, Ian, and Hana pass apartment towers to the right, crowded with Puppets milling in the parking lot, meandering past the buildings. Smaller buildings in the next block burn. The scene is familiar, and not at the same time.

Ian, in the lead now, stops to watch Puppets at the intersection. Hundreds of them.

"Gotta cut into the park," Tanis says. "I'm not up for a party that big." He stares at the shocking amount of walking dead people, feeling sadness surface, seizing all his movement.

"Me either. You can take solace in the fact that we don't have a choice," Ian agrees.

Hana takes the lead. "Move it, men. Time loves a couple of space cadets, and so do Puppet crowds.'

The three cross the parking lot for the baseball and soccer fields. Puppets stumble around like drunk assholes after a Saturday night game.

"This is my park," Tanis says. "I learned to play baseball on that field, flew my first rocket over there, crashed into those trees." His eyes burn. *I gotta get home—*

The Puppets all turn toward the survivors at the same time.

Tanis, Ian, and Hanna hurry into the trees, dense with cross-crossing trails.

"This park is huge," Ian mumbles, almost irritated.

"Heck yeah, it is. Forest Park is big enough to get lost. Hell, I have a few times, even though I walk my pup here almost every weekend."

A car had driven off the street, crashed down the trail, smashed into a tree, and probably burst into flames if a charred body hanging out the window was any clue. More signs of panic and self-destruction litter the forest park. The three keep running, passing a small group of women, children, and men, old and young, all sightless corpses, rotting, awake in their bios-like shells of consciousness.

Ian heads right at one of them and bashes the butt of his shotgun into its face. The crack of bone makes Tanis's skin crawl. He didn't have to. Could have run around the puppet. Frustration makes him do it.

"Come on, stop messing around." Tanis takes the lead, cutting through the park, Ian grunts but he and Hana following closely. Hana slides to a stop on the slick leaves.

Tanis's shortcut over a small hill across Myrtle Avenue is blocked.

"Too many," Hana says, catching her breath. "Just too many of those damned things."

"Where do we go, Tanis? Quick!" Ian blurts.

Tanis turns around.

"Retreat is a bad idea." Hana reminds Tanis. "The

Puppets we've passed haven't stopped, taken a break, or been distracted. Our noise calls to them."

"Yeah, I know. We've been collecting them as we pass, like iron filings trailing a powerful magnet. Pieces of shit," Tanis snaps, thinking hard how to get home. "Um. I think…we have to make a big half-circle, cut around most of them."

"Let's do it," Ian says, jumping into a clump of ferns, bushwhacking as fast as he can, using the shotgun to part the heavy vegetation.

Hana guards their backs.

Finally, the low growth clears, replaced by tall, thin trees; Tanis takes the lead again, picks up the pace, and finds a decent crossing at Myrtle Street. Ian has only two Puppets to dispatch.

A clear path presents itself all the way to the railroad tracks. "Man, I used to love this place. It's like we're…"

"On Earth?" Hana quips.

Tanis smirks just a little. "Right. The city should feel like an alien planet. The forest should feel like earth, but it's kind of the other way around for me because I grew up in the city." He stops, bracing his hands on his knees. The dark steel train tracks stand out because they're surrounded by white stones. Tanis picks up a stone and puts it in his pocket. It's as good as any photograph.

Finally, they clear the forest. Transitioning from forest to city is like flipping through TV channels. They fly by some Puppets that stumble around a café, knocking over tables, and cross Metropolitan Avenue. Tanis runs flat out down one street and crosses to another. "Here's my street, finally," he says.

Four wrecked cars block the intersection. Tanis recognizes his neighbor's Ford. Mrs. Garfield steps out from behind her door and reaches for him, her hands and forearms covered in black splatters like she'd just finished making a blackberry pie, beating the berries to death first. Tanis liked her because she'd pay him twenty bucks to shovel her sidewalk after snowstorms. He approaches her slowly.

"Ma said Mrs. Garfield whittled her days away, peeking into neighbor's windows and criticizing front yard flower arrangements," Tanis mumbles. He looks her over. "She looks like she always does, wearing the same orange flower-patterned housecoat she liked so much. All except for the pits where her eyes should be. But she's always been pale with tissue-thin skin. So creepy. Must have died in the morning." Tanis pointed to her pink plastic tube hair curlers.

Ian lunges forward, holding his shotgun turned butt-down aiming to cripple her knees.

"Wait! I know her," Tanis yelps.

Ian stops.

Mrs. Garfield's mouth opens, her hands reaching for Tanis, a smell worse than rotted flesh coming from her mouth. Sticky, grayish foam clings to her stained teeth and the corners of her lips.

Tanis pushes her away, not wanting to hurt her. "I wish she could have a proper funeral." He doesn't want to bash her up and break her bones, but a voice in his head tells him it is the only way. Tanis wishes he could see her eyes and see if any of her is still alive.

She stumbles and comes back toward him, screaming like she's frustrated.

Nope, she's totally gone. Tanis bolts, leaving her to her horde, her kind, her new brothers, and sisters.

He looks back once. A dark feeling slides down his spine and fills his veins like a corrupt server saturating the net with malware. Tanis can't stop the infection and can't control the spread, but he can run harder. He's never run so far, so fast before. He's practically flying. He can't feel his feet anymore as his lungs suck in the warm, wet air. He doesn't even notice his asthma. *I don't want to die to be one of them.*

He slows down and stops yards from his house. Ma's crappy white Honda, the ride she's had since she was pregnant with him. Her first baby, she'd called it.

Tanis likes his house, a narrow, four-story saltbox with a steeply pitched roof. The walls are white, and he'd painted the window trim dark brown a few summers ago. Tanis runs up the steps to the front door, his house keys in his pocket and his backpack on, like he's just coming home from school. However, he's never been scared of what's on the other side of the door before.

He opens the door slowly, feeling the subtle creak in the tips of his fingers. The house is dark and cold. "Ma!" Tanis yells. Nothing. "Kat!" Nothing. He runs upstairs, two steps at a time, and bursts through the door to his parent's room, but no one's there. The bed is a tangle of sheets. "This isn't like Ma. She'd never leave the bed like this." Tanis sees her cell and car keys on the bedside table, a calling card of the damned.

Tanis puts his back to the door, and the jam band slides to the floor. "Shit, man. I…I," he sits in the doorway and cries, sobbing so hard his body shakes.

Hana kneels and wraps her arms around him. He squeezes her until he can't breathe.

"Guys!" Ian yells from downstairs. "We have to go!"

Hana whispers to Tanis, "Your mother would want you to stay alive. You know that, right? That's what all mothers want." She gives him thirty seconds, then helps him stand. Hana ducks into the hall bathroom rips off a section of toilet paper, and hands it to Tanis.

He's embarrassed but knows he shouldn't be. "Everyone I know is dead. My friends. My parents," Tanis says; the simple act of saying the words aloud releases more tears and a stream of snot.

"Maybe they got out. Maybe they're on their way to a safe zone, just like us. We can assume anything. We have to do our part. Keep going. For us and the ones we miss."

He nods, appreciating her efforts to give him hope, a reason to go on. It works. "I feel like Ma could be alive and waiting for me, wanting me to survive. It's possible."

"It is. She would want you to fight like hell."

Tanis sees the door to his room. His posters suddenly look dingy and childish. One says, "Trespassers will be shot, survivors shot again." The other sign says, "Due to the increasing cost of ammo, warning shots will not be fired."

He kicks the door open and steps in. Clothes are strewn about, along with a baseball, books, and an old computer he'd ripped apart to turn into a Linux server.

An ornate broadsword sits on the wall, gleaming like a precious stone. A Christmas gift, an authentic, handmade re-creation of a Middle Ages broadsword from a blacksmith in West Pennsylvania. It isn't very sharp, but it's the only weapon he has besides his .22 rifle.

Hana laughs, "You're planning on chopping them up, huh?"

Tanis swings the sword around. It's heavy and almost as tall as he is. "I guess not." He looks at his closet where the gun is. "I don't want to bother with my rifle either. Way underpowered, and it has only one shot. What I need is a flamethrower, not a peashooter to kill those Puppet-things." Tanis snaps his fingers, drags his camping box from the closet, and retrieves a hatchet, flashlight, poncho, and first aid kit.

He pours half the bottle of fish food into the tank

and says goodbye to Birdy.

"One more thing." He carefully removes the photo of Ma and Dad from a picture frame on his desk and stows it in his pack. "I'll betcha Ma is holed somewhere. She's pretty resourceful."

"I agree. Your mother couldn't have raised a kid with as much brains as you without some smarts herself," Hana says.

The two run back downstairs. Ian's still in the entry, watching the street through the front door window. "We need to go out the back," Ian says. "The fucks followed us here."

"Of course they have. How the hell can they do that?" Tanis complains, pissed. "We ran out of their sight!" He peeks through the window. "They're like hound dogs or somethin' that can smell us and track us."

"Yeah, it is strange," Hana replies, looking over her shoulder.

Ian runs to the back door. "Let's hop some fences. At least we can make it hard for them."

The breakfast table still has Tanis's bowl of cereal sitting on it, along with his copy of Wires And Circuits Magazine. The milk crusted at the edges, fuzzy white with mold. His Ma usually picked up after him. He sees her date book, open to a list of numbers for her doctor's office. The page edges are covered in dark, dried mucus. Tanis bites his lip and turns away.

Ian slides the glass door open.

Hana puts her hand on Tanis's shoulder, the pressure makes him close his eyes.

Ian steps onto the back porch. "Sorry, man. I know this is hard."

Tanis opens his eyes. "My ma would want me to go on." He looks at Hana. "Right?"

"Yes, above all else." Hana raises her hands. "I need a weapon other than my pistol, something that can chop them in half. Do you have anything?"

Tanis nods, sniffling, and runs out the back door to the side shed. He hauls open the rusty door. The shed is filled with sharp, useful yard tools. He looks at his tiny hatchet, decides it's too small for a primary weapon but good enough for backup, and clips it to his belt.

Hana grabs a shovel with a sharp, rounded tip. "Too weird," she says and jerks the stiff, metal rake out of its hanger on the wall.

Tanis grabs a short pitchfork Ma used to spread

straw over the back yard before winter frost.

Ian tugs off the drop cloth covering a few mountain bikes and smiles. "These might just be our way out." Three bikes in total, two older models, stand next to Tanis's sleek red and black one. "Got a pump?"

"Hell yeah."

Chapter 1.24

Markus
The Stone of Allah

One more balmy night in Tunisia before it's time to escape. Markus feels ready but also unprepared.

Mitchell and Markus dress in stolen robes; Mitchell ties a turban around Markus's head so he looks more like a local.

"I've no idea how long you've been in the CIA, but you're good at this, very good," Markus says.

"I am good at this," Mitchell says. "So why are you still shaking?"

"God will deliver us from here. But he never promised icy nerves." Markus grips his hands together to try to stifle the seismic activity.

The two wait for everyone to leave for the stadium to hear their great scholar.

"You still willing to help me uncover this secret?" Mitchell asks.

Markus nods. "I'm nervous but excited. I will gather strength from this purpose." Imagining the danger that lies ahead, he comments, "I think God would have me carry a gun."

"God's will, right?" Mitchell replies as he peeks out the front doorway covered with the stolen curtain.

"Yes, God would want his humble servant armed to the teeth," Markus whispers, Laughing softly. *Oh, if only Marian could see me now, she'd slap me upside the head and tell me that only fools need guns.*

Mitchell hands Markus the small revolver he usually keeps in his boot. "You're right. You need this. These guys aren't hippies. They believe in killing for what they want."

"I had a run-in with a gang that extorted money for the Genovese family of New York, or what was left of it anyway."

"These guys are ideologues, not thugs," Mitchell clarifies.

"Not sure I understand the difference," Markus continues, with or without Mitchell's attention. It calms his nerves to speak while they wait. That could be why he became a preacher. "I moved to New York to fill the shoes of a dear friend who died. His shoes were tough for me to fill, coming from the South and a small congregation. His church supported a huge community I never knew existed in New York." Markus paused, searching for words. "I stumbled upon a devious scheme plaguing my parishioners. While I rolled a large black cart up and down the streets, the younger kids would run around picking up trash. The older ones trimmed trees and raked leaves. I was three streets from the church when I noticed a trend. All the cars had little envelopes on the windshields. They were about half the size of a business card. No one knew or wanted to discuss what they were until I asked little Becka. She was reluctant but confessed. If her mother hadn't put twenty dollars in one of those envelopes, something bad would have happened to her car.

"I gathered a group of neighbors together and confronted them. At first, no one said a word. Then the truth spilled out. Gang bribes. Pay off the gang so their cars wouldn't get keyed, stolen, or smashed up at night. I was horrified. I told the police, and a month later, four men were arrested while collecting the money.

"Then my house was broken into. I was sleeping like the dead when two men burst into my room. They scared me and my wife nearly to death.

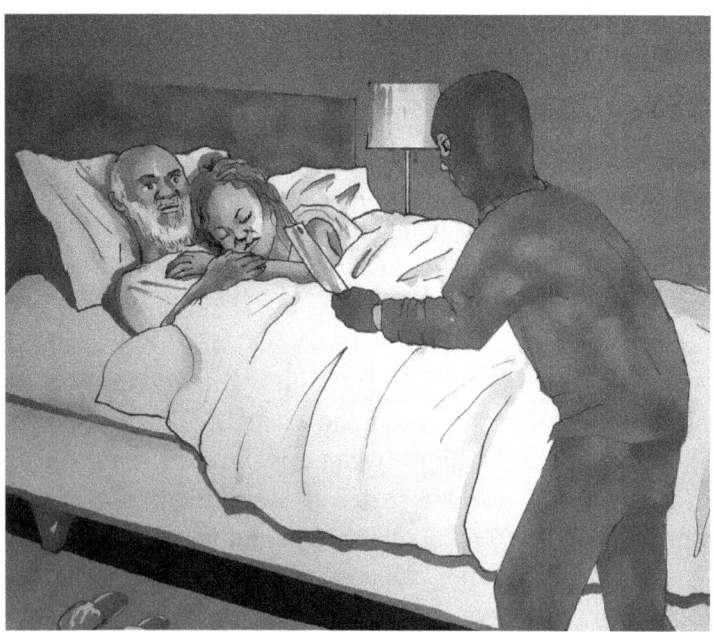

"They wore masks, of course, and brandished big blades. They bound my hands behind me and took me to meet their boss. I was forced to kneel, blindfolded. The man I saw stayed in the shadows, said he'd lost over five thousand dollars because of me, and said he was going to kill me. I believed him, so I pleaded for my life. They let me go with a warning to stay out of their business, and I did.

"The next month, I saw the little envelopes on all the cars again. I lost some parishioners. They were probably scared to come to church. But, even worse, I'd lost their trust and respect because I caved. Eventually, we didn't have enough people to run the mid-week services."

"Sounds like the Mafia to me," Mitchell says. "They *were* scared of you, though. You were in America. We're not now."

"I know that." Markus clears his throat.

"So what's your point?" Mitchell asks.

"I'm not a coward anymore. I've matured into what my wife calls bull-headed stupidity." Markus is pacing the dirt floor, eager and anxious to escape the shack's confines. He whispers a prayer.

The mosque horns blare—not the call to prayer, but another hypnotic, peaceful melody. The villagers fill the streets, walking in the opposite direction from the mosque. Twenty minutes later, the dusty streets are clear except for pockets of people here and there and a few European cars. The majority of the locals have departed.

Mitchell peeks around the fabric in the doorway again, hesitates, pokes his head out, and looks in all directions. He steps back inside, shushes Markus, and waves for him to follow. Mitchell runs, half-crouched. Markus's heart seems to stop, but he follows out onto the dusty, narrow roads.

The setting sun turns the sky bright orange and

pink. The fresh air is blessedly cooler than it was in the hut. Markus looks at every God-given detail of every wall, street, tree, and car. He blinks, his eyes watering.

Mitchell leads, stopping next to a tin shack similar to the one they left behind. It's empty. The two creep from shack to mud hut to house to housing complex until they're out of the slums.

They run through an ancient Medinine neighborhood of small, dome-shaped mud huts built right next to one another, some on top, stacking three stories tall. Narrow stairs snake up and over doorways, leading to upper-story huts and down into alleys.

"If I weren't scared for my life, I would explore and take photos," Markus whispers. "Not this trip."

"Shhh. Focus."

They turn a corner onto a narrow cobblestone street of nicer dome-shaped huts. Potted plants are set adjacent to doorsteps, and lampposts are just over the street from the top huts. Markus marvels at the contrast to the modern world. The ancient vista is ruined by an ugly Western-style apartment building on the horizon.

Mitchell stops at a shopping plaza in an updated part of Medinine. The square is paved with sandy pavers, and newer brick shops, wagons, and vegetable vendors fill the plaza's perimeter. Colorful tapestries shade plastic bins and wood crates full of oranges as bright as the sun, dates, and pomegranates.

Ornamental light poles surround the square and illuminate a curious piece of artwork: a rusted pail pouring water into a smaller pail pouring into two yet smaller pails. Mitchell translates the single word inscribed on a plaque: "It says rebirth."

They run around to the shadow of the large pail, where another plaque reads, *From the heavens came the sword*. Markus reflects on the sign for a moment, on how both the Bible and the Quran preach the end of the world. "The Quran says that Allah will wash the Earth clean of all the sinners or nonbelievers and restart a new society of love and peace. A road of destruction will be torn across the world, preparing for the coming of the twelfth Imam who will cleanse the world in totality." Markus's old friend introduced many Quran verses over the years. "Bible says the Four Horsemen of the Apocalypse will arrive and begin the cleansing wars in very much the same way."

"We'll get enough dopes to believe something, and they will make it happen. That's the contradiction of prophecy." Mitchell takes off toward the mosque.

"Hmmmm." Markus follows. He's so tired; he doesn't know how he's been able to run for so long. God must be working miracles on his cardiovascular system.

Finally, the Ali Ben Abid Mosque is in sight, the classic eight-story octagonal tower rising majestically into the sky. Markus takes in the ornamental arches in the lower portion of the tower, small windows on each level, the walkway encircling the eighth floor like a lighthouse, the apex topped with a traditional roof, and four loudspeakers.

Mitchell pauses in a shadow. "Wait by that small, gray, ten-year-old Kia. Got it?"

"Of course."

Mitchell runs toward the mosque's side entrance until he is out of sight. A moment later, he pokes his head around the corner and waves. Markus runs to him. Mitchell stands at the back door. Three guards, dead or out cold, lay on the pavement.

How in God's name did Mitchell subdue these heavily armed *men, still wearing their combat vests filled with bullets, grenades, and who knows what else? This is definitely* God's *hand.*

Mitchell strips their gear and takes the men's guns.

He hands Markus three weapons and proceeds to use a key card to open the door. The two drag the soldiers inside and roll them out of the way. Markus stacks the weapons in the far corner of the room. Markus and Mitchell are finally inside, safe for the moment.

Markus closes the door, shutting out the failing evening sunset, leaving him in darkness, his adrenaline peaking. His heartbeats echo in his ears, and his eyes adjust slowly to the darkness. *Oh, God, why have I chosen to be here, decoding history's obscurities? I should be home with my parishioners and wife, spreading Your Word.*

The lights flick on. The entire room is a metal-walled vault, without a single window, perhaps ten feet wide, fifteen feet long. Every wall is filled with papers, notes, and diagrams. Markus examines the most colorful diagram and recognizes a detailed map of Western Europe during the Middle Ages. He can't read the Arabic captions but wonders if the map represents the time of the Black Plague. A map of Caesarea is to his right, and the wall opposite has a map of Tunis and Medinine. The last wall holds a map of the world, dated 1918, with red marks all over it.

Mitchell reads the paper over Markus's shoulder, scaring the Holy Ghost out of the preacher. "Influenza outbreak in 1918 killed more than forty million people. More fatalities than WWI."

"You don't say," Markus mumbles. Both of them move to the map on the opposite wall. "What does this say?"

Mitchell interprets. "A dysentery plague in Tunis in 1943 and here in Medinine in 1985."

"King Louis may have died of dysentery," Markus says, recognizing the pattern.

"Yeah, so there are a few cases of dysentery. The bug's been in the historical record since the beginning." Mitchell moves to another wall. He reads, "1818. Dysentery again. This time, it was in Chicago. When did King Louis die?" Mitchell asks.

"1270," Markus says.

Other sites of dysentery are highlighted on the world map and cluster around the subtropical latitudes. The final poster illustrates a constellation and orbital pattern circling the solar system. Mitchell studies the diagram.

"Looks like these guys think there's a connection between meteor showers and viral outbreaks on Earth. But the dates don't line up. If dysentery came from a meteor shower, there would be a regular orbital pattern. The outbreaks would happen on a predictable schedule."

"Meteors can carry viruses?" Markus asks. "Doesn't it get too hot burning through the atmosphere?"

"Somebody should tell these guys that." Mitchell reads some more. "Here we go. There's a centurial orbit of asteroids plotted here that intersects with the asteroid belt just outside of Mars's orbit. Oh my god. They think the collisions of two different asteroid belts pushed some of these infected meteors to Earth. Weird."

Mitchell moves to the large safe in the far corner, pulls out a device the size of a credit card, and slaps it in the safe.

"CIA can do just about anything?" Markus ads.

"Yup. Your lovely tax dollars at work. We must know the world's secrets." Mitchel pushes buttons on the device and slowly spins the dial.

"Because the world is constantly plotting against you and the USA?" Markus's voice was toned with sarcasm.

Mitchell looks up from the device, as serious as he can get. "Yes. That's it exactly."

Markus continues to look around until Mitchell pops the safe door and pulls out an object wrapped in silk.

"You got it!"

Mitchell snickers like a boy. They admire the black and gold silk covering the object and unwrap it slowly and carefully, his hands trembling slightly. "This is the million-dollar secret." His voice is a rough whisper, his smile triumphant.

The stone is clear with tiny, barely visible cracks. The edges are not precisely cut, but the facets are smooth

and polished-looking. Unusual foggy shapes in the center mar the stone's clarity and beauty and are run through with delicate, golden veins.

Markus admires it but won't touch it. "This is the stone that killed John the Mighty, might have adorned the Holy Crown of Jesus Christ, and maybe even killed King Louis IX and countless others. Wonder what these ... things in the center are."

"No idea, but they look a little like fungus. This rock has been a secret for over seven hundred years," Mitchell adds. He rewraps the stone in the cloth. "We have to go now, Father."

"I'm not a Father. Just a preacher."

"Whatever you say." He stuffs the stone in his backpack. "My people will want to test this and see if it really is a killer stone from God."

Inspired, Markus rips down the maps and papers on the walls, shuffles them together, and rolls them like a scroll. He sees a red envelope on the desk, grabs it, and runs to Mitchell.

Mitchell smiles and nods, child-like mischief spreading over his face as he grabs Markus's hand. "When we leave this room, bow your head and barely peek at your feet. We're gonna run as fast as we can. Got it?"

"What is going to happen?"

"This is the hardest part, okay? Just do as I say."

Markus prays instead of arguing. *Something bad is about to happen. Please don't take my life, oh Lord.*

Mitchell flings the door open and runs right into a squad of very angry Tunisian soldiers.

Markus bows his head, almost closes his eyes, and looks at his feet, just as Mitchell had ordered.

CHAPTER 1.25

ISABELLA
SHOPPING FOR BOMBS

It's close to noon on an already hot bitch of a day. Humidity levels are through the roof from the rain last night. Isabella can't complain too much—cramped in the little rowboat was worse than sweltering heat and dank air. Hell, she'd rather have her nails ripped off than have to spend one more night in that glorified canoe surrounded by a million rotting, bloated corpses. *No, I gotta keep some perspective.*

The stores are full of shit the survivors need, and no one around to stop her from taking it. Well, except for the Puppets, but she's got them covered.

Isabella leads Markus and Josh up the path, away from the kiddy dock to the nearest road. Her mission is to find a market and stock up on food and water, lots of it. She passes a grove of trees and follows a ramp connecting to Cross Bay Boulevard.

Tanis, Hana, and Ian had already taken off in the other direction.

So far, the only sounds are the wind in the trees, waves on the beach, and the small noises the trio make. No Puppets yet.

The three walk fast and steady through the urban jungle. She is alert and in warrior mode. A mode she became familiar with while fighting in Iraq. The only difference is, then she had to slow herself and her squad and take methodical moves. Now, speed is the game. Here, there are no enemies sniping or pointing rocket-propelled grenade launchers from balconies. Advancing with speed when years of training tell her to stay low, go easy, and be watchful adds to her anxiety. Isabella scans at every window, every gap in the vegetation, every car, her Beater and M-16A at the ready.

Josh carries his small electric chainsaw, oddly enough not killed by the EMP, and Markus's bat rests on his shoulder, ready to swing. The trio is ready for a fight, but avoiding one is her first priority. She doesn't need any more wounds.

Isabella wouldn't mind beating down a few hundred Puppets, but she's tired and sore, the mission comes first. She can crash for a day or two once she brings her squad back safely.

The first Puppet pops up after a half-mile, more stumbling from the bushes along the right of way. She wants to bash all their little heads in but runs past them instead.

She leads Markus and Josh past a small strip mall.

None of the businesses look promising: a tile shop, a tuxedo shop, a Mexican restaurant, and a bait shop.

The next block housed a pizza joint and a wave-runner shop. "A wave-runner would be nice."

"But they're just paperweights now, after the EMP," Josh argues, huffing and puffing.

"No shit, captain obvious," Isabella replies.

"7-Eleven!" Josh says. "Convenience stores are gold mines."

"Twinkies and fried chips and melted candy. Let's try to find real food first," Markus replies. "We'll come back to it if we need to."

Further down the street, Josh parallels Isabella. "You ever wonder why we're the only ones still alive?"

Isabella nods. "Uh huh, but not when I'm in the lion's mouth. Let's wonder which god did the miracle and why when we're on the ship wading through boxes of food and pills."

Josh shrugs. "Hmmm."

Isabella sees a Duane Reade drug and grocery store and stops across the parking lot from the front door. Fifteen Puppets stand around under the awning, lingering like they're waiting for the door to open so they can buy their energy drink or photo prints off their USB sticks or grab a pack of smokes.

Isabella motions for Josh and Markus to join her in a semi-dark doorway of a law office; they watch the Puppets mill around.

"They look bored," Isabella mumbles.

Josh answers–he seems to always have an answer. "Probably looking for something to attack. I wonder what they will do when everything is assimilated."

"Fucking finally die."

Markus drinks from his bottle and then says, "Will

those things ever truly die? If they do, will they drop to the ground and rot away?"

"Hopefully, they will rot into the mud," Isabella says.

"Maybe the Earth will retake this place, break down these monsters into fertilizer, feed the crops for the next civilization," Josh says.

Isabella grits her teeth. "We can't let the Puppets win, can't let them take everything."

Markus puts his hand on her shoulder gently. "Our Eden is out there somewhere. That's something."

"Food is something. Let's circle around to the back," Isabella says softly and moves out. She leads Markus and Josh behind a toppled delivery truck and then hustles to a smashed sedan. "It's clear. But keep your eyes open. I don't want any fuckers to see us go in."

"You and me both," Markus says.

After watching the tree line, the visible car wrecks, and the street for a minute, Isabella bolts to the back door. Markus and Josh, though taken aback, follow her. She hands her Beater to Markus, tells him and Josh to stand back, and shoots five rounds into the lock. It disengages. Josh helps her pry the door open; the three slip inside.

"This place is ransacked." Josh looks around.

"Still, there might be shit we can use." Isabella closes the back door and crams a doorstopper under it.

"We need medicine," Markus says. "Whatever is left, by the grace of God."

"Good. Josh, you get water, as much as you can fit in a shopping cart. Pile it high," Isabella orders. "I'll get food."

Isabella finds a cart, stops at the first-aid aisle. Her injuries are healing, but if she doesn't get clean bandages on them, they'll end up festered. She's not about to go out because of an infection. She finds the last bottle of hydrogen peroxide, cleanses her uncovered wounds, re-bandages them all.

She tosses the rest of the first-aid supplies, especially the antiseptics and antibiotic salves, into her cart.

After playing nurse, she loads up on canned soup, tuna, chicken, and sweet beans. A dozen kinds of beef jerky are magically still on the shelves, and she takes them all with a smile. More food is around the corner, so she pushes her cart down the aisle, sweeping the shelves with her arms and dumping everything into her cart.

She passes a bin of discount DVDs, and her eyes linger. The shitty movies aren't her type, but the luxury of sitting on a couch and watching a movie is entrancing. *Everyone, including the poor people, had it better in this country than* almost *everywhere else. But did they know it?* She spent time in the Middle East with families that had so little. She also knew people who had never crossed the borders or flown to another country or overseas and who didn't know what the rest of the world was like. *Political pricks and media boobs talk so much about poverty, but very little real poverty exists here. Americans are just poor in their hearts, maybe because they've had it too good ... spoiled.*

She chucked at her thoughts. *Now, we're all equally poor, thrust into the dark ages by something tiny, powerful, and indiscriminate.*

The wheels of her cart roll over dried blood and bump over a magazine promising a better sex life and a six-pack. She passes a cooler filled with tubs of liquid ice cream and popsicle sticks floating in colored water.

She finishes her rounds. Her cart is overstuffed with food and first-aid stuff–she even grabbed a handful of fresh surgical masks for Josh. She stopped loading, knowing that making it back to the boat gets exponentially harder with the more weight she's got to manage. She meets Markus and Josh at the back door. Josh has duck-taped potholders to his upper and lower arms, has a novelty Giants helmet on his head, and a bent cookie sheet strapped to each thigh. He still has his white medical mask on, too. It makes Isabella laugh, but she doesn't say a word. *Whatever keeps your heart tickin'.*

Isabella opens the back door. "Let's make a run for it."

Markus and Josh nod.

Predictably, hell has gathered outside. A pack of twenty Puppets is waiting, and hundreds more are shambling toward the building. They rush forward, pushing to get inside the doorway. One gets its hand into the crack, so Isabella slams the door repeatedly until the hand comes off.

It comes off way too easily, and the puppet doesn't react—no scream of pain or howl of rage, no change in its expression. Nothing.

"How did they? Damnit! What do we do now?" Josh shrieks. "I mean, what the fuck do we do! We can't push past them with all these carts! We're stuck here. Stuck!"

Isabella smacks Josh across the plastic helmet. "Shuts your trap and take that thing off. It doesn't protect your head from anything but respect.

He's telling her with his eyes that the smack wasn't completely necessary. Isabella tells him with her eyes that it was.

"We do need a plan," Markus says.

"Don't you have the Almighty on your side? Where are His answers?" Isabella snaps. She's getting pissed. "How the hell are they following us? Huh? They can't fucking see us. Their eyes are just white root things. Can

they hear us?"

"God only knows," Markus says.

"Be right back." Isabella runs to the front door.

"Hurry up!" Josh yelps. "The Puppets are mobbing the parking lock as if this were Black Friday."

Isabella wishes she was in that Bradley fighting vehicle, unloading that cannon into the center mass of every single one. "I'd blow them all to stew-sized chunks."

However, the Puppets aren't as crowded at the front door as they are at the back door. "Markus! Josh!" The two run up to her, expecting to see something terrible. "Look, they're following us. They're gathering at the back door because that's where we went. Maybe if we get them to come to the front door, we can make a break for it when the herd at the back thins out."

The three bang on the front sliding glass doors surrounded by thick windows. Too thick to be broken, she hopes. Ten minutes later, they have the crowd foaming at the possibility of tearing them apart.

"Do it," Isabella yells, runs to the back door, cracks it, and finds a bunch still back there. "Shit, this doesn't make any sense. Some fell for it, but these didn't. Why? They must have stronger memories." She slams the door shut, turns, and round-houses an empty energy drink display off the pharmacy checkout counter.

"That plan sucked. We wasted thirty-five minutes," Josh whines. "And there's more coming every minute!"

"You come up with something, Doof," Isabella shouts, wanting to smack him again.

"They seem to dislike fire. Maybe we can start one," Markus says.

"That's actually a good thought, Pops." Isabella looks around. "Big hot fire is what we need."

Josh runs ahead, yelling, "Camping, aisle nine!"

Isabella takes an empty cart to the liquor aisle and grabs a handful of T-shirts on the way.

Josh and Isabella meet at the back door. She has a case of hard booze that had gone overlooked by previous looters, and Josh has gas canisters. Isabella smiles, twists open the booze bottles, tears the T-shirts into pieces and stuffs the rags into the bottles. Twenty-two Molotov cocktails.

Markus nests the bottles side by side in an empty cart, and Josh fits the fist-sized camping gas canisters among the bottles.

Isabella lights the T-shirt wicks, watching them burn

slowly. "This better work, fellas. Otherwise, I'm using one of you as my distraction."

"I appreciate the warning." Markus opens the back door, and the three shove the cart outside as hard as they can. The cart collides with the pack and stops. They push harder, slowly moving the Puppets back until the door is able to close. Markus leaves the door open just a crack, kicking the doorstop under the bottom. He dashes back, hiding next to Josh. Isabella aims her rifle through the gap.

"Cover your ears!" She flicks the safety off the M-16A and breathes. "Big fire, please," she whispers and pulls the trigger.

The bottle of Everclear she aimed for bursts, showering flaming fuel outward. Fire instantly ignited the rest of the rags. The entire cart is burning. Isabella's second shot punches into the heart of a gas canister. She spins away from the door opening as a powerful explosion rocks the building, spreading shrapnel from the cylinders and the shopping cart in every direction. Another canister is thrown high in the air, landing hard on the asphalt. That, too, explodes, along with three others. The explosion blows the door open and breaks the tempered glass, twisting the metal frame.

"Shit. That was big. All the canisters went off, right?" Isabella says. She peers into the smoking mess. The Puppets nearest the blasts were blown to pieces; those farther back are on fire and scattering. "Now's our chance. Run!"

Each one of them grabs the handle of a cart and collectively shoves them out the door.

Markus and Josh follow Isabella around the debris field of shrapnel and some body parts and onto Cross Bay, heading back to the ship. The rattle of thick plastic tires and janky metal frames draws the dead like a siren's call.

Isabella rams a puppet in a Red Hot Chili Peppers t-shirt and knocks it over. His buds are still in his ears, and the cord is no longer connected to his iPod.

The carts vibrate even louder wildly on the pavement.

Josh loses a jug of water.

Isabella's mind is in survival mode: her glands spit out adrenaline, endorphins pump into her body, and heat flows from her like a dragon's breath. The fuel lets her move fast. Much faster than the Puppets. Even Markus and Josh lag.

The horde definitely can't keep up, falling farther and farther behind. Isabella slows as ankle pain fights past her sledgehammering heart. She looks for something else to focus on in order to ignore her complaining wounds.

The wheels on the carts, made for smooth floors, rattle like an insane monkey locked in a cage. The sound reminds her of the rapid fire of a nail gun. She huffs as her brain seizes an old image, old feelings, dragging her back to the poverty of her childhood. Every now and again she goes back there, allowing the wound to reopen and the remorse to have its harvest.

Isabella remembers walking in on one of Father's interrogations. It was late Sunday night when she was twelve. She was in the kitchen, getting a glass of water, when she heard a thud. The floor jumped under her feet.

The basement door was open. Another thud, followed by a scream that was silenced as quick as it came. Isabella remembers that night in bright detail: the squeaking cellar door, damp odors flowing up the stairs, her white, velvety Mary Jane slippers.

Isabella tiptoed down the stairs and stopped when she could see Father. A single lamp on a desk lit the basement. Father and cousin Lorenzo had their backs to her, their shadows stretching out across the concrete floor like monsters. A guy was strapped to a chair with a sock crammed into his mouth. Blood was all over his face, and his eyes were wild.

Her father hissed at the guy, but she couldn't hear what he said over the thumping in her ears. Lorenzo had the nail gun. He shot a nail into the ceiling. "You gonna get one in the other leg, so help me God. Maybe in your family jewels next time."

Father pulled the sock from the man's mouth and waited.

The man coughed blood on Father's face.

Lorenzo brought the gun to the man's leg and pulled the trigger. THUNK!

The man's cry was cut short by the sock crammed back into his mouth.

Isabella yelped, turned, and ran upstairs.

Father stomped after her, yelling her name, busted down her bedroom door, pulled her off the bed, and smacked her across the face. "Do not go where you should not be." He'd hissed, looking and sounding like the devil in the darkness of young Isabella's room. It wasn't the first time she'd met his evil side. When he was in a rage, he looked like an Orc with red eyes and deep wrinkles.

He hit her repeatedly. "I have to show you with pain how not to stick your nose in business you don't understand," he yelled.

She never cried again when he hit her. It hurt, but she didn't let herself cry. Sometimes it would piss him off that she wasn't sobbing.

This same man, on Sundays, would act like he was God's favorite son. He'd hug old ladies, give money to the church, and pray. He liked talking about family and strength, but he was the weakest of all.

Isabella wonders if he's dead, and if so, did he ever see his true self? Or did he die wrapped in the costume of his own lies?

###

Isabella, Markus, and Josh continue running down Cross Bay toward the ship; Isabella sees Markus trailing, so

she slows.

Markus heaves, "I–can't run–anymore."

"Fine, but don't lag too much. Otherwise, see ya,"

Isabella groans because they are so close to the beach. Josh huffs and gasps, too. He chugs from a bottle of water.

Finally, they reach the path to the shore. No Puppets. The heavily loaded carts wobble and sway on the rough terrain, but the three manage to get to the beach, winded, sweat pouring off their bodies. They stop for a moment to rest, chests heaving, throats dry.

"Okay, we only have a little way to go," Isabella says, shoving her cart with her whole body. The cart stops and nearly topples when the front wheels sink into the soft sand. She calls quietly, "Get closer but stay out of the sand. The wheels are too small."

Turning to look for a better route, blocking the sun with her hand, Isabella sees a tall figure moving toward them at top speed…*Ian on a mountain bike? Hana and Tanis following him, a dog running with them?* The hairy white mutt, with brown and black patches in its matted coat, looks happy. *Fuckin' dogs always look happy.*

Josh jumps up and down.

Ian skids to a stop and runs to Isabella. "Hey, nice work." A metal rack with two five-gallon gas cans is strapped on the back of his bike, and two are on Tanis's bike.

"Looks like you did okay, too." Isabella smiles for the first time since she outsmarted those goons in the Bradley fighting vehicle.

Ian looks at her cockeyed like she's a mute who just spoke English. "Nice smile."

"Shut up." She turns away, but Ian keeps staring, his smile wide and infectious.

"Don't make me smack you upside the head." Isabella is barely resisting laughing.

"Right," Ian says, still smiling.

Hana pulls up to Ian's side. "Nice to see you brought the groceries," she says. "Let's get off the mainland, shall we?"

"Yeah, let's," Josh says as he pets the dog.

"This dog comin' with us?" Isabella doesn't like dogs much. The mutt sniffs at her and licks her shoe. She shoos it away. "I'm off-limits, mutt."

Tanis rides past her slowly. "My dog's name is Kat." He laughs and rides to the dock, shouting, "The boat's floating away!"

Isabella runs to the water's edge. The rowboat is bobbing in the water, slowly moving away. Before Isabella has a chance to react, Ian dives into the water. She considers joining him because he swims as slow as a cripple.

Markus says, "The Puppets are gathering. If we don't get that boat, we'll have to swim to the *Pioneer* and carry these groceries in our pockets."

Ian reaches the rowboat and tries to haul himself into it, making it rock and take on water. Finally, he gets his right leg over the gunwale but doesn't climb into the boat. Panting, Ian slides his arms under the mast thwart, looks at the water, curses, and kicks his left leg hard.

Isabella's blood surges in her body as she watches Ian struggle. She wades into the shallows. "Never send a man to do a woman's job. For fuck's sake, Ian! You look like a wus!"

"Something's got my leg!" he shouts. He kicks again, harder, and heaves every part of his body except his left lower leg into the boat.

Isabella yanks her pistol free flicks off the safety and aims.

"Don't shoot me!" Ian shouts, his voice coming in gasps as he reaches for an oar but can't free it from under the seats. Ian reaches for the next seat and pulls himself farther into the boat, the Puppet hand clutching his ankle rising higher above the water's surface.

"Then don't move!" She aims for the wrist curled around Ian's leg. *Damn, he's moving too much.*

The Puppet tries to drag Ian back into the water. He wraps his arms around the center thwart and tries to bend his knee up, but the grip is tight, the Puppet heavy.

Isabella takes a breath. He's only ten yards away, no problem. She taps the trigger. The gun's explosion echoes in the stillness, the sound reverberating several times before it dies away.

The hole in the Puppet's forearm leaves only a thin strip of Puppet skin holding the hand to the end of the bloody stump. The hand sinks under the water.

Ian swallows hard, shakes his head to clear it, sits up on the thwart, frees an oar, and rows toward the dock.

"That was a cool shot, Isabella," Josh says. "Very cool. Where's a vid recorder when you need one?"

"Yeah," Tanis agrees.

Ian shouts, "Get the gear and groceries to the end of the dock and be ready."

"Disturbing, " Markus says. "They aren't drowning. That one was under the water, waiting."

"Speaking of waiting," Hana said, "Those things aren't going to stay back much longer. We have to get these carts to the dock and fast."

Markus and the others cluster around the three overloaded carts, but no one can say immediately how they're going to get them through the sand.

Ian shouts, "Hey! Help me!" He's dragging the rowboat out of the shallows onto the sand. "Load the stuff in here, and we'll drag the boat back to the water."

No one argues, and all six of them pitch in, empty the carts into the boat, finally loading the fuel cans and Kat.

Tanis points at the dog, "Stay, put."

Puppets are thirty, maybe forty yards off, filling the

path, bush-whacking through the thickets. Tanis wonders for a moment if these Puppets used to be his neighbors, maybe his friends' parents.

Isabella looks behind them. "Get a move on it!"

Finally, the boat is in the water, riding very low with the heavy load. Isabella stands at the edge of the shallow surf, Beater poised, guarding their retreat.

A Puppet lumbers close enough to grab Isabella's arm with fingers much stronger than the others. This Puppet's clothes are skimpy, her fake tits lopsided, her skin bluish and pale. Her sunken cheeks are practically skeletal, but Isabella sees something worm-like moving under the dead chick's skin. Roots already protrude from multiple places on her body, some like hooks, others stretching and reaching like tentacles.

Isabella raises her Beater and points it at the Puppet's face. Before she can strike, the Puppet reaches for the Beater with surprising agility. Isabella dodges and says, "I am so damn tired of looking at your ugly mug, bitch!" and thrusts the Beater into the face; the thing's skull cracks like an eggshell. The thing lunges for Isabella despite its brain matter falling out.

Isabella shifts to her right, sweeps her Beater behind the Puppet's legs, and watches it fall onto its butt. The Puppet gets up awkwardly, pathetically. Isabella jabs it in the chest, feeling the ribs crack, yanks her Beater back so it doesn't get stuck. A strange, gurgling noise bursts from the Puppet's throat, exposing a long root coming out. Isabella keeps the sickening creature at the end of her stick, forces the thing to the water's edge, and shoves hard. It stumbles and falls, floundering face down in the water.

Isabella sees her own weakness working against her. She doesn't like fucking up something so weak, so twisted.

She's not totally cold inside.

"Come on, Isabella!" Ian yells.

Another Puppet reaches her, some ugly dude. She grabs his shirt sleeve and spins him like a top, backs toward the boat, jabs the next Puppet's knee, and its whole leg breaks sideways. It's not able to stand anymore and topples over, the sand absorbing its black blood.

Isabella splashes out to the rowboat as the others scrunch together to make room for her. Josh leans over the gunwale, hand extended; she grabs hold of him and clambers into the boat. She stumbles, lands hard on cans and boxes, whacks her injured ankle, and makes it throb.

Ian rows hard, his chest, shoulder, and arm muscles bulging, sweat rolling down his face and neck.

The chick with the fake tits sloshes toward them. It can't swim, but it sure is trying.

"Come on," Josh complains. "Let's go faster."

Ian roars like a wounded bear, "We're dragging."

"Yeah, I feel it, too," Hana replies.

The Puppet, sloshing toward the boat, submerges itself up to its head but still keeps coming for them.

Josh, arms spread to the gunwales to help balance the overloaded boat, shouts to Ian, "The Puppet is still under us! Don't let it grab your oar!"

Hana and Ian keep rowing, but the boat isn't moving at all.

"There's more than one below us, Ian!" Markus calls out.

CHAPTER 1.26

MARKUS
THE BIG CAMEL

Mitchell and Markus run out of the Ali Ben Abid Mosque straight into a squad of Tunisian soldiers, their leader barking orders and gesturing emphatically.

Mitchell holds Markus's hand like a vise. Markus, head bowed, peeks at his feet and runs as Mitchell instructed. He glances up for an instant and regrets it immediately: ten machine-gun barrels stare back at him. His heart sinks.

Cringing, waiting for bullets to tear through his body, Markus prays, asking God to protect Mitchell and comfort Marian.

Explosions burst in front of him like fireworks.

Brilliant white light washes all color from what he can see. A pressure wave hammers him, and he sways on his feet, shutting his eyes tighter. His eardrums hurt, sounds are muffled and far away.

Mitchell squeezes Markus's hand, pulling him sideways. Markus tries not to stumble.

The light is still incredibly bright. Markus's closed eyelids are almost neon pink, not red. The light fades, and his eyes open.

Mitchell is still holding tight, urging Markus to

follow him. The soldiers are shooting, but wildly. Bullets whine around them, kicking chunks of the walls and pavement into the air like shrapnel. The machine gun bursts still sound muffled.

"Run, old man!" Mitchell yells. The two race around a building, duck into a corner and stop to rest. Mitchell grips Markus's upper arm firmly; the preacher looks at his rescuer, sees a hypodermic needle in Mitchell's hand, and feels the sharp jab near his shoulder.

"You have to run as fast as you've ever run in your life. Got it? Follow me." Mitchell peers around the corner, looks in all directions, and says, "Come on!"

Markus runs in Mitchell's footsteps. Markus breathes easily, no longer gasping for air. His muscles and sore knees stop aching; his body is lithe and strong, better than when he was a fit, athletic young man. He wants to sing!

Mitchell looks back, smiling.

"What was that?" Markus calls, marveling that he can run and talk simultaneously without huffing and puffing.

"What was what?" Mitchell increases the pace.

Markus sprints to catch Mitchell. "I'm running like The Flash, no idea I could do this." His arm is tender where Mitchell jabbed him. "You drugged me!"

"CIA sweet stuff!" Mitchell says as they run in step, both grinning. "Experimental. Gets you going! I saved it for our escape. Don't worry. Side effects are a headache and nausea!"

The stuff is sweet, fantastic. Markus's clothing snaps in the cool wind, sending tingles through his body. They zigzag through the neighborhoods; the few people in the streets stay clear. The two run through the neighborhoods of old dome houses, around a manufacturing plant, and past apartment buildings.

The sun sets. Lamps flicker on, lighting sections of the streets, leaving long stretches of cobblestone dark. Markus and Mitchell zig and zag, taking advantage of the moonless night.

They slow to a fast trot when they reach the edge of town, still wary of followers. Mitchell stops at a huge wooden gate into a fenced compound, the red paint weather-beaten. Mitchell lifts a key tied on a length of thin cord from his neck, unlocks the sturdy modern padlock, pushes one side open on well-oiled hinges, and they walk into a large stockade, where Markus sees two camels, waiting patiently, bulky packs already loaded on their backs.

Markus regrets doubting Mitchell, grateful that the CIA man is resourceful and prepared for the two of them to escape. The Lord is shining on them. Markus feels like hugging Mitchell.

Markus struggles to mount the kneeling camel, surprised at just how tall the animal is. He holds on tight as the beast raises its back legs and then its front legs. Because of the drug, Markus feels like he wants to jump out of the saddle and run to the moon.

Mitchell mounts the other camel and leads the way. Twenty minutes later, Mitchell points to a small guard station in the distance. "See those bushes? You're going to hide there, with the camels, until I get back. And whatever you do, be quiet and do not move until I tell you to. Got it?"

Mitchell helps Markus position the camels, climbs off his beast, and disappears into the night. Markus waits, praying for Mitchell's safety.

Ten minutes later, Mitchell returns, blood splattered on his hands and forearms. Markus prays for the souls of the people Mitchell wounded or killed.

The stars are out in full force. Markus always watched the sky at night growing up in Alabama. Living in New York City, he felt estranged, disconnected from the sky by the light pollution. Pity. The stars are so majestic

and beautiful. His drug-induced happiness is so intense he thinks he's going to cry.

Markus watches Mitchell and tries to copy the way he lets his body move with his camel's. They pass a large natural-gas-fueled electric power plant at the edge of town, lighted like a carnival.

Markus looks behind him and sees the lights of Medinine. Helicopters fly around the city, searching wide swaths of the neighborhoods with powerful spotlights.

Mitchell plans to go south into the heart of the Sahara Desert. Markus doesn't want to go into the Sahara. He whispers a verse from Psalm 121 to himself: "The Lord shall preserve thee from all evil; He shall preserve thy soul. The Lord shall preserve thy going out and thy coming in from this time forth, and even for evermore."

An hour later, they reach the edge of a large lake. Markus is mesmerized by the reflection of the rising moon and bright stars in the water. They ride on the water's edge so the lapping waves will wash away their tracks.

"So beautiful!" he yells to Mitchell. Markus sees beauty everywhere, except for the stench coming from the power plant. This is an enchanted place. He raises his hands. "Oh, if Marian could be with me! She would be filled with romance. Oh, oh, if Sister Jordan could see this. Jordan was my secretary and had a wandering heart. She wanted to see the world more than I."

"Beauty is skin deep here. The lake is completely dead," Mitchell replies. "Poisoned by a chemical factory fifteen years ago. They dumped chemicals into underground rivers which flowed into the lake."

Markus shrugs. "Still beautiful." He does some thinking while riding his camel, gazing at the stars. He imagines what the Apocalypse will look like. Who will be the Four Horsemen? Who is the Antichrist? Will he be the president of a country or the head of an international corporation? His head buzzes and tingles with so many possibilities. The stars seem to dance like fireflies on the edge of the Alabama River. *Is God trying to talk to me?* He listens to the twinkling lights for a while.

The camels continue to move along into the night, walking easily on the soft sand. Besides a grunt now and again and an odor, they are quite pleasant.

The night goes on, and eventually, the moon sets. Pressure grows in Markus's head. The stars aren't so pretty now, and neither is the moon. All the light around grows coarse and jagged, with long, exaggerated spikes emanating from every source.

"You okay?" Mitchell asks. "You're not cooing over the view anymore."

Markus doesn't answer, slumped in his saddle. Pushing air from his lungs seems too arduous a task. The nausea kicks in. He loses his stomach over the side of the camel in heaving convulsions.

"Light nausea!" Markus screams at Mitchell, wiping his mouth. *Oh, if the Lord permitted me violence, I'd kill Mitchell for drugging me even though he saved my life.* The muscles in his legs tighten. He tries to rub them, but his hands ache too much. Pain follows until he slips from his camel like a sack of stones and passes out before he hits the ground.

Markus wakes up to the bright sun. The air is still cool, but that will change soon. His head thumps. He reaches up and pulls a tattered wet rag off his forehead.

"You feeling better?" Mitchell asks, between sips from a cup of coffee.

"I will once you share that coffee with me." Mitchell hands Markus a small blue metal mug. It's some of the best coffee on Earth. "Wow," he says, sipping eagerly.

"Arabian Java," Mitchell says, smiling. "Very fresh."

"You've been holdin' out. We haven't had fresh coffee this entire time."

Mitchell nods. "Saved it. I knew we'd need the boost on this trip. We have to cross about five hundred kilometers of desert to get where we're going."

"Please, I'm American. How many miles is that?"

Mitchell laughs, "About three hundred."

"That sounds better, even though I know it's the same distance." Markus feels safe now, safer than he'd felt in a long time despite the fact that there is nothing but sand dunes everywhere. "And where are we going?" Markus asks, sipping the warm, heavenly coffee.

Mitchell points toward the rising sun, "A secret drone base outside of Touggourt, Algeria."

CHAPTER 1.27

BEN
KILLING FOR PARMESAN

The clock ticks in Ben's head. He wishes he had a real clock to look at because the one in his head is usually wrong, and he can't be sure what time it is or how long Ian and the others have been gone. Ian, Tanis, and Hana went to find the kid's house, a fool's errand. Isabella, Josh, and Markus went for supplies. Ben hopes they bring back some good shit. And he really hopes they bring tequila because he's stuck on this boat with crybabies Rice and Andy. She paces the deck like a caged walrus, but thankfully, Andy is passed out in one of the rooms.

Ben looks for a shady place to sit. It's getting shit-hot under the sun. He climbs down into the belly of the boat, but it's like stepping into a sauna. His pits instantly become sweat sprinklers. *Windows. Gotta open some windows.*

The first area is the big kitchen. Four stainless steel sinks line the wall to the left. Two double-door refrigerators gleam at the rear of the kitchen. There's a bench to the right and two food prep tables in the middle. It's an impressive galley. *Galley, I think that's what* fishhead *sailors call it.* Polished redwood covers the walls and the floors.

Ben opens the two side portals and four ceiling hatches to get a cross-breeze going. The kitchen is pretty awesome. Lots of drawers filled with every kinda cooking tool. He opens the refrigerator. Empty. A cookbook hangs next to the fridge on a hook. He thumbs through the pages and reads aloud, "Crostini-filled mushroom caps, bacon-wrapped shrimp. Holy shit, that sounds good." On the next page, "Cornish game hens with a blackberry sauce, veal served over wild mushroom cream, and a salmon and wine dish." His stomach growls and rolls.

Rice comes down the steps, "What's going on?" She's clearly bored out of her mind.

Ben can suggest something to take her mind off things. Something hard. He laughs to himself. "Party boat for rich dudes and their dudettes," He says, staring at Rice. She has a pretty face, for sure. Puffy from all the crying. He'd definitely play with her ta-tas. Rice turns away. He hands her the menu, "Check out what's for dinner."

She takes the book. "Are you going to cook this tonight?" she asks nervously but playfully.

Ben shrugs, "I'd love to. Let me pull a game hen out of my ass."

"Oh, I'll have the veal. Got one of those in your you-know-what?" She chuckles and loosens up.

"Nice choice." Ben takes the book back and hangs it on the hook. "I just hope they stop at Romeo's Delectable Market for some fresh pasta."

"I shop there too sometimes," Rice says. "They have chicken parmesan I'd kill for."

"I love their Nine Cheese Rosatti." Ben salivates as he leaves the kitchen and heads deeper into the boat. "Nothin' like it in the world," he says over his shoulder.

"Nine cheese?" she comments easily. "That's a lot."

Ben enters the dining area, where two eight-person tables sit on either side of the walkway. Bookshelves here and there are filled, and a flat-screen TV is mounted in the center. Along all the edges of the room are cushy benches.

"I can get used to this." Rice agrees. She continues down the hall to the bedrooms. Ben peeks in the first room. It's got double bunks for stick people. "Jeez," he mumbles.

"I don't think I'd fit in these beds." Rice laughs. She knows what he means. She's a big fish like he is. "Good thing we have a kid and a skinny nerd with us." Andy sleeps soundly on the bottom bed, so Rice carefully and quietly opens the portal above him.

The breeze gets stronger. Fresh air hits Ben's face. The beads of sweat that have formed on his temple cool his skin. God, it feels good. He closes his eyes and breathes. His head gets quiet. He loves it when his thoughts stop.

"You okay?" Rice asks.

She totally rips him from his Zen.

He grunts and moves from the room. He usually hates talking to people. Occasionally, he'd count how many people he had to talk to in a day. It was a good day if he didn't have to say a word to anyone. He'd feel like an invisible man like he was watching his life on television for the fun of it. He loved every minute of his solitude.

But now he feels the walls closing in on him. There's

one wall in particular, one behind him, that doesn't stop coming closer and closer. Nervousness whips through his heart, and he shudders. *This fucking sucks.* One minute he feels relaxed, and the next, he's freaking out and trying not to show it.

Rice just smiles, which exaggerates her dimples. She has a good smile. Ben likes that she's here distracting him from being smashed by the darkness around him.

The following two rooms have twin beds. "One of these is mine," Ben proclaims. "I'm gonna block out that sun and sleep for a week."

"Big rooms." Rice peeks in. "Very nice. I've never been on a boat this big."

"Me neither. I've just been on speedboats, racing boats that burn through the water and make your nipples stand up." That was a lie. Ben has never been on anything other than a rowboat. He looks at her to see if she sees through the lie. She doesn't. At any rate, he's probably kicked someone's ass that's been on a boat this big.

There's a full bathroom with a tub behind the next door. "Rich people got it good, even at sea," he exclaims. "This is an f-ing million-dollar yacht!"

Rice moves in and tests the water. It works. "Oh shit, I can take a bath! There is a God, after all. Oh, I have to tell Andy. He loves baths."

"No hot water, though," he reminds her.

"I don't care. I just need to get wet."

"Oh, yeah?" He says and gives her his orgasm face. She shoots him a frown.

Ben pretends to smack himself across the face. "Sorry, that didn't come out right."

She shrugs. She's definitely a prude.

Ben moves to the room at the end of the hallway. It's the master bedroom. He runs to the huge bed and cannonballs onto it. The mattress is so soft. "I change my mind. *This* is my room."

Rice follows and pokes her nose in the bathroom and all the drawers. "Eight people, seven beds. This will be fun."

"You wanna rock this king-size luxury bed?" Ben pats the cushion.

"Keep dreaming," Rice replies but flashes that cute

smile again.

If he can chill out the creep inside, he might be able to get into her pants. "Joke, just a joke," He pleads forgiveness with a puppy-dog face and opens the hatches at the head of the bed. After a sweet moment of silence, they leave the room.

Andy is awake. He runs to Rice's side and grabs her arm like a lifeline. They head to the upper deck and sit together on the settee between the two masts. The sun has gone behind a thick, dark cloud of smoke, so they get a little relief from the heat.

The ropes and metal pulleys tap against the mast in the wind. Tink, tink. . . tink, tink. The rhythm echoes like a clock. Ben wishes he had a joint.

A few Puppets stumble to the end of the small dock where the rowboat is tied up.

"What are they doing?" Rice asks. Ben shrugs.

One of the dead fucks looks over the edge of the dock at the rowboat. It loses its balance and falls into the water. "Whoa! Look at that sack of skin!" He laughs at its clumsiness.

"What are they doing? No one's even in the boat." Rice rushes to the cabin and vanishes for a minute. She returns with a pair of binoculars. They take turns looking through them.

A different Puppet walks down the beach and steps cautiously into the water. It moves into the small waves until it's nearly submerged, sloshes to the rowboat, and grabs onto it. Another one fiddles with the line until the boat gets untied. "Oh shit!" The boat slowly floats away from the dock but stops a few feet away. Six more Puppets stumble into the water. The damn things are keeping the boat right where it is.

"How can they breathe underwater?" Ben mumbles.

"They're dead, remember. They don't need to breathe."

Andy runs to the railing. "What's going on?"

Rice puts her hand on his shoulder. "I don't want you to worry. Okay? Ian and the others will be just fine. Maybe you should go below. Explore the boat, find something to play with."

Andy nods and runs to the ladder. He pauses a moment before going below.

"Those Puppets are just gonna stay there, holding the boat still until Ian and the others get back?" Ben can't believe this crap.

"They're setting a trap." Rice starts to cry.

"No shit," he replies.

Shortly afterward, Isabella comes down the path, pushing a cart full of stuff. Markus and Josh are behind her, and Ian, Hana, and Tanis are on mountain bikes. And they have a dog.

Rice and Ben jump up and down. "It's a trap! Puppets under the boat!" They watch Ian dive into the rowboat. Ben yells again, but the group can't hear. Ben can't do shit to help. He's stuck on this boat without so much as a BB gun.

Rice wails.

Ben screams so loud he gags himself.

All they can do is watch.

Ian manages to get the rowboat ashore. They load the boat with the shit as Isabella bitch slaps the Puppets into piles of twitching lumps. When everyone gets in the boat, they push off the beach with the oars and row toward the *Pioneer*.

Hana and Ian pull at the oars. They don't move much.

Ben watches through the binoculars and yells, "They're under you!"

The Puppets pull the boat on one side and flip it over. Everyone is tossed into the water, along with all the supplies. Ian and the others thrash as the boat drifts away, splashing.

"What do we do?" Rice cries out, grabbing at Ben.

"I can't swim that far. My fat ass would drown," he says. "We're stuck here." Rice wouldn't be able to swim it either, so they watch. All they can do is watch.

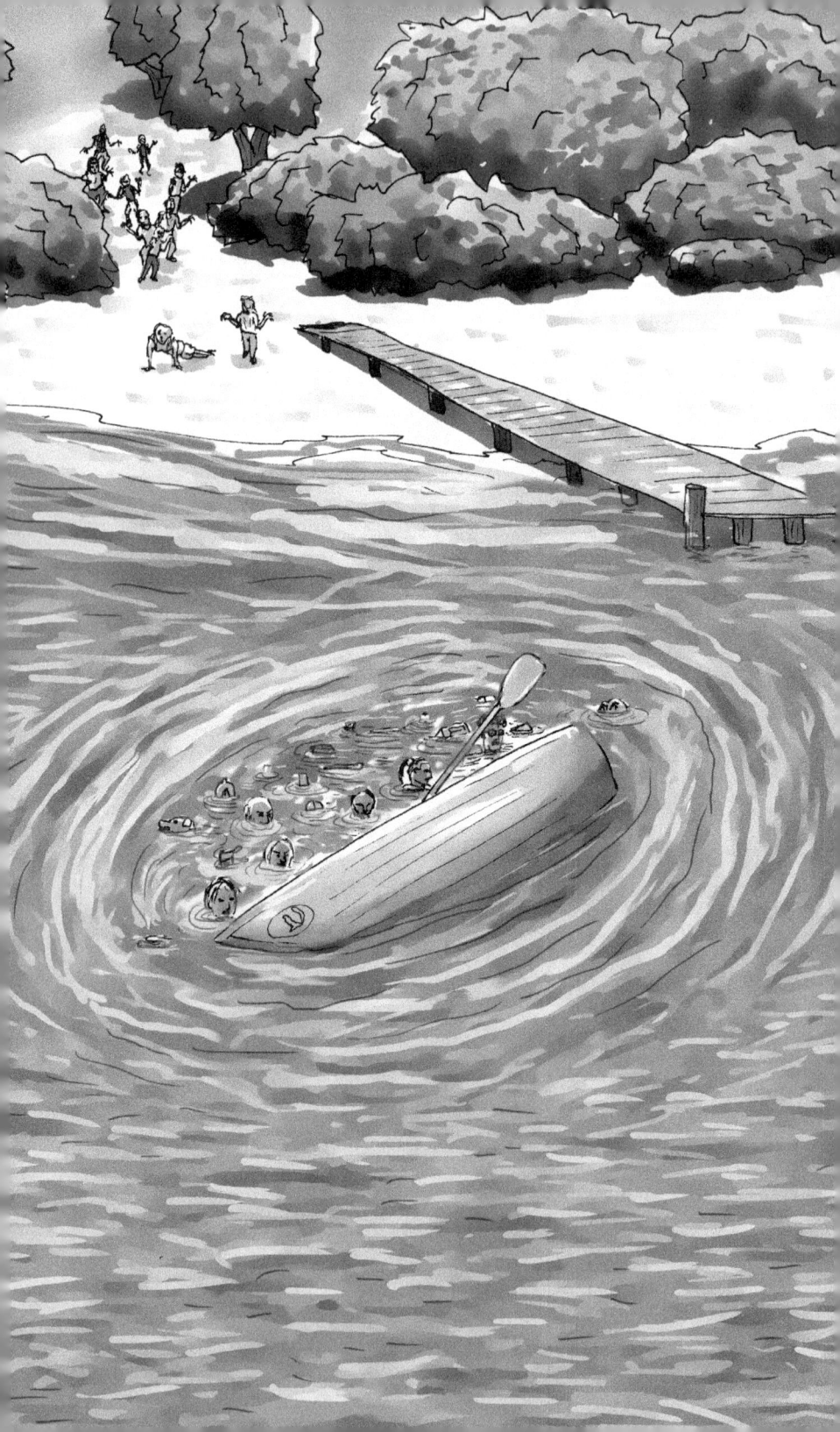

CHAPTER 1.28

IAN

HOPEFUL CALCULATIONS

The rowboat flips over, spilling food, water, fuel, and the passengers into Jamaica Bay. Water fills Ian's lungs as he splashes and reaches for the surface. Someone grabs him as he opens his eyes. Even though it is dark, swirling, and chaotic, he can see an emaciated, vein-covered hand pulling him under. Multiple hands reach through the turbulent, bubbling water and claw at his skin. The surface is only a few feet away, but he can't reach it!

Ian twists like a corkscrew, and the water helps him slide right out of their grip. His head bursts into the air, and he gasps. Isabella is also free and swimming for shore. He locates Markus, Tanis, Hana, and Josh. They've all slipped the trap. When his feet touch the muddy shore, he catches his breath.

Ian turns to Hana. "Are you okay?"

She nods. "I hate those things."

The Puppets rise from the water. Drenched and washed of the dirt and blood, they look like starving, pissed-off old folks. The worms protruding from their eyes twitch and flap in agitation. There are six.

Ian grabs a large rock from the muddy shore and repeatedly bashes a Puppet's head.

"The knees, Ian!" Isabella shouts.

Ian kicks the knee, and it breaks backward. The thing falls on its stomach, face down in the shallow water. Ian grabs its left wrist and twists it until the arm pops from the socket. The other arm dislocates just as easily. The Puppet can only flop around. Ian sickens seeing the human form so disfigured but still fighting.

Ian helps Tanis beat his Puppet. Everyone stands triumphant over their kills. The Puppets' little ambush failed, but backup came.

"Get our stuff back on the rowboat! Isabella and I will distract them until you've got it all," Ian says, hoping the Puppets didn't understand English.

More approach from the city. Isabella and Ian lure the group away from the salvage area. The Puppets follow Ian and Isabella into the shallows, which slows the Puppets further. Pertinacious fuckers! Ian jumps over the small waves and runs away. Isabella blasts one in the face with her shotgun and snaps a few of their knees with well-placed kicks.

When Markus calls out, they dive into the water and swim to the rowboat.

The group helps the two into the boat, nearly tipping it over again. Ian feels the tension in his chest ebb. "Did you get all the gear?" he asks, watching the horde splash into the water, still coming.

Markus nods. "Thank God the gas tanks float! I thought they'd sink for sure."

"Petroleum is lighter than water," Josh clarifies.

Ian's muscles burn, his body is exhausted from fighting. Hana puts her arm around him. Her warmth relaxes him, as does her steady breathing.

They row to the *Pioneer,* and unload.

Chapter 1.29

Tanis
Maat, the God of Truth

Kat is an Australian Shepherd mix, weighs about forty pounds, and is mostly white, marbled gray, and brown hair. He has a long white nose, small floppy ears, and big, soft brown eyes. He's a great dog. Tanis tucks Kat under his arm and climbs the ladder to the deck of the *Pioneer*. Kat doesn't seem to mind all this. Even when Tanis threw him into the rowboat and he had landed on a bunch of canned food, he didn't yelp or anything. He's just happy to be with his master.

Tanis felt so alone when he and Ian and Hana helped

him search his house. His parents were gone, and everything seemed hopeless. He'd grabbed his bike and helped Hana pump the tires up. They were riding down the driveway, by a crowd of dead people when Kat jumped over the neighbor's shrubs and caught up, barking like crazy. Tanis risked stopping to say hi. After that, Kat kept up with them the entire ride, running like Superdog.

His paws hit the deck of the *Pioneer* and he runs off, checking the place out. Such a good dog.

"Whoa!" Ben says. "That dog's gonna shit all over the place."

"I'm gonna shit on you!" Tanis snaps. "On your face," he says, under his breath.

"Don't be a jerk," Hana says to Ben, sticking up for Tanis. "It's the kid's dog."

Josh pets Kat. "I should've grabbed some dog food at the store. There was tons of it." Andy runs over, so happy about having a furry friend on board.

"Dog's gonna starve. We don't have food for it," Isabella says. "It will be your share that he eats," she snarls.

"I'm fine with that," Tanis says. "He can have all my food if he needs it."

Ben rolls his eyes, "You say that now."

"Yes, and you are responsible for him," Ian reminds Tanis. He's starting to act like he's everyone's dad.

Kat explores the boat's deck. "He loves it!" Tanis yells, but no one hears him.

The rationing is calculated. If everyone gets a quart of water a day and a two-thousand-calorie diet, they have enough food for two weeks provided none is wasted. Regardless, it isn't enough.

Ian starts the engine and heads for the open sea, hoping that farther down the coast they'll find either the quarantine line or small towns with sources of food and water to salvage. Ian feels hopeful. They're safe out here. The sea is their salvation.

Tanis helps Kat down the ladder and lets him run around below deck. Dogs are so connected to happy things. It's no wonder humans gravitate to them as companions.

Tanis claimed one of the bunks earlier so he sets his bag on it and takes out the photo of his parents, wedging it in a crack on the side of the bunk.

The kitchen gets loud as everyone brings in the food and water. Tanis joins them to see what they got. Ben takes control of the kitchen. No surprise there—big guy, big appetite.

"Yeah!" he exclaims as he takes out a bag of cashews. "Buttery goodness," he smells the bag.

"There's about five pounds of chicken in there. It was in the freezer and didn't feel completely thawed yet. It should be good," Markus says. "The rest of the meat is in cans."

Ben tosses a can of spam in the air, "I love this stuff with eggs."

Rice and Josh look eagerly at the food and Tanis is so hungry he could eat his own fist. "Can we chow now?"

"I got this," Ben says. "I watch the cooking channel all the time." He looks over the food. "How about lunch stuff? Some chips and tuna sandwiches?" He holds up a box of individual mayonnaise packets. "Perfect, this stuff will last for years."

"I'll help," Markus offers.

The *Pioneer* turns around and heads out of Jamaica Bay going south. Ben hands Tanis a sandwich, and he gives half to Kat. They both want more, much, much more. Oh well. He's already used to being hungry.

Later, Josh and Tanis finally get the water heater going. They work together to bypass the fried circuit board and rig the heater to run directly off the batteries. It's a simple heating unit, so it will run as long as the batteries hold. It'll drain the juice faster, but Hana says the motor has its own start-up battery so she isn't worried about using all the hot water. Markus finds a storage box with eight brand-new replacement batteries. They're set.

Rice is the first in the shower. She sings the entire time like she's in some soap commercial. It's annoying but makes Tanis smile.

Ben bumps Tanis's shoulder, "She fingerin' her lady harp in there or what?"

Tanis laughs.

They all take turns in the shower. Quick turns. The meter that says how much water is in the tanks is fried, so they don't know how much is in there.

A week passes as they keep sailing south. The stock is running low on food and drinking water. Tanis hates rationing. He drinks his part and is still thirsty. He eats his share and he's still hungry. He doesn't tell anyone, but he only feeds Kat once a day.

Ian tries to find a place to dock the ship, every time they get close to the shore, they attract thousands of Puppets. The survivors are like fugitives on their own planet.

Isabella says it would be a suicide mission if they try to get food. She, more than anyone else, knows when they're outmatched.

Tanis believes her, and the others agree. The food and water rations are recalculated as they continue pushing for Cuba.

Everyone takes shifts to make sure they stay on course. The nights are dark. Spooky dark, like the water swallows the light.

Stars are everywhere, and a sliver of a moon glows.

Tanis tries to see the shore, but there are no lights on the mainland. No one talks much, and everyone goes to his or her bunk as the silence and the night lengthen.

Tanis lies on his bunk, petting Kat. He can't sleep. He doesn't even like closing his eyes. A few hours later, Hana opens the door.

"You sleeping?" she asks. He shakes his head. "It's my shift. You want to go up top with me?" Tanis jumps out of bed and goes with her. Kat follows.

"I feel like I'm sleeping right now. . ." Tanis says as Hana takes the wheel and sends Ben to bed. Tanis slumps on the bench next to the helm with his head lying on the back. "–and that I'll wake up and be in my bed at home. Ma will be downstairs, and Dad in front of the TV watching football or something."

Hana says, "I was dating this guy before all this. We'd gone on our third date three nights prior to everyone getting sick. He's probably one of those Puppets." Hana sighs. "My parents were pretty old. They were really good people. Tried their hardest to do things right. They didn't deserve what I did."

"What did you do?" Tanis's pulse quickens and he sits up. She shrugs.

"Nothing. I mean, they didn't deserve to die."

"There won't be a funeral or anything. Not for anyone," Tanis mumbles.

"Well, your soul goes where it's gonna go with or without a funeral," Hana replies, trying to make him feel better.

"The Egyptians didn't believe that." Hana didn't know what to say to that. "I'm kidding," Tanis mumbles. "I did a project on the Egyptians last year. They were pretty crazy about the afterlife. It was kinda boring at the time. Now I get it. Death wasn't the last stop; you know? It was like a waiting room for the next place. You'd get resurrected into the final world. That is, if you passed all the tests."

"What sort of tests?"

Tanis racks his brain, "Well, I remember it was dangerous. The dead had to be protected from all kinds of demons so they could pass through seven gates. Finally, Osiris would judge your life. You had to tell a ton of different gods why you had a good life. Why you should get into the gods' world. You'd go in front of Anubis, the god of death. Then it was Maat, the god of truth. Then I remember Amemet would devour your heart if it wasn't pure, and Seth would finish you off."

Tanis looks into the darkness all around. He feels like they're passing through death into the afterlife. Maybe they're dead right now and don't know it. The darkness presses on him like he's being squeezed. This creepy feeling fills him and tears threaten to burst from his eyes.

"Well, I'm confident they're all in a better place," Hana says softly.

Tanis notices she looks more like a woman standing at the wheel than a cop, without her thick belt and gun.

"I like your necklace," Tanis says.

She touches it lightly. "Thanks."

The boat rocks gently after a gust of wind passes. Water slaps the hull regularly, like a clock.

Tanis sees Ma in his head. She's looking at him without saying a word, just looking. It's hard to picture her any other way, though he tries. "I wish I knew my parents were in heaven. Like, *really* knew, like you do."

Hana shrugs. "Well, there's a little skepticism in me, unfortunately."

Markus comes up the cabin ladder and sits on the bench. He'd heard them talking. "Even representatives of God feel doubt. Jesus cried and prayed all night before he was crucified. And he was the Son of God."

"That doesn't make me feel better." Tanis picks up the end of a rope and fiddles with it. "You know, the day before all this happened, I caught my dad fuckin' with another chick in his office. They forgot to lock the door." Tears flood his eyes, finally.

Hana snubs the wheel so it can't turn by itself and gives Tanis a hug. She sits next to him. "I'm so sorry."

"I was so mad at him that I didn't care what happened to him," Tanis says through snot and tears. Here he is, crying in front of Hana again.

She returns to the wheel. "We have to believe there's a place after death for us to go, a place where everything is better. Where people are forgiven. But even if there isn't a place like that, we can forgive and forget."

"So why even live on Earth at all, if there's a place like that?" Tanis asks.

Markus smiles. "Earth is our chance to feel a physical body. To feel things that our spirits don't get to feel, like pizza and snow. We also get to feel the bad things, like death and hate. Opposing forces pull and push us through this physical existence. We become more aware and enlightened, and we take that with us to the afterlife. We finally become whole." Markus can see the doubt on Tanis's face because he changes his tone. "Scientifically speaking, there's no reason to believe multiple dimensions that carry our souls between worlds don't exist."

"Like the Egyptians thought," Tanis says.

Markus chuckles and nods. "Kind of. See, those thoughts you have in your head? They're your body and your soul working together to give you intelligence. When you die you leave your body behind, and your soul passes from one dimension to another, along with all the knowledge you've gained."

"I've never heard a preacher say it like that," Hana says.

Tanis shrugs. "I just want to know. Really know. That way, what I did won't be—" Tanis catches himself.

Markus puts a solid hand on his shoulder. "We all want that. If you need to know how to pray, you come talk to me. I'll teach you, it helps." Markus goes below to get

some sleep.

It's just Tanis and Hana again. He walks away, but she follows.

"Earlier, you said something about what you did. What did you do?" Hana asks, looking into his eyes. He leans on the back safety-line and pets Kat lightly, but he doesn't have enough energy to play. Kat doesn't have much energy either. Tanis feels guilty for not giving him food. He must be starving.

Hana doesn't have to watch where they're going, it's too dark. Anyway, all she has to do keep the ship on the compass heading due south– it's hands glow in the dark.

"You can tell me. We won't get near land for a long time, and the ship will be fine for a little while." She lifts a strand of hair off his face and tucks it behind his ear. Tanis's Ma used to do that. He used to get so mad when she tried to groom him like he was a poodle. Now, he'd give anything to feel her touch.

"What if Cuba is like the U.S.? Too many Puppets to land?" he asks, barely able to push air through his voice box.

"Let's cross that bridge when we get there," Hana insists.

"I have a bad feeling about this." Tanis takes a deep breath. "I need to tell you something. Just in case. I need to tell someone."

She rubs his back. "Go ahead, but I promise you, we'll be fine."

Ian walks up, interrupting what Tanis was about to say. He'd been off on the dark side of the boat.

Hana stands. She doesn't have the energy to do anything but stare. "Shift is up. You guys can go to sleep."

Tanis hurries down to his bunk.

Andy, lying on the top bunk, clicks his flashlight on

and shines it toward Tanis. "Hey."

"Why aren't you sleeping with Rice?" Tanis cringes at the brightness, ducks away from the illumination and lies on top of the sheets. It's way too hot to bundle up.

"She snores and takes the sheets. I'm old enough to sleep by myself." He plays with the light on the ceiling. "Do you miss your mommy and daddy?"

"Yeah. Go to sleep." A moment later Tanis adds with a sigh, "My parents were cool. I was lucky. Some of my friends' parents were freaking wankers. Did you have good parents?"

"Uh huh. My mommy read me stories and made the best cupcakes, and my daddy liked to swim with me. He was going to teach me to dive when he and Mommy got back from their 'parents only' vacation."

The sinking feeling comes over Tanis. It has become so familiar it's like an old friend, swarming over his thoughts and body, turning the darkness into a tight space. He wants to take back what he did. He imagines that moment when he stuck the USB into the computer port, but this time, at the last instant, he changes his mind. The world doesn't end and he goes home like any normal day.

"My dad taught me all kinds of stuff. He was the smartest guy I knew." Tanis wipes his nose on his sleeve. "Hey, I'll teach you to dive if you want."

"Really? I'm scared to dive."

"Yeah, everyone is scared at first. But you just jump. And you remember that you're falling into water. It's like falling into pillows. You're not scared of pillows, are you?"

"Nope."

"Then you'll do awesome. The next time we stop we'll go diving."

"Yeah!"

"Now really, go to sleep, dude." Tanis can't shake

the thought that he has nothing but this damn photo of his parents. He's alone. Even though he doesn't want to believe it, the only thing that makes sense is that this is it. There's nothing after that light goes out. Nothing that lasts forever. No laughing or good times in heaven. But nothing means there are no sad things, either. Maybe when that day comes for him, he'll be fine. He'll fall into that endless nothingness and everything will be gone. It scares him shitless thinking about it. He presses the photo of his parents to his chest.

CHAPTER 1.30

MARKUS
BOOK OF REVELATION

Markus's rear end is sore and raw from sitting on this camel day in and day out. According to Mitchell, they'd entered Algeria an hour ago. All he knows is that his posterior needs salvation in a big way, and the temperature must be over one hundred degrees. His doctor will smack him across the face for being stupid with his old bones. The horizon, nothing but sand and hills, is still quite a sight, yellow in contrast to the blue sky, the shadows in the hills crisp and dark.

When the hills level out, Markus sees the famous mirage run along the horizon and stay there, just out of reach. When the sun vanishes, they camp. It truly is in the middle of nowhere, without a tree in sight, another night in the isolation of miles and miles of sand. Only their voices, their rumbling stomachs, and the breeze keep them company.

The temperature at night drops to near freezing, so cold Markus's muscles cramp, and he shivers in fits. He and Mitchell sit around a small coal fire, but it's hardly warm and will be their last because there is no more coal. Mitchell pours hot water into Markus's mug and stirs in a spoonful of sugar and instant coffee. They drank the last of the good stuff yesterday.

Mitchell studies the red folder, distracting himself by looking at the Stone of Allah and examining the paperwork they'd stolen. "It seems like these guys were mapping the flow of a virus across the United States." He shows Markus the diagram. "They illustrate multiple infection points. It seems they thought the best place to release a virus is New York City, giving it the best chance of spreading across the continent from there."

"New York, huh?" Markus comments. "The city that never sleeps."

"Millions come and go every day, two international airports and hordes of people shoulder to shoulder." Mitchell scratches his beard. "Why would someone want to kill the world?"

"God doesn't want the world to end, but He will sacrifice it one day to make a Heaven on Earth. See, it's not about death; it's about redemption. It's not God's will; it's His truth. God doesn't live by our definition of time. He's already witnessed the Apocalypse. It cannot be stopped because the death of everything has already happened."

Mitchell looks surprised. "Have you lost your marbles, old man?"

Markus shakes his head, "The Apocalypse will

come. Some think the signs are happening today. We should all live pure lives in preparation for the Second Coming."

Mitchell waves Markus off, "I'm not a religious man. To me, that sounds like the same crazy stuff radical Muslims blow themselves up for."

Markus wraps his long robe around his chest in a vain attempt to keep his body warm. "There are Four Horsemen of the Apocalypse: Conquest, War, Famine, and Death. Conquest has already come. The Book of Revelation says, 'I watched as the Lamb opened the first of the Seven Seals. Then I heard one of the four living creatures say in a voice like thunder, Come! I looked, and there before me was a white horse! Its rider held a bow and was given a crown; he rode out as a conqueror bent on conquest.' The arrow symbolizes advanced technology. If you had a bow in those days, you were advanced. The bow and crown symbolize modern technology and greed, spread across the world in the ultimate conquest. Some call it globalism.

"The second horseman is War. Again, Revelations says, 'When the Lamb opened the second seal, I heard the second living creature say, Come!' Then another horse came out, a fiery red one. Its rider was given the power to take peace from the earth and to make men slay each other. That would be the Antichrist. The man who fits that description is Liam Gershald. He's the CEO of the Cantel Corporation. The Cantel Corporation hired a military to fight rebels in Somalia to protect its assets, a historical first for a corporation. Now, because the rebels were really bad guys, the world did not protest or sanction the action. Gershald is working to get the United Nations to depose the Sudanese and the North Korean governments. Some say he's been influenced by the Trump Presidency. They talk about building the largest army in history to do it, a private army, fighting three wars financed by corporate interests."

Mitchell huffs, "Conspiracy theory. Blah, blah, blah. You can't prove it, but you can't disprove it. Convenient for your argument."

Markus continues anyway. "The Third Horseman is Famine. 'When the Lamb opened the third seal, I heard the third living creature say, Come! I looked, and there before me was a black horse! Its rider was holding a pair of scales in his hands. Then I heard what sounded like a voice among the four living creatures, saying, A quart of wheat for a day's wages, and three quarts of barley for a day's wages, and do not damage the oil and the wine!'

"This period of famine is important. It's not a famine of food, you see; the famine is energy. The oil is drying up. The world hit peak oil production years ago. We use over five billion barrels a day. Oil will become so valuable it will ignite small wars on the planet that eventually lead to one big war and the final days. We already have five conflicts over oil in Africa. Three belong to the Cantel Corporation and the United Nations alone.

"When the Fourth Horseman arrives, it will bring Death. 'When the Lamb opened the fourth seal, I heard the voice of the fourth living creature say, Come! I looked, and there before me was a pale horse! Its rider was named Death, and Hell was following close behind him.' They were given power over a fourth of the earth to kill by sword, famine, and plague, and by the wild beasts of the Earth. That's when most of the people on this Earth die. It may end a lot of suffering as well as bring the righteous to God and restart humanity."

"That sounds lovely, but isn't it true that in every century, there are signs that the Second Coming is on our doorstep? Weren't the Crusades started because the church thought that the war over Palestine was the war that will return Christ to Earth?" Mitchell asks rhetorically, clearly a well-read man. "During World War II, people thought the same thing."

"Yes. It is true." Markus takes a bite of bread. "Whatever God's plan is, I'll always be His humble soldier. I do not pretend to know what His plan is."

"You do that."

Markus flips through the red folder, finds a particular page, and points to the Arabic writing. "What does this say?"

"'The Stone of Allah is the hammer of Allah. It has brought death. It will bring death again.' So, these guys think this stone will pave the way for Allah to return?" Mitchell muses.

"Well, in truth, our version of the end of times and the Muslim version aren't that different. Details differ, but the outcome is the same. The righteous will survive," Markus says. "You see, God plans. There are reasons for things. A purpose to all that we do."

Mitchell takes the red folder, "So, you were destined to find this stuff? Why?"

"I will know in the days to come." Markus tries to sleep in the icy, dry air, wondering why God has sent him to this place and this time.

He finally stops shivering and relaxes, his body pressed into the soft, still-warm sand, and stares at the stars. The Milky Way stretches across the heavens like the most intricately sewn silk embroidery, perfect in its light and vastness. God is so much bigger than humans. "His plan for us will be known, and He will take care to make our path clear."

CHAPTER 1.31

HANA
THE GHOSTS AT SEA

Hana wakes up in one of the *Pioneer's* staterooms. The ship's rocking back and forth is such a nice feeling. She stretches and yawns … and smells bacon. She leaps up, throws on her dirty sports bra, checks her hair in the mirror—regrets looking—and hurries to the galley for breakfast.

Ben is cooking again, humming, flipping, stirring, and mixing. He serves up fake eggs and bacon, all smiles. Hana guesses cooking cures the idiot in him or maybe pushes it below the surface. Either way, he's more pleasant to be stuck with now that he's got some way to contribute.

The survivors have been on the *Pioneer* for two days.

Most of her worries and apprehensions are fading. When the survivors started this voyage, she felt like she was approaching a vehicle she pulled over. A traffic stop is one of the most dangerous places when you're on the beat because cops never know who is in the car or their state of mind. She relaxes when she finally sees the person as an ordinary, calm citizen. Hana is feeling that release of tension now. *We're all dealing with this tragedy remarkably well.*

She helps Markus and Josh clean up after everyone eats. Ian sips coffee and stares into space. He says exactly what Hana is thinking, what everyone is thinking: "Why don't I feel terrible? Billions of people died just days ago. Shouldn't we still be in mourning?"

"You don't know how many people have died," Rice says. She scoops the remainder of her eggs and bacon onto Andy's plate. "Maybe it only affected the states."

"Well, technically, the virus could still be crawling across the globe. Maybe reaching more secluded places by now. We're probably still in the middle of the event," Josh concludes.

"Event?" Rice snaps.

Ian goes up top, and Hana joins him.

Fog surrounds them, and she's surprised at how thick the murk is.

Ian looks over a map. "I'm hoping we get to Atlantic City by nightfall. That way, we can drop anchor, and no one will have to keep watch."

Because it's early morning, a cool breeze flows over the boat. Hana feels it on her skin and smiles. She looks at Ian. He smiles back. "Now, this is sustainable living," he says. "Too bad we have to use diesel fuel and not a renewable energy source like solar panels."

"I'm sorry, but this is far from sustainable," Markus says, sitting on a cushion beside the wheel. "We will run out of fuel eventually."

"Already burned half the tank," Isabella mutters. She's pacing for some reason. "And we're not even to Atlantic City yet."

"If we run out, we get more," Ben says, joining the group up top. "Shit, we'll need more gas for the stove, eventually. Those four tanks won't last us that long." He's sipping on rum left in the galley stores.

"Going to the store is a huge challenge. It's not like running a quick errand." Markus says.

Andy and Rice make their way up top. "We're not gonna be on this boat forever, are we?" Andy asks.

"No, just until we find safety. Even if that's Cuba, that's not that far south," Rice answers.

"But I like it on the boat. There are no dead people." Andy's eyes are full of worry and fear.

"Eden won't have dead people either, little man. It's the survivor city," Ian says and winks.

"Isn't there a chance we get there, and it's gone, too?" Josh asks. "What keeps them from getting sick?" His hands are shoved deep into his pockets as he shifts nervously.

Markus says, "A thousand shall fall at thy side, and ten thousand at thy right hand, but it shall not come nigh thee.' That's from Psalms."

Tanis ignores Markus. "So, we're gonna join a bunch of survivors in Cuba and restart the human race?"

"As long as they have hot water, I'm in." Rice takes Ben's rum and sips it. "We rebuild society and have some babies." She looks at Ian. Hana wants to laugh, but she doesn't. So Rice has a crush on Ian. He's a good-looking man and smart, too.

"Maybe make some changes while we're at it," Ian adds. "No more capitalism. We'll just live off the land, keep everything fair, and outlaw pollution of any kind."

"What a pipe dream!" Ben snips. "Keep smokin' and pass what you've got over here so I can puff-puff, too."

"Shut it," Isabella says. "Ian's right. We make new rules. Ones that change things for good."

Rice shakes her head, "You two sound like communists."

Josh points at Rice. "I'm with you." Then he looks at Ian. "Sounds like you want fairness, which is an inherent impossibility. There are genetic differences that determine all our abilities. Some are smarter than others, some are stronger. It's a matter of survival of the fittest. Always has been. We're just animals with opposable thumbs. Fairness is an illusion. Children use fairness to get what they want. But adults shouldn't fall on impossible ideals."

"You sound like my father," Ian replies. "And the only reason you think there's no fairness is because you're programmed to protect the system by the very school that taught you about the world. You let people get so rich they take over countries and pollute entire hemispheres, all because you've been taught that being dirty rich is the American dream."

"No," Josh retorts. "I've got my own mind. I can look at the evidence and weigh reality and consequences. I've also learned from historians how corrupt all communist governments have been. Talk about fairness. If you were the government, you always had more than the little people because the little people were under your boot. In fact, the communist governments were the worst polluters of all. They just hid it from their people through control of the media. I've done the research. Even socialism creates more poverty than it saves."

"People should always have the right of self-determination," Markus adds. "That is why capitalism worked for so long."

"Before it killed the world," Ian injects.

"Some stupid virus killed the world, not capitalism," Josh corrects. "You wouldn't kill the world for profit because money becomes useless. Where's the incentive for that?"

"Got a point there, Brainiac." Ben laughs.

Josh goes on, "Tom Palmer understood that libertarianism is the application of science and reason to the study of politics and public policy. That is, libertarians deal in reality, not magic. The government doesn't have magical powers. They can't ignore the laws of economics and human nature."

"Ah, but capitalism did get out of hand," Markus clarifies. "Greed took over. Television and entertainment warped the minds of too many people. Eden should be pure. The rules should be strict, but according to God's will."

"No way!" Ben snaps. "No way I'm living under religious rule. They'd off me for sure."

"Yeah, I still like the idea of freedom," Josh says. "Natural rights are always the same, no matter what president or leader is in power. No matter what system you have, the natural rights are life, liberty, and property. When you break those rights, your system fails because people will eventually fight to regain their natural rights. We know what they are because we all understand them at the very core of us."

"But our system was so corrupt," Tanis replies. "Our natural rights didn't mean shit. And we couldn't do anything about it. No one's vote really mattered. Every election since Taft was rigged. Democracy is a joke."

"It's only corrupt because every election becomes more controlled by the government!" Josh snaps. "The more central control over our lives, the more the politicians and the rich work together to enrich themselves. You keep blaming capitalism for our problems when the problems originate with federal meddling and manipulation. More socialism, more corruption. It's clear if you look at the facts."

"How would you run a government?" Ian asks.

"You just make a bunch of rules that work, and that's it. No messing with it," Tanis answers.

"That's what a constitution is, Dork." Ben laughs again.

"Yeah, but not some outdated thing written by posers in wigs." He throws a cookie at Kat, who is going from person to person, sucking up attention.

"I've got some ideas about what should be in a constitution," Ian says.

Josh steps in again on a role. "A theory called spontaneous order has yet to be disproven. Basically, it means that most of the order in society, from language and law to the economy, happens naturally, without a central plan. The constitution should only protect the laws which protect the freedoms."

"Well, it needs to level the playing field, too. Because true democracy could get oppressive. Especially to minorities," Hana interjects.

"Trouble comes in when you strip rights from one, say rich people, and give to the other. That's not fair. You can't fix unfairness with more unfairness. That is logically flawed," Josh says. "The U.S. grew one of the largest middle class groups in history. That's how I know it was as 'fair' as was possible." Josh sighed. "Look, if you expect government officials to fix millions of lives, you'll be disappointed every time unless you're delusional. There are, what, thousands of policy makers in our federal government. They have to write rules to govern three hundred million lives! They can't. They can't save poor Sally because when Sally gets her free money, Nancy goes poor. That's why business has been more successful in solving problems. Millions of businesses are solving issues out there. Capitalism and free trade give us more choices than we can fully appreciate. Businesses should be left to solve Sally's poverty problem. I like those odds better."

Ian hands the wheel to Isabella and stalks off, giving up on the conversation. Hana watches him, all the way to the stern, knowing he's feeling confused and scared and empathizes. Even in the morning light, darkness surrounds the ship, an eclipse that blocks all hope. She sits in the middle of the ship, trying not to think about those she's lost when Andy comes up to her. He's so young and cute. "Hi there."

He sits. "I'm hungry."

"I'd cook you the biggest cake you've ever seen if I could." Hana pokes his nose.

He doesn't smile. The boy is very traumatized. His brain needs a distraction.

"Here, let's make some food."

His eyes widen. "Really?"

Hana sees a large box full of tools and supplies near the mizzenmast. "What's your favorite food?"

"Sa   paghetti," he says, saying it wrong like every kid does. "And corn."

Hana rummages around and takes a bag and a few other items from the supply box and dumps the stuff on the desk. They pretend bolts are corn, tape strips are noodles and rubber plugs are meatballs. Screwdrivers are the utensils. They eat slowly and delicately and talk about school and friends.

Their "dinner" is interrupted by Ian's frantic calls.

"Survivors! Come quick!"

Everyone runs to the bow, stares into the heavy fog, and sees a boat deep in the shrouded horizon. It's a beautiful sight, and Hana wants to jump up and down like a cheerleader.

"There it is!" Rice yells, tears flooding her eyes.

"Can you get closer?" Markus yells to Isabella. She throttles down. A small fishing boat bobs on the waves a hundred yards off the port side.

"There are two men aboard, fishing!" Ian says.

They all jump up and down, waving and screaming

as the boat gets closer and closer. Hana isn't sure why she's so excited, they might be creeps, but then again, they might have news. Maybe they're getting close to the containment line!

Hana squints to see through the fog but has to wait until they get closer. She doesn't see anyone on board. A thick cloud of fog pushes between the *Pioneer* and the boat; she loses sight temporarily.

The fog lifts, visibility returns, and the boat is right in front of them.

Hana screams for Isabella to stop.

Everyone braces.

The *Pioneer* rams the boat. Neither one was going very fast, but the *Pioneer* is a steel-hulled ship and her bow bends back the smaller boat's safely railing, cracks her fiberglass hull and smashes the windscreen.

"Jesus!" Rice yelps.

Ian runs along the side. "Hey! Sorry! Is everyone okay?" he yells to the fishing boat.

There is no answer. The boat rocks away in the turbulent waves.

"Hello?" Hana yells. She's wholeheartedly embarrassed that they rammed the small boat and did so much damage.

No one is on deck, and it's hard to see through the cabin windows because they're foggy with salty corrosion.

"What happened to them?" Rice asks. "I thought you said there were two people on that boat."

"I didn't see anyone," Josh interjects.

"I didn't either," Hana says.

The fishing boat, *Day Job,* is rigged with nets, ice chests, and fishing poles. "Josh, I need your help." Hana runs to a jumble of ropes and untangles one.

"What do you need?"

"I need to find something like a grappling hook. I want to get alongside the boat and hook it to us."

Josh runs off.

Hana drags the thick rope to the rail closest to *Day Job*.

Josh returns with Hana's rake, the one she'd gotten from Tanis's shed.

The boat floats farther away.

Hana ties the rope to the rake pole and throws it, javelin style, to the *Day Job*'s deck. "Someone hold the end of the rope," she orders.

Ben takes the rope and wraps it around his arm.

"Anybody there?" yells Rice. Still no answer.

Ian shrugs. "I thought I saw someone. Really, I did." His brow is scrunched and his jaw clenched.

"They have fishing poles!" Tanis yells.

"If there's no one aboard, let's get what we can," Markus says. "God has given us some help."

"Tell him we need a PlayStation, too," Ben says. "Oh, and some Cajun spices."

Ian has his hand on his forehead. "There were two people there. I saw them holding fishing poles, standing next to the diving platform."

"Must be the light playing tricks on you," Josh says. "The refraction of light in these water-vapor clouds can be misleading. Probably happens all the time."

"Nerd alert!" Ben hollers.

Hana slips off her pants and shirt and jumps overboard in her underwear and bra.

The water isn't too cold, but it shocks her system. Bubbles flow over her body, tickling her. Feeling something other than fear and regret is wonderful. She breaks to the surface and breathes, salty water finding her tongue. She swims to the diving platform at *Day Job's* stern and climbs up the ladder.

The boat is a mess, with bird poop and gear everywhere. Whoever was out in this boat must have had a good catch before they disappeared. Hana studies the mess: at least two people were aboard. She sees signs of a struggle: blood splatters on the hand railing, the cabin window is broken, and a box of hooks is spilled over the deck. There are two full cups of coffee, cold now, two sandwiches in the cooler, and two tackle boxes. There are a dozen fishing poles, but that's typical.

She hears a splash, and a moment later, Ian climbs aboard.

"Need some help?" he asks. They are both standing in their underwear. She notices his thin but muscular body, then turns from him quickly, blushing, as she remembers that she's in her underwear as well.

"Yeah, um, there was a struggle here," Hana planned on becoming a detective once she did her time in uniform and perfected her eye for detail. "Looks like the two had a fight and probably fell overboard."

"I agree, but I can't believe they just fell overboard seconds ago. I must not have seen them fishing." Ian holds the top of his head and looks worried.

"Sorry, Ian. These people have been gone for quite a while. There's mold on the coffee cups, and the fish ice has melted. I don't think you saw anyone. Look at the poles. All the lines are pulled in. See the bait? It's dried up." She points to the bird poop. "Do you see how the poop is on top of the blood? So they went overboard a long time ago," she concludes. "You could have seen a—"

"Ghost?"

Hana laughs, "No, a mirage or something. Like Josh said. The fog played tricks with your eyes." She steps near him and puts her hand on his forearm. "You wanted to see

survivors. So did I."

Ian nods and looks at her eyes. Her mind clears like wiping a dry-erase board clean with one swipe. His eyes linger on hers. She can tell he's not thinking about the fishermen anymore. He takes a breath and lets his gaze slip down her face, down her neck, and to her breasts. She lets him linger for the briefest moment, then crosses her arms. He clears his throat, returns to the task at hand. So does Hana.

"Jesus! Get a room!" Ben yells, laughing from the deck of the *Pioneer*.

The two enter the cabin and poke around. Maps and books litter the table, and a ladder leads down into the belly of the boat. Ian steps down into the gloomy, moldy interior cautiously. Dirty dishes are piled in the galley sink, and fruit is rotting in a basket. Ian looks at the door leading to the stateroom, takes a few steps, and pushes the door open.

A man lies face up on the bed. The top of his head is nothing but dried clumps of exploded brain tissue. His arms are cut in multiple places, and his hand loosely grips a gun. Ian backs away and closes the door. "Not a Puppet, at least."

"I guess they weren't infected on the boat."

Ian scratches his head. "I wonder what the fight was about."

Hana shrugs because she's done thinking about it. All it shows her is that some find it easier to give up than to keep fighting. Loneliness is the most powerful demon. "I'm feeling creeped out here. Let's grab some of this fishing gear and get off this ghost boat."

They recover two tanks of propane, some rum, whiskey, lots of beer left in the cooler, and a ton of fishing gear. Ian siphons the remaining diesel fuel from the *Day Job's* tank into the *Pioneer's* tank. He fills one of the five-gallon cans, times the flow, and when the *Day Job's* tank is empty, estimates about eighty gallons to add to their supply.

Later that night, everyone crowds the deck of the *Pioneer* and shares the whiskey.

"I tell you, Ian when it was my watch last night, I saw some shit in the dark. Thought I saw a couple of boats. There might have been a light, too, farther out to sea. It flashed. On off, on off. Then it moved over here and then over there." Ben points around to illustrate. "But they weren't lights; they were too faint. I was seeing shit. I was seein' ghosts," he says, lowering his voice. "But I saw them plain as the zits on my ass."

Josh huffs. "Ghosts are impossible."

"The human soul is a powerful thing," Markus says. "Sometimes the soul can get trapped on Earth because it loses its way."

"So, we're going to be seeing ghosts all over the place now?" Tanis mutters.

Ian looks away. "I thought I saw two men fishing, but it was foggy and my brain has been in a frying pan for days. It was a simple hallucination. That's all." His eyes shimmer with moisture, and he's trying to hide. He knows their trials aren't over. They're still in the middle of the storm.

Chapter 1.32

Ian
The Great Storm

Ian has been sailing the *Pioneer* south along the East Coast for three days. He had to dig deep into his memory to remember how to sail.

When he was sixteen, he took dingy sailing classes in the Etang de Perols. Etang de Perols is a beautiful bay outside Montpellier, France. Ian went there every summer until his mother needed more seclusion. She complained about the hordes of people on the beaches until his father couldn't take her fussing anymore and took them to Fiji or Tonga for their summer vacation. His mother approved, and the islands became their vacation destination until his

mother's death.

The *Pioneer's* two main sails were easy to raise. They unrolled from the boom that stuck out of both masts. The forward jibs were more difficult because Ian had to find them and figure out how to get them up. Eventually, he got the smaller jib flying. Figuring out how to rig and operate the larger jib was more complex, so he asked Tanis to stuff it back in the sail locker where he found it. The only other sail he didn't use was the sail on the top of the main mast. It just needed to be rolled out, but no one was willing to climb the rigging that high to get to the halyard. He had no idea what sheet was used to control it, and the sheer number and types of ropes draped over the ship boggled his mind. He explained to the others that sheets tighten the sails, halyards for raising and lowering the sails, and the other lines and cords he had no idea how to use should be left alone. It didn't matter, though, because Ian got the *Pioneer* cruising at a decent pace without the diesel engine, and that's what mattered.

Ian was getting the hang of managing the sails and keeping the *Pioneer* on course for Cuba. Now and again, the wind pushed the ship off-course. At first, it was scary, but Ian learned to anticipate the gusts because he could see them coming. The wind raced across the water, creating white caps on the waves. Seconds later, the ship would rock. Turning into the wind gusts eases the hit, and today, using his tricks, he's not pulling his hair out in clumps.

Unfortunately, he's not sure where the ship is or if Virginia is anywhere close. Convenient signs like the ones on the freeways saying, "Welcome to Virginia!" aren't out here. Ian doesn't know how to read the charts, and he's not sure they have the right ones aboard anyway. He's sailing blind.

He expects the hull to hit a sandbar or rock and end this adventure, but it hasn't happened yet. The shoreline is so far away, but he's feeling great and more in control than he has in a long time. The wind is strong, and they're having a great time.

A sea bird follows their wake, gliding on an upward draft like it's a fixed-wing airplane. Its head cocks to the side, and Ian sees its eye. Another seabird joins the first one. The two scan every detail of the ship before deciding it's a lost cause and drop away. Ian gets goosebumps running along his skin like electric fire flying through his fried nerves. Dolphins play in their wake.

Tanis, Rice, and Andy yell and scream as they watch them. Hana has tears in her eyes.

Ian laughs, which feels alien, a useless vestigial emotion. Even so, the danger in the new world has been reduced to a blemish in his thoughts, like hairline cracks in an old painting. The air is sweet and gentle. He's not hungry, sad, or anxious but at peace on the waves.

Then Ben opens his mouth, spoiling the amity. Damn him sometimes. He points to the northeast, where a few lightning strikes flash in the sky.

Ian hopes to outrun the storm, so he steers closer to shore, feeling more at ease with land on the horizon.

Hours later, more lightning flashes. The sun vanishes, and darkness sets in. Trouble is on the horizon: not the Puppets or an act of God, but Mother Earth's fury.

The storm comes up fast. Ian has time to do nothing but clench the wheel, sensing the danger the storm poses to the *Pioneer* and all the souls aboard her.

Ian is tacking the ship back toward land when a stiff gust of wind whips across the tops of the small waves. The ship heels, the rail almost dipping into the water, and the ship is nearly sideways to the compass heading. Ian immediately steers into the wind and loosens the sheet to the mainsail. The ship slows, and the sails whip back and forth. He steers back toward land, letting the wind fill the sails again. He has no idea what to do next.

Another gust from the east slaps the *Pioneer,* heeling

her over again as Ian loses control.

Rice screams.

Ben's grip on the railing fails, and he falls into the mast.

The wind eventually lets up but for only a second. Moments later, a more powerful gust hits. Tanis slips and falls onto the railing as it dips into the water.

Ian lets go of the wheel and loosens the main sheet again. The boat naturally turns upwind and slows. His heart is on overload.

"Okay, if I remember right, we have to shrink the sail size!" Ian shouts over the tempest. Dark clouds come from the ocean faster than he ever imagined possible. The sea swells. The rocking increases.

"I ain't Captain Dick here!" Ben yells. "How do we shrink the sail?"

Ian hands the wheel to Isabella. "Keep it going upwind if you can." She nods.

Ian runs to the bow, and Ben follows. "We have to take down the jib! That's the very front sail!"

"Shouldn't we take all the sails down?" Ben asks as heavy rain falls and the wind gets cold.

"I don't think so! I think we need a sail even during a storm so we can steer the ship. Otherwise, we lose control."

"Whatever you say!"

The boat heaves upward as the waves continue to rise higher. The two struggle to get to the bow, water splashing over the gunwales, drenching them in salty spray. Ian's feet slip on the slick wood. The waves lift the *Pioneer* up and shove her down. The horizon disappears on the upside of the wave.

Ian grabs hold of the security line leading from the bow to the ship's foredeck and cautiously works his way to the farthest jib. He unties the halyard line controlling the jib and holds onto it to pull the jib down and save it, but the halyard rips away, and he loses his footing as the boat heels over the crest of a wave. Ian holds the security line, but the halyard flips around like a sea snake out of water. The jib whips and snaps nosily in the wind, threatening to rip from the ship and fly away. Ian can't catch the line. The sail is lost.

The ship rocks downward into the wave trough. Ian clings to the security line with every bit of muscle he's got. His stomach feels like it touches his toes. The ship is buoyed like a ride at an amusement park; a wave of water hits him, dousing his thoughts.

Ian slowly works his way back to the foremast. Ben is still following. This time, Ian grabs the halyard and wraps it around his wrist.

"Ian!" Hana yells. "We're going right toward the shore! We're too close!"

Ian pulls the halyard as hard as he can, trying to pull the foresail down. Nothing budges. He flaps the line and pulls again. It frees and slides down. Hand over hand, Ian pulls until the sail bunches at his feet. He steps over the heavy, sodden sail and yells to Ben, "You secure the sail to the boom! We can't lose it! Don't fuck this up!"

Ben nods.

Ian runs to the wheel, his steps less like running and more like dancing on the wet, slippery, moving deck.

"What can I do?" Isabella shouts over the wind, stepping away from the wheel with a snap as if Ian is her commanding officer.

The wind pushes them hard again, and the rain intensifies. "We need to tack! I need you to lower the back mainsail two spots!" Ian points out the ties a few feet off the foot of the sail.

"Too easy! Give me somethin' harder!" she yells,

looking confused at the mess of ropes everywhere.

Ian tries to sound calm in the rapidly declining situation. "See that rope?" He points it out. "It's the halyard. It holds the sail up. Untie it and pull it down until you get to those ties. Then, tie the hanging part of the sail up. Got it?"

Ian is way out of his game. If he does anything wrong, they all die. The ship will flip and drag them down into Davy Jones' Locker. Beyond the stern, the small wooden rowboat is still fast to the cleat but might not be for long, swinging violently back and forth on the waves.

Ian turns the ship back into the wind. The sail luffs wildly, snapping back and forth.

With her adrenalin-intensified strength, Isabella pulls the sail down two levels and ties the line. Now, only the small bit of mainsail is left up.

Ian has more control almost immediately; the ship isn't being pushed around so violently, but they're far from safe. The storm is still carrying them toward shore. "Unless we want to crash, we have to turn and head back out to sea!"

Markus pokes his head up from the ladder leading to the galley. "We're taking on water, Ian. What should I do?"

"Shut all the portholes! Get Josh and look under the floorboards for pumps. The electric bilge will be disconnected, but there should be manual ones! Look for a simple baseball-sized thingy that has a bar for a hand pump. Like an old well pump!" Ian hopes there are manual pumps that look the same as those on his father's yacht.

"Take that rope," Ian orders Ben. "It's the sheet that controls the mainsail." Ian points it out. "You and Isabella pull it tight until that boom is centered. Then, as I turn, let it out until I say stop." They nod. "Jibe!" Ian yells and turns the wheel hard to port. The boat rises on the back of a huge wave and turns. They soar up the swell and back over it— the mainsail flaps like a broken-winged bat. Ian turns, and the sail picks up the wind and locks into shape. Isabella and Ben let out the sheet, allowing the boom to swing out. The *Pioneer* hits the wave trough, the bowsprit plunging into the dark water. The crest of the wave is taller than they are!

Ian's stomach seems to drop like he'd swallowed lead. Only after they start back up the wave does he feel the blood pumping in his veins again. He figures they should head out to a safe distance, heave-to, and wait for the storm out. Ian desperately tries to remember how to do that. Back in France, they were taught to heave to if they were injured or if something broke. He remembers to push out the mainsail as far as it will go, turn the wheel in the opposite direction, and tie it down. It must work because sinking and using the rowboat to get back to land is not an option.

Thunder and lightning fill the sky. Ben runs to the railing and barfs over the side. Hana is sick, too. Ian can see it in her face. He orders everyone else below.

Ian is alone at the helm, drenched, watching the dark clouds roll over themselves, lightning snapping through the atmosphere, cutting the sky apart. Thunder is deafening, the rain stings his face, and visibility is nothing.

"Oh yeah, you stupid storm. I'm fucking Ahab now! I got you." Ian bellows and steers the ship into the next wave. "You're gonna kill the last people on Earth? Piss on you!" Saliva builds in his mouth.

He spits it out, his stomach tightens, and nausea nearly overwhelms him, but he keeps yelling. "God, you better do this right and kill me! I murdered your children! You know it, and I know it. It was me and Zilla!" Ian laughs. "You knew I'd do what Zilla wanted. You knew this would happen, and you didn't stop it! Fuck you!" Ian spits again with the vehemence of a million suffering ghosts. He spits blood.

A huge wave breaks over the bow floods the deck and washes Ian's feet out from under him. Gripping the helm, he pulls himself upright again, shouting, "How the hell was I supposed to know this would happen? I'm sorry, Mom, Dad, cousin Rick, and Liana, my whole goddamn extended family. Oh, Tammy, my little niece." Tears and snot diluted by the rain run down his chin. "I took down the system, didn't I? I fantasized about it, and I did it. Shit, man. I committed genocide, and I didn't even know it. *I* was the Puppet on a string."

Ian's vomit splashes into the salty water around his feet; he clenches the helm so hard his knuckles ache.

Sound is drowned, and Ian sinks into the silence as if he is underwater, submerged in pain and remorse. Thousands of lights, like fireflies, surround him, blinking and skittering, besiege him. One comes too close to his face. He flinches. Sickness forgotten while he watches the lights, fascinated. The *Pioneer* slides down, down, down into the wave trough, the fireflies swoop into the dark sky and disappear. Ian rides the ship to the wave's depths and rises with it to the crest. He's dizzy. So dizzy.

Ian fights the ocean silently until he knows he cannot, grimly locks the helm, and struggles to the main mast sheet, nausea rolling over him. His body is on autopilot, and he lets the main sheet out as far as it will go and ties it down. He struggles toward the hatch, dry-heaving the nothing left in his stomach. A wave knocks him down, and he slides across the deck like he's on ice. Water and gravity pin him to the safety rail. He ceases to feel the ship moving; everything is still, and the silence makes a white noise in his mind.

The ship rocks again, and Ian's head spins. His fingers find the rope, latch onto it without his conscious command, and pull him up until another wave buries him, rolling him against the railing like a log. Ian works harder

than he ever has in his life, fighting the water and wind until he gets to the companionway door. The boat rocks again, almost completely sideways this time, throwing him against the safety railing. The companionway is so far away it looks dwarfed.

The ship heels again, weakening Ian's grip. If he lets go, he will be tossed overboard. The temptation to let go teases him, promising peace. Maybe he deserves to sink into watery oblivion, die alone, with no one he loves to mourn him. He closes his eyes, releases the safety line, relaxes, and lets his body slide across the deck.

He slides past the wheel and the companionway door; his body slams against the opposite railing and is held by force as if by a giant hand.

The ship rolls again, starboard dropping below the horizon, and Ian is about to be crushed by another wave rising above the ship, a wall of water so tall it blocks out the clouds above. A demon's shadow emerges, looking into Ian's soul, singing his bones, coming to take him away.

Hana opens the companionway door, seizing Ian, gripping his hands, pulling him close. The wave beats on them both, but she doesn't let go . Together, they tumble through the open hatch, down the ladder, to the deck below.

Chapter 1.33

Isabella
Sand And More Sand

The fierce storm off the coast of Virginia lasted for hours, tossing the ship side-to-side, rolling and pitching so hard walking was impossible. Everyone aboard was seasick, too weak to withstand the heaving deck and crawl to a toilet or find a bucket or towel.

Vomit covering the galley deck was a smelly, slick mess. Ben's fancy chicken parmesan dish tasted good on the way down, but not on the way up.

Josh was curled up by the sink. Isabella couldn't

make it to a bed and remained on the settee, holding onto the cushion with all she had. Hana and Ian were passed out under the settee, clutched in each other's arms.

The cessation of motion woke Isabella, and the foul stench of the day's heat cooking the vomit in the galley spurred her up and out, seeking fresh air.

Kat the dog was not finicky; he licked it up the mess like melted cheese.

Isabella nearly gagged as she stepped over Hana and Ian and climbed the ladder.

Breathing the fresh air greedily, Isabella carefully worked her way around the deck in recon mode. The *Pioneer,* aground on a sandbar half a mile off the beach, showed the storm's violence in the damaged rigging and sails. A dozen Puppets gawked at the ship, more of the creatures shambling down the beach. Once the Puppets realized they could cross the sand bar, they'd swarm the ship.

She poked her head into the galley. "Hey, rise and shine, we're fucked."

Hana snaps awake, pulls herself free of Ian, intending to join Isabella, but shook Ian gently. "Wake up, Ian. We have to get moving."

Isabella, impatient at the delay, takes a deep breath, climbs down the ladder, picks her way across the deck, opens the portholes and switches on the galley vents, grateful the engine charged the batteries.

She kicks Ben, curled up on the galley deck, his arms still clasped around the pedestal of a table bolted to the deck. "Up. Help clean, now."

Ben peeks at her and moans, mutters "Okay, okay. Gimme a minute, here."

Isabella raises her foot again, threatening.

Ben slowly gets to his feet.

Isabella rouses everyone else, shouts at them until

they all work together to clean the ship. Hana grabs the deck hose from the topside, uses the foot pump which sucks up sea water in a tank, and takes the hose into the galley to spray clean the fuckin' disgusting chunks and slippery acids pooling in corners and dripping from the walls.

Isabella finds two buckets, shouts at Josh to help her. She hands one bucket to Ben, saying, "Here. Fill it with this smelly shit."

She and Josh go topside, tie a length of rope to the handle and lower the bucket over the stern rail, out of sight of the Puppets on the beach, fill it half-way with seawater, and carry it to the hatch. "Ben, hand us the full bucket, use this water to scrub a spot and we'll dump this one."

The bucket brigade was hard, stinking, hot work. The survivors took turns scrubbing the deck and going topside for fresh air while they dumped the chunks into the ocean, attracting noisy gulls who fought over every morsel.

When the galley and the staterooms and cabins are clean, the survivors climb topside.

The light bites into Isabella's brain, but the cool air flows over her sweat-beaded skin, through her hair, drying it in stiff, sticky strands. Wishing she could shower and shampoo, she climbs into the lowest rigging and, squinting in the sunshine, scans north to south, east and west. Puppets roam the beach like animals on the savannah who know prey is near, seeking a way to feed. These fuckers haven't chatted with the others in Jamaica Bay; otherwise, they'd attempt to get to the ship. When one decides to take a walk into the big blue, they all will.

Looking through the binoculars, she sees dozens cutting across waist-high grasses, floundering in the spongy tidal flood plain. She sees no homes, roads, or parks, and wonders where the Puppets used to live.

Isabella climbs down, asks Ian if a map of the East

Coast is on the ship.

He leads her to the helm, shows her the map he can't quite read, but is able to point out landmarks. "I think we're at the Oregon Inlet Bridge. See, the beach ends, starts again over there, the only place with such a narrow inlet on the map."

"Get to your point," Isabella snarls, still feeling nasty from being sick all night and working so hard to clean up the messes.

"We're by North Carolina," Ian says. "Well, this map shows tide and storm warnings all around Cape Hatteras. Major currents colliding make storms bigger, and even bigger waves."

"I hope you're saying we've passed that point," Hana joins the two. Her arms are crossed tight over her chest, and the dark half-circles under her eyes look like bruised apples.

"No, but we can use the Intracoastal Waterway to go inland from here to Florida. Safer, slower waters. Easier that way," Ian says.

"We're not going anywhere without a new ship, at least a new boat," Isabella says, her voice rough with anger. "Anything will be more difficult with all those Puppets on the beach."

"We're aground on a sandbar.

All we have to do is dig ourselves out and wait for the tide to come back in," Ian says. "Should be easy."

Isabella grunts. Her muscles feel twisted like a wrung-out rag. She grits her teeth and tucks the pain away.

Isabella, Ian, Hana, and Josh spend the next four hours in the shallows, scooping sand from under the hull. The wet sand is heavy, and the water stirs the silt and deposits it right back in the holes they've cleared, but the water is pleasant, and they can see progress as the tide rolls in, the weight of the ship compacts the sand, and the liquefaction process eases the ship deeper into the water.

Isabella, keeping watch on deck while the others eat lunch, sees one of the Puppets wade out into the waves and keep walking, making no effort to swim, its body disappearing under the surface, until its head is submerged. "We're almost out of time!" she yells.

More and more Puppets follow, slow, clumsy, but relentless.

Isabella doesn't have energy left to crack skulls, doubts any of the other survivors are in much better physical condition than she is.

They dig steadily, each one making maximum effort to complete the channel to float the ship off the sandbar. The work is dangerous, because the ship lists more to port than starboard, creating the risk the ship will roll on anyone too close when the sand shifts or a gust of wind broadsides the hull.

Late that afternoon, Ian calls a halt to the digging. Everyone is exhausted and there is little evidence the digging had done any good. The *Pioneer* remains sat solidly on the sand. "Everyone! Get aboard. We're fucking done. We can't do it. The ship is lost."

He and the others climb the rope ladder and stand at the railing listening to the constant waves.

"We didn't even make a dent in the sand," Hana mumbles.

Ben looks at the blisters on his hands. "God damn."

"This isn't his fault," Markus says. "He set the tide clock in the very beginning."

"Well, fuck him," Ben barks.

Hana gently coaxes Ben to another part of the boat. "Come on. Cool down. Grab something to eat. Barking at the Priest won't do any good."

"I'm not a priest. I'm a bishop," Markus replies indignantly as he finds a seat.

"Dry off, get something to eat if you need it, get the salt off your skin so you don't get dehydrated," Hana urges.

Ian throws his bucket across the deck. "Come on! Fuck. This…This is all bull shit." He stomps away with a look in his eyes that Isabella has felt deep within herself many times. He is giving up on this. Time to try something else.

Chapter 1.34

Ian

Off To Find the Wizard

During the night, the Puppets figure out how to get to the Pioneer. They surround her hull and claw at the painted metal, scratching, scratching into the wee hours. The sound grates like fingernails on a chalkboard.

Ian reaches his breaking point. He packs his bag with some canned food and jerky and fills two water bottles.

"Where are you going?" Hana asks, peeking into his room. "You know there are a thousand Puppets surrounding us." Her eyes were bloodshot and tired. She's probably had as little sleep as Ian.

"I know. Look, I'm done with running. I can't run like this. I've promised myself I'd do something. I should have never left New York," he snaps, his voice resolute. I need you and the others to make a racket portside. If you can get all the dead to move to one side of the ship, I can sneak off."

"Sneak off? You're going to leave us? Just like that, huh?" Hana puts her arm on the door jam to block Ian. "What about us? If we can't get off the ship, we're going to starve on it."

Ian pushes past Hanah. "You've got enough supplies to last until a high spring tide. Once you float off the sandbar, you can head south to Cuba." Ian marches through the galley and climbs the ladder to the deck. He explains his plan to everyone and gathers them up top.

"You've got shit to do in New York?" Ben snaps. "Yeah, I've got shopping and shit too, but in case you haven't noticed, there are fuckin' dead people stomping around your hometown."

Isabella doesn't say a word. Her eyes are as hard as granite. "He wants to go? Let him go. None of us are prisoners on the ship." She marches to the port side and starts whistling and smacking the hole. "Hey, you fuckheads. Come, gather around, and get some window shopping done."

Markus shakes Ian's hand. "Isabella is right. We can't stop you. But I don't feel it is right. God does not need your sacrifice at this time."

"Thank you. I made up my mind. I can move faster than the dead. When I'm done, I'll head down to Cuba and join you all."

"Come on," Tanis moans. "You can't say what you gotta do? Maybe we can help? We can bargain. Like we did in Jamaica Bay."

Ian shakes his head. "I'll catch up. Promise. Now go make some noise for me." He gently turns Tanis around towards the portside.

Ben shakes his head. "You're crazy dude. And you're gonna fucking die. Good luck, though." He shakes Ian's hand and turns away.

Hana hugs Ian hard. "This is very stupid, but it looks like your mind is made up."

Ian nods and hugs her tight. "Take care of these people. Get them to Cuba in one piece."

Hana sniffles and wipes her tears. "What if we never get off this sandbar?"

Ian looks at her with steady eyes. "Distraction and run. Just like what I'm doing. You can do this."

She walks away, her face in her hands.

Rice hugs Ian, too, and kisses his cheek, followed by Andy, who hugs his leg,"bye, Mr. Ian. Thank you for rescuing us."

Ian ruffles his hair. "Anytime."

The survivors scream and yell and spray the faces of the dead with the water hose. They effectively gather a massive crowd.

Ian slinks away to the ship's starboard side and climbs down on the back ladder. He silently slips into the water. The front and port sides are swarmed with the dead, forcing Ian to swim to the north. He finds an effortless stroke and settles into the rhythm. Swimming was always one of his favorite sports, though he hadn't made the time to find a pool near his condo. He slowly crosses the inlet and eventually hits the far shore. No Puppets on this side. He looks back toward the small light on the Pioneer, left on to attract the dead. He questions his decision but is resolute. He turns and trudges north in the dark further and further away.

I have to do this. Part of all of this is my fault. I let Zilla fuck with my head, and I don't deserve to be free and walking around. I should be in jail or dead. I should be roaming the countryside looking for brains or whatever these fucking puppets want to do. I'm gonna get Zilla, and I won't stop until I do. There's nothing else my life is good for now.

Ian finds Anderson Boulevard and follows the road, passing dark home after dark home. He stops in one, but it's been cleared out in a panic. They've evacuated, no doubt. There is no food, no water, and no useful weapons. He heads back to the road. All the houses are on stilts, and nearly all are missing their cars. He checks a few more houses and collects some soup, corn, and soda cans.

Meanwhile, he cooks his plans in his head. I'm going to start in DC. It's the seat of the American government. They've got bunkers, and they've got resources. If there's any civilization left on the East Coast, it'll be there. I can gather any resources I need and maybe look for evidence. Maybe Zilla has set up shop in DC after killing the entire government. Ian chuckles. Maybe the president of the United States and all the fucking Senators and Congress people all got syringes too.

A Puppet lumbers from under a house, but Ian had been moving slowly and carefully enough not to get seen. But not every step is easy. Another Puppet lunges at him as he passes. A short man with a sunburnt face like jerky. He had clawing hands and a snarling face with white-root eyes like the rest. But Ian easily slips away. I can't startle too many. They'll start to follow me. Ian passes a bus stop and catches a glimpse of an advertisement for Top Sail Aquarium. He imagines all the fish and reptiles trapped in the tanks, starving to death. A swell of guilt floods over him. How many will die in their tanks and cages without humans to feed them? He walks on in silence, stepping like a cat, avoiding branches and leaves.

A few miles down Anderson Boulevard, he sees the aquarium. It's a brand new, oval-shaped building addition with parking underneath. The top is adorned with signage and flags, like a crown. The parking lot has dark shapes…

Cars! His brain lights up. Man, if I could drive to DC in a couple of days, It would save me weeks of travel.

Ian dashes to the first sedan. Locked. He looks around, spotting Puppets meandering across the street at the surf shop, unfocused, uninspired. Ian continues to the next car. No luck. Not a single one in the parking lot is unlocked. I just need to break into one. I've no idea how to hotwire one, but I'll give it a try.

A large Ford F150 truck sporting the aquarium's logo was at the far north parking spot of the aquarium. They'd have keys for that truck inside, for sure. Ian checks the driver's door; sure enough, it's locked, but there are no keys inside. He sneaks to the aquarium and tries the front door. It opens. He slips inside.

Too dark to see. "Hello?" Ian says as loud as he dares. He's in the gift shop area, the original side of the building. His eyes adjust a bit more, so he fumbles to the register. No keys. But he needs light. Ian finds the back room and closes himself inside. His ears are focused on the ambient sounds, listening for threats. There is none, so he sits with his back to the door and closes his eyes. He misses his friends already.

The next morning, he wakes and sits up. He sips his water and stands. He searches the desk for the truck keys but finds nothing. He leaves the office and follows the newly constructed hallway to the aquarium showroom. Huge tanks line the walls full of assorted fish of all colors and shapes. His heart breaks again.

He turns to leave when he catches a shape in the shark tank. Ian rushes over to it. It's one of the employees floating in the water, his back toward Ian, all buoyancy lost. He is bloated but also bleeding steadily from different spots. The shark swims by and strikes out, snapping a bite off his shoulder. Blood and bits float away but dilute quickly in the murk.

Ian backs up. Well, at least the shark will have some food for a bit. Ian shivers at the thought of being nibbled on for weeks.

Then he sees it. A keychain is on the employee's belt loop. And on that keychain is an F150 key fob. "Shit," Ian says and his heart jumps. "In the shark tank. Figures." He takes a deep breath. "Guess I'm going for a swim."

The shark swims around the enormous tank and returns to its body for another bite. Its mouth snaps open, and its sharp rows of teeth jut out and snap the top of the employee's head. The bite isn't easy or clean. The shark's fins beat the water as it curls and bucks, trying to take a piece off the man's skull. It succeeds, opening his skull, and then swims away.

Ian watches in horror but, oddly enough, can't take his eyes off the tank.

The employee's floating body slowly turns to face Ian. Ian's throat seizes, and he jumps back, knocking a display off the wall. The glass shatters, but Ian barely registers the loud noise. He's focused on the floating dead guy. The body has been nibbled for days, bit by bit. Not only are his gaping wounds extensive and horrific, with parts of skull and bone exposed, but dozens of white worms extend from his body, reaching out into the water like an explosion frozen in time. But they aren't frozen. They're twitching, looking for something to grab onto to dig into.

Ian backs up, stepping on broken glass. "Damn,

damn, damn. I need those keys." His stomach turns. "Forget it. Not worth it." He heads back to the exit, deflated and unnerved, feeling alone again.

There is noise in the gift shop. Ian moves behind a rack of shirts and listens. He hears scratching on glass and muffled screeching. Oh no. They followed me. I thought I was so quiet. God damn it!

Ian sneaks to the door and peeks outside through advertisements and store hours.

The parking lot is full. Three dozen Puppets at least and clambering at the door.

"Fuck."

Ian searches the building and finds a back door that probably leads to a yard. It has a push bar for emergencies, but there is also a locked deadbolt for some reason. "What the hell?" Ian moans. "Fucked off the building codes, huh? Assholes."

If I can open the door, I could make a run for it. But if I bust it down, the noise will call the dead like a siren's song.

He turns and leans against the door. "I guess I'm getting the keys off the floating dude after all."

Resolute, Ian hurries back to the aquariums. It doesn't take long to find the access doors. He steps up the steel stairs to the catwalk. He is now on top of three large tanks. The shark one, a reef tank, and one for penguins. Coolers line the wall, one of which is open. The stench is unbearable. Ian gags. He pulls up his shirt, covering his nose.

"You can do this. That truck is your only way out of here. I'll just make the play Isa, Josh, and Markus made at the drugstore. Make a shit ton of noise at the back door, drawing the crowd. Then, sprint to the truck in the front and drive off. Easy."

Ian then grabs a pole with a metal loop on the end and reaches it into the shark tank. He hooks the employee's body and pulls him closer to the catwalk.

The worms twitch with excitement. Ian turns the body around so he can see the keychain on his belt. With care, he sticks the hook into the man's belt and pulls him up toward the surface of the water. The body moves easily in the murky water.

Ian reaches for the keys.

His fingers are only an inch from the key fab when the shark comes out of the dark, bloody water and grabs the employee's body. Ian lunges and grabs the keys at the last second. The shark does a roll, ripping at the dead tissue.

Ian has the keys, but they're hooked to the belt loop by a carabiner.

The shark thrashes.

The body jerks hard, and Ian falls into the water.

Panic fills Ian's body. But he holds onto the dead body. He can't see the shark, but the tank isn't that big. Ian tries to hold the dead body at arm's length and to keep it between him and the shark, but the tentacles are swimming toward him. Fuck.'

Ian reaches behind him, grabs the catwalk, and pulls himself to the edge.

Movement.

The shark shoots from the murky water, teeth barred.

Ian pulls the body over just as the shark bites down. The teeth sink into the shoulder of the employee.

Ian's thumb hits the carabiner's latch and twists it off the belt loop as the shark flails, trying to tear off a chunk of meat.

Ian spins and pulls himself out of the water.

He is on his hands and knees, gasping for air, trying

to still his panicking heart and catch his breath, when he notices white roots on his forearm. He smacks it off and jumps to his feet. He searches the rest of his body, but he's clear.

"I'm outta here," he spits as he runs to the steps.

At the bottom, he looks at the keys in his hand. The key fab, plus a few more building keys, are on the loop. He heads to the back door, and one fits into the deadbolt. He unlocks it and pokes his head out the back.

The day is overcast and hot. Ian sneaks to the edge of the building. Across the street, a puppet stumbles toward the front, heeding the call of his friends.

"Hey, shithead," Ian yells. "Dinner. Me. Come and get it." He bangs on the side of the home, then on the nearby garbage can.

The Puppet sees him and takes the bate. He stumbles across the street toward Ian.

Ian makes his racket until the first Puppet is nearly upon him and slams the back door closed. He continues to bang on the door but not too loud.

Then he waits. Hours later, Ian sprints to the front and checks the truck. The Puppets are all gone.

Ian opens the door and sprints to the truck. The truck's driver's door is open already, but when Ian gets fully inside, he hits the lock button on the door. "Yeah!" Ian yelps with glee and relief. "let's do this! DC, here I come. Zilla! I'm back on your fucking tail." He reaches out and smashes the start button.

The truck doesn't start. He hits the button over and over, but it's no good. Ian pulls out the key fob. The light on the fob flashes when he presses the lock button, but the truck doesn't respond.

These are the right keys. "Come on! I hate this shit!" Ian blurts. He hammers the steering wheel over and over in rage.

He reaches for the handle when he stops. The Puppets have the truck surrounded again, and more are coming. Ian is trapped.

Ian sits in the truck, his thoughts a whirlwind of despair. "The possibility of finding Zilla is so far from possible. I would waste what was left of my soul and achieve nothing." Now, trapped in this metal cage, the weight of his choice to leave his friends and pursue revenge presses down on him like a suffocating blanket. The world outside is deadly and indifferent to his quest. There would be miles and miles, decades and decades of searching with no solace or escape from his anger unless he leaves his anger behind now. In this truck. Forever.

"I will never see Zilla behind bars or at the end of a rope. He's won." Ian cries.

Puppets pound on the glass, the hood, and the doors. They screech and wale.

With a heart heavy with resignation, Ian realizes he is not only giving up on finding Zilla but on life itself. Hopelessness consumes him. In a final act of desperation, he screams so primal, so visceral, his larynx feels like it tears. He doesn't care. His cry echoes through the cramped cab, bringing no relief.

Chapter 1.35

Tanis
No tide

Tanis sits at the bow of the boat. He has a fishing pole in his hand, one he'd grabbed from the ghost ship they had stumbled upon days ago. Over the edge are the ever-growing horde of dead Puppets, all looking up at Tanis with their root eyes and screeching with their dead voices. Tanis is lowering the fishing pole end to the nearest Puppet and then, at the right moment, whipping the top of its head and teasing it. It was amusing at first, but now he's doing it out of sheer boredom.

Kat is next to him, lying down, looking sad and

hungry. Tanis pets his head. "Waiting for a spring tide to lift us off this sandbar is the thing that's gonna kill us, huh, Tanis mumbles. He thwaps a Puppet's head again. "It should only take a week. That's what Ian said." Tanis grunts. "But he didn't sound too sure. I'm not sure he knows what he's talking about."

Tanis takes the pole away from the dead and drops it next to the railing. "I can't believe he left us."

Kat mews in agreement.

Tanis happens to be looking at the starboard side, which is the same side Ian snuck off. The shore he swam to is so far away. "I wonder if he made it. I'd freaking drown," Tanis says to Kat. "I wish I could call him up and be, like, hey, you okay?"

A dark feeling overcame Tanis. Worry. He'd come to really like Ian. "He's the freakin' captain of the boat, right? Who's gonna sail it? Isa said she could. But has she ever?" He stands and paces. "What did he have to do that was so important anyway? Everyone just let him go. No one stopped him. I didn't stop him." Tanis had an uncontrollable vision of the ship sinking eve, anyone dying, and Ian being torn apart by Puppets.

Tanis puts his head on his shoulder and tries to calm himself. But it isn't working. He is as anxious as he's ever been, and the feeling doesn't go away. Tanis lies next to Kat and hugs his dog. He's sweating, and his heart is beating so hard he feels sick to his stomach. There is nothing to do but lay next to his dog and cry.

After a half hour of panic, Tanis has a vision of his dad talking about anxiety.

"Anxiety is fear. Fear is unknown. The only cure for the unknown is to know. And that takes steps. You take steps to know what you need to, and the fear goes away. Make moves. One step in the right direction will make you feel better almost instantly. That and deep breathing." His father used to ruffle Tanis's hair. He hated it, but would give anything for one more ruffle of his hair.

Tanis sits up. "I'm going to go get him."

Kat whines.

"I can do it. I'm not the best swimmer but damn it. No one else is gonna go get him, so it has to be me. I'd rather drown out there than leave Ian behind."

Kat licks Tanis's hand.

"Yeah, you can go with me. I need your nose. The only way we find Ian is for you to take me to him. I'll figure out how to make something that floats so we won't drown."

That night, Tanis and Kat sneaks out of the pilot house. Earlier, he had tied four large water bottles, half full of water, to the side of the pack so they would act like a floatilla. Then, he had loaded the pack with supplies. Just the act of packing and planning made most of Tanis's anxiety vanish.

Ben is on watch but has a habit of sleeping through his watch. The Puppets are still clamoring at the base of the hull, an unstoppable undulating mass of dead tissue, but they avoid the rear of the ship during high tide because of how deep and rough the water gets.

The escape off the ship is easy. Tanis picks Kat up with one arm and lowers himself down a rope he'd tied knots in and slips into the water. Kat seems to know they have to be quiet and doesn't seem to mind the water at all.

Tanis is only wearing shorts and is expecting a cold blast of water, but the chills hit him harder than expected. Shaking erupts throughout his muscles, and his teeth begin chattering. "I got this. I got this," he echoes.

But he can't let go of the rope. After what feels like forever, Tanis starts to climb the rope. But he stops. He's paralyzed by indecision. What would Ian do? Would he come get me? Hell yeah. Just swim. You know how to. You're just being chicken.

The dark water feels ominous, like it's hiding sharks or leviathans that will eat Tanis up in one gulp. It's not hiding anything. That's the same as when I thought a monster was under my bed. Never was. No matter how many times I checked.

He tells himself to go a dozen times. He wants to scream at himself, but he has to be quiet. There's nothing there!

Just start. I can always come back if I lose my nerve.

Kat has his two front paws on the floating backpack waiting patiently, but probably also wondering what the holdup is.

Tanis kicks off the Pioneer's hull and swims away in the dark with only a dark tree line at the base of a night full of stars to guide him. He picks a star and heads toward it. He and Kat use the flotilla as support and are kicking hard with their feet and paws.

They're not making much progress, but he doesn't expect to. He's not a good swimmer. He's just thankful the incoming tide is helping him and not fighting him.

He warms a little, and his teeth stop clacking in his mouth. His backpack is floating behind him, full of clothes, water, and food. The half-empty water bottles are full of air, acting as ballasts.

"We're doing it! See, not too hard. Just keep moving forward. You were all worried, huh, boy."

Tanis can't believe he's actually in the ocean at night. Assisted by the current, he and Kat find themselves across the channel in less than twenty minutes.

Suddenly, something hits his foot. "What the hell was that?" Tanis thrashes and tries to swim but loses all momentum. "It's nothing, right? Just some seaweed?"

The two continue.

Tanis is yanked underwater.

Something has his leg. Tanis kicks and flails but is held on tight. No pain, just tight pressure around his ankle. He reaches down. It's a goddamn Puppet!

Tanis struggles but can't free himself. He looks around, but everything is inky dark. He's using up his oxygen. Didn't get a chance to get a good lungful of air. Chest hurts. Shit. I'm gonna drown. I knew this would happen. This is why I stayed out of the fucking water!

Tanis lets out the little air he'd had in his lungs. He's fighting not to breathe in water, but his lungs pull on his throat to open up. He reaches down again and grabs the dead hand but can't break his grip. The Puppet's other hand is trying to seize Tanis's other foot.

Splashing.

Tanis is going to pass out. He can't see anything.

Splashing under him.

Suddenly, he's floating upward. He beats his hands, kicks his legs, and breaks the water's surface. Gasping for air. Coughing.

Kat is next to him, and they're swimming again toward the shore.

Tanis's feet find mud and grass, and he sprints out of the water as fast as he can, though it feels like he's trying to run through honey. He falls to his hands and knees on the sandy rocks. "Holy shit. Holy shit. Kat. Where are you?"

Kat mews and is right next to Tanis, licking his arm. "We made it. Barely. Holy shit. That was close. What the hell happened?" He wishes his dog could tell him. But the pressure on his ankle starts the explanation.

The Puppet's hand is still clinging to him. Tanis pulls at the fingers, which are stiff and locked in its grip. He breaks one off, then another, and finally, he pulls off the hand. "Something had bit through its arm, taking off the hand?" He looked at his dog. Was that you?"

Kat shook himself off, flinging water in every direction.

Tanis hugged his dog. "Yeah. That was you. Thank you. I'm gonna find you the biggest doggie bone I can find. Not a Puppet bone. A nice cow knuckle or something."

Kat licks Tanis's face.

Tanis dries off and dresses, though the air isn't too cold. It's still hot and muggy. But getting dry feels as welcoming as a fire in the winter.

The two start up the beach. "Okay, boy. Do your thing. Let's go find Ian."

Chapter 1.36

Hana
Grounded For Good

Hana sits at the galley table eating a bowl of cereal with water and powdered milk. Josh sips his coffee and then proceeds to hand grind more coffee beans, making a second cup for Hana. Isabella slumbers out of her room, takes Josh's cup of coffee, and makes her way to the ladder.

"Yeah, you're welcome," Josh mumbles.

"It's good. You make good coffee," Isabella retorts.

"Guys?" Hana says. "I think we outta come up with another plan. It's been three days since Ian left, and the tides are no different. What do we do if there is no spring tide? And we're grounded here for good?"

Isabella stops on the ladder, "he said it would take a week or so. Don't you think we oughta wait a week or so to find out? We have enough food and water."

Hana nods. "I just want to prepare Plan B, that's all."

"Fine," Isabella replies, "plan B is sneaking off the boat and heading down the coast to find another boat. Now I'm going up top to do my workout."

"Okay, whatever," Hanah mumbles.

Josh pours hot water over the coffee beans in the French press. "I get it; you're a little worried. I'm feeling a little stir-crazy, too. Plus, it feels a little like a ghost town on the ship. I'm used to Ian walking around doing stuff like fixing things and organizing ropes. He didn't exactly tell us how to sail this ship very well before he left. Plus, I'm used to a dog on board, always begging for food and licking my legs. I don't remember when I saw Tanis or his dog last."

Hana stands up from the table and walks down the hall, stopping at Tanis's door. There is a note taped to the door that says do not disturb. She snatches the note and rips it off the door. "Tanis? You okay?" She grabbed the handle and turned. It's unlocked, and swings open easily. The room is empty.

Hana spins and heads down the hall. She opens Rice's door, she tends to sleep late. No Tanis. "Where is that kid?"

Tanis isn't in Marcus's or Ben's room either. They have the night shift. She tries not to wake them but can't help slamming the door in agitation. She turned and marched through the galley and the kitchen and up the ladder to the deck. "Isa, have you seen Tanis? He's not in the ship." She turns and looks around. "Tanis? Kat?"

"Not up here," Isabella says.

"Where the hell would he go? What a little snot

head." Hana barks. She goes to the railing and looks overboard. "Would he have really just ditched us without saying anything?"

The survivors got together at the wheel. They had discussed options but couldn't come to an agreement. Hana paced, crying. "So, we don't know where Tanis went, we have no way of tracking him, so we're just going to let it be. Let him march off into the dying planet with just a dog and a backpack full of who knows what. I hate this."

Ben rubs his eyes. "It doesn't seem like he wanted to be followed, just like Ian. I guess he had better shit to do. We can't do anything about it."

"If we're not going to do anything about Tanis as a group, will anyone go and look for him with me?" Hana asks.

"It's just a bad idea," Isabella says. "Think about it. Tanis doesn't like to swim. He would never have crossed the channel the way Ian did, which means he went in the opposite direction, but there is no opposite direction. He could've gone south. He could've gone southwest. He could've gone west or a little southwest and then turned south. We're in fucking North Carolina flood land. There's probably 3 miles of mud between here and anything that resembles a town."

"Yeah, Ben adds. "I'm betting he'll turn his ass around and come on back."

"I will have to agree with Ben and Isabella," Markus says. "You will more than likely return when he does not find what he is looking for."

"I can't believe he would do this. First in and now Tanis." She lowered her head and made the cross sign on her chest. "I hope they don't die." She looked at Markus, "can...can you say a prayer?"

"Yes, I will."

Andy picks his head off Rice's lap and sniffles. "Tanis was my best friend. And his dog, too, can't we find them? I want to find them now."

"I'm sorry, baby," Rice says. "I guess they just wanted to be alone for some reason."

Chapter 1.37

Ian

No Good Options

Ian sits in the truck's cab, cradling Isabella's 9 mm pistol. She had insisted he take it, though it was no good on Puppets. He wouldn't have left it behind anyway. It is the pistol he planned to kill Zilla with.

Ian had slept in over twenty-four hours. He couldn't sleep because he couldn't close his eyes. When he did, the screeching and scratching and inhuman sounds of the dead would cut into his nerves.

There is no escaping this truck. The only reason I'm alive was to get some sort of revenge. But that's simply not possible, so I'm done. I deserve prison or death." Ian laughs.

"This is one hell of a prison." He hammers the side of the door glass., wishing he could actually punch the Puppet that was snarling at him in its ugly face. "Who am I kidding, I would never survive prison."

Ian pulls back the slide of the 9 mm pistol and checks to see if there is a bullet in the chamber. There is. He puts the gun to his temple even as tears pour from his eyes and blur the world around him. He has so many regrets. The one thing he wanted to do with the remainder of his life was make amends somehow.

His finger tightens on the trigger. "I'm sorry for everything. Mom. Will I see you now?"

Tap. Tap. Tap.

Ian opens his eyes to the sound coming from the front windshield. It was a note taped to a rock suspended by a string that read, "Need some good news for once?"

Ian blinks the tears from his eyes and pockets the pistol. He looks out the windshield and follows the string to the roof of the aquarium.

Tanis hangs over the edge, waving and smiling.

Ian waves back. "Holy hell, overwater! Hell yeah, I need help!" He wipes tears off his cheeks.

Tanis sprints across the roof and disappears for a bit.

Ian waits and weights. "I don't know how you plan on getting me out of here. But you better not get your ass killed in the process."

Tanis returns to save Ian in the most miraculous way.

Chapter 1.38

Isabella
No Way

One week after Ian left the Pioneer, the decision was made to abandon ship. The tide never got any higher than the first day they wrecked. With solemn resignation, the survivors packed bags, food, and their weapons.

Ben, Rice, and Markus pound on the ship's starboard side, trying to get all the Puppets over to one side.

Isabella has a rope ladder ready on the port side. She and Hana will get off the ship first, then make a run for it. They will take over, making noise and drawing the crowd away from the ship so the others can sneak off. No one likes the plan but sweating it out and being trapped on the Pioneer is the worst of the two options.

"Don't fall behind," Isabella says to Hana.

"I won't. Don't you know me by now?" Hana replies.

Isabella half smiles. "Yeah, I do." She peeked over the edge. "Ready?"

Hana nods. "I'll go first."

"Fine by me." Isabella tosses over the rope.

Hana leaps over the railing like a jackrabbit and scampers down the ship's side.

Isabella hears the splash of water and nearly springs into action herself. She pauses, hearing something.

The rope ladder thuds and is taught again.

"Hana?" Isabella draws her weapon and turns to aim it overboard to help Hana fend off a Puppet.

But Hana is on the ladder. She reaches the railing, out of breath.

"What is it?" Isabella asks.

Hana points to some trees a hundred yards away. They break and fold like twigs and get pushed out of the way as though some huge dinosaur is running their way. But it's not a dinosaur. It's a tractor.

"Fuck me," Isabella mumbles. She pulls up her rifle's scope. "It's fucking Ian and Tanis!"

"Are you serious?" she grabs the rifle and takes a look. "Ian!! Tanis!! Oh my God, it really is them. They're okay. They've come back."

The word spreads as the rumble of the tractor gets ever louder. The survivors on the Pioneer jump up and down and whoop and holler. There is so much relief on the ship, a feeling that hasn't been felt in some time.

The tractor has four large wheels and a large scoop. Ian drives it into the shallow surf and scoops out the sand.

With the tractor's power, the Pioneer is freed from the sandbar in less than an hour.

Tanis and Ian swim to the Pioneer as she slowly drifts away from the beach. After Kat is lifted up, they take turns climbing the rope ladder.

Hugs are enthusiastically given, including a punch to Tanis's arm from Hana. "I am so glad you are back and safe. But if you ever leave like that again, I will kill you."

CHAPTER 1.39

ISABELLA
INTERCOASTAL DEATH TRAP

"Good. Now I know Isa could have handled this ship without you, but we all need to know how to sail her. If any one of us dies, we need to be prepared," Hana says.

Ian teaches everyone how to "trim the sails," as he calls it. Everyone takes turns maneuvering the *Pioneer* for the rest of the day and through the night slipping between the barrier islands and the mainland. The waterway dampens the big, deep waves and break up the heavy wind gusts of the open Atlantic.

The following day the Pioneer sails smoothly, the

intense rocking gone.

Isabella is over her seasickness, but she's still sick of Ben doing nothing except being himself. She's close to taking her pain out on his face.

The weather is still calm the next day when Harker's Island, on the far eastern shore of North Carolina, slides by on the horizon. Isabella is getting the hang of finding landmarks. Ian helps some, but Josh is best at what he calls "spatial dimensions."

Following the Intracoastal Waterway takes them west through Bogue Sound. Isabella lets her hair fly in the breeze, which makes her scalp tingle. She lets her mind go blank, savoring the gentle rocking in every muscle, every cell, absorbing the pleasure. Zero stress is like a warm bath, and her nipples stand up and tingle. Her skin is cool, and her back is loose.

Tanis sits next to her. His dog licks her feet now and then, like kissing her ass or something. Tanis asks her how she became such a good fighter.

"I trained to fight in the military, and when I got out, two nights a week, I trained in Tai Jujitsu. Fighting comes easy for me. I love it. Don't ask me why."

"But you're a—" Tanis pauses.

"A girl? Yeah, so? I can still kick ass. It's not about your junk; it's about doing what you want. I want to fight. It's like running for some. I feel good, strong, and in control when I fight."

"Can you teach me some moves?" Tanis's hair covers his eyes.

"Okay, but you can't cry if you get scared, okay?" She stands. "The first thing you have to learn is how to fall without hurting yourself."

Tanis is attentive and works hard to copy Isabella's much fitter, stronger, and more flexible body. Two hours later, when Tanis is bruised and aching, she says, "I'll show you a new move every day, so you can help me kick some Puppet ass. It's my turn at the helm."

"Deal." Tanis vows to find a safe, out-of-sight place to practice.

Isabella joins Ian at the wheel.

"I think that shadow in the water is the bottom," he says, looking over the starboard rail. Ian summons Hana and Ben: "I need you two to look for rocks or reefs or anything in the water that might damage the hull or the rudder."

Isabella looks at the map and the compass. "We're going southwest now, probably by Myrtle Island. We're at a weird spot with lots of little islands around. The channel we're in is pretty deep, but it's narrowing."

Ian slows the ship and rounds the island, steering in the deepest part of the channel.

Isabella points out docks jutting from the beach, near houses on wide, grassy lots on the water, small sailboats, and motorboats everywhere. Some have been sunk, but most are rotting in the sun.

The island is still and perpetually quiet at five in the morning, and there is no sign of a containment line or safe zone. Deep silence settles on the boat. No one wants to talk about how the virus traveled so far and destroyed so many people. Puppets, the new beasts, are everywhere.

Isabella is antsy now that she's thinking about how fucked they really are. She needs a distraction but expects everyone on board to be asses, rude, and need to be put in their place, but they're all tired and discouraged. None of the survivors talk much; everyone is getting along. Isabella can't stand it, but she's enduring the others' idiotic behavior, so clearly, she *can*. Maybe she should go ashore, bust some heads, and burn off her excess heat.

Markus shouts and wails, and everyone but Ian runs

to starboard. Sea birds, dead ones, lie in piles like raked leaves. It still isn't clear why, and it might never be.

Isabella is not into nature much, but she is sad. "The virus got 'em," she says. "That means that other animals are vulnerable, too."

"So that's why we're not seeing animals," Josh says. "They're running scared or infected. I'd like to know more about the head-worms."

"So we can fight them," Isabella adds.

Rice sobs.

Kat barks at the dead birds.

The puppets are sparse out here and seem distracted. Isabella wonders if the rest of the once-human creatures are chasing something else.

Ian calls to her. She returns to the helm and takes up the map and her navigator's duties again.

"We've run out of shoreline to follow," Ian says.

Isabella follows the channel with her finger. "We either go left here, out to the Atlantic," she says, "or we go right and stay in the narrow channel." She sets the map aside and stands again to scan their surroundings, her hair tangling in front of her face. She gathers the top into a short ponytail like a samurai.

"I don't mind following the channel, but we'll use fuel, and we've already been under power for over two hours because this inlet is so narrow."

"We'll get more fuel," Isabella says without hesitation.

"I agree. We've passed a lot of fuel docks. No fuel out at sea, we're vulnerable to the weather, and navigation is harder." Ian shakes his head. "I'll never forget that storm around Cape Hatteras."

Ian chooses the channel, leaves the mainsail up, reefed halfway to catch the breeze to hold the ship steady in the current and use less fuel.

Ian motor-sails under a high bridge, the masts clearing by only feet. Puppets stumble around on the road, some leaning over the safety rail like fishermen.

Ben points at one near the end of the bridge, "Sucker's just walking in circles!" he says, laughing.

Josh runs to see Hana and Tanis close behind him.

"So, if a Puppet isn't clawing somebody or has nothing to chase, it just moves around?" Tanis asks. "That's messed up."

"No rest for the wicked," Markus mumbles.

Isabella is unsure why Markus said that. Maybe it was his version of a joke.

"Yeah, well, let's hope they start to eat each other. Then we'd be fine in a week or so," Ben adds.

"They don't seem to eat for sustenance," Josh said, watching the Puppets, his face serious. "I think they're... driven to get those white root things into our bodies to spread the infection."

A fisherman, Puppet, looks down at the ship passing under the bridge–as if you can call it looking. Its face locked on the mizzenmast, it screams, but the *Pioneer* continues up the waterway. More and more Puppets stagger out of the brush and trees.

Isabella goes on alert. The Puppets can see the ship in the narrow channel and follow it. She watches them the way she watched for suspicious people approaching when she was on guard duty. This bunch is different. These Puppets are not moving randomly, as they were when the survivors first saw them on the bridge. Isabella squints, a vigilant lookout, searching for tell-tale signs the hostiles are communicating with one another, coordinating their attack.

Hana interrupts. "I'm thinking the channel might be a bad idea," she says.

"Scared?" Isabella asks.

"Worried."

"Let 'em try somethin'," Isabella replies, turning back to her sentry post. She remains at her station for an hour without figuring out how the Puppets are anticipating the ship's movements. The *way* the Puppets move is purposeful as if they have a plan. Not all of them, though: one tries to jump off a small dock, falls into the water, and flounders stupidly.

Tanis shouts something to Hana, and she leaves Isabella and Ian alone together. "I heard you last night," she whispers, "during the storm, when we almost sank."

Ian pretends to not know what she's talking about. "Hum?"

"You were fighting the storm and yelling at the clouds or God or somethin'," Isabella murmured. "What were you saying?"

Ian's cheeks are pink, like a little boy's. "I was just freaking out. No big deal."

"You have to tell me," she said, leaning closer. "Tell me. I don't want to be your enemy."

Ian turns to her, eyes hard, jaw clenched.

Isabella sees her threat backfire and softens her voice. "I know what you said. Just clarify it for me. I don't want to tell the others. Give me your side."

Ian takes a deep breath.

Isabella senses his need to tell someone what's on his mind. She usually wouldn't give a shit, but she was damn curious to know why Ian said he killed the world, murdered God's children.

Ian runs his fingers through his jet-black hair.

"Cough it up, man," she urges.

"Nothing. It's nothing. I just miss everyone. Even the people I thought I hated."

Isabella folds her arms, determined that one way or another, he'll tell her his secret.

"You're getting too close to the beach!" Hana yells.

Ian corrects the ship in the very narrow channel. He rubs his temples, fighting for self-control. "First, we have to survive."

"No shit," Isabella replies. She sits next to Ian, silent, until near sunset, the sky blooming with reds and oranges. "I don't want to be on this channel after dark. After the rough night, cleaning up the barf fest, and diggin' out the boat, I want to sleep hard. I don't want to worry or have to fight right now."

"Same here. Is there a place to stop soon?" Ian asks. "With enough of a buffer between us and the Puppets?"

"Nope."

The ship passes a village of small houses with tiny yards, many small docks poking into the water. This time, yards, docks, and the shoreline are crowded with hundreds of agitated Puppets, straining like leashed hunting dogs onto their scent.

Isabella stands and paces, winding herself up. She can hear those fucking things screeching like vultures.

The rest of the survivors gather on deck to see. The Puppets look less and less like people and more like plants. The white roots are growing through the skin to the outside of their limbs, longer and thinner, like hair or maybe grass. One Puppet steps over the channel's high bank and splashes into the water without leaving a ripple.

The ship passes a pivot bridge, the center section open all the way, completely loaded with the dead.

The ship veers, the bow too close to the shore, clearly exciting some of the Puppets, like creeps outside a college bar at closing time.

Ian throttles the engine higher.

The channel narrows, the Puppet crowd moving faster, no longer stumbling fawns. Some are speed walking, shaking their asses, and others run together, like squads on the parade grounds.

More homes and small docks line the channel, but the crowd of Puppets is much bigger than the population of the villages along the channel could hold.

Ian stays in the center of the channel, his hands

sweating on the helm, as the ship approaches a huge, half-submerged drawbridge platform, surrounded by the twisted steel and concrete rubble left when the bridge was destroyed.

Puppets climb all over each other like roaches, massing on the warped, buckled metal.

Isabella watches them, back in sentry mode. She doesn't believe the Puppets just want to get a glimpse of the ship.

"They're using their brains," Josh says. "I've been watching their behavior, and they definitely have motivations and memory. Maybe they've reanimated their hosts' brains." He pauses and says, "The bodies can be reanimated, so the brains can be, too."

Isabella agrees with Doof. The Puppets are after the survivors and want them in a bad way. "They're moving like they've smelled our blood and called up the reserves," she says. She's edgy but thinks they're safe on the ship. Right?

Isabella is drawn to the bow rail to watch the dog pile of Puppets at the edge of the drawbridge, wondering if the ones at the bottom are being crushed. It wouldn't matter, though, because they're already dead. The Puppets create a towering structure by clinging to one another in a grotesque parody of an acrobat's pyramid. The Puppets squirm, their bodies torqued in unnatural, impossible positions, limbs bent back on themselves, others upside down, the roots in their eyes moving toward the sky. Some Puppets scream and gurgle like frothy lunatics. Isabella runs to the seat behind the pilot wheel and pulls up the cushion. She grabs her cleaned, loaded M-16 and flips the safety off.

"What are you doing? You're gonna start shooting? Won't that just upset them?" Rice is panicky.

Isabella runs to the rail, braces herself with one foot, and pops a few rounds in the growing tower of bodies. The

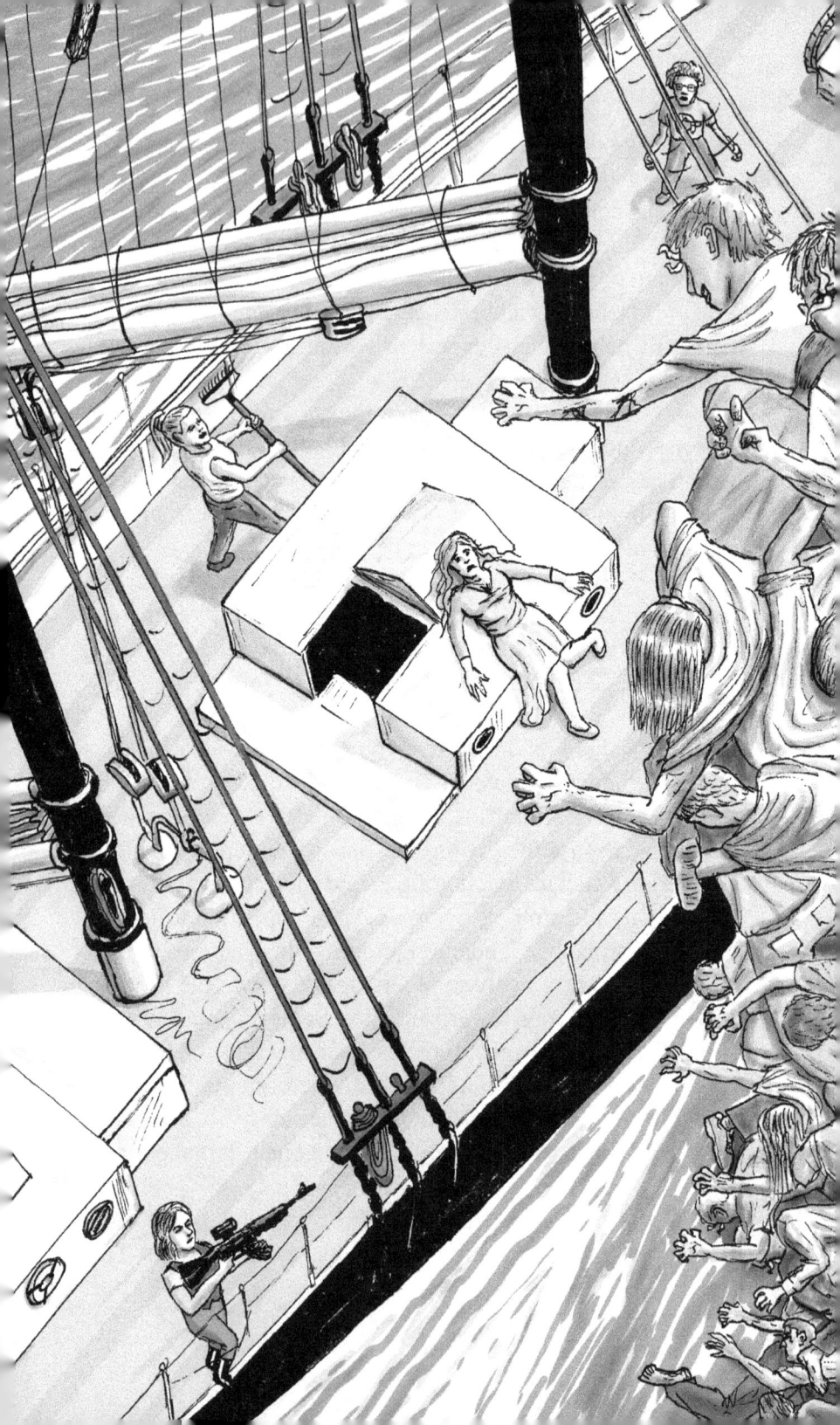

squirming increases and the tower leans over farther and farther until the tower of bodies arches over the channel waters, bodies crashing onto the ship's deck.

Rice is caught under the mass of falling bodies.

Tanis is struck a glancing blow and thrown into the port railing.

The ship rocks heavily and rolls against the opposite canal bank, splashing water upward.

Isabella stumbles and falls.

Puppets waiting on the opposite side, mouths watering, leap from the bridge platform onto the boat.

Ian puts the engine on full throttle, and the *Pioneer* careens down the canal, overloaded with the infected. The bodies untangle like a muscle relaxing, stand, and fill the deck between the companionway and the settee like they're lining up for burgers.

Isabella guesses her shift guarding Ian is about to begin.

White-knuckling the helm, Ian manages to get the ship back into the channel.

Hana and Ben, on the port side of the cabin, count survivors: Rice is buried, Josh and Tanis are at the bowsprit, and Markus is below.

Markus fights his way up the ladder, weapons in hand.

Hana takes the rake and holds it like a battle-axe.

Isabella hangs the rifle on her back, grabs her Beater from Markus, and shouts thanks. The first ugly fucker gets a jab to the jaw, cracks, and folds inward like bungled origami. She knows she can't kill the thing, so she knocks it into the railing and pushes it over. The next one is shorter, with a lower center of gravity, and won't go over so easily. Isabella knocks its grabby hands away, turns it with her foot, and smashes it between the shoulder blades. Her Beater pierces the frayed shirt and sinks into soft flesh between the ribs, releasing a gush of black blood. She pulls the Beater free, snatches the thing's ankle, and flips it over the rail, exposing herself. Another Puppet grabs her but can't hold her. She jerks loose, strikes it across the cheekbone, kicks its chest, and shoves it down hard on the deck.

Ben screams. He and Hana are overwhelmed, and he's clutching a wound on his arm. The two fight back-to-back, trying to protect one another against nasty odds.

Isabella turns back to her line of Puppets and moves faster, flipping them like cards over the rail, one after the other, not bothering to listen for the splashes. She clears her side of the cabin, inching her way to Rice, who's in the center screaming for help. Isabella works her way to the terrified woman, smashing knees and tossing Puppets off the deck, one after the other.

Markus, behind Isabella, is swinging his bat fiercely, keeping the Puppets off her right side.

Tanis climbs into the shrouds, over their heads, and kicks field goals with the Puppets' skulls.

"Everyone, hold on!" Ian yells.

"Grab something!" Isabella shouts, repeating Ian's warning, and grabs the nearest rail.

Ian turns the helm to starboard, rocking the entire ship. Puppets on the rails are flung away. Others fall like dominoes, but regain their feet and continue clawing at the survivors.

Isabella finally reaches Rice and pulls some hairy guy off her. The girl's cheek is split, and her ear hangs loose, barely attached to her head. Her blouse is shredded, blood oozes from everywhere, and she's covered in worms. Isabella grabs Rice's hand and pulls her close, shielding the girl's body within the Beater's arc. No place on the ship is safe enough to leave Rice unprotected.

Josh and Tanis get the deads' attention by screaming and flailing their arms.

Ian orders, "Hold on!" again. Brings the ship about sharply again, flinging a few more Puppets overboard, but not enough because they're hanging onto the safety line.

Markus has his back to Isabella. "I'm tired. I might not—"

Hana's scream distracts Isabella momentarily, and one Puppet grabs Isabella, then another with strong hands. *This isn't working*. Isabella shoves Rice behind her, pushes the Puppets away, and, with Markus helping her, backs all three of them into the narrow space between the cabin and the railing. The sails are down, bundled on the booms. Black shit covers the deck in splatters and chunks.

Josh fights the Puppets off with the anchor bar.

Good boy. Isabella waves Josh to her, Markus, and Rice. Josh ducks under the grabbing arms and snarling faces. He jumps on the settee, bashes two Puppets off the mizzenmast seat, and leaps to Isabella.

"The anchor!" she shouts.

"I can't pick that thing up!" Josh replies.

"The fucking smaller one! Kedge or whatever it's called! It still weighs twenty-plus pounds!"

Josh is smarter than he looks and understands what Isabella wants him to do.

Josh rams the Puppets, crowding around Isabella, holding onto the smaller but still bulky kedge anchor. Isabella kicks away the fucks grabbing at him until he's at her six, next to Rice. Josh pushes Rice into a crouch, her arms protecting her head.

Isabella picks up a section of the kedge anchor chain and wraps it around the neck of the ugly puppet in front of her. "Toss it!"

Josh hefts the anchor over the railing, letting it drop

and go taut, sweeping a half dozen puppets to the bow, smashing them into the lifeline.

"Ian! Hit the gas!"

"I'm going full speed!"

No matter. A moment later, the kedge anchor bites into the bottom of the canal, turning the anchor line and the lifeline cable into a scissor. The dozen Puppet's soft bodies are cut in half, their heads and torsos fly into the canal, and their legs crumple to the deck, spilling their rotten guts and a gaggle of worms.

"I'm dragging!" Ian yells. The boat slows. He doesn't know it's the kedge anchor.

Markus and Isabella attack the remaining Puppets and beat them into broken sacks.

Josh works the windlass and eventually pulls the anchor free of the muck.

Hana and Ben also make progress, joining Isabella and Josh at the mizzenmast and pushing the last seven or eight Puppets toward the bow.

"Oh shit! Another Puppet tower!" Ian shouts.

Isabella whirls toward the stern and sees another mass of bodies rising high on the canal bank. A dozen more Puppets topple onto the back where the wheel is. The ship rocks, and momentum pushes the *Pioneer* toward the channel bank, nearly aground.

Ian leaves the helm and runs to the fighters at the mizzenmast.

Snarling dogs sprint over the canal bank, leap, land on the stern, howling and biting at one another.

Isabella steadies herself against the dogs, pushing through the Puppets toward the fighters. They, too, have roots hanging out of their eye sockets. Only the dogs appear more frightening, with sharper teeth, faster, harder to stop.

"Get below," Ian bellows, and Markus opens the

hatch.

"No! Get them off our boat!" Isabella screams. "I'm not gonna retreat and leave the topside full of fuckers. We'd be sitting ducks. This is our stand!" she screams, reaching into the equipment locker next to the mast. She pulls out handheld signal flares and hands some to Markus. They light them all and pass them out.

The dogs stop advancing, and so do the Puppets.

"Got your attention now?" Isabella swings the burning flare in wide arcs at her enemies, backing them away step by step, screaming, "You like this pretty fire? Huh?"

Ben and Ian sweep the Puppet body parts off the foredeck. Hana helps Tanis off the rope ladder.

Markus and Isabella push all the fuckers to the stern, where they cower and screech at the flames. Isabella shoves her flare close to a Puppet's face, getting close to the white root. It jerks and shrivels, falling limp.

The Puppets on the canal banks stop, too. Isabella sees them stop. "They really don't like this shit."

A dog bolts toward Ian, but he jabs the flare into its face, driving it, yelping, back toward the other dogs. The dead crowd the helm.

"Feel the fear, you fuckers!" Isabella advances, stops next to the hatch, senses movement inside, and glances through the porthole. Andy's coming up top!

The boy swings the companionway door open, facing the Puppets and some vicious-lookin' dogs. He freezes. "What's going on? Kat is barking and crying and scaring me!" he says.

"Get your ass below!" Isabella screams.

The fifteen remaining Puppets attack, fronted by six undead dogs, surging forward like a machine. One snatches Andy off the ladder and drags him into their ranks, kicking and screaming.

"No!" Isabella drops the flare and swings the Beater at a dog leaping toward her. It sinks its fangs into her arm. Her blood sprays. She falls back, rolls, grabs the dog's throat, punches her thumb into its larynx, and snaps its neck. The jaw slackens and releases her, giving her the opportunity to throw it overboard.

Andy screams.

"Kid!" Ben yells.

"Get more fire!" Isabella orders. The Puppets move closer, one step at a time. The bastards at the back seem to be protecting their catch.

She looks at Ben. "Pants, now!"

"No fucking way!" he argues.

"Pants, or I throw you at *them*!"

"Andy!" Hana calls to the boy, bashing the Puppets with her rake without effect. Her rake simply isn't sharp or strong enough.

Ben unbuckles his belt and rips off his pants.

Isabella feverishly ties them around her Beater. "Light it!"

Ben shoves his flare into the pants, lighting them on fire. Isabella hands the fiery stick to Ian.

Ian jabs at the Puppets with the makeshift torch. Over and over, screaming back at their shrieks of terror. The fire works, for now. They hate it but are afraid.

The plant people retreat to the helm again.

Isabella sees Andy lying at their feet, silent and still. Rage fills her so fast she nearly explodes. She wants to be the Phoenix, to devour them all, to fly that kid out of here, to a better place. But he's probably already gone.

Isabella glances at Ian.

Tears fill his eyes. He stops, closes his eyes, and sways where he stands.

Isabella's attention snaps back to the horde crowding the deck of the *Pioneer*. "Get them off our fucking boat, Ian."

Ian reaches down, grabbing a line. "Which way is the wind?"

She spits on a finger on her bloody hand and holds it up. The breeze tickles her skin. "Port."

"Pull that mainsail halyard up as fast as you can. Hana, untie the main sail." Ian orders, still swinging the fire.

Ben and Isabella grab the halyard as Hana unties the sail, pulling the thick rope hand-over-hand until the mainsail rises into the sky like a majestic flag. Ian grips the railing. "Anchor yourselves!" The wind fills the sail so full it cracks with a sound like a whip. The line connected to the boom tightens, and the boom swings to port so fast that Isabella almost misses seeing it bash a couple of Puppet skulls. The boat heels hard toward the middle of the canal, dumping the rest of the Puppets and the dogs overboard.

Isabella leaps forward, slides in a pool of slick black blood, and grabs Andy's shirt.

The ship yawls and nearly tips on its side before the sail slackens. As quickly as she'd floundered in the pools of blood and ick, the *Pioneer* rights herself. Wind bellies the sail once more, and she pitches herself upright.

"Pull the sail down." Ian orders, releasing the line wrapped around the winch.

Hana helps Ben pull down the sail, and the boat rides upright in the water.

Ian sprints to the stern, pushes the throttle to full, and the boat speeds down the canal and away from all the Puppets in the water and on the channel banks. The ship passes through the rest of the narrow channel, the survivors waving flares at the Puppets crowding everywhere. The mutants can't touch the survivors now, but Ian is certain the creatures are trying to figure out their next move.

Hana checks Andy's pulse. He's gone. The most innocent of them is gone. Hana looks destroyed.

Ben and Markus carry Rice below, leaving a trail of

blood in their wake.

Isabella is glad Rice is unconscious for now, but when she wakes up, she'll fall apart all over again.

Josh and Tanis stand amidships, statues of disbelief. "What made Andy come up top?" Josh asks.

The survivors assemble in the cabin Andy shared with Tanis, nearly suffocating in the heavy silence and confusion, to wrap Andy's body in a flowered sheet. The boy's blood soaks through immediately.

"We have no place on this ship to stow Andy," Markus says.

The rest of the survivors nod and murmur, debating where to put the sweet little boy to rest.

Markus prays aloud, asking God to accept Andy's soul and give him peace in death so that he might remain an innocent child, uncorrupted by the Devil's spawn of Puppets.

Eventually, the decision is made. The survivors head back up top.

Tanis and Hana tie Andy's body into the sheet and slide his body overboard. The small body splashes in the canal's still water, maddening the currents for a moment. Soon, his body sinks into the depths to forever rest, spared from a second life.

Ian, Isabella, Hana, Tanis, Ben, Markus, and Josh are all speechless as they stand at the lifeline.

Isabella cries but doesn't understand why. *I'm all wet-eyed for some kid I met only a week or so ago.* "He didn't deserve this," she mumbles.

Josh replies. "None of the people mutated against their will deserved to be turned into things, maybe more plant than animal."

Ian is next, "Not one of the millions of children poisoned by the virus, their bodies taken over, deserved this fate."

Tanis tries to speak but can't. Markus repeats the last rights.

Isabella vows silently. *I fucking vow I will hunt Zilla down like the dog he is and kill him like the dog he is. Only I'll make sure Zilla feels every bone in his body snap, every cell saturated with pain, before he croaks.*

The survivors disperse throughout the Pioneer.

Isabella paces in the mess, trying not to feel the hate in her veins.

Markus tends to Rice's extensive injuries. He's never far from her side.

Hana is sobbing in one of the cabins.

Isabella stops behind Markus and feels the wind whistling through the open porthole touch her face. *I need something to do, or I'm going to lose it.*

Rice lies on the starboard bench, Markus leaning over her. She moans, her blood soaking the makeshift bandages. Markus doesn't hear Isabella's approach and doesn't interrupt his soft, kind explanation to Rice. "There were small white roots in the wound," Markus says. "They've crawled inside you, infected you, but I can still save you."

Rice doesn't respond. She's dying, bleeding out.

Markus shows her the red syringe in his hand and injects it into her arm. "There, now you will recover. You're saved."

Isabella reaches out and grabs Markus's hand.

He drops the syringe, and guilt covers his face like a kid busted stealing cookies.

"Where the fuck did you get that syringe?"

Chapter 1.40

Markus
Algeria Goes Dark

The camels shuffle along in the sand, slowly but steadily.

Markus and Mitchell crest the last dune and spot the secret military drone base in Algeria after two days in the Sahara Desert without food or water.

"I pray the camp on the horizon is not a mirage," Markus mumbles as he struggles to keep his eyes open and his back straight.

He's been watching the horizon for days, seeing the shimmering silver refractions rising toward the sky. But the dark spot he sees on the hot golden sand isn't slipping away.

"We're here, ol' man. We made it," Mitchell replies.

An Apache helicopter roars over Markus and Mitchell's heads. The camels shy at the racket but do not stampede. Markus wants to cry, fall to his knees, and thank the Lord, but his dehydrated body can't form tears.

A Humvee tears through the dunes, filling the sky with plumes of dust. It skids to a stop a dozen yards away. Four soldiers, armed with machine guns, leap from the vehicle and march toward the two, weapons ready.

Markus and Mitchell raise their hands high and, when ordered, slowly lift their robes to show that they aren't armed or wired to explode. Apparently satisfied, the squad sergeant says, "Okay, boys, park your camels and dismount. I wanna see your ID before you take ten steps."

"Permission to retrieve my credentials from my camel's pack?" Mitchell asks.

The sergeant carefully checks Mitchell's badge and ID card, holding the photo inside the leather case next to the CIA man's face.

"I, uh, lost my identification to the ruffians who kidnapped me," Markus says.

The sergeant looks wary. Mitchell vouches for Markus, referencing case numbers and protocol.

"Checks out," the sergeant says after speaking into his radio. He waves to the soldiers. The squad lowers its weapons and welcomes the two travelers. They pile back into the Humvees, and two men stay behind to bring the camels to camp.

Markus slumps in the back of the Humvee and accepts water from a soldier. The preacher closes his dry eyes and thanks God a thousand times. The Humvee's air conditioning is cranked down to such a low temperature that Markus thinks his face is burning for a moment.

Mitchell and the Humvee driver chat away like schoolboys as the base gets closer.

Markus stares out the window. "Smaller than I expected."

Mitchell turns around. "It's a military drone base and can be taken down or assembled in hours, airlifted from place to place in pods. It's bigger than it looks." He faces the front again.

The buildings look like a futuristic spaceport on a distant moon, with satellite dishes on the roofs, pointing in all directions. The two-story tower above the central command center is a lookout post with a large artillery piece mounted in a turret.

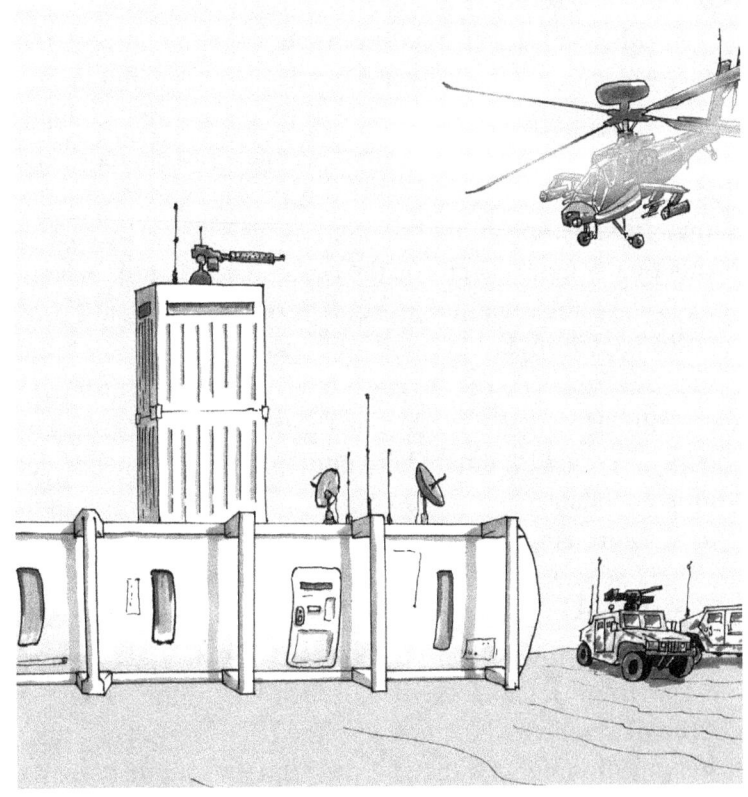

The pods are connected in a circle like a doughnut, the "hole" shaded by a tent. The narrow windows are heavy-duty bullet-resistant acrylic. The door's edges are rounded like an air-lock entry, even sporting an iris scanner mounted at eye level.

The Humvee parks next to the base, and the Apache helicopter lands near a handful of other tan desert-camo Humvees. Markus and Mitchell are led into the base and out of the heat.

The structure's interior is simple and utilitarian—narrow metal walkways about three feet wide, with doorways and narrow windows. The walkway leads to the single, large command center filled with electronic gear, dozens of TV screens, and technicians at workstations.

Mitchell hands over the Stone of Allah and the red folder to Colonel Lorey, a hard-eyed, clean-shaven marine.

Markus is shown to his very clean, albeit small, quarters: a single bed, mirror, and one drawer under the bed. He gratefully strips off his filthy clothes and takes a hot shower in a bathroom that doubles as a shower. His energy is practically gone; he sits on the bed and nearly falls asleep.

A young man in uniform taps on the door and opens it. "Sir, I've brought you food and water and clean clothing borrowed from one of our guys. He's just a little bit bigger than you." He sets the clothes on the bed and hands Markus the tray. You are to remain here until an officer comes to get you. Understand?"

Markus nods and takes a big bite of the roll.

The man leaves. Markus says a prayer of thanks, eats and drinks slowly, savoring the food, and itches to call Marian.

Hours later, a crew of other CIA officers and a couple of scientists land and join the base crew. They take turns questioning Markus and are kind and inquisitive. At no point did he feel interrogated.

Markus is allowed to call Marian three days later. However, due to the time difference, he can only leave her a voice message.

Though Markus has been quite comfortable these last few days, his impatience is building like a storm on the horizon. He can't open the door, is not allowed to see Mitchell or anyone else, and doesn't have access to a phone, but he prays.

Late on the fourth day of isolation, Markus is taken to another small room, where he's questioned by different people who record everything and take blood samples. He's escorted back to his quarters, where someone delivers food and water.

"What is going on? Will somebody tell me?" Markus asks, and not for the first time.

Marian is in Markus's dreams, on his mind constantly, and in his prayers. He worries about her safety and asks God to protect her. He hopes she's not too mad at him.

###

It's six o'clock in the morning when alarms go off, jolting Markus from a deep sleep. Red lights flash from the top corner of the room. He pounds on his door, but no one answers him. The alarms continue. Panic fills his body.

Markus shoulder-butts the door over and over, but it doesn't budge. His shoulder will give out first. He inspects the locking mechanism and gets on his back. He kicks at the lock over and over, as hard as he can, until the metal door bends outward. Finally, it gives, and the door swings open.

He steps into the narrow hall, limping, his ankle sore from the kicking.

An army guard is throwing up, skin pale and almost blue, mucus flowing from his nose. He looks at Markus, eyes reddened and strained. Shouting from the other side of the base startles Markus. He sprints down the hall.

Mitchell emerges from a room, holding his stomach.

"What's happening?" Markus shouts over the alarm.

"Get back to your room!" Mitchell orders through coughs. The whites of his eyes swirl with blood.

Markus runs back to his room and closes the thin door. The broken latch barely holds. He's sweating more than he should be. He looks in the mirror, noting his skin looks too dark. He sees red in his own eyes.

More shouts, unintelligible words, but the fear in the voices is plain to Markus. He hears an explosion. The base rocks like it was hit by an earthquake.

Markus hides himself in his quarters and vomits in the toilet, seeing blood in the bile. Whatever is plaguing him is going to kill everyone. This is the Stone of Allah's curse. *Oh God.* Dysentery. Markus curls into a ball on the bed and covers his ears, trying to block out the alarm. He waits for hours. Finally, the siren goes off, but the light still flashes. He listens, but there are no more screams or shouting. His skull feels like it's going to cave in. When he can't take the pain anymore, he pulls himself off the bed and opens the door. The walls hold him up and guide him down the hall. *Give me strength, Lord.*

The command center is empty. Blood on the back of a chair and papers strewn on the floor frighten him. He continues down the hallway slowly, hand over hand, leaning heavily into the wall. The red light submerges the entire base in its blood-red reflections. His heart races and hurts, and his muscles are weak.

He sees the phone, the secure line he's been using to leave Marian messages. He has to call her. *Fingers. Do what I ask.* The phone rings, and his cousin answers.

"Where in God's name are you, Markus? And you do not get to tell me you ain't comin' home." She's irate.

Markus's head hurts badly. He can hardly speak. "Where's Marian?" he mumbles. Thick mucus rolls down his throat, and he coughs.

"She's dead, Markus! She was in a wreck a week ago. It wasn't an accident. Someone cut her brakes! Where the hell are you?"

Markus drops the phone and sinks to the floor. "God would not take my Marian away from me." He's spinning and in need of medical care.

Markus struggles to his feet and keeps walking. The next room has four bunks, a man in each one. Three look dead, and the other is dying, choking on thick, yellow discharge oozing from his mouth and eyes.

Every room Markus passes is filled with sick or dead people. The last room he stops at is the medical unit. Mitchell is on the table.

Markus checks his pulse. He's dead.

The doctor lies on the floor next to him, also dead. Markus puts his hands on Mitchell's chest and prays. "You became a good friend, Mitchell. The reason I'm still alive."

"Thank you, brother, for saving my life," he whispers. "I'll never forget you." The room spins. Markus kneels next to the doctor and throws up blood. If Marian is gone, he'll see her now. He feels closer to her than he has in weeks. "Here I come, my love. Here I come."

He opens his tear-filled eyes and looks at the counter across the room. A light and magnifying glass are positioned over the shimmering Stone of Allah.

A hammer and chisel lay next to the stone, a chip removed.

The light on the counter brightens, filling the small

room with a warm, white light.

Markus sees double. There are two stones and two lights. His heart skips beats.

The light intensifies, outshining all the other lights, and turns blue.

The Stone of Allah is the light source, brilliant, glowing brighter and brighter.

A deep vibration in his chest steadies his vision and makes his ribs tickle; the pain goes away, and the nausea stops.

Markus reaches out to the blue light floating in front of him now. This is his time to meet God. He falls to his knees and smells a fragrance like incense, and the blue light forms into an orb.

A burst of color and cool air pushes him off his knees onto his butt. He blinks furiously so his tears won't taint his vision.

A translucent wispy figure emerges from the orb, fluctuating in tandem with the vibration in his chest. The figure pulses like something under the surface of clear, rippling water. The shape morphs, focuses, and then blurs until a magnificent horse with pure white hair and sculpted muscles emerges from the light, its mane so long and silky it hangs nearly to the floor.

The rider is a featureless shape, like a shadow, only white and surrounded by blue light. *God. I am in the presence of the Almighty.*

The white horse kneels reverently, flickering in and out of focus.

Markus is overwhelmed by the presence, prostrates himself, and cries.

The light is so bright and intense he can barely keep his eyes open.

Markus raises himself to his knees, keeping his

eyes on God as He stands and reaches out with His glowing white hand.

A small white light rises and presses into Markus's chest, clutches his heart, and holds it still. So warm. The rest of his body feels cool and still until warm blood fills Markus's limbs with a sensation he can only describe as hope.

God finally speaks. His voice is deep and airy, solid

yet gentle, "You are my White Warrior. A crown is placed on your head, son. With justice, you will judge. Lead this world back into my body, for you are my White Warrior."

God's hand withdraws, and his horse stands.

His image flickers in and out, and he looks at Mitchell.

"And you will be my sword. Together, you will bring my children home, for there is a war in Heaven, and I need their love returned."

A red syringe rolls across the floor and stops at Markus's foot.

God leaves in that instant. Markus feels a moment of clarity, though the pain returns violently. He injects half the syringe's contents into his arm, turns and plunges the other half into Mitchell.

CHAPTER 1.41

ISABELLA
CASTING THE FIRST STONE

After the tower of dead people attacked the Pioneer, the survivors wrapped Andy's body in a sheet and slid it off the stern to a watery burial.

Isabella had gone below, beaten, tired, and angry until she saw Markus saving Rice's life with an injection from a red syringe, the same sort of syringe she'd gotten when she launched the EMP rocket.

"How did you get that?" Isabella demanded of the preacher. "Syringes like that don't come from the corner drug store."

The boat rocks, and she leans against the bulkhead to steady herself. She's slick with black gunk but doesn't care. What she cares about is the preacher with moon-white eyes who has contraband she didn't think she'd ever see again in this new world.

Josh joins the two in the dining room, dripping black gunk from his makeshift armor and medical mask.

Isabella gives Josh a steely look.

He freezes. "What'd I do?" A glob of brain matter rolls off his splattered medical mask.

Markus puts the syringe into a medical pouch and then tucks it into his pocket. He takes a deep breath. "I got the syringe, and two others like it. They were mailed to me about two weeks ago, along with a note. It said I was saved. That God loved me."

"Why'd you get three of them?" Isabella asks. Her fist tightens.

Markus shrugs. He puts a hand on an unwounded part of Rice's leg and holds it there. He takes a deep breath. "The note said they were from Zilla. I assumed I was meant to save some souls," Markus answers.

Isabella doesn't know what to think. *Who else was given syringes? Who else was chosen to survive, and why?*

"What's in the syringe?" Josh asks.

"It must contain an anti-virus or a cure," Markus says.

"You have *vaccines*?" Josh blurts—black shit spatters everywhere as he flings out his skinny arms. "I almost died!" he yells. "Infection rate is over ninety percent! I. . . I've been wearing this mask the entire time!"

Markus shrugs. "I'm sorry, son. It seemed like the virus stopped spreading. Now the white worms are doing the work. I would have shared with you if you had gotten infected like Rice. You are a part of us, too." He looks at Isabella. "I don't know why I got three. Maybe I touched someone's heart. I had a big congregation, a prime-time spot on Sunday morning television, but I wasn't always successful."

"You're a liar," Isabella scowls. She never trusted Markus and never knew why. Maybe it's because he claims to talk to God. She takes her rifle off her back and points it at him. "Somethin' not right about you."

Markus holds his hands up.

He doesn't look scared. Maybe because he's fucking crazy.

"I lost my faith for a while until I went to Tunisia. I found my faith again and returned to New York to rebuild my church."

Josh reaches out. "Can I have the dose? I don't want to wait until those worms crawl into my skin or the virus sneaks into my body."

"I'm sorry. I can't give it to you," Markus says. "You're not infected yet."

Hana comes down the ladder, similarly splashed with Puppet blood and guts. "What's going on with Rice?" She pauses.

Isabella can tell she's feeling tension in the air, like a lack of oxygen.

"Markus has three doses of the vaccine. Never said a word." Josh is so angry Isabella expects steam to burst from his ears any second. "I get a dose. I need it!"

Tanis and Ian rush down the ladder. "What the hell?" Ian asks.

Hana says, "Markus had three vaccines in red syringes and just dosed Rice with one."

Ian looks at Markus. "You care to explain?"

Markus calmly explains himself for the third time.

Ben pokes his head into the entryway. "Something wrong? It's all stuffy and smells like bad breath down here."

Isabella glares at Ben. "Zip." She turns to Ian. "No one gets the anti-virus."

Ian agrees. " I'm sorry, Josh, but that makes the most sense. You are probably immune to the virus. And I have no doubt the worms could kill us all if enough of them get inside us. If you show signs of infection, get the dose."

"But!" Josh yelps. "I want to know why he's got three vaccines! It doesn't make any sense. If…if there *is* a cure, why did everyone die? Where was the CDC? The government? We can reproduce the vaccine somehow so we can all get it."

Isabella is still pointing her gun at Markus. "You got that right, Josh. This is some fucked up shit here. That red syringe is inside stuff. You got to be close to Zilla to get one of those. Maybe you were really good friends with the boogie man himself to get three."

"Zilla?" Josh says, his head cocking like a dumbfounded puppy.

"Oh, you know the name, too?" Isabella's finger tightens on the cold, thin trigger. "Ben, get the Bible."

Ben returns with Markus's Bible.

"I wasn't sure before, but now I am. I watched Markus writing a few days ago, and it reminded me of somethin'. Ben, flip the book open to any page with notes in the margins and show it to Ian."

Ian inspects Markus's writing. "I…studied his note—every letter, curve, slash. I wanted to make sure I could identify Zilla in any way possible. The only clue was his note."

"I'm fucking right, aren't I?"

Tanis takes the Bible. Hana and Ben look over

Tanis's shoulder.

Ian folds his arms across his chest. "So, you're Zilla?" he asks Markus.

Josh snatches the book, inspects the writing, and looks up, his jaw hanging.

Markus wipes black crap off his cheek. He takes a turn, looking at everyone on board. "I am but God's humble servant."

Isabella bashes the butt of her rifle on his head, a glancing blow that splits his skin. He falls from the settee to his knees.

Tanis leaps at Isabella and grabs her shirt. "Stop, Isa!"

Isabella takes hold of Tanis's neck and kicks at his knee. Tanis falls, yelping.

Ben comes at Isabella, but he stops when her eyes fix on him. She turns and points her gun at Markus. "You're dead, old man!"

Hana kicks the weapon, but Isabella loses her grip. The gun clatters and slides in the slick black muck that pools on the galley floor.

Isabella turns, but Hana is fast. Her elbow bashes Isabella's head. She pulls back and brings up her hands.

Ian yells for the women to stop, but they don't.

Isabella steps twice toward Hana, fakes a kick, and then punches. Her fist cracks Hana's nose.

Isabella punches again. Hana grabs her wrist and twists her arm around her back, locking Isabella in place. Isabella knows the move and slips out easily.

"Hana! Isabella!" Ian stands in between the two. He tries to grab Isabella, but she slips past, spins, and sinks her fist into Hana's stomach.

Ian falls on Isabella, bending her over the countertop. Isabella's head snaps back, and she butts his nose. She steps into the center of the galley and fists up. "Fucking get me off this boat!" she screams. She slips on the black blood but maintains her stance.

Hana lifts her gun. "I *will* shoot you, Isabella."

Great, the fucking cop is on her throne. "You're gonna have to."

Ian approaches again with his hands up. Blood spills from his nose and slides down his black-splattered forearm, turning purple. He looks at Hana. "Markus needs the end of your gun."

Hana nods.

Ian turns back to Isabella and lifts his hands. "Markus is at gunpoint. He's not going anywhere. If you would calm the fuck down for a minute, we can figure this out."

Isabella's blood pumps hot. *I can throw off all these assholes and take this boat to Cuba by myself. I should—*

Isabella sees Tanis on his knees, crying silently and holding his neck.

A wave of guilt rushes over her. She doesn't make a habit of hurting kids.

"We have to survive *ourselves*," Ian says. He gets closer, within range of Isabella's fury, but she's cooled without even knowing it. Ian puts his hands on her shoulders gently. "This has always been about surviving."

"Markus is Zilla. I know it. I think you do, too." Isabella lowers her fists and feels like crying again, but she holds it in. "He deserves to die."

"I agree with you. I know that handwriting." Ian turns to Markus. "Now that we know you're Zilla."

Markus stands tall and points to Isabella. "And who art thou? To cast the first stone? You, Isabella, fired off the EMP for *money!*"

He points to Ian. "How about the virus you spread? It wasn't a coincidence that the police and the Guard got sick first, was it?

"Oh, young Tanis? I love how you installed the virus on your father's computer. You see? We are all Zilla. We are but humble servants of God."

Isabella turns to Ian.

"You got control back?" Ian asks.

Isabella nods and grabs Markus, pushing him to the ladder. "Up top," she orders.

Markus climbs up, followed by everyone else. Isabella pushes Markus to the safety line.

"And Hana! I love that you opened the quarantine, letting a horde of infected out into the world against orders," he says over his shoulder.

"And Ben. Ben… You poured the bacteria into the water at the behest of a sexy woman in a red dress. Did you think she would fuck you?" Something changed in his voice. Turned gravelly. You're God's swords. We all are!"

Isabella, shocked, backs away. *Everyone on board had a part in Zilla's game?*

"You were all so eager to believe the propaganda Zilla fed you. You're like children. Ian, you float between anarchy and socialism, and you don't understand either. You can't have it both ways! You bought every paranoid conspiracy theory you ever read."

He turns to Isabella. "Your greed got you far in life, didn't it, Isa?"

She punches Markus in the side as hard as she can.

He coughs but continues. "Ah, Ben. You were easy, weren't you? Busy blaming everyone else for your failings. Mad at the world for the actions of the lost souls around you. You all have no principles to guide you, except for maybe Josh over there. Your wandering hearts keep you all lost and afraid and confused. It is why God chose you to do the hard thing. To help him return his children to Heaven."

Ian leans close to Markus. "Why did you do this? Why?" His voice cracks. "Why?"

Markus lifts his chin. "It was already done. In God's plan, it was always going to be this way. We can live our lives in His service because we are the chosen ones. We will be at God's side for eternity." Markus's eyes widen, strain and bulge in his madness.

Ian turns away from Markus. "Fucking horse shit. Why let people be born in the first place? Why let everyone suffer like this?"

"Religion is not logical but ideological," Josh says. "Just as fucked up as fascism and communism and any other idea that justifies one person killing or stealing from another." Josh glares at Markus, eyes crying. "You killed my mother. Why not me?"

Markus does not answer Josh.

"What do we do with him?" Tanis asks.

"Kill the idea. It's a virus, no less real than the one this piece of shit used to kill the world," Isabella suggests, looking at Hana. She closes her eyes and lowers her head. Isabella knows Hana agrees now.

Isabella punches Markus in the side again. He bends over and turns to the safety line, waiting out the pain. Like a thief, Isabella slips her hand into his jacket pocket and pulls out the case with the anti-virus syringes. Markus doesn't try to stop her.

Isabella desperately wants to smash his face into a cobbler-like substance and throw him overboard, but she doesn't. Some invisible hand stops her. "We're not far from a horde of Puppets. And if he makes it to shore, they'd tear him up. It might be what he deserves."

Hana stares as still as a wax figure, the wind lifting

her golden hair off her shoulder like a flag. "I can't fight you, Isabella. No one on this boat can." Hana shakes her head slowly, imparting her rational charm to them all. "So, what are you going to do?"

Isabella's shoulders relax. Ever since her father's fists stopped hurting her, she's always known how strong she is, but Hana is strong in her own way. She's smart. "Fuck it," Isabella mumbles and backs away from Markus and the group. It takes another kind of strength to admit you're wrong. "I'm sorry, Hana, sorry, Tanis," Isabella tells them. "It was wrong to fight you guys, my crew. You're not a bad group to ride to the end of the world with. Do with him whatever you think is right."

Hana raises her gun and steps toward Markus. "Hands behind your back. When we get to Cuba, every survivor will know the face of Zilla. You'll get your trial, then. It will be all the survivors who get to judge you next time."

"But he can't go with us to Cuba," Tanis says, his face as tight as a knot.

Josh stomps off, clearly confused and pissed.

"Lock him in a stateroom for now. We need to figure some things out." Ian looks at Hana. "I want him to stand trial, too, but we've got some dirty laundry ourselves."

"We're victims here," Hana spat. She shook visibly, so she holstered her pistol.

"I know, we are victims. But we're partly responsible, all of us. We didn't think." Ian heads to the bow as Hana and Ben escort Markus down below.

Ian hoists the anchor with the winch, and Isabella and Tanis set the sails.

They sail south but with a different air around them. Now, there's a dark secret aboard the ship, like a gaping wound covered by a tiny Band-Aid.

Isabella wishes she could rewind time. Go back to how she was living when she was Cott's bodyguard. It was easier then, taking orders and following protocol. She didn't have to think much. Of course, not thinking much led her to launching the EMP for cash that didn't exist. She chokes back tears as the wind caresses her face and toys with her short hair.

The *Pioneer* slips past rows of grand homes, their dark windows looking like the eye sockets of skulls. The yards and docks are full of watchful Puppets. The survivors are the parade of the living, and the dead hate them for it.

Isabella's not too pissed that she didn't shoot Zilla in the face because she knows what lies ahead for him. He'll get his justice one way or the other. Maybe they'll throw him to the Puppets, let the worms crawl into his skin, and take his body. He might be immune, but he should still die at the hands of his children, the dead that walk in his image, a reflection of his twisted soul.

Ian pulls out a hose, steps on the foot pump, and washes himself clean with salt water; Isabella takes the next turn. Everyone cleans the boat with the hose, buckets, and sponges and purges the sadness from her teak, tackles, winches, and lines. Cleaning the ship is familiar and cathartic, done in silence and reverence to her protection.

As Isabella scrubs the gunk from the nooks and crannies, she thinks about Zilla. The master game he played and won. She thinks about her life before the extinction event. No part of her mind or body feels like her old self. Before all this, Isabella was a phantom on the Earth, a mind in a foreign object that went from place to place. Now she feels every muscle, every scratch, every wound. Her body is different, and so is her consciousness. Yeah, she's different, and because of the emptiness around her, she feels

vulnerable, like a scared little girl who can't seem to wake up from the scariest nightmare anyone has ever dreamed of.

CHAPTER 1.42

IAN

INTO NYX, THE GODDESS OF NIGHT

Ian orders everyone to gather around the helm. The wind is warm, the light bright. Fatigue sits on his shoulders and begs him to sleep, but he can't. Not yet. His fingers run along the smooth wheel, and for a moment, he forgets to steer.

Hana sits next to him, and so does Tanis and his dog. He can't go further in life without addressing what Zilla said. It can't hang between them and grow into cobwebs because they will forever be trapped by their guilt and secrets.

Isabella and Ben approach, smoking and sipping whiskey.

Ian clears his throat and prepares to be judged. "What Markus said was true. I got a syringe. I'm vaccinated."

Isabella blows out her smoke. "We all know he was telling the truth. Except for Rice, Andy, and Josh, the main reason we survived is because of the shots."

Everyone takes turns sharing the finer details of their roles and how they collectively ended the world.

Josh listens, in shock, looking small and thin and alone.

Ian hears the water lapping off the boat's sides. Finally, he says, "So, you get the shot, Josh. You're saved," Ian mumbles. "That leaves one dose for anyone we come across."

Hana gives Josh the shot.

Josh laughs. He hasn't said a word since the confessions. Finally, he mutters, "You guys are like the Four Horseman of the Apocalypse."

"There are five of us, you know," Ben adds. "Six if you count Zilla."

"Whatever, you're the fucking Six Horsemen of the Apocalypse. If I had just one more month, I'd have blown the story open. Maybe I could have stopped all this," Josh says, thinking about how he and Gigglypuss69 were hot on the trail of Zilla's master plan.

"I want to know how a minister becomes a mass murderer," Ian says.

Ben sips the whiskey and passes it around.

"I thought that shit was what the Muslims wanted to do, hasten the return of the Mahdi or some shit," Ben says.

"Anyone can twist their mind to justify whatever they want. Markus twisted Christianity into a pretzel so he could make his God however he wanted. I've seen every color of criminal do it." Hana takes a drink, wincing as the burn hits her throat.

"We've all twisted ourselves up to justify what we've done," Isabella says. "I don't like people, but I didn't want to off them all."

"I didn't know what I was doing, either. I thought I was helping!" Tanis mumbles. He takes a sip of whiskey and chokes on it.

"We were manipulated by a psychopath," Ian says and sips. The warmth in his chest doesn't calm his nerves but sets them on edge.

Hana stands. "He was right on one point. We didn't have any principles to guide us, to help us make the right decisions. The first principle is, do no harm."

She is about to continue adding to the list when Ben interrupts, "Maybe the first is not to believe bull crap that comes out of people's pie holes." Ben walks away from the group.

"I should have verified what Zilla was saying, but he just said all the right things." The ship rocks gently. The wind and weather is calm and cool. "I don't know how he went crazy or why. I don't think we'll ever know unless Markus tells us," Ian says.

The horizon accepts the sun as it sets. It will be a long night, but all nights are long. They all disperse, wearing cloaks of shame.

Ian heaved-to for the entire night and stayed near the helm.

Isabella remains at the bow until she walks amidships and stares at the dark shore.

Ian wonders what she's thinking. She looks ready to give up.

The next day, Ian sets sail as soon as the sun rises. He doesn't know about everyone else, but he didn't get much sleep.

The day passes slowly while the clouds race across the sky.

Ian sees a sign on the channel marking South Carolina waters and keeps at the wheel to prevent himself from cracking into a million fragments.

Everyone else finds their own part of the boat to be alone. The heavy silence feels shitty.

The survivors keep sailing south. The United States has been overrun, and no containment line exists—at least, not along the eastern shore.

Ian decided to go to Cuba after Isabella retrieved him but still hoped to see an army, a group of survivors, someone alive.

Their water doesn't hydrate them enough, and the food doesn't satisfy them. The fact that they are still breathing hardly changes their moods. Everyone is stuck in sadness.

Now that the truth stands in front of him like a phantom that he can't leave behind, Ian wants to drop the sails, drain the fuel into the ocean, and float over the horizon to whatever afterlife awaits.

But he doesn't. Instead, Ian hugs every last person on the boat, even Ben. He lets himself cry, not caring how the strain and tears twist his face or how weak it makes him look.

They work as a team, trimming the sails and adjusting the course of this everlasting southern migration because that is what they set out to do.

Eventually, Ian feels further away from that phantom. Is it behind him now, or is he too tired to see the shadow it casts over his mind? Either way, he feels the breeze on his skin again, which cools his soul. He swims when he sets anchor and lets the saltwater pull the moisture from his skin until he's wrinkled and faded.

They pass by Miami and watch thousands of Puppets stumble and hunt.

Someone hung a banner reading "Survivors Inside" on a high-rise condo, but when Ian searched the windows with binoculars, they saw darkness, burn marks, ruins, and Puppets skulking on almost every floor. Ian or the others could not possibly get through the horde to the tower, anyway, unless they had incendiary bombs or a tank.

Eventually, the Florida Keys disappear over the horizon, but the effect on Ian is minor. They're on a course for Cuba, and even though they don't have enough food or water, Ian doesn't care that they're leaving sight of land.

Ian contemplates Markus's behavior and how he used his religion to justify his dark desires. Markus was no different from Ian, each blinded by his point of view, biases, and hubris and hobbled by his inability to use reason and common sense. Ian never sought out the opinions of those who tried to disprove the conspiracies and never took the time to consider or discover alternative explanations. He absorbed the lies because they were packaged so nicely.

Ian must do better from now on and help rebuild what he helped take down. He has to find his salvation in Cuba, where the radio chatter says there are survivors.

###

The first day in the open sea, the night comes too soon. The isolation is a strange feeling, but not as scary as Ian thought it would be. It's better to be out of sight of the shattered modern world and all its sharp edges.

An hour past nightfall, the moon rises, so huge it fills the horizon like Nyx, the Greek goddess of night. She pulls on his chest like she pulls on the tides. He's not afraid of her power. Zeus was, supposedly, but he didn't survive an apocalypse and go days without food or water.

Ian is at the helm but hasn't touched the wheel in over an hour.

Another day passes, a day of ocean swells, eerie calms, and a freak squall. Now Ian is done, given up, waiting to die.

Water a mile deep and a million miles across surrounds them, and they can't drink a drop of it. They're out of bottled water and booze, and the only food they have will dehydrate them, so no one will eat it.

Ian feels he will close his eyes tonight and not open them again. His eyelids get heavy, and he stares at the reflections of a shattered moon on the ocean ripples.

Ian has no real identity anymore. He is a community organizer with no community, nothing to rail against, and no corruption to fight. He wonders how much of the corruption and injustice was imagined. Humans are out for what they want and nothing more. Society, cohesion, and altruism happen because they benefit people as individuals in some way.

Ian sits up. Cuba can't be too far away. He will fight Nyx. "You can't take me yet, baby. Not yet," he says. "I won't go into your arms, no matter how warm you tell me they are."

The compass shows the ship drifting; Ian corrects the course away from the drift west in the trade winds. He stands on the seat at the helm, holds onto the main sheet, and stares at the horizon, but it's as straight as the blade of a sword.

CHAPTER 1.43

IAN

FINALLY FOUND

Ian is about to sit when someone makes a noise at the bow. He didn't know anyone else was up top.

"Ian! Ian!" It's Josh. He sure does love that bowsprit. Ian sees Josh's curly hair in the moonlight, coming at the helm like a battering ram. "We're here! We've made it!"

Ian hops off the helm seat and runs to Josh, who grabs Ian and points over the port side.

"See that?" he yells into Ian's ear. "Lights, awesome lights!"

Ian recoils at his volume but squints at the horizon. There's a light, then another! They drift up into the sky like balloons.

Josh disappears.

Ian runs back to the wheel, pointing the ship southeast toward the activity, and runs to the main sheet. Ian winds the sheet up in the winch, the ticking reverberating in the bones of his thin fingers. The sails tighten like muscle fibers, and the boat tips as the *Pioneer* picks up speed. Ian runs to the forward sheet and does the same, then tightens the jib sheets.

They're close-hauled now. The *Pioneer* finds her comfort zone and spears through the placid ocean. She heels farther, and her side rail touches the water, splashing with enthusiasm.

Everyone comes up top, looking like skin and bones in the moonlight.

A dozen more lights lift into the sky, then more and more, until Ian loses track of how many.

The *Pioneer* remains on her side and sails faster than Ian has ever sailed her. She makes great time.

Closer to the source of the lights, Hana turns to him. "Oh, Ian, they're lanterns with the candles in the middle!"

They rise into the night sky before burning out, sending glowing embers back to Earth. Everyone jumps and screams and hugs and anything else they can do to express their joy. It is Eden!

They see the island of Cuba an hour later.

Ian turns the ship into the wind and the sail stalls. He slows in the rocking waters.

"Why are we stopping?" Hana asks, barely able to curb her excitement.

"I can't sail upwind, so I've got to tack back and forth to get to the lights."

"What about the engine?" Ben asks.

Ian shakes his head. "Out of fuel. It's okay, I got

this. We'll be there in no time."

A dozen more lights blink to life on the left, the port side, probably from hotel windows and campfires.

"They have a survivor city!" Hana yelps. "It has to be safe to have all the lights on. We've made it. We're finally saved." Hana fires off a flare. The red light barrels high into the sky, and she reloads and fires again in excitement.

Ian knows they need to be closer to get someone's attention, but with plenty of flares, he lets her have her fun.

"Watch out, Ian!" Tanis yells. "In front of us!"

Ian turns to look where he's going and sees the dark coastline at the last moment. The shore comes out of nowhere! Ian spins the wheel to head upwind, the ship turning slowly.

The dark closes too fast. Ian's eyes widen as he realizes how fast the ship is going. "Hold on to something!"

The *Pioneer* runs aground. Ian slams into the wheel, knocking the wind out of him. Everyone else falls or hits something hard. The boat tips and turns, and a gust fills the sails, tips the ship over, and dumps everyone like a bucket turned on its side.

Ian falls and hits the shallow waves. Hana and Ben hit the water next to him. Tanis and Isabella were holding on, but they let go and fall. Markus and Rice are still in the belly of the *Pioneer*.

Every wave pushes the boat farther on shore. The ship tries to right herself, but the wind keeps catching her sail and pushing her over again. She moans, her lines ticking in the wind like she's crying.

Ian gasps and sits up, the waves bashing into him. "Hey, everyone okay?"

Everyone moans.

Josh pokes his head up from midship, hanging onto a railing. Blood spills from his left forehead, but he seems in good spirits. "We're okay!" Josh helps Rice off the ship into Ian's arms. She is still covered in bandages but healing nicely.

Josh turns to go back into the ship. "I'm getting Markus!" He disappears from view.

"Ah, leave the fucker," Isabella mumbles as she gets to her feet.

"He's probably dead already. No one's peeked in on him since we ran out of water," Ben says.

"Heads up!" Josh yells. He pushes Markus out the cabin door, and the frail old man slams into the surf.

Hana drags Markus out of the water. He gets to his feet, stumbles to the sand, and falls. He's thinner and more frail than everyone else.

Josh tells Ian to move aside so he can jump down.

Ben points to the lights on the horizon. "Great parking job, little off the mark though."

"Eden can't be more than a couple of miles away. We follow the beach and be there in no time," Tanis says.

Isabella climbs the side safety line like a ladder, reaches the settee behind the wheel, and trips the cover latch with her finger. The lid opens, and her M-16A, shotgun, and pistol fall into the water. She retrieves them easily and shakes the salt water from their breaches, barrels, and clips.

Hana, with her pistol on Markus's back, pushes him in front of the group. "You first."

They head toward the wonderful lights of Eden.

The lights pull on Ian's heartstrings like magnets, and he knows they'll be there shortly. He's starving and thirsty, but his mood is pure sugar.

A dark shape comes at the group from the tree line. At first, Ian thinks it's someone who will help, but the shape stumbles unnaturally and reaches out, cries an unnatural cry. Another comes from the dark, then another. A mass of figures stumbles from the tree line, shrieking with glee.

"Shit, dudes!" Ben cries. "They're here, too! Jesus fucking shit!"

"Fuckin' Puppets," hisses Isabella. "Can't leave us alone, can they?"

"Back to the ship," Ian orders. Even practically on its side, *Pioneer* is still a place to hide. They all turn to run.

"Hey! Markus!" Tanis yells.

Markus isn't able to keep up. He drops to his knees and raises his clasped hands in the air. "Go, let them have me. I'll distract them."

"God damn it," Ian snaps, shaking his head in disbelief. *Where was this selflessness when it mattered?*

Hundreds come from the darkness, fall on Markus, and drag him off the beach and into the jungle.

"Oh, man," Tanis cries out.

Hana takes his shoulder. "Zilla is gone. His fate is what he deserves."

"Hurry!" Ian pulls Hana and Tanis. "On the ship. It's safe there."

The *Pioneer* rests awkwardly on the beach, but she'll give them shelter.

Ian hopes this is low tide and that high tide will free them from the sand. He doesn't want to have to wait for another spring tide like they had to last week.

Hana gets Tanis to climb the ladder. "We need to pull Rice up, fast."

Isabella stands ready, gun aimed towards the jungle, waiting for the first Puppet to rear its ugly face. "We won't be able to dig out this time. The Puppets can stumble right to the hull. They'll surround the ship, and we will never leave."

The crack of Isabella's gun splits the air like bolts of lightning, and the light leaves green spots on Ian's eyes.

Hush mumbles, waiting for Rice to struggle her way, in pain, back onto the ship. "Eden is close, so close. We've stepped out of the bear trap and into the pack of starving bears."

"I guess this is what we deserve," Ian mumbles. A horde is coming right for them, their dark silhouettes ululating like a single organism.

Without warning, the tree line bursts into bright orange flames. Ian shields his eyes from the brightness. He peeks again and sees the fire rise and turn red. The flames seem to come from a dozen places.

Ian and other survivors run and hide behind the *Pioneer's* massive hull.

"What the hell, dude," Ben barks.

Ian stands waist-deep in the surf and tries to remain on his feet, but the waves have other ideas. He's so tired.

The flames die down, and the orange reflections vanish like the flip of a switch.

"What're we gonna do? I can't swim for shit." Ben mutters.

"We survive this, just like we have before," Hana says, hanging onto Tanis with one arm and gripping Ian's sleeve with her other.

"I can't see good enough to hit the fuckers," Isabella says, breathing hard.

Ian sees the rowboat still tied to the *Pioneer's* stern, bumping the hull noisily with every wave as if tapping his shoulder. "The rowboat. We can row to Eden." Ian runs to the rowboat, jumping through the water's thick grasp, and grabs the painter. "Isa, give me your knife. I need to cut the line free."

"I have one." Hana holsters her pistol and removes a pocket knife from her police belt. "I hate this little boat. I hate how cramped it is."

"I know."

"Come on, Tanis, come on, Rice. We're leaving the *Pioneer* here."

Ian looks at the dark tree line. The Puppets are still screeching and yelling, but he can't see them from this side of the *Pioneer*.

Isabella climbs into the small rowboat, as do the others.

Ian is just about ready to jump in when he hears a voice.

"Hey, you!"

Ian turns and sees a man sprint down the beach, leap over the first set of waves, and splash toward the rowboat, rifle in hand.

Ian pushes the boat away from the shore as hard as possible and jumps in. "Go!"

Hana and Isabella row hard.

The man has some kind of tank strapped to his back. "Wait! Hold on!" he says, diving into the water and swimming to them.

Isabella leans over the edge and points her M-16A at him. "Ian, we don't know this guy."

"Hold your fire," Hana snaps.

The Puppets reach the beach, tripping over themselves as they clamber into the waves.

The man in the water reaches up and grabs the gunwale, gasping for air. "Help me! Come on! I just lost five of my guys trying to get to you."

Isabella tips the muzzle of her rifle up, looks at Ian, and Ian shrugs. "We got room for one more."

They help the man into the boat, and Isabella immediately strips him of his flame thrower.

Each of the survivors looks at the newcomer, wondering if he is a friend or an enemy.

His short brown hair, thin beard, strong-looking arms and shoulders, and square, tight jaw show no signs of infection. "Thanks." He spits sea water over the gunwale. "I was hoping for a more peaceful welcome, but that'll have to do. Welcome to Eden. My name is Mitchell." He points toward the lights on the horizon. "Home is east. If it's not being overrun."

"So, Eden isn't safe?" Tanis says, clearly disappointed.

"It was an hour ago. I saw your flare and left with a few jeeps and some men to come get you. We cleared the infected area a week ago, so I wasn't worried. I saw you run aground before the infected came at us from all directions. We had no idea they were there. It's like they were hiding and for who knows how long. They're smarter than you think."

"Yeah, no shit," Ben says.

Ian looks at the lights of Eden. We will make this our new home, but it looks like we're gonna have to fight to keep it.

That much will probably never change.

TO BE CONTINUED....

Hello, dear reader. I sincerely enjoyed my story. It has been a labor of love and a fantasy that I hold dear. It began as a dream and ended as a full-fledged novel. If you don't mind, don't go away so soon. Please help me out by posting a review on Amazon.com, Facebook, Goodreads, or your blog. It only takes you a minute, but it will help me out for a long, long time.

Sincerely,

Anderson Atlas

Visit my website at **AndersonAtlas.com**

Deeper into the folds of Fools' Apocalypse: Beyond Symbiosis

1. Why did people die in huddled groups holding each other? What would this symbolize?

2. Was giving the survivors the red syringe a compassionate act?

3. Ian railed against consumerism, but when his stuff is stolen how did having nothing make him feel?

4. How did Markus use people to get what he wanted?

5. What did you think about Josh's research about how socialist states eventually collapse and zero free market states have? Did you know this is a real fact?

6. Do you think the author intended the zombies to portray an element of society? In what way?

Thank you for reading *Fools Apocalypse! Beyond Symbiosis!* There are many aspects of the puppets that have yet to be revealed. Why did the dead end up in piles? What was in the red syringe? How did Markus get so much power? What happens on Cuba? Is the entire world dead or just the East coast of the USA?

Thank you to all that supported me through this novel, including my family, for putting up with my writing and drawing zeal. Thank you to my critique group members: Pam, Elaine, Kate, Marilyn, Elise and to Karl and Brian, my first beta readers.

About the Author

Anderson Atlas is a graphic artist, illustrator, and writer who lives in Southern Arizona with his family. He loves to read, sail, hike and watch movies. When it comes to his own books, he writes and illustrates them himself, and he especially likes writing character driven stories with fun and unique twists. He has written many books from Children's books to Young Adult books to Adult novels.

Visit **AndersonAtlas.com** for more about me!

www.ingramcontent.com/pod-product-compliance
Lightning Source LLC
Chambersburg PA
CBHW052347020726
47503CB00001B/146